Doors to the Past

T0002278

In
SPOTLIGHT
and
SHADOW

RACHEL SCOTT McDANIEL

BARBOUR
PUBLISHING

In Spotlight and Shadow ©2023 by Rachel Scott McDaniel

Print ISBN 978-1-63609-476-2

Adobe Digital Edition (.epub) 978-1-63609-477-9

Scripture quotations marked NRSV are taken from the New Revised Standard Version Bible, copyright 1989, Division of Christian Education of the National Council of the Churches of Christ in the United States of America. Used by permission. All rights reserved.

This book is a work of fiction. Names, characters, places, and incidents are either products of the author's imagination or used fictitiously. Any similarity to actual people, organizations, and/or events is purely coincidental.

Cover Photograph: © ILINA SIMEONOVA / Trevillion Images

Published by Barbour Publishing, Inc., 1810 Barbour Drive, Uhrichsville, Ohio 44683, www.barbourbooks.com

See the series lineup and get bonus content at DoorsToThePastSeries.com

Our mission is to inspire the world with the life-changing message of the Bible.

ecpa Member of the
Evangelical Christian
Publishers Association

Printed in the United States of America

Praise for *In Spotlight and Shadow*

McDaniel takes a stellar cast of characters, adds humorous sparkle, an intriguing mystery, and delivers an emotionally engaging and entertaining story that showcases why she's one of my favorite authors! *In Spotlight and Shadows* ranks as one my favorite reads of the year!

-Natalie Walters, award-winning author of *Lights Out*, and The SNAP Agency series

I was captivated by the first page and couldn't stop reading until the very last. With the suspenseful romance set in a dual timeline, reading this book was medicine for my soul. Love, forgiveness, and acceptance poured off the pages, and I made sure to drink every last drop.

-Shannon Hargreaves, @the_reel_bookery

Romance entwined with mystery, it had me turning the next page and lying as I told myself, "just one more chapter." There isn't a good stopping point; you will be wanting to clear your schedule for this dual timeline. Read this book—it'll satisfy that romantic craving.

-Hannah McDaniel, @the.book.maiden

Intriguing, mysterious, and thoroughly romantic, this dual timeline about two women separated by a century but bound together by secrets will have you believing that people, and love, deserve second chances. A must-read for any fan of historical romance!

-Marilee Merrell, @marilee.loves.to.read

This book satisfied every need in my variety-hungry soul, and I couldn't love it more! It's deep without being somber, witty without being overdone. It's a perfect balance of romance, intrigue, and suspense, with some historical elements thrown in, all wrapped up in glorious Christian principles that feel natural and uplifting. Once I started, I could not put this book down! I never guessed at the threads that tied the two stories together; it was even better than I imagined! This book has easily catapulted into my category of top favorites, and I know I will enjoy reading over and over through the years.

-Jessica Harwood, @lovelybookishdelights

DEDICATION

To Jane,
Thank you for always loving my stories. You left this world
before I could give you this one, but you're walking the
paths of angels with views I can only dream of.

CHAPTER ONE

ELISE

January, Pittsburgh, Pennsylvania

*H*istory didn't haphazardly repeat itself in the chapters of Elise Malvern's life. It copy-and-pasted in the most irritating fashion. But if one were to flip through this proverbial book, most of the pages would be blank. Because important people—the ones who were supposed to fill her life—never showed up. Some bowed out even before day one.

It was a predictable story. One that Elise wouldn't five-star on Goodreads. Wouldn't recommend to her fellow book club members. And would abandon the book for a Netflix-binge, because who would torture themselves with such a repetitive narrative?

But today, she'd encountered a severe plot twist.

Someone had shown up. Most surprisingly.

Her boyfriend of five weeks suddenly appeared when she sat down on a frigid bench to inhale her lunch. Foster Trent was totally breaking trend, but he was doing way more than that.

"I know this seems fast." He flashed a handsome grin and lowered on bended knee right there on the busy sidewalk, his right hand holding out a ring that sparkled far too much under overcast skies. "But I can't wait any longer. Elise Layne Malvern, will you marry me?"

She squinted, her gaze transfixed on the prism exploding inside the solitaire-cut stone. This wasn't how she'd expected her lunch break to unfold. Her plans had included only her routine stalking of the taco truck on Penn Avenue followed by cramming enough MSG in her system to get through the long stretch of video editing at work. A proposal was not on the itinerary.

Rogue snowflakes pricked her face. Ugh. Forget cusses, snow was the worst four-letter word. She had a not-so-healthy hatred for the evil white stuff, but she couldn't let old memories cloud her focus. Her eyes connected with Foster's, and she rallied for courage. "We've only been on eight dates. No, seven." Her last boyfriend waited two-and-a-half years to pop the question. Over a hundred dates. She and Foster haven't even reached double digits.

"It's quick. I know." He switched to his salesman voice—that confident tone he employed to persuade clients to forgo any reservations and sign on the dotted line. But Elise wasn't purchasing a timeshare in Tahiti for a week. If she agreed to this deal, the terms were for life. "I got a good feeling about us."

The only feeling she had was a sharp pinch in her gut, squeezing her street taco back up her esophagus. Foster Trent could be "the one," but it was too soon to tell. She'd only known him for two months. "I—I need more time." Because no one second-guessed their second guesses more than her. Overthinking wasn't a pesky habit; it was her way of life.

His brown eyes dimmed. "I'd like an answer pretty quick." He abandoned the whole kneeling gig, grimacing at the wet spot on his jeans, and reclaimed his seat beside her. "There's a job opportunity in Dallas. I'm hoping to move by the end of next month."

So not only would she be getting married, she would be moving a thousand miles away as well? She fidgeted with the wispy ends of her scarf, the same shade as her pale green eyes. Eyes that no doubt betrayed her hesitation. "I don't know what to say." She'd heard of relationships that began as whirlwinds and lasted the long run, but she wasn't wired for impulsivity. No, her motherboard had a very slow processor. While the rest of the world made decisions at 5G speed, her pace was more AOL dial-up.

"Say yes. Come on this adventure with me."

Her gaze roamed the towering skyscrapers, the jagged lines of buildings poking the gray sky. "But then I'd have to leave Pittsburgh." Where her only remaining family lived. Where all her dreams were anchored. She interned at the legendary Heinz Hall as a creative marketer, but she wanted more. Since she was fifteen, it had been her hope to win a second violin seat in the Pittsburgh Symphony Orchestra. To play on the same stage as her mother.

If only she dared grab the chance to sign up for an audition. But no,

Elise Malvern didn't just have cold feet, they were frostbitten. Too frozen to run after anything out of her comfort zone.

A car horn blared in the distance, and she returned to the moment. This utterly absurd moment. She scrunched her nose. Shouldn't she be maniacally happy? Or excited? Something? Truth was, they'd bypassed key relationship markers. Such as, she'd never cooked for him at her apartment because she was a culinary failure. Did he know she ate cereal most nights for dinner? He'd never seen her without makeup or with unruly hair.

And she didn't know his hopes and dreams, if he wanted any children, or his method of changing a toilet paper roll. Important couples' details! They hadn't even exchanged "I love you's." *Did* she love him? How could she? She hardly knew him.

But what was most odd, besides the ring, was that Foster hardly showed any interest in her on their first few dates. He wasn't that into her. It wasn't until she accidentally spilled about—

Her spine straightened. The engagement stone sat between them on the bench, directly beside the remains of her beloved taco. She unclenched her teeth. "Okay, Foster. I'll marry you."

His smile stretched wide. "You just made me the happiest man alive."

"And I'm happy you don't mind that I'm broke. Probably will be for the foreseeable future, since I'm currently an intern with no other work experience." She forced a perky smile. "You'll have to support us both until I find a job. I'm thinking three or four years. Maybe longer. I'm extremely picky about my place of employment."

He jolted. "But—"

"But what?"

"I. . ." His gaze dwindled to the snowy sidewalk, a crease forming between his blond brows. "I thought you had a trust fund."

Ugh, knew it. "You did?"

He gave a stunned nod. "Or that you will." He rubbed the back of his neck. "Doesn't it become yours in March, when you turn twenty-five?"

"Oh, that?" She gave a careless shrug, gleaning from that one theater class she'd taken her sophomore year at Carnegie Mellon. "I can't touch a penny until all my college loans are paid off. Which is roughly the amount of the trust. After those are clear, I may have a few dollars left."

His jaw slacked.

"Of course, I'll have to use whatever's remaining toward a modest wedding. What are your thoughts on imitation crushed velvet?"

"For your, uh, dress?"

"No, your tux. For my dress, I'm going to repurpose my prom gown. Do brides wear neon-pink zebra print?" She tapped her index finger on her chin. "Doesn't matter. We'll make it work."

"Elise, I—I thought that—"

"Though we might need to postpone the honeymoon until we can afford one." She gave his shoulder an exaggerated squeeze. "But I firmly believe our undying love for each other can get us through any financial strain." Her attention shifted to the solitaire. "Or we can just return this gorgeous diamond. I don't need a fancy, extravagant ring. We can live off the several thousand dollars it's no doubt worth." She made a play for the ring box, but he swiped it from reach.

He darted to his feet as if the park bench had grown fangs and bitten his backside. "You know, you're right. We hardly know each other. I'll just hold on to this." He quickly shoved the box into the pocket of his puffer coat.

"Seems you know a lot about me already, Foster. My middle name, my favorite food truck." Probably from being a social media creeper. "And when I break for lunch." She didn't want to contemplate how he'd obtained that information. "But what you failed to discover. . ." She leveled a gaze on him, abandoning her feigned flaky attitude. "Is that my family owns one of the leading auction houses in western Pennsylvania. That diamond is as phony as your proposal."

His face blanched, and she was pretty sure the lady on the nearby bench lowered her magazine.

Elise recognized his *busted* look. She'd seen it repeatedly on the faces of those trying to pull one over on her grandfather. Many tried to pass off their paste jewelry as genuine. But Pap was sharp, and he'd taught her everything he knew. How to sift the fake from the authentic. If only she had that talent in selecting boyfriends, there wouldn't even have been a second date with Foster-the-fortune-hunter.

His shoulders curled forward. "I'm sorry, Elise."

"For what? Being a scammer? Offering up a dollar-store diamond?" It was a good fake; she'd give him that. But he'd picked the wrong girl to swindle.

"That business opportunity, the one I mentioned in Dallas. It's for my own travel agency. But I need eighty grand to buy it. The banks won't loan me anything."

"And you thought to take my dead mother's money to finance it? How charming." She snatched her purse. "Don't call. Don't text. Don't come near me again. Because just like that ring, you're worth nothing to me."

❦

Sunlight fought free from the oppressing clouds and poured into the arched window, bathing the grand lobby of Heinz Hall with light.

Elise took in the scene through the lens of her camera. The fifty-foot vaulted Venetian ceiling hovered over marble floors and staircase, the gilded pillars lining the balcony like tall, decorated soldiers. This space always reminded Elise of a European palace. The classic and elegant atmosphere could rival any fancy ballroom depicted in a Jane Austen novel. And while Elise had always hoped she'd meet her Mr. Darcy, today she'd encountered a modern-day version of George Wickham—the villain who pursued heiresses—well, more like he pursued their fortunes.

She bottled a sigh, squeezing her fingers tighter on her camera. Then, keeping steady, she leaned back to fit both chandeliers in the frame. These sister pieces were original to the theater. Almost a hundred years old and weighed a ton each, yet breathtaking. They only proved weight and age never decided beauty. Elise snapped the shot then nodded her approval.

She switched to recording mode and panned out. Every inch of this space was a work of art from floor to ceiling. She stood for several long seconds in this regal spot. After her crazy lunch break breakup, she needed normalcy. She needed peace. She needed—

"Did you honestly wear a neon-pink zebra print gown to your prom?"

She needed to think twice before confiding so quickly in Kinley, fellow marketing intern, apartment roommate, and routine prier.

Elise lowered her camera. "This should be enough material." She and Kinley were responsible for attaining footage of different areas of Heinz Hall for a quick educational video. "*A virtual field trip*," her supervisor called it. "What do you think?"

"I think you're ignoring me and my very important question about your awkward fashion choices." Kinley crossed her arms with a huff.

"I never actually wore it." Because Elise never went to her high school prom. She'd been stood up by Pierson Brooks. And while she received an explanation from Pierson's grandmother, the stooder-upper hadn't reached out to her in the following days. . .or the following nine years. Which wouldn't have hurt so much if they hadn't been best friends.

Elise looked through her camera again. Maybe she could get a better angle. Not like she didn't have a million shots of these chandeliers already, but being behind the camera was her comfort. "And is that all you caught from my monologuing? There's a bigger factor here. Like the one where Foster tried to rip me off."

"For the record, I never liked him. He looks like a man who irons his socks." Kinley placed a hand on Elise's elbow, her brows lifting in concern. "How are you coping?"

She drew a calming breath. "I'm okay. Just weirded out by it all." She hadn't expected a proposal today any more than she'd planned on being dateless for tomorrow night. But since her plus-one had been Foster, she'd rather go solo to Dorothea Hart's elaborate birthday party. Not ideal, but she couldn't think about tomorrow. Or Dorothea's grandson. She'd spent enough time dwelling on him and her botched prom night. That was ages ago, she was past it, and even though they'd been close for a few years in their teens, he most likely didn't remember her now. And most likely wouldn't be at the party. "Did you contact those names of potential donors for our Theatre Throwback promo?"

"Didn't I tell you?" Kinley grabbed the camera bag and handed it to Elise. "I finished that two weeks ago. I got ahold of everyone on your list. Some have photos they'll scan and send, and others have playbills they're willing to donate."

"All from the Loew's Penn?" Elise couldn't hide the excitement in her voice. Theatre Throwback was her baby. Every Thursday, she posted a picture about Heinz Hall's history on Instagram. The account had gained popularity since she started highlighting the early years when the building was Loew's Penn Theatre. Back in the day, people came here by the thousands, and a fifty-cent admission secured hours of entertainment—a live stage show followed by the latest silent film.

"All from Loew's." She gave a triumphant smile. "We just have to keep our eye on the mail. Things should start pouring in soon."

Elise finished her work in the lobby and spent the rest of her shift editing footage from last night's symphony performance while shoving down the longing to perform on that stage rather than film it from behind her camera. She closed her laptop and glanced at the calluses on her fingertips, resulting from her vigorous rehearsing. Like an athlete in pursuit of a championship, she drove herself to practice her violin day after day for hours on end.

Kinley chatted the entire walk home, not seeming to pause for breath until they reached their apartment door, where a box was propped against it.

Elise stooped and read the label. "It's for me."

"Who from?"

"There's no return address." She shifted her purse on her shoulder and lifted the package, which was surprisingly light for its size. Elise moved aside as Kinley opened the door, and they filed inside.

Elise stepped out of her heels, and her pinky toes sang in relief. After discarding her coat and scarf, she eyed the box. Who would send her anything? It wasn't her birthday, and it couldn't be anything she'd purchased. She'd cut back on retail therapy after finally getting her credit cards under control from her Christmas shopping last month. The package was a mystery. And just like surprises, she didn't like mysteries.

Kinley now sat cross-legged on the carpet beside the package. "The scissors are in the drawer under the silverware."

Chuckling at her friend's impatience, Elise located the orange-handled scissors and sliced through the packaging tape. Placing the box between them, she lifted the flaps and removed the packing filler, only to discover a stack of papers. "It's playbills."

"Old ones!" Kinley picked one up carefully and inspected the yellowed, warbled program. "It's from a stage show."

Elise leaned in. "Look right there." She pointed to the black-inked letters. "Loew's Penn Theatre." But it didn't make any sense. Had Kinley accidentally given the donors their home address? Elise zeroed her gaze on the playbill's date. "This is from 1927." Her excitement tripled. "You know what that means, right?"

"That this paper is really old?"

"The Loew's Penn Theatre opened in 1927. These are inaugural playbills." Her mind started exploding with ideas on how to incorporate these gems for Theatre Throwback. With delicate movements, Elise opened the playbill and read the cast list. Unfortunately, she didn't recognize any of the actors' names.

"There's more in the box." Kinley dug deeper into the cardboard pit and withdrew what looked like a strange sort of coat. While tugging it free, something else tumbled out of the box.

A miniature violin.

Unlike the ancient playbills, the trinket looked new. Elise picked it up. She smiled at the curved, wooden body complete with four strings attached to tiny tuning pegs. It was as if someone had taken her instrument and shrunk it. A yellow ribbon was attached at either end, causing her to realize it was a Christmas tree ornament.

But Christmas was three weeks ago. If this wasn't an antique or didn't have any connection to the Loew's Penn, why had someone put it in the package? She turned it over and found an engraving.

You're never without my love ~ your father

She almost dropped the ornament.

It couldn't be. Yet the box was addressed to her. Did that mean this was from *her* father? The man who'd been absent from her life from the get-go? Almost twenty-five years without a word from him. No cards on birthdays. No present on holidays. No attendance at any of her graduations. Her gaze dropped to the engraving, her chest burning hot. Never without his love? Yeah, right. If that was love, she wanted no part of it.

"What's wrong?" Kinley's voice bled through her thoughts. "You should see your face right now."

Elise shook her head. She didn't want to discuss the ornament or her AWOL birth father. "Is there a note or anything?"

Kinley gently rustled through the blank newsprint used for packing. "Nope."

Okay, why hadn't her father left a note? Maybe the inscription was the message he wanted to send. She inspected the mini violin again. The present year was etched under the words, confirming its newness. Yet it stirred old feelings of rejection. Caging a sigh, she returned the ornament to the box. This was why she hated surprises.

"What do you make of this?" Kinley all but shoved the jacket into Elise's hands.

With what transpired over the past few minutes, Elise had forgotten about the bulky coat. The seams were long, and the fur was fake. It had all the makings of a stage costume. "I wonder if this was used for the live show." She searched through the pockets. Nothing. And then she opened the coat to search for a tag. But instead of a tag naming a designer, there was a small, yellowed paper pinned to the inside of the collar. "There's something written here."

"Really?"

"It says 'Sophie Walters.'"

CHAPTER TWO

SOPHIE

*I*t was quite tiresome getting arrested every night of the week.

"I caught the thief!" The policeman's fingers dug into my wrists, pinning my hands behind my back.

I jerked, but his grasp only tightened.

With a grunt, he urged me forward. "Found her climbing out the rear window of your estate, Miss Townsend."

Through the dark veil concealing my face, I saw a woman approach, her bright blue eyes narrowing in disgust. "What have we here?" With quick movements, she searched my coat pocket and withdrew the necklace I'd stashed earlier. Her manicured hand lifted the chain high, the gaudy stones glittering in the light. "My jewels! These are priceless!"

The policeman shifted behind me, his chest pressing into my shoulder. "The Townsend diamonds are irreplaceable. Glad I was able to be of service."

"Unhand me!" I writhed and kicked to no avail.

"Let's unmask this criminal, shall we?" Her evening gown swirled about her long legs as she circled me like a high-society vulture. She snatched the hat from my head, and I was thankful the netting didn't catch on my nose.

She gasped. "It's you!"

"Of course it's me." Because I, Sophie Walters, always played the villain. Both onstage and off. The blinding spotlight tore into my vision, the audience a dark blur in my peripheral. "You stole from me." A fiery curl fell over my left eye, and I tossed it back with a jerk of my head. "It's only right I return the favor." And so concluded my lines in this play. All seven of them.

My pretend ex-fiancé, the other lead role in the show, Gerald Franklin, stepped forward and wrapped a protective arm around the leading lady. His gaze raked over me in a disdainful perusal. "She didn't steal me. You and I were over." He raised his chin, giving the crowd a glimpse of his handsome profile. "I could never marry you."

I'd heard Gerald's last line since opening night, and each time it stung. Because five long years ago, I wrote those exact words to the man I once loved. . .then abandoned. So acting pained came naturally.

Lina Landis shot an adoring look at Gerald. Not entirely an act either, considering the two had been sweethearts since the first day of rehearsals. With a mocking smile, Lina scooped up my discarded hat and slapped it on my head. Hard. "Take her away, Officer."

The curtain closed on my exit while the main leads passionately embraced. Dick Leibert played the final notes on the state-of-the-art pipe organ, the massive instrument that could produce the sound of every orchestra piece with the volume of a fifty-man symphony. That feature alone drew the masses, for it was billed "the greatest musical instrument the world has ever known."

Basically, it was loud. But not as loud as tonight's audience. They roared their approval, the thunderous applause rising to the gilded ceiling. The energy was so palpable, I wouldn't be surprised if the elegant chandeliers shivered. All because love triumphed. The couple secured their happily ever after. Such a pity this kind of ending was reserved for the stage. I wasn't as fortunate.

With a sigh, I lifted the netting over the top of my hat just before the curtain reopened. We took our bows. Gerald and Lina stepped forward to receive their due recognition.

"How are you feeling, Sophie?" Violet Salter asked through her cemented smile. "When Lina smacked that hat on your skull, I could practically hear your brain rattle."

My temples throbbed in agreement, but it wasn't Lina's fault. "She has to make it believable."

The remaining company of twenty retreated another step as Lina and Gerald gestured to the pit band in a show of respect for their musical accompaniment. Dick stood from the organ bench and bowed. The audience responded with increased clapping.

Violet snorted while keeping her glowing grin in place. Impressive, really. "Lina doesn't make anything believable. She only has the lead role because the director's batty over her."

I acknowledged her words with a gentle smile. No need to add any fuel to Violet's fire concerning Lina.

With one more exuberant wave to the crowd, the cast retreated another step back while the curtain closed. "Finally," I muttered, and worked on removing the stifling duster coat. Though I couldn't blame my wardrobe for this suffocating feeling pressing into my lungs. I'd had this sensation ever since I left California and set heel back in Pittsburgh. I swore I would never return. Yet here I was.

Lloyd Harris, former vaudeville star and our director, waved his arms, garnering our attention. "Hold it, folks."

My fingers stilled on the second button of my coat.

"Don't run to the dressing rooms yet. I need you all to go upstairs to Rehearsal Room D for a meeting."

"Oh great," Violet whispered while tugging her satin gloves off. "I don't think I can stomach another soliloquy about how fabulous Lina is and how awful the rest of us are."

Violet was cast as Lina's best friend, but off stage it couldn't be any further from the truth. The two were rivals, and I suspected it had something to do with Gerald. Both of them seemed to have taken a shine to the man. But to be honest, Violet seemed to take a shine to every fedora-capped gentleman within a twenty-mile radius.

Fran Jackson moved beside me and whispered, "What do you think this is about?"

I shrugged. With Lloyd, it could be anything, but knowing Fran, she'd already imagined a variety of scenarios concerning this meeting. We'd been friends from grammar school, and I'd learned Fran had two talents—acting and jumping to unwarranted conclusions.

Lloyd gestured to Gerald and Lina. "No signing tonight."

The couple paused, their expressions twisting in confusion. Since opening night, Gerald and Lina had signed autographs while the production crew prepared for the silent film feature. The stage door led to an alley where they greeted those brave enough to leave the plush seats during intermission and squeeze into the narrow space in hopes of a handshake and signed playbill.

As a group, we climbed the stairs to the rehearsal room. Joe Neville appeared at my side.

"Here, Sophie." He took my hand, pausing my steps, and dropped two white pills into my palm. "This will help you feel better."

I flicked a skeptical glance at the tablets. While Joe may play a policeman in the play, he wasn't the most upstanding regarding the law.

He grinned at my raised brow. "It's only aspirin. I promise."

"Thank you, but I'm fine."

"You were rubbing your temples a second ago." He nodded at Fran as she passed, then returned his attention to me. "I figured you had a headache."

"That's very thoughtful of you. Though I don't need anything for my head." I handed him the pills, and his thumb lingered longer than necessary on my knuckles.

Fran and Violet waited for me at the entrance of the rehearsal room. We walked inside and stood at the back of the group.

Once everyone was accounted for, Lloyd ambled to the front of the room. As far as directors went, his disposition leaned on the mild side. Yet he swiped at his brow as if to rub away agitation. Then he straightened his already perfect waistcoat.

My forehead wrinkled, and I exchanged a glance with Violet.

Lloyd cleared his throat. Twice. "Last night, not only did we have a sold-out crowd, but Mr. and Mrs. Stoneberry, the owners of Stoneberry Tires, were our distinguished guests."

Hardly the disturbing news I expected. Since the Loew's Penn opened six weeks ago, the theater had received plenty of well-known personages, such as steel mill tycoons, railroad owners, and bank presidents. People came from all around to glimpse the breathtaking structure. It could almost be considered a museum with all the imported decor. Crystal from Vienna. Artwork by Renaissance masters. Silk damask drapes from Europe.

I turned my attention back to our director.

"Last night, Mrs. Stoneberry was robbed."

I covered my mouth with my hand.

Lloyd's gaze darted about as if searching for a place to land. "Now, I'm not accusing anyone. The robbery took place at Mrs. Stoneberry's home in the night hours, but since this was the last place she visited wearing the jewelry, it's obvious that questions be asked." He motioned to someone in the connecting rehearsal room. "Detective, please join us."

My gaze drifted stage left. A man emerged through the doorway, and my diaphragm squeezed so hard, I fought for breath.

Violet nudged my elbow. "If that's the fella asking questions, I volunteer to go first. I may even confess to a few crimes." She snickered, but I couldn't summon a smile. I could barely move. I'd never experienced stage fright, but I was certain it couldn't be as vicious as the dread roiling through me, freezing everything from bone to cell.

If I could ever regain dexterity, maybe I could tug the veil back over my face. Or drop to my knees and crawl out the other door. "Violet." My voice was a reedy yet desperate whisper. "Shield me."

"What's the matter?" Her black brows pinched.

"I can't let him see me." But it was too late. I locked eyes with Sterling Monroe. The man I'd left at the altar.

I was an actress. A professional pretender. I could do this. It didn't matter if my knees crumbled like stage powder. Such were my thoughts as I'd paced Rehearsal Room D, waiting as my fellow cast members were questioned, one by one, in the adjoining space.

Now it was my turn, and my stomach swirled so rapidly, I feared it had knocked all my organs out of place. I draped my coat over a chair but left my hat on, taming my bobbed curls. My simple frock did my curvy frame no favors, tugging in all the wrong spots. But it didn't matter if I was dressed in potato sacks. I would lean on all the years of theatrical training. My determined steps brought me directly in front of Sterling. Yes, I could look straight into his dark eyes and act like his powerful presence had no effect on me.

For I was a woman of the arts.

"Miss Walters."

I was also a woman with a voice for silent film.

My mouth opened, but no words filled it. All that came forth was a faint squeak. Wonderful. So much for being casual. In control.

I blamed Sterling's voice for the absence of mine. There was no degree of recognition in his tone. Any onlooker would judge Sterling and me as strangers, not two souls that almost linked for a lifetime.

Miss Walters. Not Sophie.

The formal greeting stung, but I deserved it. And much more.

"It is *Miss* still, isn't it?" He must've misread my silence, for his sharp gaze dropped to my left hand.

I clamped my lips together and ran my tongue along my teeth to be sure the muscles in my mouth still worked to form words. Satisfied, I tried again. "G—Good evening, Sterling." As for his question, I let my bare ring finger speak for me. I couldn't approach the topic of my unmarried state. Because the last time I saw him was the day before *our* wedding. Before it all went wrong.

Time hadn't altered him. From the strong angles of his cheekbones to the broad definition of his shoulders to the arms that required the seams let out in all of his jacket sleeves, every facet of Sterling revealed strength.

And in his eyes, I'd proved myself the weakest sort.

"Please call me Detective Monroe." He corrected my informal address. No coldness marked his eyes. Just indifference. Which was worse. "Have a seat." He gestured to the chair closest to the table, yet he seemed inclined to stand.

This rehearsal room was arranged like the other ones. A handful of chairs grouped around an oblong table filled the front of the space, leaving most of the area as an open floor necessary for staging scenes.

I lowered onto the chair. "You're not in uniform. Are you no longer a sergeant?" Had he been promoted? Five years ago he was in charge of the police investigative department. But today he wore a dark brown tweed suit tailored perfectly to his large frame.

He flicked open a notepad, a blatant dismissal of my question. "Mrs. Stoneberry went backstage to congratulate the cast members last evening." His eyes raised from his notes and peered at me from under his hat. "She visited for about twenty minutes. Did you see her?"

"No."

His gaze trekked across my face, no doubt searching for any signs of deceit. "Did you see anything suspicious?"

Everything in my line of work was suspicious. I performed with twenty other people whose united skill was make-believe. Most didn't even go by their real name, me included. But he'd meant if I'd seen anything about the robbery. "No. I left right after the curtain closed."

"Why?" His hooded stare relayed no emotion. Well, other than boredom.

This really wasn't fair. After years of silence, this—this!—was my first conversation with Sterling. An interrogation. Him, the man I was supposed to marry. His name, the one I was supposed to take as my own. His face, the perfect arrangement of eyes, nose, and lips that I was to wake up seeing every day.

I had nothing to do with the robbery, but I'd committed a crime of the heart. What kind of woman abandoned her fiancé at the altar? I humiliated him. I crushed his spirit. And I was forbidden to speak about it. "I left because I *had* to."

His gaze snapped to mine, his dark slanted brows inching north.

Had he caught the undertones of my words?

He blinked, and the flicker of intensity present in his eyes a second ago was replaced with disinterest. "Care to expound?"

I sighed. While I couldn't detail my actions five years ago, I could explain my reason for leaving after last night's curtain call. "I had to meet someone."

"A rendezvous?"

"An obligation." I intended to specify further, but something in his expression stopped me.

He flipped a page in his notepad and studied it. "What's your role in this play?"

"One of no consequence." I've had my share of rejection both in Hollywood and Broadway, but was it wrong to hope again for more? I had dreams of stepping out from the shadows of my past and into the spotlight of my dreams. My heart was set on seeing my name on a marquee, having my own dressing room, landing that role that catapulted my career and proved once and for all that I had a purpose for being here. I had already lost Sterling. Was it wrong to want a consolation prize of attaining one life goal?

"What's your character's name?"

Why did that matter? "I'm nameless." I shrugged. "My role is that of a jewel th—" My lips pinched tight.

He took a commanding step, hovering over me. "A jewel thief?" He rubbed the turn of his jaw lined with late-day stubble. "How very interesting. I'm here investigating a jewel theft, and you're the robber."

"In the play." I leaned forward in my seat, my voice squeaking a bit. "Only in the play. But I'm not a very good one."

"Actress?"

"Robber."

His arms folded across his chest, and his handsome head tilted as if to say, *Enlighten me.*

I crossed my own arms and smacked my elbow on the wooden armrest. Not the same effect. "For one, I wear this oversized driving duster."

I motioned toward the other room as if Sterling could see the bulky coat hanging over the chair. "Who would rob a house in something you can hardly move around in?" A soft sigh escaped. "But I didn't write the play. I just do what the script says."

He watched me, one brow slightly higher than the other. "Looks like I'm done here." He shoved the notepad into his trouser pocket. "Unless there's anything else you can add."

"There is one thing."

His gaze met mine.

I stood to my feet. He was only a touch away, but there was much more distance between us. "I'm sorry, Sterling. For everything."

His eyes drifted to a discarded playbill on the table. "Looks like you got what you really wanted."

He thought I chose my career over him? Of course he did. It was safer to allow him to believe the lie. Because the truth was far worse.

CHAPTER THREE

ELISE

$\mathcal{T}$onight Elise was going to party like it was 1959.

She stepped in the classy William Penn Hotel dressed as someone who stepped out of a *Happy Days* episode. Dorothea Hart, a longtime friend and card-playing partner of Elise's grandmother, turned eighty today, and the birthday girl wanted a fifties-themed party in the swanky, historic ballroom. Of course, Dorothea could afford it. Or rather her grandson could, and footing the bill was undoubtedly his atonement for not attending her octogenarian celebration.

Pierson Brooks had a habit of not showing up for things.

Which didn't bother Elise. Because after yesterday's bizarre breakup with Foster, followed by the surprise package from her could-be birth father, she was in no mood to see her adolescent best friend who'd ghosted her and ended up a platinum recording artist.

Elise adjusted her grip on Dorothea's gift bag, and her free hand slid down the blush-pink fabric of her swing dress. Fresh out of poodle skirts, she'd rummaged her closet earlier this week in hopes of finding something vintage-looking, only to come up empty. Amazon Prime for the win. The sweetheart neckline and fit-and-flare cut paired nicely with her mother's pearls and a cream belt.

"There you are." Her grandmother, Nancy, matriarch of the Malvern family, retired schoolteacher of forty years, and current wearer of tight leather pants, met Elise at the entrance to the ballroom. "Dorothea's looking for you."

"Grancy." Elise had accidentally stumbled upon the moniker when she was three years old and attempted to say Grandma Nancy. The name *Grancy* had emerged. But now she wasn't attempting to say a difficult word, she was just trying to utter something in response to her eccentric grandma's wardrobe choice. "Red leather pants? You look—"

"Neato?" She struck a pose. "Keen?"

"Yep, exactly what I was going to say." She linked arms with Grancy, and they stepped into the grand ballroom. This hotel was just as historic as Heinz Hall and equally elegant. The two-tiered room boasted a balcony decked in gilded, gold-leaf accents. A dozen chandeliers hung over a group of seniors doing the Loco-motion. It was the perfect way to spend a Saturday evening.

"Oh, there's Lucy Mansfeld." Grancy pushed her glasses up her nose and peered in the direction of a dainty older woman. "I didn't think she'd have the courage to show her face after the thrashing I gave her last night."

"Poker again?" As if it could be anything else.

She nodded. "Of course."

"Do I need to remind you what the scriptures say about gambling?"

"It's all in good fun."

Elise rolled her eyes. Dorothea and Grancy were always playing poker or making wagers of some sort. Thankfully, they never bet money. Elise was saved from a response by her phone. "Give me a second," she said, spying Kinley's name on the screen.

Grancy frowned. "Don't be long. Dorothea's waiting."

Elise nodded with a smile and answered her cell as Grancy joined her friends. "Hey, Kinley."

"Don't hate me."

Nothing good ever came from a greeting like that. "What's up?"

"Remember how a second violin seat opened for the symphony a few weeks back?"

How could she forget? "Yes." That familiar disappointment slid from her heart to her stomach. Oh, how she'd waited for a chair to become available, only to hesitate when a spot finally opened. She had everything ready to submit—recordings of her performing, recommendations from her professors at Carnegie Mellon. But there'd been a flood of applicants, and the audition coordinator closed submissions after one day. Twenty-four hours of reluctance poked another hole in her dreams.

Was it wrong to ask God for another chance when she'd ruined the first opportunity?

Kinley's nervous chuckle rattled through the phone. "Well, I kinda did something."

Another song blared through the speakers as though the DJ had upped the volume. Elise readjusted her grip on the present's handles and pressed a finger to her other ear. "Hold on, Kin. I can't hear you over the doo-wops." She hustled toward the door, keeping a careful eye on her steps. The last time she wore these heels, she took a spill at Sunoco and got tangled in the fuel pump hose. She also didn't want to inflict a bone fracture on some unsuspecting partygoer by plowing them over, so her gaze volleyed between her toes and right in front of her.

She reached the door, and someone called her name. Dorothea? Elise glanced over her shoulder and smacked into someone.

Faster than you could say "hip replacement," her phone as well as Dorothea's present crashed to the ground. Elise reached out, hoping to break the fall of the elderly victim.

But she gripped muscle and leather. Humiliation burning, she raised her gaze and locked eyes with a Grammy Award winner.

Pierson Brooks.

Sturdy fingers wrapped Elise's bare upper arms, rippling warmth to her pinched toes. "You showed up." She winced at the obvious surprise in her tone.

Pierson's gorgeous blues blinked back at her.

"Hello," she muttered, wishing she could become invisible.

His gaze searched her face as if trying to place her. And failing. He had no idea who she was. *That's fine. It's fine.* His perfectly molded lips opened then closed, and he just stared at her like she had lipstick on her teeth. *Did* she have lipstick on her teeth? Too late now.

She had changed a lot since he'd last seen her nine years ago. Her braces were gone. She'd learned how to tone down her frizzy hair and level up her makeup skills. But had her appearance altered that much...or was she that forgettable?

He released her with an easy grin. "Sorry, my fault. I wasn't paying attention."

Seriously? Not one shred of recognition? Well, she wasn't going to embarrass herself further by stumbling through an introduction.

He dressed casually yet fit the party's theme in a leather jacket coupled with jeans and a white T-shirt. His dark, late-day stubble contrasted his cobalt eyes, giving him a bad boy look. He had that rebel aura like

James Dean, while she was the modern version of June Cleaver.

Her gaze fell to the ground. Dorothea's present! She hunched over the crumpled gift bag. "No, no, no." Scooping it up, she peered inside. The book wasn't ruined. She exhaled, but the weakened bag ripped in her hand. The book tumbled out.

Pierson reached and caught it. His head lifted with a smile. "Seems like you're struggling."

That could be her epitaph. "Yeah." She snatched her phone from the floor. Hesitantly, she placed it to her ear. "Kinley? You still there?"

"Yep!" Her voice sounded far away. She must've put Elise on speaker.

"Sorry, but I gotta go. I'll explain later." Elise quickly ended the call and caught Pierson's gaze. "I'll take that off your hands. Thank you." And since he didn't remember her, she could proceed with her evening plans—wishing Dorothea a happy birthday, eating her body weight in cake, and avoiding country music superstars.

But his gaze dipped to the gift he still held captive. "Is this for my grandmother?"

"Yes." She smoothed a hand over her hair, detesting the nervous itch crawling over her. "It's just a book I made." A downplayed move that didn't work because her voice squeaked.

He studied the abstract cover she'd designed, then opened to the first page. "That's her childhood home."

Elise was proud of that particular shot. She'd snapped the redbrick house at sunrise, a metaphor for the dawning of Dorothea's life.

Pierson's long silence made her shift.

She cast a nervous glance over her shoulder. She needed to find a way to remove the book from his careful study and return to the party. "I should probably give Dorothea her present now."

"Is that?" His gaze bounced from the page to the hallway. "That's right there."

She knew what picture he referenced—the lobby of this hotel. "Where Dorothea met her husband. They both worked at the William Penn." Which he would know. It was the very reason her party was here.

"Amazing." He flipped through the pages at a leisurely pace. "You told her life story through pictures."

"I tried." And she also tried not to let the awe in his southern drawl affect her. While she was pleased with how the book turned out, it probably appeared amateurish. But what could she give the woman whose grandson got her whatever she wanted? Pierson might be busy with his career, but he'd always had extravagant presents delivered to Dorothea. That lady was the only woman Elise knew who drove a Tesla to bingo night.

"Elise?" His gaze lifted from the photos. "Elise Malvern?"

Oh man. She'd forgotten she'd written a special birthday message on the last page and signed it. There was no avoiding this now. All she could do was nod.

He shook his head, a smile building until his perfectly straight teeth gleamed under the fancy lights. "It's been years." He stepped closer with an impressive swagger. "How have you been?"

She thought he intended to return the book, but instead he drew her into a hug. Her cheek bounced off leather and woodsy cologne.

She pulled away with a nervous chuckle. "I'm well." As well as could be expected for a twentysomething whose internship was ending with no job in sight.

His gaze tracked the terrain of her face. Eyes that had locked with A-list celebrities, peered out upon thousands in stadiums, and stared into TV cameras. Her face felt relatively plain in comparison, yet he still looked at her. "You've grown older."

Oh, that did wonders for her already shriveling pride. She tugged the book from his hands. "Those kinds of lyrics won't win you any awards."

He tipped his head back with a laugh. "I didn't mean that as an insult. It's just that you look—"

"Oh wow!" A high-pitched squeal sounded from behind Elise.

She turned to find a starstruck woman. The petite blond was probably a few years younger than Elise. College student, maybe? True to her generation, the woman wasted no time whipping out her cell to snag a picture.

Pierson tensed, his discomfort as noticeable as his set jaw. Didn't he deal with these situations every day? Maybe he didn't want anyone knowing he was in Pittsburgh? Or perhaps he left his bodyguard at home. Elise did a quick check around. Unless Pierson's hired protector was an eighty-plus gentleman armed with Tic Tacs, he was on his own.

Phone posed for a direct shot, the young woman waved her other hand, fanning her face. "You look just like—"

"That guy from *Price is Right*?" Elise stepped in front of Pierson and smiled a cheesy grin. "Sorry, but he's not Drew Carey. No bidding on his showcase today."

Pierson snorted behind her.

The woman lowered her phone, finally glancing at Elise, confusion marking her perfectly penciled brows. "Um, no. I was going to say Pierson Brooks. He looks just like him."

Elise gave an exaggerated wave. "There have been rumors Pierson Brooks is in a special clinic in Cleveland. Something about deworming. Messy stuff." She grabbed Pierson's wrist and dragged him into the ballroom. "Nice talking to you," she called over her shoulder.

Amusement lit his eyes. "Deworming? That's the best you could come up with? That doesn't do much for my persona."

"I didn't make it up. The tabloids did." She *had* said it was a rumor. "Besides, it's an improvement from your current rep." The words ripped from her lips without thought. Why couldn't she have a filter like most people? Grancy's influence, one hundred percent. "I'm sorry. You don't deserve that."

"Yeah, actually I do." His gaze shifted to his boots, but not before she caught his haunted eyes. "It's no secret about my tanked reputation."

Over the past few months, Pierson's life had been smeared all over the tabloids, painting him as an arrogant, entitled star. Word leaked that he broke a promise to a college friend to sing at a local charity ball only to advance his career by performing at a major sporting event instead. Then things had gotten worse from there. Accusations of auto-tuning his voice and other damaging rumors.

They stepped farther into the ballroom, and no one looked his direction. Unlike the scene in the hall, these folks didn't care that a famous person had strolled into the room.

All except Dorothea Hart. The woman of the hour. "Is that my grandson?" She rushed over in a whirlwind of floral perfume and smothering affection.

Pierson tugged her into an embrace. "Ah, I missed you, Gram." He kissed her rouged cheek. "Happy birthday."

She squeezed him tighter, and Elise took the opportunity to study Pierson's profile. A view she'd had often during her teen years sitting beside him during music lessons. He claimed she'd grown, but she hadn't added an inch since she was sixteen. Perhaps she was a tad curvier, but mostly she'd only progressed in maturity. But him? The man was an easy six feet. He filled out his jacket and jeans. His hair was cropped short on the sides and back, blending into the top length, which was artfully mussed. Time had perfectly chiseled Pierson Brooks.

She'd seen him on every media possible—television, magazine, internet, pictures on Dorothea's phone. But flesh-and-blood Pierson was a sight to behold.

Processing this updated version of her adolescent friend, Elise set her book down with the other gifts.

Dorothea and Pierson reached the main table where Grancy and Pap were already seated.

Elise followed behind, determined to speak her salutations and flee. "Happy birthday, Dorothea. You look gorgeous on your special day." She hugged the older woman then straightened. That single chair in the far-right corner beside the dessert table had her name on it, but a not-so-feeble hand ringed her wrist.

"Thank you, sweetie. But don't hurry away." Dorothea pointed to the empty seat next to where Pierson now sat. "Your place is right there with us."

No, not going to happen. Her social battery was rapidly draining, and she didn't have enough charge to survive a night of awkward small talk with Pierson. Last evening's shock with the engraved ornament from her father lingered at the edges of her mind. She hadn't mentioned it to Grancy or Pap because she was still processing it all. Probably would be for the foreseeable future. Plus, she needed to escape before getting questioned about—

"Where's Foster?" Grancy stuffed a Wheat Thin into her mouth, some crumbs flaking onto her black blouse. Next to her, Pap was clad in a blue-checkered dinner coat.

Elise surrendered and claimed the chair between Grancy and Pierson. A distraction was in order. "Does this DJ take requests? How about a reprise of the Loco-motion?" She glanced around the table. "This time, Pap, you can lead." Mainly because he was the only one who could spill the beans. She'd told him everything about Foster this morning when she visited the auction house to update the website.

"You were supposed to bring Foster tonight?" Dorothea looked to Grancy, who was suspiciously eyeing Pap.

Huffing, Grancy snatched Pap's plate of cake away. "Tell us what you know, Leroy."

Pap stared at the empty space where his dessert once was, his plastic fork still raised. He turned his head slowly, and his gaze bypassed Grancy, settling on Elise with resignation. He was about to turn traitorous. Sold out over cake.

Grancy sighed and returned the plate. "Never mind, Leroy. I can take my losses gracefully." She unhooked the glitzy chain from her spectacles. "Here you go, Dorothea." She held out the glasses cord. "You won fair and square."

Elise choked on her own breath, her cheeks burning hot. "You wagered on my relationship with Foster?"

"Last month got a little boring." Grancy patted Elise's hand and looked sympathetically into her eyes. "I'm sorry things didn't work out with you two. But this is a bet I'm glad to lose. I never wanted Foster to propose in the first place."

"But he did."

"Pap!" A strangled sound came from somewhere in the vicinity of Elise's throat. This conversation needed redirecting. "Did you know this place had a speakeasy under the lobby?"

Grancy was unmoved. "He proposed?"

Elise waved to the ballroom doors. "With a tunnel that led to the road in case of a prohibition raid. They recently restored it to its former state. We can all go see. Right now sounds great."

"Leroy." Grancy had that tone she used when turning away persistent telemarketers. "What do you know?"

Her grandfather shoveled the chocolate cake into his mouth as if he sensed its imminent capture. He swallowed and dabbed his mouth with a napkin. "Foster proposed to her yesterday."

"Pap!" Elise groaned. "O-nay alking-tay."

Pierson chuckled. "Did you just speak Pig Latin?"

"The English language isn't working." She sent another pleading look to Pap, but he wasn't paying attention.

"Foster tried to use a phony rock to get her to say yes. Elise can spot a fake from a mile away."

She slid lower on her chair, debating whether to sink under the table and hide for a million years. They had a country music star at their table. A total tabloid target. And these people singled her out? She lifted her lashes and found Pierson's gaze on her. Oh, the humiliation of this day.

Unfortunately, Pap continued. "He asked her to marry him to get his grubby hands on her trust fund. She told him to take a hike." He reached across Grancy to give Elise a high five, which she met half-heartedly.

"See? This is why you need to take over the auction house. You have a good head on your shoulders and can—"

"Not today, Leroy." Grancy reached for her glasses chain from her friend. "Looks like I won the bet after all. Now that's settled. We need a new wager, Dorothea."

Elise cast a longing look at the dessert table. "Preferably not about my love life."

"Your last one before Foster didn't turn out as we bet either." Grancy shoveled more crackers into her mouth. "I had such hopes for Roland."

"Rylan," Elise corrected. Poor Rylan. They dated for two and a half years, but Elise hadn't been able to take the plunge into the next level in their relationship. So much for a fun Saturday evening. Her arms fell to her sides, and her left hand was scooped up in a warm, manly one.

Pierson's.

He gave her fingers an encouraging squeeze. Because he too knew that one never escaped the antics of meddling relatives.

"I have an idea." Dorothea observed the exchange between Elise and Pierson with a satisfied smile. "The next wager should be about matchmaking."

Elise flinched, knowing where this was headed and feeling helpless to prevent it. The Loco-motion wasn't a strong enough deterrent. Nor the story about the speakeasy. She needed the intervention of. . . "Pierson, don't you think it's time to sing that special song?"

He turned confused eyes on her. "What?"

She treaded dangerous waters, but she wasn't about to let any bet be placed on her and Pierson getting together. Their history was over. They had nothing in common except meddling grandmas with a penchant for gambling. And a very close mutual friend. That was all. He was guitar. She was violin. He was Nashville honky tonk. She was elegant concert halls. Other than the CMAs, cowboy boots and stilettos didn't mix. "Yes, that song you prepared for Dorothea. *Now* would be a great time." She gave him an imploring look.

His lips twitched as he leaned toward her. "I'm guessing you need me to run interference."

She nodded. "I'm desperate."

"Okay, Malvern." He grinned. "But you owe me."

Her stomach clenched. If he did a solid for her here, she supposed she'd quit sticking her tongue out at every magazine cover he was featured on at the pharmacy checkout.

"You're going to sing?" Dorothea's hand pressed over her heart. "That would be the best gift."

Pierson's eyes softened with affection. "I have the perfect one for you, Gram."

The famed singer brought every woman over fifty to their proverbial knees with his rendition of Elvis's *Fools Rush In*. Dorothea and her late husband danced to that song on their wedding day. Dorothea cried. Grancy leaned her head on Pap's shoulder. And Elise sighed with relief at the timely distraction.

Her phone chimed with an email alert, pulling her attention away from Pierson and his smooth voice. Kinley had forwarded something from the Pittsburgh Symphony.

Elise tapped the notification, and her fingers tightened on the phone. She scrolled the email, disbelief parting her lips. The message confirmed that her application had been accepted, and her audition was scheduled. Her previous, clipped convo with her friend came to mind. *Oh, Kinley, what have you done?* This wasn't just the audition of a lifetime, but the awakening of the inescapable nightmare that came with it.

CHAPTER FOUR

Sophie

*G*o in. Grab Violet. Get out.

I'd stepped inside the William Penn Hotel before but had never entered the building through an underground tunnel leading into the basement. More specifically, the speakeasy.

Sterling once told me over five hundred gin joints were stuffed within Pittsburgh's borders. And that was over five years ago. The number surely had increased as Prohibition dragged on.

I paused a few steps into the forbidden room as I took in the sophisticated atmosphere. This sublevel establishment seemed to match the grandeur of the hotel lobby directly above it. Papered walls in muted gold and black tones framed the space. Decorative sconces threw pale dots of light on the fancy tin ceiling. The only splash of vibrant color was the furniture, couches and chairs upholstered in rich scarlet.

I drew a breath and almost coughed. Cigarette smoke clashed with notes of various perfumes, my nose tingling at the odorous onslaught. A cluster of young women with glittering headpieces and tinkling laughter pranced past.

None of them Violet.

I tugged at the neckline of my gray sequined dress. It was one of my finer gowns with intricate stitching and coordinating wrap. I'd dug it out this evening to blend into the crowd, but I initially purchased the dress for an important audition with Metro Goldwyn Meyer. Having been dismissed by all the other studios, I thought I had finally caught a break. Yet I never made it to the general manager's door. The contract was given to a young Swedish actress named Greta Garbo.

Before reaching twenty-six years of age, I was rejected by Broadway and Hollywood. A failure from coast to coast. Not quite the legacy I'd hoped for.

I pushed back the rising sigh and continued my search for my friend.

A golden-haired man approached, his drink sloshing in his hand. "Hiya, gorgeous. Wanna dance?" He motioned toward the heap of fast-moving limbs connected to gyrating bodies crowding the center of the room. Jazz music performed by a three-person band bounced off the fancy tin ceiling. He inched closer, his ice-blue eyes attractive but predatory. "I'll make it worth your while."

"No. I'm not here to dance." I gave him my best I-could-claw-your-face-off look Sterling had taught me. "Or anything else."

He retreated a step.

"I'm looking for a friend." A friend I was going to throttle. Of all the dumb things Violet could do. Lloyd had warned us to avoid gin joints or he'd remove us from the show.

A familiar, high-pitched laugh sounded a few yards away.

"Excuse me," I muttered to the man and cut through the crowd toward the dark-haired woman. "Violet."

She whipped her head toward me. "Oh my dear, Sophie!" She blew an exaggerated kiss. "'Bout time you joined the fun." She fussed with fake pearls draped around her neck, then with half-lidded eyes, regarded the young man beside her. "This is my sweet friend, Miss Walters. She's an actress too. But a bit of a fuddy-duddy." She snorted at her words.

The man's gaze slid over my form, and I worked to keep my temper in check. I ignored the note of masculine approval in his eyes as well as Violet's unkind remark. I'd come to aid a friend who appeared unaware of the damaging consequence of the situation. She would indeed be sorry if Lloyd found out. Even though my role was small, there came a certain prestige with working at the Loew's Penn Theatre. Violet and I were easily replaceable.

"Time to go." I tugged the glass from her hand, earning her scowl, and set it on the table behind her. "We'll grab a strong cup of coffee on the way back."

"She doesn't have to leave." The gentleman stood a little taller. "I'll escort her home."

"How chivalrous." I turned toward the man who had more oil in his smile than grease in his slicked-back hair. "Are you also willing to pay her rent and all her expenses when she gets fired for visiting a speakeasy?"

He sputtered. "Well. . .I. . ."

"That's what I thought." I didn't wait for Violet's response but wrapped an arm around her, keeping her steady and propelling her toward the exit.

Once we were through the tunnel and on Oliver Avenue, Violet released a contented sigh. "That was great fun." Her words had no slur in them. "We don't need to stop for coffee, Soph. Not unless you want to."

I froze on the sidewalk. "Wait. Your speech is back to normal. You mean, you're not—"

"Juiced to the brim?" She laughed. "So I fooled you too? I'm getting better." She linked her arm in mine. "I wasn't drunk at all, my friend. It was an act."

My brows scrunched. "Why?"

"For fun, of course." She tugged her cloche hat. "Don't you ever pretend for the thrill of it? Why, just last week, I had an entire café convinced I was a British heiress." She squeezed my arm. "I'm sorry I called you a fuddy-duddy. I didn't mean it. Though you could afford to liven up a bit." She sent me a sympathetic smile, as if my staying away from gin joints was a pitiful stance.

"I prefer to keep my job. If Lloyd finds out, you could lose your part." As would I, for the simple act of retrieving her. "If I was—"

"If, if, if," she lightly sang. "My mother always said, 'In the center of life is the word *if*, but don't let that keep you from living.'" She curled an arm around a streetlamp and spun around it as if the metal post were her partner in a silent dance. "That's it! I'm going to make you my project, Sophie. I will help you step out and embrace the moment."

"Thank you for the kind offer, but all I want to embrace is my pillow and sleep." I hadn't slept well last night or the one before. I blamed Sterling for the dark circles under my eyes. It had been two days since I'd seen him at the theater. Not only had I failed at extricating him from my heart, but he'd now taken residence in my head. Sterling Monroe was consuming me piece by piece.

Violet's mother was right. In the center of life *was* a big "if." Those two letters held the power to haunt. What if I had never gone to that terrible place the night before my wedding? What if I had spoken up? What if I had never left the man I loved at the altar?

We continued our walk to the boardinghouse where Violet, Fran, and I rented rooms.

Violet nudged my shoulder. "How'd you know I was at the William Penn?"

"Joe Neville told me after tonight's show." I had run to the dressing room to catch Violet, but she'd already left for the speakeasy. "He was concerned."

She snorted. "Like he should talk. Why just last week I caught him—" Her mouth crimped shut.

"What?"

"Nothing. I'm not a tattletale like Joe is." She raised her chin. "And I didn't tell him. He must've overheard me asking that dishy detective to join me."

I inhaled a sharp breath. "Detective Monroe? Violet, he's a policeman. You should be grateful he didn't come tonight to arrest you."

She stared at me. "No, he's not."

"Not what?"

"He's not a policeman." Her smug smile revealed her pleasure in knowing Sterling better than I. "He's a private investigator."

My jaw slacked. When had this happened? Sterling had been determined to climb the ranks of the police force with dreams of becoming commissioner. Violet eyed me as if awaiting a response. No chance I was about to confess my history with Sterling. "Oh, I just assumed he was a cop."

"I'm disappointed he didn't show tonight. I made it a personal goal to make him smile. Not that I don't admire the brooding look, but I bet he's even more handsome if he loses the scowl." Violet paused in front of a dress shop window.

All the stores were closed for the evening, but that didn't stop Violet from eyeing the displays in the weak glow of streetlamps. While this section of the city was relatively safe, I wasn't comfortable dawdling on the sidewalk this close to midnight.

My stomach was still a tight coil from having to step foot into a gin joint, and this conversation about Sterling only knotted it further. "What do you think about the robbery? Do you think they've caught the thief?"

"That thing is positively hideous." She pointed to a large—somewhat gaudy—brooch on a cream-colored shawl. But like everything else, the storefronts didn't hold her attention long, and she quickly grew bored. She hastened her pace, nearly skipping. "Wasn't it thrilling to be questioned about a jewel theft? Too bad I didn't have any useful information for Detective Monroe. I was only backstage for a handful of minutes the night of the robbery."

"Who all was there?" I stepped over a crack in the sidewalk. "You know, when Mrs. Stoneberry was backstage?"

"Me, Gerald." She counted on her fingers. "Lina, Joe, Fran, and a few of the extras."

I opened my mouth to respond, but Violet kept talking.

"Mrs. Stoneberry didn't care too much to chat with us ladies. Her attention was fixed solely on the gents." She wrinkled her nose. "She was practically pawing Gerald. You should've seen Lina. If I wasn't so disgusted at Mrs. Stoneberry, I would've enjoyed the sour look on the prima donna's face."

"Did you tell the detective all this?"

"No. Like he really cares about Claudia Stoneberry's flirtations." She rolled her eyes. "Besides, I left almost immediately. Her trilling laugh got on my nerves."

"And Lina?"

"Probably left too. I don't exactly watch Lina's every move." Her tone was sharp, then as if realizing her snappish mood, she gave an apologetic smile. "But none of that counts for anything. It's a cinch none of us stole that woman's jewelry. My money's on a disgruntled Stoneberry employee. Some maid probably gave herself a hefty raise."

"I suppose that's more likely."

"Pity it's not someone from the cast. Then the detective would poke his nose around more. And what a perfect nose. It matches the rest of his face." She sighed, and I tried to stifle my annoyance. I had no claim on Sterling anymore.

By the time we reached our rooms, there was a chill in my bones. I quickly changed into my nightdress and slipped under the bed covers. My fatigued body sagged against the mattress, but my mind proved more difficult to quiet. Sleep proved slow in claiming me.

A sharp knock yanked me from a fitful dream. Muted sunlight pushed through a gap in the curtains. I glanced at the clock on my bedside table. 8 a.m.

Another staccato rap at my door. "Open up, Sophie. It's Fran."

Yawning, I tugged on my robe and trudged across the thin carpet. I turned the handle, but Fran must've been leaning on the door because the tall blond stumbled into the room.

I took in her distressed brown eyes. "What's wrong?"

"It's not in the papers." Her gaze darted around my room. "But I heard it from Hannah. Who heard it from Joe because he'd just come from a meeting with Lloyd."

I rubbed my forehead as if the action would clear the fog in my brain. Hannah Price was a fellow boarder, and she carried a torch for Joe Neville. But what did that have to do with Joe's meeting with the director? "I don't understand."

"It doesn't matter how I found out."

"Found out what?"

"There was another jewel theft last night. Only this time it was at the Dresdens'."

Hector Dresden owned several railways. And he and his wife were at yesterday's performance.

Sterling was in the grand balcony. I'd felt his gaze on me every time I stepped onto the stage. Thankfully, it was only rehearsal. He'd shown up at the theater this morning to investigate the area the Dresdens were seated in the previous evening.

I didn't expect him to find the jewels tucked into the folds of the chairs, but I did hope he wouldn't linger for the entire play.

He did.

After Lloyd's final notes and suggestions for tonight's show, I rushed to the women's dressing room. I hung my costume on the rolling clothes rack, but not before checking the pocket, making certain I'd returned the paste necklace.

I changed in record time, but it wasn't fast enough. Sterling was waiting outside the door, leaning against the opposite wall as if he'd been there all day. Was he waiting for me? I'd fooled myself into believing my heart trembled the other night only because it was our first encounter since our separation. That once I got over the initial shock of seeing him, I'd have no reaction to his presence.

The chaotic trip in my pulse disproved that theory.

Violet stood in front of him, chatting away. Too bad Sterling was of tall stature, for he peered at me over Violet's bobbing head. I lifted my hand in a weak wave and then darted down the hallway.

"Hey, Sophie." Joe moved in front of me, blocking my retreat.

My breath whooshed out. "See you later, Joe." I stepped to the right, but he moved with me.

"I was hoping to catch you before you left. Want to grab a bite to eat? Lottie's, on the corner of Sixth Avenue, makes the best omelets and hot cakes." His lips eased into a luring grin. "My treat."

Wasn't Joe interested in Hannah Price? "That's kind of you, but I already have a prior engage—"

"Miss Walters."

Without my mind's permission, my body swayed toward that familiar, deep voice. Sterling approached. His navy pin-striped suit was neatly pressed, his matching tie perfectly centered. From the top of his crisp homburg down to his polished oxfords, Sterling gave the impression of someone tame and docile. Yet he was anything but. He was untapped strength, both in his mind and body, placing him on the dangerous side of safe. Yes, with his sharp intellect and powerful form, I felt protected in his presence. But his intense gaze seemed to have the ability to sift through all my secrets and detect my every weakness. Sadly, my main weakness was him.

Sterling's dark gaze flicked to Joe then back to me. "If you have a moment, Miss Walters, I need to speak with you."

Joe leaned close. "Maybe another time, kid." He gave a parting wink and sauntered away.

Sterling waited until Joe was out of earshot. "I have a few questions I need to ask, if you don't mind."

His words, so politely spoken, set me on guard. And now I glimpsed the lethal side of Sterling. No, he wouldn't dare harm me, but the pain was inwardly inflicted. For it hurt to look at him. Hurt to hear his voice. To be near him. I pulled in a breath. *I'm an actress.* How many times would I need to remind myself? Pretending was my profession. "I'm sorry, but there's somewhere I need to be. I can't keep them waiting."

"Is this appointment important?"

I nodded.

"Can I escort you, and we can talk along the way?"

"Certainly." I tempered my tone, as to not reveal how unnerved I was at his nearness. We exited the building and moved toward the streetcar stop.

Sterling spared me a glance. "This is more convenient, since I don't want to be overheard."

"Why?" I'd forgotten how long his strides were, one for my every two. "Do you think the thefts are related to the theater?"

"Possibly."

Surprise lifted my brows. I'd thought it an unfortunate coincidence that both robberies occurred after the victims were at the Loew's Penn. If Sterling believed the robberies were connected, did that also mean he suspected someone at the theater to be the thief? "What would you like to ask me?"

"About your relationship with the woman who watched your show and then was robbed only hours later."

"Mrs. Stoneberry? I told you I never met the lady."

"No. Mrs. Dresden."

I blinked. "I haven't met her either. Why would you think I have any connection with her?"

He reached inside his jacket pocket and withdrew the show's playbill. "I found this in Mrs. Dresden's seat." He pointed to the cast list. My name was circled in black ink. Beside it, in a decidedly feminine script, were two letters connected to my past.

A team of thirty workers was hired specifically to clean the auditorium during the late-night hours. Had the janitorial crew missed the hidden paper? But what was more troubling was why Mrs. Dresden wrote those letters in the first place.

"There are no other markings on the paper. What's her purpose in circling your name?" His gaze penetrated mine. "And what do the initials *M H* signify?"

The curtain closed on my pretense.

My lifelong secret had just claimed the spotlight.

CHAPTER FIVE

ELISE

*H*ow was the party last night?" Meredith Wittenhouser, Elise's former music teacher and honorary second mother, directed her warm smile at Elise. "I wanted to come." She set her cross-stitch project on the armchair of the plush sofa. "But I don't move around as easily."

Elise lowered onto a stylish chair adjacent to Meredith. "I don't know which is classier, the William Penn or this place."

Meredith's new accommodations at Legacy Towers was an open concept design with a modern aesthetic. Bright white walls, marble and light wood accents, and Elise was fairly certain the foyer boasted natural stone flooring. Yet there were subtle cues to senior living. Such as sturdy furniture and wider archways to accommodate those in wheelchairs and walkers.

Over the years, Elise's musical mentor had lived comfortably, but not at all extravagantly. And this place was the Ritz Carlton of nursing homes. Hopefully, Meredith's insurance covered her stay and wasn't gnawing into personal funds.

"You're stalling." Meredith laughed softly. "I asked about the party."

Elise tugged the hem of her sweater. "It was. . ." Surprising. Then humiliating. Then. . . she wasn't exactly sure. Kinley's little stunt had shocked Elise. As if she wasn't already struggling with the mysterious package possibly from her birth father and the presence of Pierson Brooks, followed by the actions of her meddling relations. Why not throw a life-altering audition into the mix? "It was interesting."

With a knowing smile, Meredith examined her manicured nail—manicured?—did they have a spa here? "Pierson showed up at last."

Elise nodded. "That he did." And no, she didn't want to discuss the megastar or how he hadn't recognized her. "Anyways." She held up her violin case. "I brought this per your request on my last visit." A visit that had taken place at Meredith's quaint house. Her change in residence was done quickly and entirely without Elise's knowledge. This morning, Meredith phoned and gave Elise the new address. And what an address it was. "Are you playing checkers with Sally Field later?"

"Shush, you." Her eyes sparkled with amusement, and she gestured toward the violin. "You're stalling again."

Yes, she was. She practiced every morning. When most women her age hit the gym with kettlebells and dumbbells, she hashed out Mozart and Strauss. Yet, her musical muscles hadn't seemed to strengthen. What if she'd plateaued? "What would you like to hear?" Elise unlatched the case and withdrew her mother's violin.

The smooth curves of its spruce body. The bow her mother had held so many times. Holding the violin once again reminded Elise of the engraved ornament in the mystery box. Was this a nudge from God to finally look for answers concerning her father? She couldn't ponder this now. She had to survive the next five minutes. With a sigh, she settled her jaw on the chinrest, and the familiar dread pulsed through her.

"Play whatever's on your heart." Meredith's thin mouth pressed into a hopeful smile.

Elise could do this for Meredith. Clinging to a meager scrap of confidence, she played the piece she'd rehearsed only a few hours ago—a sample from the audition repertoire. Technique? Check. Accuracy? Double check. One reason why she loved sheet music? The notes were firmly set in black on white. Orderly. She played the arranged procession, obeyed the markings, followed the transitions. It was methodical. Unlike life, which constantly shifted. Circumstances could bend in less than a second, but the notes on the page didn't change. Sheet music was predictable and dependable.

She ended the song and slid her eyes closed. That was a victory.

Clapping that was not from Meredith's small, weak hands echoed off the walls. Her eyelids popped open.

A masculine throat cleared. "Nicely done, Elise."

She dropped the bow onto the plush carpet, her stomach seeming to plummet further.

Pierson had joined them. More tragically, he'd heard her play. Hand cupped over her mouth, she darted toward the bathroom and slipped inside. Only to discover she'd barged into a closet.

She could *not* vomit on Meredith's shoes!

It was Elise's fault for not exploring the suite's layout before dashing behind door number one. Nervous she'd smack her violin into something in the dark, she tugged her instrument close to her roiling stomach. She focused on her breathing until the queasiness subsided.

A knock at the door jolted her.

"Everything okay in there?"

Pierson. No doubt his dark blue eyes, the same shade as his hooded denim jacket, were brimming with laughter.

She would not give him the satisfaction of seeing her embarrassed. Again. "Yep, just checking for cracks." Her fingers skimmed the walls for conscience's sake. "You can never be too careful when it comes to high-rises."

"Might help if you can see." Pierson flung open the door, and light flooded in.

"Looks good." She patted the wall in approval. "Completely solid."

"Unlike your story." Pierson popped a shoulder against the jamb, his mouth curving in amusement.

Refusing to take his goading bait, Elise stepped from the closet and away from Pierson's teasing stare. "I should be going, Meredith." She retrieved her bow from the floor and tucked everything back into the case. "But I'll be by next week unless Robert Redford is visiting."

"Oh stop." Meredith actually blushed. "But don't run off. It's been years since I've had both of you together." Her gaze toggled between them, and her dull eyes glossed over. "It may never happen again."

Elise froze in her steps and exchanged a concerned look with Pierson.

He sat next to Meredith, his brows lowering. "Are you feeling okay?"

"Oh, yes." She gave a dismissive wave. "I only meant that you've been busy touring the country. This reunion might not happen again for a while. You two are my only kids who visit."

Meredith had no biological children, but over the years she'd poured her heart into dozens of students.

Nothing like a side of guilt to go along with the present awkwardness. But it hadn't always been this uncomfortable. Some of Elise's favorite memories had occurred during those music lessons. While Pierson and Elise attended different schools during the two-and-a-half years Pierson had lived in Pittsburgh, they'd spent two evenings a week at Meredith's house because they shared an hour slot. But before that, Elise had first met Pierson at church. Dorothea had dropped him off at youth group, and Elise—at the prompting of her mom—reached out to him. Who would've guessed the wounded, angsty teen would one day entertain millions with love songs?

"Yes." Meredith's soft voice trickled into Elise's thoughts. "Having you both here is like old times."

"Do you want to catch me sneaking Skittles from Elise?" Pierson grinned and shot Elise a look that was sweeter than rainbow-colored candies. "Because she probably has some."

Elise eyed him warily. "You could *not* know that."

"Am I wrong?"

"Are you talking in general or about the Skittles?"

He laughed. "You would always carry them in your purse." He flicked a glance at her secondhand Coach bag hanging by the door. "Or should I say duffel? What do you have stuffed in that thing? The Pittsburgh offensive line?"

Elise snorted. "I wish."

"Still have the hots for men in uniform?"

"Still borrowing slang from the nineties?"

The slow curl to his mouth was like something straight out of a movie. Only Elise was without buttered popcorn and complete darkness to hide her rising blush.

It was at that moment she realized their eighty-two-year-old teacher observed their exchange with interest, just like their grandmothers had the day before.

Not again.

At least Meredith wasn't a matchmaker.

"So." The way her teacher stretched out the word had Elise reconsidering her previous assumption. Meredith wasn't going to start meddling, was she? "A little birdie told me a second violin seat opened at the Pittsburgh Symphony."

Her stomach seized. "The birdie's right." Elise should have known Meredith would be informed of the seat vacancy. The woman may be confined to this place, but she had international connections to the symphony world. Uncovering details about a building only a stone's throw away would be simple.

"And?" Meredith prompted. "You got an audition, right?"

Breathe in. Breathe out. "Well, about that—"

"Wait. The Pittsburgh Symphony?" Pierson's gaze landed on the violin case, then swung to Elise. "That was your dream, to play there."

The man hadn't recognized her at the William Penn, yet he recalled her life's goal with perfect clarity? A thousand snarky remarks danced on her lips, but her insides weren't behaving, and Meredith seemed to be awaiting a response. Too bad Elise's vocal cords were fused to her throat.

"I understand." Meredith's gentle expression only made Elise feel worse. "I know how quickly those slots fill. Don't be discouraged, honey. More auditions will open, and you'll get another chance."

"I. . .uh. . .have an audition in February."

Meredith gasped. "That's wonderful."

The nausea in her stomach charged north. Elise reflexively squeezed the handle of her case, her knuckles draining white, probably like the rest of her.

"You okay?" Pierson stood as if she were going down in an epic faint.

"I need to go. I'll call you soon, Mer." She grabbed her violin and jacket, exiting in a flurry of drama and regret.

She reached the elevator. Her escape was in sight. She focused on her breathing, steadying her heartbeat, thinking calm and orderly—

"You forgot this." Pierson held out her bag.

How did she not see him approaching?

The elevator doors dinged open. It didn't matter if he materialized out of nowhere because she was about to perform a disappearing act. "Thank you." She tugged the tote from his hand and ducked into the elevator. "So long, cowboy."

"Wait up." He slipped inside before the doors closed. Great, she was now trapped with Pierson. "Are you feeling okay?"

"Fabulous." She stabbed the Lobby button.

He continued his scrutiny. "You're pale."

"It's January, Piers. Not everyone spray tans."

He ignored her jab. "I'm driving you home. You look awful."

"Wow, you sure can sweet talk."

His grin turned wolfish. "Darlin', you couldn't resist my sweet talk if I made an effort."

"You're right. I'm going to be sick."

He laughed, and she pulled in another stabling breath, thankful her stomach was settling again.

The elevator reached the lower level, and Pierson tugged the hood of his jacket over the back of his head. If that was his disguise, he really needed to up his game.

She stepped out first. "Thank you for your concern, but I'm good."

"Trying to get rid of me?"

"Yes, but I'm being nice about it."

"Man, Elise." He trailed her through the lobby. "Deny it all you want, but I saw you. First running into the closet and then dashing out of Meredith's room. You're not feeling well. Let me see you home."

His sincerity stole the fight from her. "I'm not sick." She stopped her mad dash past the front desk and faced Pierson. "Trust me."

"I'm trying to be a decent human."

"But I'm fine."

"Let me help."

"You can't."

"Give me a—"

"I get stage fright." And just like that, her secret was out.

She'd kept silent about her unfortunate failing for two years, and who was the first person she confessed to? Her polar opposite when it came to performing. No way Pierson would understand.

Her plans were to walk to her apartment from Legacy Towers, but all her energy drained at her admission. Reluctantly, she allowed Pierson to drive her home in his souped-up truck.

"I know you used to get nervous before recitals." Pierson flicked the blinker and entered the crazy Pittsburgh traffic. "But I don't remember you having stage fright."

"Because I didn't." She tugged her peacoat closer, and Pierson turned up the heat. "After I graduated college, I auditioned for any violin seat across the country." Her dream destination had always been Pittsburgh, but she was open to any position with a symphony. "I drove to Tucson, Portland, Grand Rapids, Atlanta. Everywhere."

"And?"

"I got rejected. I wasted lots of money on traveling expenses." Her heart grew heavy. "More than that, I lost my confidence. At an audition in Chicago, I started shaking and couldn't finish my piece." Her cheeks burned at the memory. "I thought it was a one-time thing. A fluke."

"But it happened again?"

She nodded. "It reached the point that even the thought of auditioning makes me nauseous. It's weird, but the only person I can play in front of is Meredith."

"And when you saw me?"

"Turn left at the next intersection." She pointed to the upcoming stoplight. "When I saw you, I thought I was going to retch."

"Not usually the reaction I get from women, but can't win 'em all."

She smiled. "I'm not easily won over. Don't forget I knew you in your defiant stages of fashion. Remember your mullet? I have pictorial evidence."

"That's enough to blackmail me." He chuckled. "I'm yours to command, Malvern."

Her nerves hummed at his words. Something she couldn't allow. "How long are you visiting?"

"Not a subtle subject change, but I'll roll with it."

"Much obliged."

"I promised Gram at least four weeks." He turned left as she'd indicated earlier and pulled onto the avenue leading to her apartment complex. "I have to meet with the record label on February ninth."

Which would be a Tuesday. She knew because February ninth was the day of her audition. She willed back the waves of dread flooding through her.

"I toured the past eight months, and this is the first break I've had. I didn't want to stay in Nashville. It's a lion's den right now concerning me."

The bad publicity. "Is it true?"

"Partially." A frown darkened his brow. "I made mistakes. Several key ones, and I let people down."

She understood that one.

"My press agent believes any publicity is good, even if the subject is bad. We disagree there." He slowed to a stop in the parking garage of her apartment and flashed a smile. "How about I hire you as my publicist?"

"We're not workplace compatible. I don't own a Stetson."

"I'll get you one. You'd look amazing in a cowboy hat."

She rolled her eyes at his flirty wink. No chance she'd fall for shallow charm. She'd been around that block so many times her Skecher prints marked the pavement.

"Although I could always hire you to inspect my closets for cracks."

"Structural integrity is a passion of mine."

His chuckle was low and husky. "Seriously though, your grandmother bragged about your marketing skills at the party. That you've been running the auction house site and increased web traffic. Plus all your work at the symphony. Impressive stuff."

Her pulse stuttered at his compliment. "I've been posting content that gives a better look behind the scenes—wait, that's it!" She shifted in her seat, facing him. "I think I can help you."

"Interesting." Pierson tugged the keys from the ignition. "I was about to say the exact same thing to you."

"I'm glad Kinley's at work." Elise set her keys on the counter in her apartment. "She loves your music."

"Kinley's got good taste. Does she know of our connection?" His gaze drifted about, taking in the space.

Hesitancy nipped her steps across the small living room. No doubt Pierson had a home fit for the stars. Her apartment was tidy and functional but outdated. She set her violin case down by the sofa. "We really don't have a connection. You didn't even remember me at Dorothea's party."

He shot her a look she couldn't decipher. "We're connected. Our grandmothers are best friends. We sat under the same music teacher. You wrote about me endlessly in your diary."

She scoffed. "I never kept a diary."

He shrugged. "Just seeing if you're paying attention."

Oh, she was. Too much. Like the way he said her name in that southern drawl. Or how his full lips tipped at the edges, always ready for a flirty smile. But Elise was not fifteen anymore. Surely there was an expiration date on crushes. She needed to focus on the future. More specifically, her audition. She hazarded a glance at Pierson. "Do you really think you can help me overcome this?"

His eyes met hers. "I like a challenge."

"But my audition's in a month, and I've been battling this for two years." Which was why she'd taken the Heinz Hall internship. It proved a great distraction and gave her fresh purpose.

He sank onto her sofa. "Then we should get started. We'll need a pencil and paper."

"And a miracle."

"Oh, ye of little faith."

There'd been a day when her faith was solid, but just like her dreams, God felt far away. Instead of replying, she retrieved a notepad and pen. "What are these for?" She sat beside him.

"A list." He wrote Elise's name at the top and numbered to ten. "We're going to attack the source, not the symptoms."

"Which means?"

"Instead of treating the symptoms of stage fright, we're going after the root."

"You lost me."

"I'm talking about facing your fears. You, Elise Malvern." He wagged the pen at her. "Are going to learn to take risks."

"You have no idea what you're asking." She groaned. "It's easy for you. You go on stage and exude confidence. Like that Christmas TV special at Madison Square Garden. Did you even break a sweat?"

His smile grew. "You watched?"

"My Hallmark movie was on a commercial."

"I see." He lightly tapped her knee with the pen, causing heat to flood her cheeks. He shouldn't be casually touching her with writing utensils. "But I wasn't always comfortable on stage. I was nervous for my first television appearance."

"Being nervous and shaking uncontrollably are two separate things." She buried her chin in her hands and spoke through her fingers. "How about we abandon this and work on helping your career. Let's get those junior high girls back to writing your name in Sharpie on their limbs."

"Don't give up before we start." He nudged her shoulder with his and let the closeness linger. "C'mon, champ. You can do this. Let's make a list of risks."

"I'm allergic to risks."

"Name something that pushes you out of your comfort zone. What makes you uncomfortable?"

"Prying Grammy winners?"

He gave her a longsuffering look. "Nice try, but no."

Her eyes strayed to the mystery package. He wanted to know something that made her uncomfortable? How about the number one thing?

Pierson nudged her shoulder again. "What's that look for?"

"Nothing."

"That was definitely something."

She sighed. "A few days ago, I got a box with no return address. Inside were items dating back to the Loew's Penn Theatre. That was the name before it was Heinz Hall. But that's not what's strange about it." She walked over to the cardboard tormentor and withdrew the ornament.

"At first, I thought it was an anonymous donation for a project at work. Kinley and I've been contacting people. So I figured one of us accidentally gave this address instead of Heinz Hall."

"Makes sense."

"Though it was addressed only to me." She reclaimed her seat and handed him the engraved piece. "And I found this."

Pierson read the inscription. "You're never without my love." His gaze latched onto hers. "This says it's from your father."

A shiver coursed through her. "Yeah."

Pierson rubbed his chin. "Your mom never mentioned him, did she?"

She shook her head. "Anytime I asked about him always resulted in this. . .awkward, painful silence." Although Elise's story wasn't too different from Pierson's. She recalled he had an absent father too. Only Pierson's dad had dropped in and out of his life like a parental yo-yo. "I haven't told anyone about this."

His blue eyes darkened with interest. "So between this and your stage fright, I'm your secret keeper."

"I'm questioning your phrasing."

"Guardian of your inner whispers."

"Definitely not."

"We can debate my new title later. But for now, I think we found the path leading out of your comfort zone." He glanced at the blank list in his hand as if it were a map to Atlantis. "Let's locate your birth father."

CHAPTER SIX

SOPHIE

*T*he ashen sky hovered over us, darkened with soot from the various mills. In a city overrun with steel factories, sunny days were as rare as Sterling's smile. Once upon a time, I'd been able to coax several out of him, but now it seemed I only inspired frowns and questions.

His thick fingers held up the playbill. "Why did Mrs. Dresden search for you last night?"

I hastened toward the trolley stop. "She did?" So much for those initials by my name being a bizarre coincidence. Had I met this woman and not realized?

He nodded. "The main usher said Mrs. Dresden went backstage looking for you." He turned those dark eyes on me. "Why?"

"Why aren't you on the police force?"

He stilled. "I'm the one asking questions."

"Now I am." I folded my arms with a pert smile. "I don't see why you get to have all the fun interrogating people." I leveled him with my most intimidating glower.

He tapped his fist over his mouth. Was he covering a smile or a scowl? "You look as if you slammed your fingers in a door."

My nose wrinkled. "I may be a lousy investigator, but it doesn't take keen skills to ask you what happened with your job." My voice softened. "You loved being a policeman."

"I loved a lot of things." His words were a direct hit to my sore heart.

My lower lip trembled as the trolley slowed to a stop. "I did too."

"Just not enough."

I turned my head, directing my focus on the opening trolley doors so he wouldn't glimpse the anguish on my face. Thanks to Fran's letters,

I knew the rumors. *Sophie can't commit. She never cared for Sterling. She's afraid of love.*

I wasn't afraid of love but of being able to handle it. Because when I cut free the strings of my heart, it flew from my reach, free from restraint. I'd lost that part of me five years ago, and it was agony to move on without it. Of course, I felt the natural pulse of the organ, but the core of me was gutted. Ever since I boarded the train out of Pittsburgh. "Goodbye." I managed a weak wave. "Thank you for your escort." I turned away and concentrated on clearing the lofty trolley step. Strong fingers clasped my hand, helping me into the cable car. Sterling removed his touch as quickly as he'd offered it and followed me up.

Surprise pinched my words, pitching my voice higher. "You once hated cable cars." I fished for coins in my purse.

"Still do." Sterling deposited money in the slot, paying our fares.

I smiled my thanks.

"But you didn't answer my questions."

Oh. Right.

I located the only empty space, and Sterling crammed beside me. He stretched his long legs into the aisle, but there was no helping the sides of our bodies melding together on the tiny bench.

The clanging of the moving car, the chatter of other passengers, and one wailing infant charged the air.

I set my hand on his arm, drawing his attention. "Fran told me about Percival. I'm sorry."

His jaw locked, and he accepted my condolences with a tight nod.

Percival Simmons had been Sterling's partner on the police force. Fran had written that he disappeared one night while working his rounds. His body surfaced weeks later in the Allegheny River, almost unidentifiable except for the tattoo on his shoulder. "Did they find the person responsible?"

"No."

"Is his death the reason you're no longer a policeman?"

"No. Did you see Mrs. Dresden backstage?"

And we were back to that again. "I have no idea. There were a lot of people shuffling about after the show."

His gaze flicked to the left side of my head, and I knew exactly what he was checking. I have an oddity—when I lie, my earlobes flush red. Sterling knows it. Fortunately, my hair covered both my ears.

He let out a heavy breath. "She was wearing a turquoise gown. Does that help?"

"Oh. Maybe I did see her. Did she have a peacock feather in her turban?"

"Yes, that was her." He glanced at his pocket watch. "Was she wearing the jewelry that was stolen?"

"I wouldn't know. You didn't tell me what was taken." My gaze narrowed. "Which you purposefully concealed to trick me."

He didn't deny it. "Why do you think she asked for you specifically?"

"Maybe she was overcome by my performance and wanted my autograph. I deliver each of my seven lines with such brilliance."

He was unmoved by my sarcasm. "You mean your role as the jewel thief?"

"It's my role on stage. In real life, I've never stolen anything." I waited for his reaction. There was none. I blew out a breath. "Can I see Mrs. Dresden's playbill again?"

He shifted, pressing his thigh into mine, to withdraw the playbill. He scowled and handed me the paper.

"What's Mrs. Dresden's first name?"

"Lavinia."

I winced. "Was her maiden name Larsmont?"

"Yes."

Now it all made sense. "The initials here aren't *M H*." I rotated the playbill clockwise and returned it. "Read it this way."

"*H W*?"

"The H stands for Hildi. My aunt. She and Lavinia were friends."

"And the W?"

"My aunt's last name." My lips pressed together, and I hoped he wouldn't further question me. I'd already confessed more than I should have. "It's been fifteen years since I last saw Lavinia. I didn't know she married into the Dresden family."

Sterling remained silent.

"I'm sorry for wasting your time, Sterling. I truly didn't recognize her." My fingers smoothed the fabric of my skirt. "But I'm certain she'll confirm my story." And that was all she could do. There was no danger in Lavinia Dresden leaking our family secrets because my aunt never told a soul.

He gave a tight nod, but other than that, he was stoic. The man had his answers. What more did he want?

"You never mentioned any family." His voice fell quiet. "Except for that note." His gaze trekked over my face, and I was terrified to know what he found there.

I wrote two notes on the day of our wedding. The first, I hired a message boy to deliver at the church. Each word had burned into my soul. *I couldn't possibly marry you.*

The second, I left under his apartment door—explaining I'd changed my mind about our relationship and gone to live with my sister. All of it a lie. I'd repented of my wrongs but struggled with forgiving myself.

"This is the stop." I stood abruptly, knocking Sterling's leg with my knee.

He rose to his feet and gestured for me to lead the way. I didn't expect him to accompany me any farther, especially now that he'd gotten the information he wanted, but he followed me off the cable car.

"It's just over there." I pointed to the dilapidated building.

The sidewalk was as uneven as it was narrow. Our fingers brushed, and Sterling slowed his pace so we wouldn't be elbow to elbow.

His gaze roamed the littered alleys and run down structures. "Do you come here often?"

"No." I stepped over a broken bottle. "This isn't the best part of town, but it's all she can afford."

"She?"

I nodded, and he almost seemed relieved. Who had he thought I was meeting? We climbed the planked staircase, which led to Prudence Jamison's flat. I stopped at her door and dug into my purse.

I retrieved the envelope and gently pressed it through the mail slot. Satisfied, I faced Sterling. "Okay. Let's go," I whispered and tugged his sleeve, but he wasn't budging.

"That's it?"

I tugged again. "Come on. She mustn't see me."

Sterling's brows lowered, displeased.

"I'll explain when we're out of sight."

He exhaled a heavy breath and finally stepped away from her door. I rushed down the steps, Sterling not far behind, and quickened my pace on the walk. A gentle yet large hand wrapped mine. I froze at his touch, at the familiarity of his fingers on my skin for a second time today.

"Explain." Once he had my attention, he removed his hand, and I tried not to sigh my disappointment.

"A young woman came to the stage door a few nights ago. It was right before showtime, and our director thought she was sneaking into the theater. He wouldn't give her a chance to speak. Just turned her away."

"Does that happen often?"

"Some people try to skirt the ticket booth by using that entrance, but that wasn't the case with Prudence." I rubbed a spot on my arm. "There was something about her expression. She looked. . .desperate. So I went after her."

"A complete stranger?"

"Yes. Because she reminded me of. . ."

"Of what?"

"Myself at that age." Sadness crawled into my tone. "She told me all she wanted was an audition. She's young, Sterling. Seventeen at the most. She ran away from home and has been looking for work. I gave her money to attend the play and asked her to meet me outside the stage door afterward."

"And that's where you were the night of the first robbery. You said you left directly after the show."

I nodded. "I took her to get a warm meal, and she shared her story with me. I can tell she wants to return home but doesn't have the money for traveling. I offered to help, but her pride got in the way." Thankfully, I'd retrieved her address before we parted ways.

"So you left cash inside her door."

Knowing him, he probably thought her a swindler, but I'd heard the regret in her voice. Not even the finest actress could emulate it. "I had to wait until payday. Only hope it's enough to buy her way to Norfolk."

His dark gaze clamped mine. "How much of your pay did you give up?"

"All of it."

"Stay right here," he demanded before dashing up the walk and bounding the apartment staircase two steps at a time.

What was he planning to do? Pound on the door and demand my money back? What if Prudence wasn't there? Surely he wouldn't break down the door. He had no right. It was my money to keep or give.

Ignoring his orders, I chased after him. My T-strap shoes, clopping loudly against the wood, made quick work of the steps. I reached the top, my lungs burning with each jagged gasp.

Sterling rushed to meet me at the landing. "Everything okay?" His gaze darted about as if searching for whoever was chasing me. "What happened?"

"I'm fine." I sounded as winded as I felt. "I came to stop you."

His brow arched. "From what?"

"From. . ." I waved my hand about. "Doing whatever you were doing."

"I see." He took pity on me and offered his arm for support. Between low amounts of sleep and high amounts of nerves, my body wasn't prepared for sprinting up thirty steps. "I'm afraid what's done is done."

My shoulders curled forward. I'd just have to return to Prudence's soon without Sterling.

"It appears you still possess that talent, Sophie."

My head lifted at his use of my name. "What talent?"

"Of emptying my wallet."

Sterling and I parted ways on Penn Avenue—he to the car he'd left parked on a side street near the Loew's Penn and me to the theater to speak with the director. Sterling's kindness in helping Prudence only emboldened me. If she chose not to return home, I hoped she'd use the money to lease a better apartment. But extra funds only lasted so long, and she needed work. This afternoon, I'd attempt to secure her an audition. Since Lloyd usually held meetings with the producers on Fridays, this would be my best opportunity to catch him.

The day watchman let me in through the stage door, and I made my way toward the offices. These vacant halls would buzz with activity in only a few hours. Lloyd had seemed concerned about possible low attendance because tonight's silent film featured lesser named actors. But I'd met Stan Laurel and Oliver Hardy on my way out of an audition, and I wouldn't be surprised if they made it big one day.

Movement to my left jerked my attention.

An elderly cleaning man exited the costume and prop room. He tugged his cart over the threshold, and it nearly toppled, sending a few cleaning bottles tumbling to the concrete.

"I'll get those." I hastened my steps and scooped them up. "Here you go." I set them on the tray.

The man wore gloves, but his hands were shaking. Was it a sign of old age or was he distressed over the mishap?

"Thank you, miss." His frail voice quivered into a wracking cough.

I stood helpless as the man's frame shook violently. "Are you okay? Would you like some water?"

"No, no." He turned away, coughing into his elbow. "I'll be fine."

"Here, take this." I offered my handkerchief.

He took it. "Thank you, miss." Now wheezing, he pushed the cart down the hall.

I realized he'd left the light on in the prop room. Lloyd was adamant about keeping that door locked except during show times.

I stepped inside to shut off the light, but something caught my eye. My duster, that odious coat, had slipped from the hanger and puddled on the floor. I picked it up and brushed off the dirt and lint. My fingers skimmed the open pocket. Open? My brow scrunched. The coat had snap fasteners for each pocket used for keeping the paste necklace secure. My hand slipped inside the felt-lined crevice.

Empty.

I crouched and searched the concrete. Nothing. I was certain I had stowed the jacket with the necklace safely tucked inside this morning after rehearsal. But now it was gone.

Someone had stolen my paste jewelry.

CHAPTER SEVEN

Elise

*E*lise had a severe case of risk-taker remorse. With a quiet huff, she scrolled over the Loew's Penn contributors list. "It has to be a mistake."

"What?" Kinley breezed into the office they shared.

"I'm trying to find the mysterious donor who sent this." Elise gently patted the duster coat. She'd brought the costume to snap photos for Instagram. But its constant presence taunted her about its sender and the absurd deal she'd made with Pierson to locate her father.

It had been only forty-eight hours since she'd agreed, and she was already grappling for an escape. She'd hold to her end of the agreement—help him with his image—but as for finding the man who'd skipped her entire life? She'd rather leave that drama for Lifetime movies.

"I already contacted them all." Kinley plopped onto her desk chair. "Everyone I spoke with verified what they donated. Your anonymous sender isn't anyone from our list."

So much for that. Elise exited the spreadsheet and closed her laptop. "Thanks for checking." Her resigned tone matched her mood. "If you need me, I'll be in the auditorium. I'm staging photos with this coat." *Among other things.* She loaded her webcam, laptop, tripod stand, and costume onto her trusty rolling cart.

Elise shot a parting smile and pushed the cart out the door, down the hall, and to the side entrance. When she popped the door open, she found Pierson waiting. She stifled a laugh at the odd combination of his cowboy hat and boots paired with the puffiest parka she'd ever seen. It was zipped high, shielding the lower half of his face.

"Are you afraid of paparazzi or hypothermia?"

"Both." His coat muffled his voice, his raised cheeks the only visible part of his smile. He shifted inside, his gloved hands cradling his guitar case.

She reached around him and relocked the door. They'd both agreed the side entrance would attract less attention. "Anyone on to you yet?"

"That I'm here in Pittsburgh? No."

She gave a pointed look at his guitar. "They will after today. You sure you want to do this?"

He tilted back his head, jutting his chin over the jacket's zipper. "Absolutely not. But you're the genius. I trust you."

She wouldn't pick apart and examine his last three words. "Here." She took a step closer. "Let me hold your guitar so you can climb out of your sleeping bag."

"Laugh all you want, Malvern. I forgot how cold it gets here." He unzipped his parka to reveal faded jeans and a black, long-sleeved ribbed shirt sculpted perfectly to his form. "How do you survive this?"

A wave of his cologne hit her, as if all that beautiful scent held captive under his jacket was now free to invade her breathing space. She needed an emotional Epi-Pen because her entire system shut down around men who smelled good. "Thick skin, my friend."

"I know all about that. Gotta have it to survive tabloids and vengeful ex-girlfriends."

"Oh, you poor famous person."

"No sympathy from you?"

She laughed, returning his guitar. "Not even courtesy pity."

His gaze swung to the costume on the cart. "And you're making fun of *my* coat? At least mine doesn't look like it once hibernated."

She snorted and moved behind the cart, motioning him to follow. "It's nearly a hundred years old."

"Impressive. It looks well preserved."

She nodded. "I think it's from the inaugural show when this place was Loew's Penn Theatre." Her voice dropped to almost a whisper. "This coat was in the box with the ornament."

His raised eyebrows disappeared under the brim of his hat. "The one from your dad?"

She paused in front of the auditorium door. "What if we're reading too much into everything? It could be some weird mix-up." It was better to discuss this before investing more time and emotions into a bogus search. "What if the package isn't from my father?"

With his coat pinned under one arm, he adjusted his grip on his guitar case. "How do you explain the engraving? Or that the package was addressed only to you?"

"That's why I can't dismiss it altogether. But wouldn't he give his name? Something?" She tapped a rhythm on the cart's handle. "If he really wanted to reach out, he would've made a way for me to contact him."

"Could be intentional. Maybe he doesn't want to overwhelm you and is slowly inserting himself into your life."

"Then I don't have to search for him. We can forget about my side of this. . ." She motioned between them. "Bargain."

He looked at her as if she'd confessed to toilet-papering Graceland. "You want to back out of our plan? This is to help you beat your stage fright." Pierson was convinced her fear of risks had a direct link to her panic in performing. Unfortunately, he was probably right.

Her lashes lowered, that familiar pain sinking in with sharpened claws. It wasn't as if she hadn't tried to overcome this. She'd amassed mega reward points at her local bookstore from her self-help book purchases. Had four different counselors in her phone contacts. Had all the scriptures about fear and anxiety highlighted in her Bible. She'd prayed every prayer she knew to pray, but there was a disconnect between her and God. And she knew it was all on her side. What was she doing wrong? Shame twisted through her. "What if it doesn't work?"

His gaze melted into tenderness, one that traveled back to their time as best friends. "What if it does?"

Was it wrong to draw strength from the confidence in his eyes?

Yes, yes it was.

She couldn't allow herself to hope. It would only cause more disappointment in the end. "Let's work on your end of the agreement now. We'll tackle the other later." Like in the next millennium. "Deal?"

He bumped her arm with his elbow. "I don't remember you being this bossy as a teen."

She nudged back. "You don't remember many things." As in her existence for the past nine years. Yeah, he hadn't recalled who she was at Dorothea's party, but that didn't hurt as much as his vanishing from her life. It was best to set that fact on her brain's repeat, because after four weeks, he'd return to his glittering life and forget about her. Again.

His head tilted in question, but no way would she satisfy him with an answer.

Instead, she tugged down the hem of her gray sweater and opened the door. She'd first stepped into the Heinz Hall auditorium when she was in middle school. Fourteen years later, Elise still paused in awe. The chandeliers, the balconies, the gold accents. All of it stole her breath. It was a place of music and wonder. The arched ceiling hovered high above the wide expanse of seats. "Two thousand seven hundred twenty-six."

"What's that?" Pierson eased beside her.

"That's how many seats there are. Two thousand seven hundred twenty-six." The only seat she wanted was the one on stage. But they weren't here for her. She faced Pierson. "Do you remember where we sat that night?" At her apartment the other day, they'd discussed his Reputation Rescue Plan, as Elise had dubbed it. Pierson had mentioned an important instance that occurred during one of her mom's symphony rehearsals.

"We were on the main floor. Left of the stage." His smile turned sheepish, and he led the way down the red-carpeted aisle. "Right here." He patted the aisle chair in row K.

"Give me a second to set up." She set her laptop on the tripod stand and plugged in her webcam. "I need to find the best angle."

"All my angles are best."

"Debatable."

He chuckled at her unimpressed expression and unzipped his guitar case. "Same plan we discussed the other day?"

"Yep. You play and I record you live." Pierson had given her access to his Instagram account. "It'll give your fanbase the chance to see you unplugged and without all that—"

"Auto-tune?" His eyes held a challenge. "That's a rumor."

She looked through her camera lens. "I was going to say smoke and flourish." A shift to her right centered him in the frame. Perfect. "There's no spotlight. No backup singers or band. This is just you and what made you who you are." She gave a reassuring nod. "Let's give this a go."

He hooked his boot on the side of the seat and perched his guitar on his bent leg. "This isn't easy for me." He strummed, then shook his head in dissatisfaction. "I don't like talking about my past." His left hand slid to the fourth fret and tested the strings. He twisted the silver tuner peg, then strummed again.

"It was the day before my fifteenth birthday. I was in the school cafeteria. And some kid kept throwing spit wads at a girl with special needs.

She just sat there, crying." He continued tuning his guitar. "All the other kids were laughing, and I got real angry. Warned the boy to quit, but it only encouraged him." He sighed. "I picked up the kid's notebook and smacked him upside the head. It didn't hurt, just startled him. Then he punched me, and. . .I punched back. Earned my first black eye that day, remember?" His eyes sought hers.

Elise nodded but didn't want to break the moment.

"Then we came here. Into this auditorium. The orchestra rehearsed some concerto, and it made me cry." He casually shrugged as if he wasn't baring his soul. "I felt stupid because I was beside this pretty girl." He lifted his gaze from his guitar and winked at Elise. "But the pretty girl just squeezed my hand and said, 'Your heart was right, but the way you expressed it was wrong.'"

She held in a laugh. Her fifteen-year-old self watched too much *Dr. Phil.*

He strummed again, and this time, he nodded. "That memory is the basis for my song 'Right Heart in the Wrong Place.'" Then he played it.

Her fingers froze on the camera. She'd had no idea. That song was a chart-topper. She never realized she'd helped inspire it. Pierson's voice was smooth as velvet as his fingers slid along the fretboard. He didn't look at the camera, but it was better that way.

He finished the song, and his gaze crashed into hers, the emotion on his face overwhelming her. "And that's the story behind the song."

She stopped the recording. "Perfect." Her voice barely audible.

"Think that'll work?" He leaned over his guitar. "Are we ready to film?"

"The video just went live."

His boot slipped from its hooked position on the chair. "What?"

She laughed. "I told you to 'Give it a go.'"

"Yeah, but I didn't realize you were going to film right then."

"I pressed PLAY right in front of you."

He lifted his Martin guitar. "I was tuning."

And he'd looked ridiculously attractive doing so. She was confident his female fanbase would agree. "It was unrehearsed and brilliant."

He reached for his guitar case. "So much for my signature smolder into the camera."

"People tell you to do that?"

"People tell me to do a lot of things."

"You shared your heart, and that's what you needed to do." She glanced at her computer. "Look, it worked. Your cyber audience is gushing with likes and comments."

He stowed his guitar and joined her. The reception was mostly positive. There were a few remarks that would make even Grancy blush. And some devoted fans pledged their lives to him. "Do you often get proposals on your posts?"

"Yeah." His full lips tipped into a smile. "Jealous?"

"Very much." His brows flicked north, and she chuckled. "Slow down, cowboy. I'm not envious of your admirers but how easily you performed. If I went live, I'd be ten shades of green. You were amazing, Piers. I can see why you made it big."

"Thank you. I still have a lot of ground to regain."

"But this is progress." She shifted the laptop stand toward him. "Now talk to them."

He blinked. "What?"

She swept her hand over the keyboard. "Comment back."

"I never do that. My publicist always says—"

"Well, your *bossy* friend says do it. You won't be able to answer everyone, but make an effort. Let this be the day the Nashville prince showers his loyal subjects with emojis."

His low rumble of laughter made her heart skip. "I hear that sarcasm and will try not to be wounded." He moved in front of the laptop and started replying.

"While you're working on that, I'll be on stage taking photos of the hibernating coat."

He glanced up. "What for?"

"I've been posting about the Loew's Penn every week."

"Is it a throwback Thursday kind of thing?"

"Exactly. Only it's Theatre Throwback. I've been taking pictures of past props, costumes, and playbills, and then I caption the post with the history of each item. Kind of like an online museum exhibit."

"What's the story behind that coat?"

"I'm not sure. There's a name—Sophie Walters—pinned to the inside collar, which matches an actress on the playbill. I'm guessing this was her costume. I googled her but found nothing." She glanced at the coat as if it held the answers. Sadly, there were only more questions. "If the mystery giver *was* my dad, why would he send me this?"

"Maybe he's related to this Sophie person. Which would mean you are too. Or maybe he acquired it to contribute to your work here."

"Those are some pretty big maybes."

He shrugged. "It's not a stretch to think your dad has connections to this place. After all, your mom worked here. He might have met her in the symphony."

"Possibly." But Elise was ten years old when her mother finally got hired on as a second violinist. "It's more likely Mom met someone when she went to Julliard, since I was born a year after her graduation."

"That makes sense. Have you asked your grandparents?"

"Yes. Mom never told them either." She looked at the coat, the possible link to her father. "Grancy always said he must be someone not worth calling Dad."

"Yeah." He pocketed his phone. "I understand that sentiment."

She nodded in sympathy. Pierson's father had a substance addiction that broke his family. It drove his mother into the arms of other men, causing her to abandon her own son when he was fourteen. Pierson's father remarried shortly after, and Pierson moved in with Dorothea for a time. Last Elise knew, no one had heard from Lorraine Brooks in twelve years. This poked strangely at Elise—why would Pierson encourage her to find her father when his own mom had been MIA for years? "Are you still in contact with your dad?"

His gaze fell to the scarlet carpet. "He only visits when he needs money."

"I'm sorry."

"Yeah." He adjusted his hat. "Let me help with your photos."

They both reached for the coat, and in her clumsiness, she knocked it off the cart. She scooped it off the aisle floor, then grimaced. "There's a tear in the hem."

"Not surprising, seeing how old it is."

She angled the bottom left corner toward the light, examining it further. "The material's thinner here. As if. . ." She slipped the edge of her pinky inside the gap. Her gaze snapped to Pierson. "Something's in here." Whatever was inside must've rubbed against the lining, weakening the fabric over time.

He moved close, his arm brushing hers. "What is it?"

"It's hard to tell without seeing it." A coarse cloth scraped against her pinky. Burlap? Yet there was something decidedly solid wrapped in it. "Metal, maybe."

"Why would someone hide something in a coat?" He dipped his head, his nearness making Elise aware of the copper tones in his stubbly jaw. "That was from the prohibition days, right? Maybe it's a flask."

"Doesn't seem like it." She perched on the edge of the aisle seat and set the coat on her lap. "I don't want to rip it any more than it already is."

"Why not?"

Her mouth dropped. "It's almost a century old. The fabric's too worn to stitch back together. I could ruin the thing."

"Where's your risk list? I'm adding this to it," he teased.

"Maybe if I work whatever it is toward the hole, I can ease it out." She gently kneaded the fabric. "It's close."

With their heads bent toward each other, they waited to see the mysterious object hidden in an old stage costume. She gave one more push with her finger. "Ugh. I tore it more."

Then something slid into Pierson's palm. He peeled back the cheap burlap.

It was a necklace.

"Look at these obnoxious stones. It's like something from the dollar store." He shook his head with a laugh. "All that for a stage prop."

She ran her fingers over the glistening stones, raising the chain to the light. "Pierson."

"What?"

"This isn't paste. These are real emeralds."

CHAPTER EIGHT

Sophie

Fran stood beside me offstage, her brown eyes riveted on the singing trio. "One day," she whispered, "I'll be the main attraction, just like the Rhythm Boys."

I smiled and lowered my voice. "I don't doubt it." But I was certainly doubting my sanity lately. I could've sworn my necklace disappeared the other day. Yet when I checked my coat pocket later that night, it was there. Why would someone steal the necklace only to return it? Perhaps no one took the prop, and I was somehow mistaken. Was my lack of sleep affecting my faculties? I shook my head, pushing aside the discomfort.

"Don't you like these fellows?" Fran had misread my irritation, but I wasn't about to tell her about the necklace. Not when I didn't understand it myself.

I risked a glance at the stage manager. He allowed us to watch from behind the curtain, but he could change his mind if he heard us talking. I leaned toward Fran, who stood enamored by the all-male singing group. "I think they're swell, especially the gentleman on the left. What's his name?"

"Bing Crosby." Her breathy words were part murmur, part sigh. "Handsome, ain't he? And what a voice. I could listen to him sing all night."

I nodded. Mr. Crosby's vocal range proved a mixture between bass and baritone. His performance was bound to be highlighted in tomorrow's papers. I'd much rather read about a young crooner than another jewel heist. The daily editions sensationalized this past week's robberies, leaving all of Pittsburgh in anticipation of who would be the next victim. The *Gazette* went so far as giving the elusive thief a moniker—the Mirage.

Fran threaded her arm through mine but focused her kohl-lined eyes on Mr. Crosby. "Violet says he's single."

I didn't miss the hitch of hope in her voice. Ah, now I understood why she lingered here instead of in the dressing room primping for tonight's performance. The Rhythm Boys ended their opening number, and the crowd responded with exuberant applause.

While the audience gawked at all that glittered on stage, they missed the production in the wings. It was equally impressive. Lines of rope climbed to the ceiling, cinching sandbags and twisting around metal rods. Stagehands, dressed in black, stood like sentinels beside the complex system of pulleys and levers, awaiting the command to lower backgrounds and raise curtains. The crew hardly got any recognition, but we wouldn't have a show without their contribution.

I pointed to the stage exit, and Fran's eyes filled with indecision. It was clear she wanted a chance to speak to Mr. Crosby, but the Rhythm Boys would be performing for only a little while longer, and we needed to get into costume. Her posture slumped, no doubt realizing the same thing. We quietly padded into the hall.

"Big crowd tonight?" Joe broke away from his conversation with a theater usher and joined Fran and me as we walked toward the dressing room. Of course, he was already in his policeman costume. As much as I loathed my bulky coat, Joe seemed to derive enjoyment dressed as a cop.

"Seems so," Fran answered. "Let's hope there's no wealthy dame out there wearing a fortune around her neck."

"The Mirage struck yesterday." Joe lit the cigarette pinched between his lips and shook out the match. "Doubt they'll rob two days in a row."

The Mirage. In ten days, the jewel thief had become a household name. My thoughts strayed to Sterling. He'd been hired by the Stoneberrys and the Dresdens to recover the jewels. Was he making any progress on the investigation? We paused at the dressing room door. "How did the newspaper find out about the robberies?" I couldn't imagine any of those wealthy families inviting the badgering press into their private affairs.

Joe blew out a stream of smoke. "The news was leaked by a maid at the Dresden house."

"Please." Fran dramatically draped her arm over her forehead. "Can we go five minutes without talking about the Mirage? It's making poor Lloyd anxious."

Fran spoke as if our director was within hearing distance, which wasn't the case. But she was right about Lloyd's nervous mannerism. He'd expressed concern about the authorities closing our show if the robberies continued. Did they have the power to do so? It did appear too much of a coincidence that every theft victim had been at the Loew's Penn only hours before each crime occurred.

Violet emerged from the dressing room, her bobbed hair sleek with pomade and her face freshly rouged. She engaged Fran in a bubbly chat, blocking the door and leaving me with Joe. Why hadn't the man already moved on? It irked me when he loitered outside the women's changing room.

Joe tipped his cigarette, and I shuffled to keep the ashes from falling onto my shoes.

His mustache twitched as he drew near. "Maybe it's not nerves causing Lloyd's strange behavior. Could be something else. Like guilt or the fear of getting caught."

My lips parted at his insinuation. "Lloyd wouldn't do such a thing."

"No?"

I frowned at this odd exchange. Joe usually conversed in flirty tones, but his eyes, demeanor, even his stance, seemed off. "I don't believe anyone in this cast would steal."

"How trusting you are. It's endearing." If his head dipped any closer to mine, the brim of his patrolman's hat would knock my forehead.

"Joe, have you been—"

A throat cleared beside me, and I flinched. When had Fran slipped away? Because in her place stood Sterling. He was tall, brooding, and. . . holding a bouquet of red roses? His gaze clasped mine, and my cheeks flushed.

"Oh, Detective." Violet fused herself to his side. "How beautiful. Who's the lucky gal?" Her sultry bat of lashes contrasted her hopeful doe eyes.

Sterling held the bouquet away from his body with a loose grip as if the flowers were dipped in arsenic. "They're for Lina."

My gaze dropped. I hadn't realized Sterling held an interest in Lina Landis. Though unsurprising. The leading lady was beautiful, elegant, and hadn't shattered his heart. But still, it pricked like a thousand thorns.

"Lina?" Violet sniffed. "As if she doesn't get enough nauseating gifts from Gerald. Then there's that secret admirer who showers her with flowers every night. Now you're eating out of her hand too?" She shook her head in disappointment. "I thought you had better taste, Detective."

"Violet," I gently rebuked.

She faced me, her eyes sparking with disdain. "You know as well as I do that Lina doesn't deserve any—"

"These aren't from me." Sterling's gruff tone stopped Violet's tirade. "A theater worker pushed these into my hands to deliver." A scowl darkened his face, expressing his stance on being made an errand boy.

Joe sauntered away. Thank goodness.

Sterling's gaze seared into me. "Can you give these to her?"

I needed to dress for tonight's production, but my heart didn't want to deny Sterling anything, even this small favor. I readily nodded. He handed me the flowers, and our eyes locked over them. Violet poked her head between us, severing our connection. While she brazenly flirted, I turned in search of Lina.

Earlier, she'd slipped into one of the main-level rehearsal rooms. Was she still there? I hustled down the hall, anxious to finish this task and change into costume. I rounded the corner only to be stopped short by Lloyd.

"Sophie, just the person I wanted to see."

Me? For the past two months, I'd been beneath our director's notice. I tried to speak with him on Prudence's behalf the other day, but he dismissed me before I could finish a sentence. "Anything I can do for you?"

His gaze slid over the roses. "It's about Lina's shoddy performances." He ran a hand through his thinning hair. "She's been missing lines and coming in late for cues."

I stood quietly, unsure how to respond. I'd noticed a mistake here and there, but I wouldn't label Lina's acting as shoddy.

"You're her understudy." His narrowed gaze swept my frame. "Brush up on her lines in case you're needed. It might be soon." He dipped his chin in a tight nod and moved past me.

I blinked at the unexpected encounter. I had Lina's lines memorized, but I never imagined I'd have a chance to speak them. While a part of me yearned to be in the spotlight, my convictions weighed heavy. Stepping into that role meant Lina stepping out of it. With a sigh, I continued to the rehearsal room. Harsh tones caused me to skid to a halt.

I peeked into the room.

"I have a right to know, Lina." Gerald stood, his stance wide, the line of his shoulders tense. "Are you in love with him?"

Lina paled, making her scarlet lipstick even more pronounced.

"Not even a denial?" He slashed his hand through the air, and Lina flinched.

He cussed. "What on earth, Lina? You think I'd hit you before curtain?"

My blood heated at his phrasing. Was he implying he'd strike Lina if she wasn't due on stage? I'd never suspected Gerald had a temper. His mild nature consisted of easy smiles and good-natured remarks. This side of him pushed a sliver of unease into my spine.

"No." Lina dashed a tear from her cheek. "It's all very—"

My bracelet clinked off the doorframe.

Both heads whipped my direction.

"I didn't mean to intrude." I took a cautious step into the room. "I came to deliver these."

"Another bouquet." Gerald's voice was a dangerous low rumble, his hand clenching in fists. "From Lina's true love." He cut her a scathing look, then stormed out of the room.

"Gerald." Lina's voice broke on a soft sob, her pain-pinched eyes gaping at the empty doorway.

"I'm so sorry." My chest squeezed at her sorrowful expression. "I didn't mean to make things worse for you."

She swiped under her eyes. "This isn't your fault." Her shuddered breath disturbed the lace on her collar. "They are beautiful roses, aren't they?"

I nodded, recognizing her intention of switching topics, but I couldn't let the matter drop without offering support. "If you need to talk, I'm here." I handed her the flowers, and her eyes widened with shock. "What is it?"

"The card. Where is the card?" Her fingers searched, almost frantically, through the rose petals. "It must've fallen out."

"Right here, Lina." I plucked the card from its tucked position between two rosebuds, though it was practically in plain sight.

"Sorry. I'm a bit flustered." She pressed the small envelope to her chest and breathed a sigh of relief. "It wouldn't do for Gerald to see this." Her tear-heavy lashes lowered against her porcelain skin. "Love is complicated, don't you think? I doubt any of us know what love truly is."

"I think this world's full of diluted versions of it." I'd certainly seen my share. But love in its full strength was something we found only in God.

Lina set the roses on a nearby table and grabbed her wrap. "I've never been blessed with good relationships."

Perhaps that was why she switched men like Violet did lipstick. Lina and Gerald had been romantically involved since the show's debut, and now another man had entered the scene. The number of flowers this gentleman had given her over the past three weeks revealed his interest.

Had Lina grown bored with Gerald? Was she falling for her admirer? We were in the theater, where we pretended to be someone other than ourselves. Yet often, those masks remained long after the curtain closed. We all hid something. Which brought me back to my conversation with Joe Neville in the hallway. Could one of the cast members be the Mirage?

CHAPTER NINE

ELISE

*T*he person who coined the adage "a picture's worth a thousand words" had never been the photographer for Malvern Auction House. Because here, a picture was hopefully worth a thousand dollars or more. Elise's duty was to capture each item up for bidding and upload it onto the website. But to her, the job was more than that.

With each shutter's snap, she told a story.

She was currently sprawled on the tiled floor in the auction house's backroom, her camera poised over her face, taking an underside shot of a two-hundred-year-old desk. It was necessary to catalog every nick and stain. The maple wood had yellowed in some spots, and the dovetailed joinery boasted a few minor splits, but Elise didn't view any of these marks as defects. Each smudge had a tale, each gash held a secret.

The desk's top flipped down, revealing multiple drawers for file storage and providing sturdy space for writing. The several ink spots could decrease the value, but it only increased Elise's curiosity. What kind of letters had been penned? Ones of business? Love notes? She hoped her pictures invoked that same intrigue in potential buyers.

Her grandfather strolled into the room, stepping around the flash and light equipment. "The artist at work, I see." He lowered onto the stool beside the card table that had been in Pap's workspace longer than Elise had been alive.

Elise scooted out from under the antique desk, careful not to smack her head. "I got all the new pieces photo-documented. After a few edits, I'll upload them on the site." Then she was off to the library. Where Google failed her in locating anything to do with the mysterious Sophie Walters, the Carnegie Library had a massive database of newspaper articles.

"Very good."

Setting her camera on the table, Elise arched a brow at the man who'd raised her. "Though I shouldn't be helping you since you tattled on me at Dorothea's party. That was mildly humiliating."

"I'm sorry for that." He didn't look the least bit sorry. "You know I can't keep anything from your grandmother. The woman's always belly-aching about age stealing her sense of smell, but she sure can sniff a secret a mile away."

"Speaking of secrets." Elise grabbed her canvas bag from the floor and withdrew the box she'd stored the emerald necklace in. "Can you take a look at this?" She opened the lid, and Pap's silver brows hiked.

He tugged his loupe, a ten-power magnification tool, from the front pocket of his shirt. "Where'd you get this pretty thing?"

"Out of a coat from the Roaring Twenties." And that was all the info he needed right now. "But I know this necklace is older than that."

"How do you figure?" That familiar glint entered his eye. He was test-ing her. Like he'd done over the years when teaching her the ins and outs of antique jewelry.

Elise rose to the challenge. "For one, the clasp. Most pieces from the 1920s and later have circular spring closures. This is a box clasp." She pointed to the two metal joiners—the tongue and the box. The tongue would squeeze into the box, locking into place. "Then there's the patina. It's sigh-worthy." As platinum aged, the metal surface adopted a satiny finish that was a badge of honor in the world of antique jewelry. That was what first caught her eye at the theater. No fake jewelry could replicate that kind of sheen.

He gave a nod of approval. "I've taught you well, Cricket."

She laughed. Pap wasn't one for accuracy when it came to pop culture quotes. "Can you pin it down to a year?" With careful movements, she handed him the necklace.

He flipped on the light of his loupe, raising the magnifier to his right eye. A slow smile hooked his lined face as he examined the pear-drop gems. "The emeralds seem in good shape." He moved on to the fittings. "I'd wager this was made at the turn of the century. Most likely between 1900 and 1905. This is a great find."

It was a baffling find. Who would hide a valuable necklace in a bulky jacket? The stuffing was thick. It was surprising she'd discovered it at all. Whoever hid the jewelry did so knowing the dense filling would brilliantly conceal the necklace. But why hide it? Did her father know what was inside the coat? And why, all of a sudden, did she want to talk to Pierson about this? Red flags waved so hard within her, she could almost feel a draft.

"It's an interesting piece." He lowered the loupe and returned the necklace. "Which brings me back to my first question. Where'd you get it?"

"I told you, I found it in an old coat." The stones grew heavy in her hand. "What's it worth?"

"A lot." He casually dropped the loupe in his front pocket, slapped his knees with an easy exhale, and stood. "Call me when it's time for lunch." He strolled away with a whistle.

Elise knew this tactic. "Not so fast, Pap."

He took his time turning on his heel. "Is there a problem?" His innocent expression was one for the record books, to be filed under "Manipulating Grandparents." To get Pap's answers, she had to leak a few of her own.

She placed the necklace back in the box and set it on the desk. "Last Friday there was a box left at my door." She recapped the past week, excluding the part about the bargain with Pierson. Reason being, her family didn't know about her stage fright or her upcoming audition. She detailed the box's contents, including the engraved ornament. "I think my dad sent me the package."

Pap's chin tucked as if dodging a conversational sucker punch. "That's quite a story."

"Tell me about it." This kind of stuff didn't happen to people like her. First the mysterious package, then the surprise audition, now an antique necklace possibly worth a fortune? What was next? Was her father some monarch, and Elise, the only heir to a kingdom? It was all up in the air at this point. "Pap, I know I asked this before, but is there anything you can tell me about my dad?"

His jowls jiggled on a heavy sigh. "Deb never told us." He ran a thumb over the jewelry box on the table. Just like the necklace inside it, her mother had held secrets. Had taken them to her grave. "But I think it was to protect you. I got the suspicion your father wasn't a good man."

Not a king then. Maybe a drug lord? Insurance launderer? One of those shady people who badgered Elise about renewing her car's expired warranty? But still, this was more revelation than she'd ever received.

"What makes you say that?"

"Her eyes." His thick lips pressed together. "Your grandma and I stopped bringing up the subject of your father because Deb's eyes were always a mixture of regret and pain. It hurt us to see it." He pressed an age-spotted hand on Elise's shoulder. "But she never regretted you."

Elise nodded. She'd never doubted her mother's affection or questioned if she'd been an inconvenience. Yes, her mom was young when she had Elise. Deb Malvern was freshly out of Julliard with a head full of dreams and a womb cradling a baby. Elise had done the math several times. She had to have been conceived around the time of her mother's graduation from the elite music school or shortly after.

"Just because she didn't tell us anything," Pap continued, "doesn't mean she never let it slip to someone else."

Elise perked. "Someone like. . .?"

"I wasn't going to mention it." Pap shifted his weight, the wrinkles framing his gray eyes deepening as he stared at the jewelry box. "But Giselle Turner is passing through town."

"Who's that?"

"She was your mother's roommate at Julliard."

<hr/>

Pierson jogged up the sidewalk that night sporting a backward ball cap and a pair of Oakleys.

The weather had climbed to forty-five degrees, and Elise was relieved the skies ceased spitting snow earlier in the day. Otherwise, she would have been forced to ask Pierson for a ride. Elise never drove in the snow, which proved tricky living in a city where winter weather spanned from October to April. Her Penn Avenue apartment kept most things within walking distance, but tonight she was meeting Giselle Turner in a coffee shop outside the city limits, closer to the Pittsburgh International Airport.

"I'm not sure if you should be here." Elise had texted Pierson this afternoon, but she hadn't expected him to accept the invite. She didn't know how rich, single guys spent their Friday nights, but she was pretty sure coffee bar get-togethers wouldn't top the list.

"Your welcoming skills need work." He pocketed his keys in his jeans. "The correct greeting should be, 'Glad you came, Pierson. I missed you the past two days.'"

She'd needed those forty-eight hours away from him. After his confession about her role in his hit song, her heart had been doing funny things. She'd decided to blame it on bad salsa and not attraction to the man before her. "Is there a clause in your record deal stating your ego needs to be as large as your album sales?"

He chuckled. "I'm detecting vibes that my presence here is unwanted."

"More like inadvisable. That live song we streamed revealed you're here in Pittsburgh." The post had surged his popularity. "I'm slightly horrified at how many social media accounts have been created for the sole purpose of Pierson sightings." And even more horrified that she'd fallen into the internet vortex of browsing said accounts. "It's like a Piers-infatuation."

"I'm stealing that for my next album title."

He'd totally missed the point. People entered and exited the coffee shop, not sparing them a second glance, but how long would that last? "What if you're spotted?"

"Thing is, Elise, most people are caught up in their day-to-day life. They rarely see beyond what they expect to see. People don't expect me to be in their world."

"Yes, us mere mortals."

"That's not what I meant."

Maybe not, but it was a convenient reminder that she and Pierson were not only in different tax brackets but totally separate universes. He may have the whole down-to-earth persona nailed, but at the end of the day, he was still a celebrity, and she was not.

"I promised to help you." He tugged open the door, and his face grew serious. "I'm keeping my word. If that means I get noticed, I don't really care."

She ignored the spark of determination in his eyes. They stepped inside, and the familiar aroma of caffeinated goodness enveloped her. Giselle Turner had said she'd be wearing a beige blazer over a navy turtleneck.

A woman matching that description sat in a booth by the window. Elise's stomach pinched. Could today be the day she'd discover more about her mother? And her father?

She nudged Pierson. "That's her."

He must've noticed Elise's reluctance, because he rested his hand on her lower back, lending support as they walked across the room.

Her steps were even and casual, but her nerves were breathing into a paper bag. "Are you Ms. Turner?"

The dark-haired woman stood with a friendly smile. "I am, but please call me Giselle. You must be Elise, Deborah's daughter." She shook Elise's hand.

"Thank you for agreeing to meet between flights." The music professor was passing through to Boston. Elise glanced at Pierson. "This is my friend, uh. . ." Was she supposed to introduce him with his real name? They probably should've discussed this detail. And the folk music blaring through the surrounding speakers didn't help. How could she think with the repetitive, twangy strumming? "Stupid banjo."

"Banjo?"

"Hmm?" Elise blinked, her brain fog clearing even as Giselle's brows raised in question. "Oh, yeah. This is Bentlee." Not a lie. It was Pierson's middle name. "But he goes by Banjo Ben because of his epic skills with the mandolin. He's a crowd favorite at the Polka Pot."

Pierson's hand slid across her sweater. He subtly pressed his fingers into her side, tickling her. She bit back the rising laugh and favored Pierson with her most angelic smile. His eyes told her he wasn't buying her innocence.

Giselle was oblivious to Pierson's true identity and to their antics, but it reminded Elise of a hundred fun moments between them as teens. The older woman shook Pierson's hand without a flicker of recognition.

They tossed around small talk, moved to purchase their food—Elise's courage demanded a white chocolate scone—and then returned to their seats. Pierson and she shared the booth bench, placing him distractedly close.

Giselle slid the cardboard centerpiece aside. "You said you have questions about your mother's time at Julliard?"

"I do." Elise fidgeted with the purse strap in her lap. "This is a delicate topic for me, but. . ." This was stepping out. More like stepping out over a cliff, but she could do this. Pierson's warm hand settled on hers over her thigh. His gesture was sweet, but his touch sent all her nerves into an awkward line dance. "I'm searching for my birth father. I'm pretty sure my mom was pregnant with me around graduation or a little after."

"She was?" Surprise widened her eyes, then her lips parted with a soft sigh. "I should've been a better friend. We were both so focused during the final semester that we drifted apart."

Something Elise could relate to. Most didn't realize that statistically speaking, it was easier to land a position on a pro basketball team than to win a seat in an orchestra. Elise had known the logistics going into Carnegie Mellon, which was why she'd minored in marketing. But this topic pinched her gut regarding her own audition in four weeks. "What was my mother like during that time?"

"Driven. We all were." Her bracelets jingled against her plate as she took a bite of her muffin. "But your mom even more so. We all were jealous of Deb's talent."

"Do you know if she had any boyfriends? Anyone she was close to?"

"She often turned heads. Like I'm sure you do." Giselle gave Elise a soft smile. "You resemble her."

Elise didn't think so. Her complexion was olive-toned where her mother's had been creamy ivory. The pale green eyes and dark auburn hair that always met Elise in her reflection were nowhere close to her mother's caramel brown eyes and crowning golden hair. Not to mention the dimple that poked Elise's cheek. But she soaked up the sentiment anyway. "Thank you."

Giselle's gaze bounced between Pierson and Elise before continuing. "She dated a man named Cedric. He went to Julliard and played the cello. But they were never serious."

Elise didn't want to hope. Yet this was her first and only lead.

Pierson leaned forward. "Do you know what happened to him?"

"I married him."

Oh.

"Then divorced him."

Pierson and Elise shared a look.

"Turns out Cedric wasn't into monogamy." She huffed a laugh. "Deb tried to warn me, but I didn't listen. I thought she was jealous because he chose me over her."

But hadn't Giselle said he and Mom were never serious? Something wasn't adding up. At first, Giselle gave the impression she and Mom had been friends, but now it seemed they were more like frenemies. Though still, Elise felt bad for Giselle's heartbreak. "I'm sorry."

"Don't be. I'm happily remarried." She lifted her left hand, showing off a large solitaire. "I'm the one who should be sorry. I'm sorry about your mom. She was a good person. I heard about the car accident when I was performing overseas in London, or I would've attended the funeral." She tucked her hair behind her ear, and Elise spotted some silver streaks.

A fresh pang of sorrow tore through Elise. Mom never had a single gray hair. Nor any wrinkles. She hadn't lived long enough. Elise picked at her scone, her appetite dwindling. "Is there anything else you can think of that might help?"

"There was one thing." Her hazel gaze turned distant. "Directly after graduation, Deb spent the summer working at Anders Music Camp. It was a last-minute decision. But what was strange was she asked me to cover for her with her parents. She'd intended to spend the summer months at my family's beach house. I never questioned it. But now I wonder if there was more to the story."

Mom had lied to Grancy and Pap. Why? Working at a music camp was awesome résumé padding. It didn't make sense for her to hide her whereabouts. "Anders. Was that in the Poconos?"

"Yes, that's the one."

"I see." Elise's shoulders slumped, and Pierson gently squeezed her fingers.

Giselle took a sip of her cranberry-colored drink. "The plan was for her to return to NYC and share an apartment with two other female musicians and me as we job hunted. But when Deb returned, she was . . .different. She told us she decided to move home to Pittsburgh. Then packed her things and left. We all were shocked but didn't press her to stay. Looking back, I should've asked more questions."

"Was Mom still dating Cedric at the time? Did he go to the music camp too?" Elise might have been conceived during her mother's stay in the Poconos. The timing fit.

She shook her head. "Cedric isn't your dad."

"How can you be certain—"

"I just know." Her voice was as tight as her features. Taut silence stretched until it was finally broken by Giselle's heavy exhale. "You see, it's a sensitive topic for me. Cedric and I couldn't have children." Notes of sadness filled her eyes. "It wasn't on my end."

"I'm really sorry."

She shrugged. "Probably for the best."

They chatted a few more minutes before Giselle had to return to the airport to catch her flight. Elise and Pierson lingered at the table.

With Giselle gone, Elise assumed Pierson would claim the other side of the bench, but he remained by her side. She glanced up and found him watching her with concern.

She pushed her plate away. "I'm not sure if that helped or made things worse."

Pierson's compassionate smile could be her undoing.

Nothing good ever came from getting her hopes up. And she foolishly had. "Do you think she was lying about Cedric? What if he was my birth father?"

Pierson idly toyed with a straw wrapper. "There's no doubt Giselle was jealous of your mom, but she didn't seem like the kind of person to lie about something that significant." He blew out a breath. "What about that music camp? Think there's anyone we can contact there?"

Elise shook her head. "No, if it's the camp I'm thinking of, they closed twenty years ago."

"No follow-up there." Pierson spoke her exact thought.

"But now I'm wondering about the necklace and the coat. I feel it's a part of all this. I just don't know how it connects." She filled Pierson in on her conversation with Pap this morning about the emeralds.

He opened the photos app in his phone and showed her a screenshot of a newspaper article. "I found this." He shrugged as if it was no big deal, but Elise didn't miss his bashful expression. "It's a story about jewelry thefts in the Roaring Twenties. But it seems like one of those sensation pieces."

A warm jolt she blamed on an espresso shot surged her bloodstream. He'd done research for her. "I saw this one too. And I agree. It's a total tabloid piece." She finished her drink. "I went to the library, but I couldn't find anything beyond this. The data tech said there was a massive flood in the thirties that destroyed a lot of records."

"Bummer."

"We know from that article that there was a series of jewel heists by a thief nicknamed the Mirage. We don't know what was stolen or if the robber was ever caught." What if the Mirage had access to the costume and hid the jewels there? If Elise searched more about the Mirage, would it lead to the discovery of the coat's owner? She shook her head. No way she was going to go all Nancy Drew on this. She needed to focus on her audition.

"The Mirage. That's some alias." Pierson dipped his head close. "Speaking of nicknames. Banjo? Really?"

He was lightening the heavy mood, and it worked. Because she sputtered a laugh. "Banjo Ben," she corrected. "I used your middle name. It was the perfect deflection."

"Perfect isn't the correct descriptor."

"I'm thinking for your next social media live you should do some pickin' and agrinnin'. Get those grannies on the Pierson train." Her smile was all tease, but her heart twinged a little. She hated to admit it, but long before his handsome face graced an album cover, she was the first passenger to have her ticket stamped and her heart boarding that fan locomotive.

She wouldn't return to that girl again. Because that version of herself was too vulnerable. Having lost her mom, then being ditched by her closest friend, she'd learned it was safest to keep people at arm's length.

The only thing she wanted within reaching distance right now was her violin.

CHAPTER TEN

Sophie

$\mathcal{T}$he shellac had long worn off the wooden planks beneath my heels. I paced the length of the narrow stage, my steps echoing in the forgotten theater. Metal rods hung from the ceiling at the mercy of rusty chains. No curtains. No lights. Just faded memories among dust and cobwebs.

Yet I loved this place.

Gentle flames danced inside the two kerosene lamps on each side of the stage, creating a promenade of light and shadow. Fran's father, Mr. Jackson, owned this building and faithfully kept empty lanterns and a jar of oil near the entrance since it wasn't wired for electricity.

Cracks climbed the cement blocks like decaying vines, but it was within these four walls that I became an actress. From reciting Shakespeare to practicing the Castle Walk dance, Fran and I had spent our formative years here. But I didn't come to reminisce. I came to meet *him*.

On cue, the side door yawned open. Corroded hinges groaned. Sunshine spilled in, carving Sterling's darkened profile in the entryway.

I descended the splintered steps. "You came." Last night, after the awkward encounter in the rehearsal room with Lina and Gerald, I'd asked Sterling if he'd meet me at the site of my "arrest." I was positive he grasped my meaning but less certain he'd show.

He stepped inside. "You said it was urgent." His gaze roamed my face, searching. The incoming light exposed the dust motes swirling in the air, an accurate reflection of my soul. Sterling's nearness stirred long-buried secrets within me, and I was scared his piercing gaze would glimpse them all. "Why wouldn't I come?"

I closed the door. "Because this place. . ."

"Was where I first met you."

"You mean first tried to *arrest* me." I smiled. "You thought I was a rumrunner."

"I might have." He dipped his chin in a tight nod, but I could have sworn I glimpsed a spark of amusement in his eyes.

"Might have? You nearly tackled me." I'd had an audition at the Shubert Theater the following day and had come here to rehearse. It was snowing heavily that evening, reducing visibility. I rushed down the side alley, eager to escape the wintry elements. With my long, bulky overcoat and scarf disguising my feminine form, coupled with my hustled steps, it was understandable for Sterling to assume I was a bootlegger on the run.

His gaze casually scanned the space. "In my defense, we had a tip that rumrunners were using abandoned buildings to store alcohol."

"Tell that to my hat you trampled." When he'd realized I was a woman, he quickly helped me up and, in the process, accidentally flattened my hat, which had fallen off in the tussle.

"I recall buying you a replacement."

"Yes, you did." A hat I still had in my possession. One I wore when I missed him terribly. I probably should have left it behind with the ring, but I hadn't been able to part with it. I'd needed a token to remember him by. Which reminded me. "I have something for you." I snatched my purse from the stage and quickly fished for the small items.

Sterling drew near, his familiar scent wrapping around me. Breathing deep, I opened my hand.

"My father's buttons." His voice was a low rasp.

"You were upset when we couldn't find them..." *For our wedding.* His father passed away two years before we met. Sterling had intended for his mother to sew his father's buttons onto his wedding suit to honor the late Mr. Monroe. But when the time came to adjust Sterling's jacket, we couldn't find the sewing kit I'd stored them in.

His fingers curled around the buttons in a tight fist. "Where were they?"

"I was going through my things last night and found my sewing kit. The buttons were still inside." Was Sterling's somber expression because of missing his father or the missing bride on his wedding day? "I'm sorry."

He dropped the buttons into his trouser pocket. "Didn't need them anyway."

Silence stretched and twisted between us.

I waited until his gaze met mine. "I never intended to hurt you."

"Why did you. . ." His voice broke, and the impassive mask he faithfully wore cracked. Sterling stood, half in darkness, half in light. So very much like him. He hid all emotion, any form of vulnerability, only showing the world his intimidating side. In a way, he was an actor much like me. His eyes closed, and when he lifted those dark lashes, indifference had reclaimed him. "Why did you ask me here?"

Disappointment warred with relief. That wasn't his original question, but my heart wasn't ready to discuss why I'd left him. Instead, we grappled for steady ground between us. "I asked you here because strange things have been happening."

He motioned toward the first row of seating, then scowled at the grime-crusted chairs. "One moment." He brushed off the worn cushion, but the dirt clung to the fabric. His full lips flattening into that signature grimace, he shrugged out of his jacket and draped it over the seat.

"You don't have to—"

"You get crabby if you stand too long."

I gasped. "Do not."

"Do too." He wiped his hands on his handkerchief. "Now, tell me what happened."

I perched on the edge of the chair, determined not to wrinkle more of his jacket than necessary. "When we returned to the theater the other day, I checked my costume, and my paste necklace was gone. I searched everywhere. What's strange is, later that night, the necklace was back inside the coat pocket."

"I see." He gave a slow nod, slipping into the detective role. "What do you suspect happened to it?"

"I'm not sure. Why would someone take it in the first place? It's not worth anything."

He barred his arms across his chest, something he always did when in deep contemplation. But without his jacket, his muscular form was distractingly accentuated. "There has to be an explanation."

I shifted in my seat. "There's one more thing. I talked to Joe today."

"I noticed."

"Yes, well, he seemed to imply our director is behind the robberies." Sterling didn't flick an eyelash. "I know Lloyd's been uptight, but I can't imagine him doing such a thing."

He shrugged. "People do unexpected things all the time."

I stiffened. Was he implying me? Or had he meant people in general?

"But your friend Joe was drinking. His judgment might've been impaired."

My eyes widened. "You knew that?"

"You didn't?"

"When he leaned close, I smelled alcohol." I didn't miss the flash of annoyance on Sterling's face. "I didn't want to say because—"

"You two are seeing each other."

I stood abruptly. "What?"

His jaw tightened, his lips pressing together as if he were forcing back words. But our gazes locked, and a challenge crept into his piercing eyes. "I just assumed—"

"You assumed wrong."

"That you are a couple." He ignored my objection. "Seeing how he singles you out every time you're around."

"Oh, two can play that game." He was at least a head taller than me and twice my weight, but I advanced on him as if the playing field were even, erasing any distance between us. "Because I can say the same thing about you and Violet. So does that mean you and she are together?"

"Why do you care?"

"You can't answer a question with another question."

He scowled. "I can if the first question's absurd."

"It's just as absurd as you thinking I'm with Joe Neville."

"You didn't deny it." His head bent toward mine, his eyes daring me to oppose.

I raised on my tiptoes, my chin tipped in defiance. "Just as you didn't deny interest in Violet."

Our heated breaths tangled. Another two inches and our mouths would touch. Something we both realized at the same time. Passion shifted. Our argument died, but awareness blazed to life. Sterling's hands lifted as if to reach for me, but he dropped them to his sides and began to ease away.

No.

I seized the front of his shirt, stilling him. Sterling possessed a physical strength that outmatched most men. He could easily break free from my fragile grasp, but he remained captive.

Heaven help me, his heart thundered against my fingertips. He wasn't as calloused to my nearness as I'd thought. If only I could lean into him.

Kiss him. Tell him through touch the sentiments my conscience forbade me to say.

The room dimmed. One of the lanterns had snuffed out. Another reminder of the pressing darkness of my past. We couldn't rekindle our romance. Too much stood between us. Heart heavier than a hundred sandbags, I released him. "I'm not interested in Joe."

His face softened. "Nor am I in Violet."

I lowered my head and stared at a water spot on the floor. Anything to keep him from spotting the longing in my face.

Sterling's knuckle settled beneath my chin, gently nudging my jaw upward until our gazes knotted. "We've been tiptoeing around this. But it's not helping us push past what we were to each other."

I retreated a step, shaking my head.

"I don't want this talk any more than you do." His face tightened. "Let's get this over with and we can both move on."

No. No, no, no.

"Why did you leave?"

Sterling waited quietly before me, but a riotous storm waged in his eyes. He deserved to know the truth, just as I deserved to be free from its weight. But my freedom came at a painful cost.

I couldn't put us through that.

My shoulders curled forward. "It wasn't because I didn't love you. Sometimes choices are forced on us."

"No one forced you to run." Deep lines bracketed his downturned mouth. "That was your decision."

I shook my head. "It's more complicated than that."

"Then tell me." A man like Sterling Monroe would never beg, but his pleading gaze broke something in me. He wasn't demanding answers. He was seeking closure, binding for a long-standing wound.

"You were a lawman. You know a case isn't valid without proof. Neither is mine." I shoved all my conviction into this argument. "I can't defend myself because no one would believe me without evidence, especially you."

"Why is it up to you to determine what I believe or not?" His jaw ticked. "What are you even talking about? This is between you and me. Not some hypothetical crime or third party."

"But there *was* a third party." My lips clamped tight. I'd revealed more than I intended. Sterling was an investigator, and I'd handed him a leading clue.

His gaze latched on to the stage beside us, the lines fanning around his eyes tightening. "Your dream." Defeat weighted his voice. "I couldn't compete with your hopes of becoming a famous actress."

My mouth opened to refute, but I couldn't. If he assumed acting had separated us, I determined to leave it at that. My ears enflamed at the unvoiced fib. Though my hair covered the traitorous blush, I couldn't savor any relief. Guilt sparred with shame, but what was I to do?

While it would pain him to believe I chose the stage over him, the reality would devastate him. And I'd hurt Sterling Monroe enough to last a lifetime. "I'm truly sorry." For allowing him to believe an untruth, for sacrificing the future we could've had, for the undertone of loss in his voice. "I lied to you."

His brow bent in question.

"In the note I left you, I said I was going to my sister in Massachusetts. I don't have a sister." Lies. Half-truths. After a while, they all blended into a mess of deceit.

"Why?"

"I didn't want you to know where I really was."

"Because I'd come after you?"

I nodded. "And I'd return with you." I'd been weak those first few months, grieving the loss of our relationship. But remaining in Pittsburgh meant I'd be forced to mourn something far greater—Sterling's death.

"Would that have been so awful?" His voice broke through the painful thoughts. "You marrying me?"

"I told you. I had no choice." My emphatic tone did nothing to erase the doubt in his face. I was right. He wouldn't believe me.

"Why did you return then?"

I finally felt safe enough to come back. "I kept in contact with Fran. She wrote about the Loew's Penn opening. Got me an audition."

"There's one more thing I need to know." Sterling's pensive stare cut through me. "If given the chance to do things over, would you still leave?"

I turned away. "You can't ask me that."

"Why not, Soph?" He moved behind me. His hands braced my shoulders. "Please tell me." His fingers slid down my arms.

My eyes pricked. His touch, the most beautiful form of cruelty. If I answered no, would he offer me another chance? My heart leaped at the thought. But that meant I had to utter a lie, with more to follow, since I couldn't explain that tragic night.

If he only knew, he wouldn't demand this of me. Because traveling back in time would change nothing. The circumstances would be the same.

He bent closer. Near enough to nuzzle my hair, but he didn't. "If you could go back to that day, our wedding day," he murmured, "would you leave me again?"

The truth twisted deeper inside, burying beneath the ashes of what could never be.

A tear labored down my cheek. "Yes."

CHAPTER ELEVEN

ELISE

*P*ierson and Elise stopped in front of a pale brick building sandwiched between an insurance agency and a nail salon.

"THE OUTLET." Elise read the painted letters on the glass door. "What even is this?" Pierson had texted her this afternoon asking if she was up for visiting a place run by one of his friends. This marked the second weekend night in a row with Pierson. And tomorrow, Sunday, was Grancy's potluck poker, and the guests included Dorothea and her grandson. She knew Pierson was making up to Dorothea for the years he'd spent catering to his demanding career, but he was also giving a lot of his time to Elise as well. "I've never heard of this place."

"You'll see." He reached for the door handle.

"Oh no you don't." She clamped his solid bicep, stopping him. "Explain." He'd dodged her questions the entire ride over. Also his text messages were vague. Kinley was convinced his mysteriousness indicated it was a date, so her best friend insisted on being Elise's personal stylist. Usually, Elise balked at that sort of thing. But she felt bad for keeping secrets from Kinley regarding Pierson and gave in to Kinley's excessive primping. The sweater dress was on the snug side, and her hair—a double-dutch loose braid that flowed into a messy bun at the nape of her neck—seemed a bit too much of an effort. Though she'd caught Pierson's gaze tracking the lines of her throat at least three times already.

She didn't relax her death grip on his arm. "Fess up, Piers. Why did you bring me here?"

He moved to place his other hand over hers, but she quickly retracted her fingers. "Let me ask you this. Do you think your stage fright gets triggered from being in front of crowds in general or only performing with your violin?"

Her suspicions soared to high alert. "I don't know. I've never performed *without* my violin."

He jerked his head toward the door. "We can find the answer."

She gasped. "No karaoke!" Because unlike him, she could not sing.

"Take it easy, Shania." He quirked a smile. "I promise no singing is involved. Unless you beg me to serenade you."

"Never gonna happen."

"I'm wounded." He flattened a hand over his heart. "But seriously, this is an improv place. The audience is seventeen and under."

"Huh?" She wrinkled her nose.

"You're adorable when you do that." He bopped her under the chin like she was five. "My friend from college owns this place. He does a lot of inner-city ministry work, but he also runs this program. It's to offer a fun, safe space for teens to spend Saturday nights. Think *Whose Line Is It Anyway* meets Nickelodeon, and you have The Outlet."

She agreed with the purpose, could get behind the vision of helping youth, but she did not love the idea of improv. "The thought of winging it makes me want to cuddle my daily planner." Improvisation was the exact opposite of her personality. Her gaze dipped to her callused finger tips. Normally, she'd undergo months of rehearsing before taking the stage. With improv, everything was made up in the moment, acting on impulse.

His gaze softened. "I thought it would be a lowkey atmosphere to work on your stage fright."

It shouldn't affect her that he seemed really invested in helping her, but it did. Especially when he looked at her like that. "I predict epic failure." But with Pierson in the room, would anyone pay attention to her? Yesterday, Giselle hadn't recognized him, but these kids wouldn't be so easily duped. "If, and I say this loosely, *if* I participate and need a buffer, you're it." She poked his arm. "Got it? Like a flashing, neon Elvis suit kind of distraction."

"I can manage that." He gave a slow wink. "I'm your hype man."

"A country guy using rap jargon. Something just snapped in the musical stratosphere."

"Just be you." He tugged her to his side for a quick, friendly squeeze. "You're easy to fall in love with." He released her and held the door open as if he hadn't just stopped the breath in her chest with those words.

Once her heart rate chilled to human levels, she stepped into the sleek space. Black brick walls paired nicely with steel accents, complete with trendy hanging lights, making her wish this hangout had existed when she was younger.

"You're just in time." A tall man with the build of a linebacker stood behind an aluminum-framed reception counter, gaze fixed on his clipboard. "We're about to begin." He jotted something on the paper, then glanced up. And yep, this man knew exactly who stood in the foyer. "Brooks?" His grin widened as he rounded the desk. "It's been a while."

Pierson pulled him into one of those bro hugs complete with loud claps on the back. "Good to see you, Combs."

The man gave a disbelieving laugh. "I never actually counted on you coming."

Pierson kept his smile in check, but Elise caught the dark flash in his eyes. He'd burned bridges in the past. People didn't trust him. That seemed to hurt him more than a bad reputation. "Just had to convince this beauty to come along. Elise Malvern, meet Jeff Combs, the worst tutor for anything English related but can cook some mean omelets." Pierson grinned at her as Jeff chuckled.

Elise shook Jeff's hand. "You have a great setup here."

"Thanks." He returned her smile. "You do any improv?"

"Not at all. I'm here to watch. And by watch, I'm talking about the kids plastering Pierson's mug all over the social media galaxy."

"For now, my man's safe." Jeff pointed to a wire basket on the counter filled with. . .cell phones? "The only way improv can thrive is through participation. Nothing stops interaction faster than the threat of being bullied or ridiculed on the web." He shrugged. "So we confiscate all devices until the end."

She gave a hearty thumbs up to that idea.

Pierson faced her. "You ready?"

She moved her hand in an exaggerated sweep toward a door she suspected led to all the action. "This is your show, cowboy."

"We'll see about that." He flashed a disarming grin.

Jeff led them into the main room. A few kids looked their way. Then came the subtle elbow nudges and shocked whispers. The domino effect took hold, and soon every teen awakened to the reality that a celebrity had joined their ranks. Pierson knew how to work the room, greeting each young person, about twenty in all.

The kids quieted enough for Jeff to take charge, and he encouraged everyone to grab a seat.

He explained the basics of improvisation. "For every skit, we'll take suggestions from the audience. Remember, no mean comments. We're all doing our best, right? Both tonight and in life. If someone freezes, we don't tear down. . ."

"We build up," echoed from around the room.

Clearly this sentiment was emphatically stressed.

"So." Jeff clasped his hands together. "What do you say we call up our guests of honor for the first improv? Elise and Pierson."

Now? Didn't they serve snacks or something? Elise's brain cells required more processing time. Pierson stood and reached for her hand. A nice, strong hand she didn't take because touching him would be another dent in her concentration.

Cheers and whistles erupted as they walked to the front of the room.

"Okay, you two, spin for your improv." Jeff pointed to a tall wheel with colored slots, each space having different activities scribbled in marker.

Elise gave Pierson an easy shove toward the circle of doom, but he didn't budge.

"Let's spin together." He linked his pinky with hers, and she drowned out the dramatic sighs from a cluster of girls.

Pierson set his hand atop hers on the wheel, and they spun it. The red pointer made a clicking noise that rivaled the pace of her spastic pulse. As the rotation slowed, she held her breath.

"Looks like. . ." Jeff leaned in as the wheel came to a stop. "Fortunately, Unfortunately." He gave Elise a grin as if she'd just won the improv lottery. "That's a great one to kick off with. Okay, guys." He looked to the crowd. "We need a topic. Could be a person, place, thing, or event."

"Event!" A dark-haired girl in a Vans hoodie waved an energetic hand. "I say prom!"

A chorus of well-meaning teens cheered their agreement even as Elise's heart shriveled and sank. Of course, high school kids would pick high-schoolish events, but no!

Elise didn't want to discuss prom—fiction or non-fiction—with the man who'd stood her up. This was supposed to help her stage fright, not send her spiraling.

"Okay, prom it is." Jeff rubbed his hands together while Elise debated a mad dash toward the door.

Nope, couldn't run in her stupid heels. Plus, Pierson had driven them.

She was stranded in improv torment.

Pierson nodded, all casual as you please, completely oblivious to Elise's struggle. But why would he care about her feelings now? He certainly hadn't then.

"Here's how it goes." Jeff angled toward her and Pierson. "Brooks, you improvise a prom-themed story, but your opening line must start with the word *fortunately*. Then Elise takes over and must begin her spiel with *unfortunately*. Then you volley back and forth."

"For example," Jeff said, "if the topic is school lunch, Pierson might say, 'Fortunately, it was pizza day, which is my favorite.' Then Elise might say, 'Unfortunately, I tripped over Pete's tennis shoe, and my tray landed on my crush's head.'"

That sparked a few snickers.

"We can do this." Pierson's mouth paved a smooth smile, while apparently his brain hitched a ride on amnesia highway. Did he not remember how awful that night had been for her? And what happened afterward?

A shame Elise couldn't forget.

She closed her eyes. Too easily, she was back in time, in her bathroom, face streaming black tears, her fingers ripping bobby pins from her hair. The sensation of unworthiness that had suffocated her that night seeped into the present.

"Here goes." He moved closer to her. "Fortunately, the gangly, awkward boy asked his dream girl to prom, and she said, 'Yes.' He was stoked."

Elise stepped away, flushing hot at Pierson's indifference. "Unfortunately, on prom night, the girl waited in her fancy gown for her date. He never showed. She spent the entire evening sobbing."

A few teens gasped. Some laughed. Pierson paled. But she wasn't done.

"The young girl soon found out from her date's *grandmother* why he missed prom. In her heart, she forgave him because it was a legit reason, but her date, who was supposed to be her best friend, ended up ghosting her for almost a decade."

"Rude!" a teen called from the back.

"Loser!" another one said.

Tears stung her eyes. Whether from repressed sadness or anger, she didn't know. But she did know this wasn't the best platform to hash things out with Pierson.

"Fortunately. . ." Pierson's voice was soft. "God gave the stupid kid another chance to make things right."

Not buying it. He'd never apologized. Hadn't even talked to her about his disappearing act. "Unfortunately, when the guy saw her again nine years later, he had no idea who she was."

"Burn!" someone called from the sideline. A few other teens mumbled similar remarks.

Pierson stood, open-mouthed, gawking at her.

Emotion sliced through her. The most prominent one, embarrassment. But how could she fix it? She inhaled and stepped toward the crowd. "The young woman realized not to place her trust in people, but in God. For God will always be there and never let her down. The end."

Without a look to Pierson, she turned toward her seat.

Gentle fingers wrapped her elbow. Pierson moved into her space. "We need to talk."

She didn't feel like having this conversation. It had waited almost a decade. What was another millennium or two? But he was right. Might as well get this over with. Reining in a sigh, she allowed him to lead her into the foyer.

Once the door shut behind them, Pierson pulled her to him, crushing her to his chest. Her cheek pressed against the button of his collar.

"I'm sorry," he murmured against her temple. "So very sorry."

Elise pulled away. "That was dumb of me. I shouldn't have gone there."

"No, you should have." His blue eyes warmed with a tenderness reserved for intimate whispers and moonlit nights. "I'm proud of you."

"For acting like an idiot?"

"No, for being vulnerable." He released her only to knuckle back her hair he'd knocked loose during his embrace. "You faced your emotions in front of everyone. That took guts. And you didn't turn ten shades of green."

He was right. She'd even been under the lights, with all eyes on her, and not even the slightest degree of faintness. "That's because I was livid."

"Rightly so. I was a jerk." His gaze hooked hers. "That wasn't easy for me either."

"What? The improv?"

"No. Returning to Kentucky."

She laid a hand on his arm. "I know why you had to go home." His dad was in critical condition from alcohol poisoning. The doctors weren't sure Clint Brooks would survive, so they'd summoned Pierson. While Elise was waiting for Pierson to take her to prom, Dorothea was driving him to the Louisville Medical Center. Thankfully, his dad pulled through.

Pierson moved into his dad's house to help with his young stepsisters as his stepmom nursed his dad back to health. As a minor, Pierson hadn't much choice in where he lived.

"I never meant to hurt you."

"We were kids, Piers."

"You have no idea how many times I wanted to reach out to you."

That was new. "What stopped you? Your silent treatment made me feel like our friendship meant nothing."

He cupped her shoulders. "It meant everything."

"You had a lousy way of showing it."

"When Gram came to visit, she talked about you and showed me your picture on her phone. It hurt not being a part of your days anymore, leaving my old life behind, so I stopped asking. The only way to push through was to keep busy. After high school, I was busy with college. Then consumed with my career." A thousand poems could be written about the emotions in his eyes. "There's really no excuse for dropping you like I did."

"You were my closest friend." The one who understood her and all she'd gone through with losing her mom.

"I'm sorry." Their gazes collided, and something lingered there. "I thought about you a lot over the years, and when I saw you at the hotel. . ." His hands trailed down her arms until his fingers caught in hers. "I could hardly breathe."

"Wait. You didn't remember me."

"Believe me." His voice was a low rumble. "I knew it was you."

Surprise parted her lips. "Why didn't you say anything?"

"I didn't because I couldn't." He gave a slow shake of his head. "I don't know what I was expecting. You were always pretty growing up, but. . .you stole my breath. My voice." His thumbs grazed the tops of her hands. "I can't explain it, but it felt like everything wrong turned right again."

"You were with your family." It would be wise to move away from his touch, but she didn't. "You were finally there to celebrate Dorothea for her big day. Of course things felt right again. Priorities and all."

"It was more than that." Noisy cheering pulsed from behind the door, and Pierson blinked. The depth of the moment shallowed. He quipped a chummy smile. "So. We good?"

"Uh, yeah. We're good."

"Awesome." He slung an arm around her shoulder in a total "pal" move, as if they were going to stuff their faces with buffalo wings and stream some UFC. "It's nice to be on the same page."

They weren't on the same page. They weren't even part of the same book. Pierson's happily ever after was in Nashville, and hers was in Heinz Hall. Their stories couldn't tangle. It was important for Elise to keep that detail bookmarked.

CHAPTER TWELVE

Sophie

*W*hat's the matter, Sophie?" Fran dusted her face with stage makeup and leaned over the vanity, checking her work in the mirror. "You've been pale since you got here. Are you sick?"

I stood between Fran and Violet while other actresses flitted about the dressing room. It seemed everything moved faster than the slow crawl of my heart. I'd left my motivation, my focus, and any hope of a relationship with Sterling back at that dilapidated theater. Sterling had left something too—his jacket. My gaze strayed to his navy sportscoat draped over one of the dressing screens.

Violet followed my eyes in the mirror's reflection. "I recognize that coat. It's Sterling Monroe's." She coated her lips with scarlet tint and smacked them together. "How'd you get it? Did sweet Sophie break the boardinghouse rules and have a man in her room?" She feigned a shocked gasp that melted into a laugh. "About time you did something naughty." Her suggestive tone made my stomach twist. "I'll gladly surrender my claim if he's smitten with you."

Both Fran and Violet gave me their full attention, expecting a response. "The detective left his coat in the auditorium." I refused to specify which one. For all they knew, it was the Loew's Penn. "I'm simply returning it. Trust me, Violet, he wants nothing to do with me." Not anymore. After my admission this morning, he'd left without a word. Not in rage or agitation but in seeming determination. As if he refused to let anything I said or did hurt him again.

If only he'd asked me how I felt today, in this moment. Would I leave him now? Never. I'd embrace the second chance I didn't deserve. But he'd pinpointed our wedding day, when circumstances had trapped me.

Fran's smile softened with understanding. She knew of my past relationship with Sterling but not why he and I had separated. "I'm judging the detective's got a vision problem."

Violet nodded. "Especially with those gams of yours, Sophie. If I had your legs, I'd raise the hemline on all my frocks."

"I didn't mean her appearance." Fran often grew annoyed when Violet acted shallow. "Only that he can't see how good a person she is."

But I wasn't good. When I tried to do right, I did him wrong. "It's okay. He doesn't—"

Lina Landis burst through the door.

Her heels lent a sharp cadence to the concrete floor, her eyes wild with fury. "Violet Salter! You've got nerve!" She thrust out her hand, which clutched an evening gown. The one she was supposed to be in for tonight's show. "You ruined my costume." She lifted the green dress high, revealing where the lace was torn from the shoulder and neckline. "Fix it. Now."

Violet's eyes widened at the accusation, then narrowed. "How dare you. I don't need to wreck your clothes for you to look awful on stage. You take care of that yourself."

Lina gasped in outrage.

"Let me see it, Lina." I edged toward the fuming woman. "I can mend it."

She handed it over but trained her heavy glower on Violet. "At least someone around here has some decency."

"Decency, you say?" Violet stepped into Lina's space, and a small crowd gathered to watch the verbal sparring. "Coming from a woman who's two-timing her beau."

Lina's face turned crimson.

"You thought you were being clever hiding behind the sets the other night, but I got a good look at who you were with." Violet's lips teetered between a snarl and a smile. "It wasn't Gerald."

Lina lunged toward Violet. I dropped the gown and gently tugged Lina's arm. Her sharp yelp stilled my hand. My grasp loosened, but curiosity gripped me. I lifted Lina's flowing sleeve. Four dark bruises lined her arm. As if someone had roughly grabbed her.

The commotion silenced. Those of us crowding Lina leaned in, examining her purpled skin.

"It's nothing." Lina raised her chin while shrinking away from me.

"I bumped it on the door the other day." She adjusted her sleeve. "Really, ladies. You look as if you've never seen a bruise before." Usually, Lina loved having an audience, but the attention on her now clearly made her uncomfortable. The vacant expression in her eyes revealed she wouldn't confide in us.

I scooped up the discarded gown. "This isn't as bad as it looks." I lifted the dress. "I can tack it on for you in less than five minutes."

She shot me a grateful look and left.

Fran sighed. "Those bruises were left by a man. An angry one."

I had to agree.

Betsy, the understudy for Violet, stepped forward, her eyes downcast. "I saw her and Gerald fighting outside the theater today. He was furious."

I recalled the argument I witnessed between Gerald and Lina in the rehearsal room. She had flinched when he raised his hand. Why else would she behave that way if he hadn't struck her before?

Fran's brows drew together. "Lloyd threatened her too."

"Loony Lloyd?" Violet picked up her lipstick and slid it into her bag. "He's eccentric, but I can't imagine—"

"I heard him." Fran's voice was emphatic. "He told Lina if she continued performing poorly, he had the power to destroy her. You know, she did forget key lines the other night."

She'd missed cues as well. My thoughts went to the conversation I had with Lloyd in the hallway when he suggested I brush up on Lina's lines. He'd seemed irritated but not aggressive. Could our director have hurt Lina?

It seemed I wasn't the only one with secrets.

※

After the show, I changed back into my frock, fatigue from the day settling into every joint. With my costume coat rehung on the rack and the paste necklace securely in the pocket, I tugged my cloche hat over my red curls. Fran and Violet begged me to go to a new dance hall after the show, but I had no desire to be on my feet longer than required.

"Sophie!" Violet's petite frame burst through the dressing room door, her gaze quickly seizing mine. "You have a visitor." She clasped her hands together and held them beneath her chin in glee.

A sharp band stretched between my shoulders. My gaze drifted to Sterling's jacket, still draped over the dressing screen. He was more likely my visitor, coming to claim his coat. My confusion turned to dread. Could I face him this soon after what I'd said to him today? "Here, Violet." I grabbed his jacket. "Would you mind giving this to the detective?"

"It's not Detective Monroe. I don't think he's here tonight."

"Oh."

"You'll never guess who asked for you." Her grin grew, and excitement lit her eyes. "In fact, I've decided not to tell you." Her dainty fingers latched onto my wrist. "It will be much more fun to see your reaction. Come on." She tugged me from the dressing room.

I tried to slow my steps, but with Violet's enthusiasm, I feared she'd yank my arm from its socket. "If this is your attempt to introduce me to a gentleman so I'll go dancing with you and Fran, I already told you I have a date with Charles Dickens."

She made a sour face. "Boring. And no, it's not a fella. Though that's not a bad idea. Say, we could ask Joe to escort you." She waggled her brows.

"Please don't," I pleaded as we snaked through the crowd, avoiding the set manager and the production assistant.

"There!" Violet pointed with a glowing smile.

I squinted at the large group of cast members huddled like pecking crows.

"As if *she* could come backstage and go unnoticed." Violet snorted.

"She?"

A tinkling laugh caught my attention. I sucked in a breath. No. Not her. Anyone but her. She and I had an agreement. One she obviously refused to honor.

"Sorry, Violet. I'm not up for greeting anyone. Please relay my regrets." Using the crowd as my shield, I broke free from her grasp and pivoted on my heel.

"Sophie." That voice. "There you are."

Too late. My jaw clenched. Slowly, I turned, hoping I was mistaken. That the feminine lilt didn't belong to the woman who betrayed me. Hands locked in tight fists at my sides, my gaze collided with Broadway's darling.

Greer Donnelly was a name many knew, but not many knew her like I did.

Her crooked finger, gracefully bent then outstretched, beckoning me. There was once a time I would have run to her, eager to gain her approval.

Those days were long gone.

I inclined my chin and held my spot. "Hello, Greer. This is unexpected." I kept my eyes from narrowing, but I was confident she grasped the undertones of my words.

She waved a gloved hand. "I heard the Loew's Penn could rival any theater in New York. I came to see if the rumors were right." Her laugh was as fake as her glittering headpiece and just as ostentatious.

There was more to Greer's visit. She never dawdled in public without a self-serving reason. I retreated a step. "I'm sure someone in the cast could give you a tour."

Joe emerged from the crowd of admirers. "I'd be honored, Miss Donnelly."

Good. I'd be free of Joe's attention and Greer's presence in one convenient swoop. The famed actress was almost two decades older than me, but she didn't look it. She was beautiful, elegant, and had an engaging aura that drew men in.

"Have a nice evening." I plastered on my brightest smile and hustled away. Let the other actors and actresses compete for that prized spot beneath her wing.

I knew the truth.

A sharp knock at my door jolted me awake. This wasn't fair. It had taken far too long to fall asleep, and now some inconsiderate person robbed me of what little rest I could snatch. I rolled to my side and fumbled for the switch to the lamp. I angled to read the clock on my nightstand, my eyes still adjusting to the light. Gripping the sides of my mattress, I leaned over more to make up for my blurry vision.

"Sophie?"

I fell off the bed.

"I hear you in there." Greer Donnelly's voice tightened with impatience. "Open up."

Something between a groan and growl rattled my chest. I hadn't seen or spoken to Greer in over seven years, and now twice in one night? I'd rather trip off the stage and land in the orchestra pit than face the arrogant actress at—my gaze darted to the clock—three in the morning.

Another round of staccato knocks sent me scrambling to my feet, which proved challenging because the lower half of my body was tangled in the sheet. But the last thing I needed was my landlord's scolding for being loud. Or worse, that she suspected I'd brought a gentleman to my flat. Mrs. Fielding had strict rules about men in the ladies' rooms.

I hurried across the carpet, tying my robe with an agitated jerk, and then opened the door. "Why are you here?" I moved aside, and she brushed past me in that annoying air of superiority.

"Hello to you too, my dear." She air-kissed the side of my face, which was all for show. Everything about Greer was dramatic and exaggerated, from her black grease-penciled brow slanting downward to her temple, to her gold-studded heels with jeweled buckles.

I gently closed the door. "And while you're explaining your unwelcomed presence, you can also explain why you reek of alcohol."

"I didn't come here to get chastised." Her gaze lazily strolled my small room. "I took a nice walk with your friend Joe."

Figured.

"He seems to know a great deal about you." Her hinting tone rankled. She glided to the faded wingback chair and lowered like a queen on her throne.

I picked up the Bible I'd left on the seat beside hers and sat.

"He told me he's been in your room."

"What?" My voice shrieked louder than intended. "He has not."

"How else do you think I knew exactly where you live? What number your room is?" She raised a dark brow in challenge. "He gave me very explicit directions. Even told me the color of your walls." She turned and skimmed a finger on the wallpaper. "Though I'd say it's more burgundy than maroon."

I shifted, and the Bible nearly slipped from my lap. "How did—" Fran. She'd told me she *borrowed* my room for a few moments the other day, but she neglected to tell me she'd entertained a visitor. Probably because she knew how I'd react. I could get evicted for this! And of course, Joe hadn't said a word to me about it.

A strange sensation crawled over my spine. Had he touched anything? Dug through my drawers? I shivered. I'd have to speak with Fran and confiscate my key. But I had to address my current predicament. "You broke your agreement, Greer."

She studied a fingernail. "I'm allowed to go wherever I want. You don't own the Loew's Penn."

"But you're here in my room," I countered. "Does that mean I get to break my end of the agreement?"

All her practiced elegance dropped with her gaping mouth. "You wouldn't."

"Why are you here?" I hated being rude, but I, more than anyone, understood the manipulating prowess of Greer Donnelly.

"I wanted to see if you were doing okay. When we last saw each other—"

"You were ruining any chance I had on Broadway." The summer after graduation, I left Pittsburgh for New York City. My aunt disapproved, warning me of the pitfalls of the acting profession, but I wanted a life like the famous Greer Donnelly. I wanted to prove my worth, to show the world I held value. Greer had promised to help, but her *assistance* had been a lethal hit to my career.

"I only said you weren't prepared for leading roles."

"To Florenz Ziegfeld." One couldn't get any higher than the mega-producer and owner of the Ziegfeld Follies. He was the only one willing to give me a chance.

"I didn't know you'd scamper back to Pittsburgh only to run away to California. And now you're here *again*." She tsked. "Aren't your legs tired from all that running, Sophie?"

She was baiting me, but I wouldn't nibble on the line she cast. I also wouldn't waste time discovering how she'd siphoned that information. Yes, I returned to Pittsburgh after Greer's sabotage in New York, and I did so again after I didn't succeed in California. I supposed there was no other platform in America for me to fail. At least I had that going for me.

"I've never cared for movies anyways." Her chin notched higher. "You can't interact with the audience. You're better off not to venture into that kind of thing." She stood and walked over to my vanity table, perusing the tray. "That little brunette, Violet, was it?" She picked up a perfume bottle and sniffed it. "Did I hear her mention Sterling Monroe?"

I bit the inside of my cheek.

"Wasn't he your fiancé?" She smiled sweetly. "Hildi wrote." She leaned in, examining her makeup, as if the topic of conversation was boring and not the very crux of my heartache. "She told me everything."

My aunt. The sting of betrayal dug deeper. But I shouldn't expect anything other from Aunt Hildi. I'd always been a burden to her. Though she'd moved into the country, it seemed she wasn't beyond Greer's seizing reach.

I rose to my feet, my thoughts clamoring.

"Since I'm in town, I should visit this Sterling fellow."

I pressed the Bible to my chest as if it could push strength into my heart.

Greer's gaze sharpened.

I wasn't convinced she'd actually hunt down Sterling, but I couldn't take that chance. I adopted Sterling's air of indifference. "You seem to know a lot about the locals."

"Joe likes to talk." She lifted a narrow shoulder. "I've met many men like Joe. He's the kind that sticks his nose where he shouldn't. I'd be careful around him." The sequins on Greer's frock caught the light, tossing glittered flecks on the wall as she walked toward me. "Just a friendly warning."

"Since when are we friends?"

Greer's head reared as if pelted by the gusty force of the icy truth.

I'd awaited this moment for years. The one where I'd see Greer knocked off her crystal pedestal. But the satisfaction I expected didn't come. Instead, my soul drained empty, as if bitterness had chewed a hole through it.

Greer reached for the door handle and paused. She looked over her shoulder, her gaze fastening on me. "I'm sorry."

Shock silenced me.

"I'm sorry for what I put you through." Her golden-brown eyes communicated more than her words.

She wasn't only talking about her remarks to Ziegfeld. No, there was more damage between us than a lost role.

Greer didn't deserve my pardon. I sure didn't feel like extending it. My thumb brushed over the holy scriptures still cradled in my hand. Forgiveness wasn't a feeling. But a choice. I squeezed my eyes closed, forcing words I hoped wouldn't burn me later. "Apology accepted."

Her eyes widened as if she hadn't expected it to be that simple. It wasn't simple. At all.

"I brought what belongs to you."

I shook my head. "I don't want it."

"But it's yours. I can't be responsible for. . ." Her sigh held more resignation than annoyance. "Never mind, I'll keep it until you're ready."

We said our goodbyes, and I reclaimed my spot beneath my sheets. The warmth of the bedspread smothered my frame, but I couldn't shake the chill coursing through me. Greer looked different tonight. I could blame the change on the seven-year gap since we'd last met, but I had a feeling it was more than that.

While still beautiful, her features had lost that delicate softness. As if her hardened resolve to trap secrets inside had a direct effect on her outside. She hid it well, but even her eyes seemed troubled. I detected it because I'd seen that unrest in my own reflection. Secrets left piled upon one's soul held the power to crush it. I didn't want to hold on to them any longer.

It was time to tell Sterling the truth.

CHAPTER THIRTEEN

ELISE

*E*lise broke her 120-month self-imposed banishment from Grancy and Pap's attic. She turned a slow circle, breathing in the scent of sun-warmed dust and faded memories. The space was once a makeshift apartment for her and her mom, but now it was overrun with boxes, dusty furniture, and probably spiders.

I can do this.

She'd come here to complete a decade-old mission—to go through her mom's belongings. Within minutes, Elise found the cardboard container marked DEB. The wimpy parts of her psyche wanted to retreat downstairs, but thanks to her bargain with Pierson, she was exercising her bravery muscles.

It was time to flex.

She would remain here and face the cardboard beast.

The sun's rays streamed through the round window, shining a natural spotlight on the box. Dust and grime coated the sides. The tape had yellowed. Everything about this box whispered *forgotten*.

But she hadn't. She'd only been scared. Because opening the lid meant reliving the pain. Her eyes fell to the Persian area rug beneath her Uggs. The hand-knotted wool was faded, but she recognized the pattern. How many times had she played Barbies or Legos on this spot?

Being here stirred more than her sinuses. In her mind's eye, she could see her mom sitting cross-legged on the rug reading Elise *The Chronicles of Narnia* or standing on a stepstool changing the lightbulb in the overhead fan. Could hear her off-key humming over the noise of the vacuum.

Elise and her mom lived in this attic until Elise's seventh birthday, when they moved into a furnished apartment.

With a sigh, her gaze swept her mother's box. Remnants of a thirty-seven-year existence stuffed into a three-cubic-foot container. That was all that remained of her life.

The edges of her vision grayed, matching her bleak heart.

I can't do this.

Boots clopped on the wooden stairs. Heavy. Precise. And somehow rhythmic.

Pierson, the king of love songs and mixed signals, appeared in the doorway.

Surprise caused her pulse to jolt. "Bad timing, Brooks. You're interrupting my neuro meltdown."

He jerked a thumb toward the stairs. "Want a couple more minutes?"

"You're here." She shrugged. "Might as well stay."

"Ah, Elise. Your charming welcome makes my heart burn."

"I have some Tums in my purse."

"I'm good." He stepped farther into the attic. "But it sounds like you're not."

Her arms fell limp to her sides. "I'm trying to rally the courage to look through my mom's stuff. I'm seventy percent certain of my uncertainty in opening it." Elise was a tight ball of emotions. But one gentle tug from Pierson, and she'd unravel. So she refused to look at him and glued her sights on the cardboard mystery. "I thought you were playing poker with the ladies."

"I didn't care for the hands."

Elise rolled her eyes. "Is Grancy dealing a trick deck again?"

Pierson neared, bringing along the scent of leather, spice, and forbidden fruit. "No, I'm talking about physical hands. That lady with the pink rollers in her hair. Martha. She keeps trying to pinch my cheek. And I'm not talking about this one." He tapped the side of his face.

"She's ninety."

"With impressive hand-eye coordination."

Her laugh broke through.

"I'm remaining next to you for the foreseeable future." As if to prove his point, he moved flush against her side. "And appointing you as my bodyguard."

She didn't want to think about having any jurisdiction over his body. "If I wait here much longer, I'm gonna chicken out." She pulled a rag from the back pocket of her jeans and swiped at the box's surface, clearing away the crud.

"What's in it?"

"Not sure. I've never gone through it." She shook out the cloth and wiped again. "After Mom's accident, I couldn't bring myself to sift through her things. It was too much of an acknowledgment that she was really gone. That life would never be the same."

"Heavy thoughts for a fifteen-year-old."

"It was a heavy time." She met his eyes. "But you helped more than you know. Thank you."

"All I did was invent stupid songs to make you smile."

He downplayed his role in helping her cope with the grief, but Elise knew the truth. Pierson had been her lifeline. Yes, he devastated her heart later, but she was grateful God had dropped him into her life.

"You okay?"

"It's all. . .overwhelming."

"I'm going to speak your language." His chin tilted as if he was going to go all philosophical. "You're looking at the entire score and getting overwhelmed. Remember, every song begins with one note. Start there. Then go forward measure by measure."

She blinked. "That's actually decent advice."

"I should take offense at your surprised tone, but I'll overlook it as long as you keep looking at me like that."

Oh no. What had he seen? Now she regretted declining Grancy's many offers to teach her the art of the poker face. Because if her expression betrayed the emotional tug-of-war going on in her heart, she was in trouble. She couldn't let him know how he affected her. "Like what?"

His blue eyes deepened in intensity, and her stomach dipped. *He knew.* His body inched closer, narrowing the space between them. "Like I'm your Mozart, Bach, and Chopin."

She huffed a laugh, popping the bubble of—whatever it was—that had been building, dropping her back into the reality that she'd been reading him wrong. *He's only trying to lighten the mood.* "You're ridiculous." She needed a flow chart to keep up with all his varied messages. "Would you lift this box to the table?"

He slid his ball cap around. "Sure." With little effort, he carried it to the old card table by the window.

Her eyes took in her mother's name written in black marker. "This could be my fountain."

"Fountain?"

"Oh." Why did she always bring up random topics? Well, random to other people, not her. "Did you ever hear about the legendary Fourth River in Pittsburgh?"

He tilted his head. "No. I thought there were only three."

The Allegheny, Monongahela, and Ohio. Pittsburgh is known for the joining of those three bodies of water. "But there's a hidden river underneath Pittsburgh."

"Really?"

"Well, technically it's not a river. It's an ancient aquifer."

"Sounds ominous."

"It courses beneath the city." She rested a hand atop the box. Goose bumps erupted. "The garden fountain in Heinz Hall's courtyard taps into it. Most walk on by without knowing." Her gaze connected with his. "What if this box taps into the secret wells of my mother's past?"

He stared at her.

She probably shouldn't ask why he openly gawked at her, but it was like ignoring an itch. To resist would bother her more. "What?"

"You."

Ugh, she'd gone deep again. This man had traveled the world, sung for royalty, been televised globally, and here she was relaying a metaphor about a hidden aquifer no one but she cared about. "Sorry. I'm weird. I can't help—"

"Don't." He cupped her face. "Don't apologize for that. It's your thing, and you're good at it."

She tried not to read into his touch. Pierson had always been a contact kind of guy. Growing up, it had always been fist bumps, high-fives, and side hugs. Now that they were older? Well, who did fist bumps anymore? "What's my thing? Making people feel awkward?"

He quipped a smile. "No, that's Handsy Martha's." His fingers worked a beautiful trail, like a slow love song, tracing her jaw, dipping to her neck. "Yours is storytelling. The way you are with words. Your expressions. From one artist to another, I think it's pretty hot."

Now she understood why the majority of country songs were about potential heartbreak. Pierson delivered a lethal dose of charm every time he opened his perfectly shaped mouth. She wouldn't examine his flirty words but could judge the ones about her being a storyteller. She wasn't. "I'm an everyday marketer and a someday pro musician."

"You're more than that." His hands skimmed to her shoulders, bracing her. He leaned in. Or maybe she did.

But what should she do with her hands? Clasp them at her sides? Stuff them into her pockets? Or option number three—rest them on Pierson's expanded chest. If his hands were on her, it was only fair, right? The second her palms flattened against him, she almost drew back. Because while the fibers of his T-shirt were soft, what lay beneath was not.

"That first time you spoke to me." His voice was husky. "We were at youth group, remember?"

She angled her face to look into his. "I was scared to say anything. You always looked angry."

"Because I was. Mom left. Then Dad remarried. And I was filled with angst and Red Bull in equal measure." He lifted his hand and playfully tugged a lock of her hair. "But then you strode up with your high ponytail and adorable dimple, launching into some story about manatees."

"I did not." She laughed. "It was about sea lions. I said you reminded me of one, and you growled at me."

"No teenage guy wants to be compared to a cute, chubby mammal."

She lightly smacked him. "It's because they have loud roars but are very friendly. And that's what I was hoping you were." She gave him a cheeky smile. "Turned out I was right." Would it be wrong to gently bow her head forward? To nestle on his shoulder? She leaned but caught herself before making contact. There had been enough touching for one day. She needed to pull back, but first. . .

"Did you just sniff my neck?"

"Maybe. Did you just kiss my hair?"

"Maybe."

She retreated a step with a teasing smile. "Then let's just 'Leave Things at Maybe.'" She quoted a title track from his last album.

He chuckled. "I'm having second thoughts about that song." He reached past her and grabbed the boxcutter from the table. "Are you ready to open this?"

"No," she answered. "But I'm a wannabe risk taker, right? Let's do this."

"Atta girl." He flashed the same grin that had graced magazine covers and handed her the cutter. "You do the honors."

With a hesitant grip, she sliced the blade through the brittle tape and lifted the flaps. The scent of paper and mildew filled the air. Several smaller boxes were crammed inside. She withdrew the top container and set it on the table.

"Photos." She read the label and shot a look to Pierson. "Okay." *Deep breaths.* "Let's check what's in here."

They browsed albums from when Mom was in high school and an envelope of snapshots from her violin recitals and competitions. Then they skimmed through the rest of the photos but didn't find anything relevant. The next box Elise opened held her mom's ribbons and plaques from her musical achievements. A small plastic container held some of her knickknacks, like a personal junk drawer.

Elise dug out the final item. "A music box? I don't remember this."

"Could be from her childhood."

She tried prying open the lid, but it was jammed. With a resigned sigh, she handed the slim wooden box to Pierson. "Can you get this?"

He gently slid the boxcutter blade under the lid and applied some pressure. It flipped open, and a folded piece of paper tumbled out. He swiped it from the ground and handed it to Elise.

The paper was lined like a page from a spiral notebook. She unfolded it and stared.

Notes.

Random music notes? Here she thought she'd find some deep dark secret—her fountain!— but no, just a scrap of paper with a hand-drawn staff with seven notes. There were two separate measures—one on the top of the page and the other on the bottom. The first bar had three notes, and the second bar had four. Whoever composed this also included a six-eighths time signature beside the treble staff.

Pierson hummed the melody, and she tried not to let the soothing rumble distract her. He looked at her with raised brows. "Recognize it?"

"No." She hummed it again to be certain. "What does it mean?" Her eyes landed on the first notation, and Pierson's earlier advice resurfaced. "Take it one note at a time."

He hovered close as she examined it with a fresh perspective.

"Oh." She raised the paper between them. "Look at the individual notes rather than the melody. It spells something."

He let out a whistle. Because he saw what she did. The first measure was Mom's name, *D E B.* And the second one read *C A D E.*

Pierson rubbed his stubbly jaw. "That's taking the whole love *note* thing to the next level."

Elise nodded. "But who's Cade?"

CHAPTER FOURTEEN

Sophie

*S*unlight danced through the large maple trees lining the residential street, highlighting the leaves in various shades of gold. The streetcar had dropped me off three blocks back, and I savored the walk. It was one I'd made a hundred times in the past.

I didn't know where Sterling currently lived, but there was someone who did—his aunt and my former landlady, Helen Parker. The Willow Courts apartment building came into view, and I slowed my steps. With its bright shutters and white picket fence, everything appeared friendly and welcoming, but I doubted any invitation extended to me. Mrs. Parker acted as Sterling's second mother. How excited she had been for our wedding. I hadn't only disappointed him but his entire family. Would Mrs. Parker slam the door in my face? Unleash five years of pent-up scolding as I stood helpless on her front porch?

My gaze dropped to the hatbox in my hand. Inside was Sterling's suit coat. Perhaps I could set it by the door and leave undetected. But what about Greer? She threatened to visit Sterling. Though would she betray my secret when I could easily expose hers?

A rustling to my left caught my attention.

Sterling.

Dressed in shirt sleeves and trousers, his sturdy form bent then straightened, dragging a rake through the leaf-strewn yard. Judging by the tall piles, he'd been outside for a while. Did he still live at Willow Courts? Or had he stopped by to help his aunt?

Watching him work in the shade of the two-story apartment building roused familiar longings. I'd fallen in love with Sterling within those brick walls. We might have met at that rundown theater, but when I became a resident of Willow Courts, we saw each other regularly.

As if hearing my heart calling to him, Sterling glanced over. He paused midswipe, the rake going limp in his hand.

I lifted my hand in an awkward wave. "Good afternoon, Sterling."

He set the rake down and met me at the fence line. "What are you doing here?"

My smile faltered at his cool tone. "I came to get your address from Mrs. Parker." I raised the box. "I wanted to give this back."

Dark eyes narrowed his stern face. "The hat I bought you? Keep it."

"No. Your jacket's in here. I didn't want it to get wrinkled." I opened the lid and withdrew the navy coat. The fence slats were only three feet high, making it simple for me to hand it to him.

"Thank you." He relieved me of the coat, seeming to take extra effort not to brush my hand. "Though you didn't have to come here."

"I haven't seen you at the Loew's Penn."

"I'm off the case. The police are handling the thefts now." His gaze met mine for a tense second.

I could only nod. A sliver of sadness cut at the thought of not daily seeing Sterling, but the sensible side of me was relieved he wasn't chasing jewel thieves.

"Goodbye, Sophie." With a brusque twist of his shoulders, he walked away.

"Sterling?" My voice stopped his retreat. "Can we talk?"

He refaced me. The shining sun contrasted the brewing storm in his eyes. "What for?" He barred his arms across his chest, his forearms on full display. "You made your stance clear."

No, I hadn't. "Please?"

His strained exhale wasn't precisely heartening, but within seconds, he was opening the front gate for me. I navigated the mounds of leaves and twigs until I reached the garden furniture. "Do you still live here?"

Nodding, Sterling set his coat on the wrought iron table and motioned toward the three matching chairs. "I never moved into our house." There was no trace of malice in his tone. "It was too much space for one person."

I'd loved that house on Herron Avenue. I thought I'd finally found a place to call home with the man I loved, but at least today, I could give some answers.

Sterling leaned against the tree trunk and pinned me with his piercing stare. "What is it you need to tell me?"

"Greer Donnelly visited me the other night." I paused, eyeing him for any speck of. . .something. He didn't even blink. "Have you heard of her?"

"No."

My shoulders lowered with an exhale. Sterling wouldn't lie. Relief washed through me, knowing I'd at least gotten to him before she had. "She's a famous actress. But that's beside the point. The thing is, I realized something when I was talking to her."

"That you want to be famous." He pushed off the tree and stalked toward me. "I know that, Sophie. If it's closure you need, you got it. I forgive you for picking acting over me. Does that make you happy?"

I rose to my feet. "You forgive me?" Though I'd said I was sorry, I never dared ask that of him. Never believed it possible. "Truly?"

His Adam's apple bobbed. "I do."

"Even though I refused to say why I left?"

He dipped his chin in a solemn nod.

I was forgiven. My heart swelled, finally free from guilt's iron clench. "Thank you." Now for the hard part. "But you're mistaken. When I talked to Miss Donnelly, my realization had nothing to do with fame. But with secrets. The woman has it all. Success, beauty, wealth. She's at the top of her field, but she's a servant to her secrets. She'll do whatever it takes to hide them. I can relate." I watched his brow hike ever so slightly. "Because that's how I am. But I don't want to be that way anymore."

Sterling's expression gentled. "You can tell me anything."

I wasn't entirely sure. But it was time. "Fran met a young man at a social event. When he found out she was a performer, he told her about his business associate who had great connections in the theater world. He invited her to meet him the evening before our wedding. Fran's father fell ill that night, and she begged me to go to the appointment in her place."

"You never mentioned anything."

"I didn't have time. Fran asked at the last possible minute."

He nodded.

"When I walked into the room, I realized—" My throat burned with the fiery confession. "It was a dice joint."

"What?" He jerked back. "Where?"

"Between some shops on Fifth Avenue." The windowfront appeared like an everyday office building, but I'd discovered the harsh truth. "I tried to leave, but a man grabbed me." At once, I was back in that hazy room.

The odor of cigars and whiskey stinging my eyes. The clink of roulette wheels. The man's hot breath coating my neck as his fingers bit into my arms. "I managed to get away, but not before he threatened me."

"Soph." I'd never witnessed alarm in Sterling's eyes. Until now. "You should've come to me directly."

"I wanted to but couldn't."

His hands went to my elbows, his tone insistent. "Yes, you could have."

"There were consequences."

"Consequences for them, you mean." His eyes flashed. "I was a lawman, but more than that, your fiancé. No one hurts you when I'm around."

"I know that. It's just—"

"I would have done anything to protect you."

"But *I* was protecting *you*." Tears clung to my lashes. "Can't you see? This was all about you. I never chose the stage over our relationship. That was a lie." It was as if my heart tore open, freeing the words I'd been forced to keep imprisoned. "He told me if I didn't leave town, he'd kill you."

His eyes widened, and the tender concern that had overwhelmed his features a few seconds ago faded. "What are you talking about? Who said those things?"

"Percival."

His touch fell away.

"It was Percival Simmons. He owned the dice joint. He didn't want me to tell you, so he threatened me." I'd only met him a handful of times before that evening, but I recognized him right away. And vice versa.

Sterling searched my face. In his profession, he peered into the eyes of the guilty and the innocent. In which category would he place me? My gaze pleaded with his hardened one.

Please, believe me.

"You're mistaken."

My hand pressed against my abdomen as if I'd been physically gouged. But hadn't I expected this? Wasn't this why I'd kept silent? Percival had known Sterling longer than I had. It was foolish for me to hope Sterling would side with me.

He stepped back as if repulsed by my lies. "Can Fran verify this story?"

"No." I shook my head, loosening a tear. "She doesn't know what happened that night." My wedding was supposed to be the following day, and by that time, I was gone. When I reconnected with Fran months later, she'd forgotten the entire thing. Yet it had haunted me every day since.

"Percival wouldn't do any of those things."

"He forced me into silence." I dashed another tear from my cheek. "He said if I didn't leave town, he'd make certain you had 'an accident.' He would have killed you, Sterling. I know he would have." The dark glint of his gray eyes had confirmed it. "Since he was attending the wedding, I decided to make a dramatic exit. So he would *know* that I left and wouldn't hurt you."

He scoffed. "Anything else?"

"You're mocking me." My tears died as frustration mounted. "I gave up everything. Everything! I lived in fear for your life and mine. You asked me the other day for the truth. Here it is."

"No. You're inventing a story to appease your conscience. And picking on Percival. Didn't the man have enough hardship while living?"

I knew what he meant. Percival had been a pilot in the Great War like Sterling. His wife left him when he was overseas fighting. "I'm not discounting what he did for our country."

He only glared.

"And what you did for him was kind." Sterling had discovered that Percival's wife abandoned him, and he invited him to Pittsburgh. He got Percival hired on with the Allegheny Police Force. They were war comrades, friends, police partners. I never stood a chance. What was I thinking coming here?

He folded his arms. "Prove it."

Of course it would come to this. "I told you I couldn't. That's what I was saying in the theater. I have no evidence. It's his word against mine."

"He's dead. How convenient."

"And I'm sorry for it. But I'm not sorry for feeling safe again."

He slashed his hand through his hair. "He can't even defend himself."

My chest rose and fell with rapid breaths. "There's nothing to defend. He ran a dice joint. He threatened your life. I left."

"You're lying."

"You know I can't lie, Sterling." I took a bold step toward him. "See for yourself."

The challenge hung between us. Sterling wasn't one to retreat from a dare, just as I wasn't afraid to issue one. So I propped my hands on my hips, awaiting his response.

Like a tiger with his prey, he slowly advanced, keeping me in his sights. His jawline taut, he threaded his fingers through my hair and drew back the sides. His pinky finger absently skimmed my earlobe. He leaned in, checking, testing my honesty. I knew exactly what he'd see or, rather, wouldn't see. My ears weren't aflame.

He muttered something, and while he held a fierce scowl, he gently untangled his hands from my hair.

I'd won the dare, but defeat echoed through me. I wished he had believed me before it came to this. "Percival was why I lied about living with a sister that doesn't exist. You couldn't know where I was. Because he'd find out and make good on his threat. When he died, I knew it was safe to return. He couldn't hurt us anymore."

He palmed the tree trunk, the tendons bulging on his extended arm, his head hanging low. "I don't know what to say."

"Say you believe me."

He angled his face toward me, eyes somber and piercing. "I can't."

The president of Paramount Films sat in the first row for tonight's show, and everything that could possibly go wrong had. Gerald had been arguing with Lina, and they both missed their cues. The spotlight malfunctioned. Joe had too much to drink and slurred his lines.

To make the evening worse, who had claimed the chair beside the silver screen mogul? Greer. For all her negative comments about the film industry, she had no qualms tonight as she practically cuddled against him.

After curtain call, we all expected Lloyd's lengthy tirade, but he waved us off, ordering our presence at tomorrow's rehearsal.

"No lecture?" Fran looked as bewildered as I felt.

"I don't understand it." I walked down the hall with her. "But speaking of lectures, you're due for one."

She put a hand to her chest. "Me?"

"Why was Joe Neville in my room the other day?"

Her lips tightened, then broke open with a sigh. "I should've told you." She tugged my wrist, bringing me closer. "He was visiting Hannah. Somehow Mrs. Fielding suspected he was in her room. I warned them just in time and hid Joe in yours because it was the closest. I couldn't let her get evicted."

"But if Mrs. Fielding saw him leaving my room, I'd be the one tossed out."

"I know. I know." Her shoulders sagged. "I'm sorry. It won't happen again."

Joe Neville seemed to share Lina's view of relationships—the more, the merrier. If anything, this reinforced my resolve to keep away from him. Fran apologized one more time before engaging in another conversation with a fellow from the stage crew, leaving me to head to the dressing room alone. I changed out of my costume and freshened my makeup. After snatching my purse from the table where we all kept our bags, I rushed out the door, only to be halted by yet another crowd gathered in the hall.

Dread gathered in my chest. I couldn't handle another Greer Donnelly encounter.

"I've had enough." Gerald's voice raised above the chatter.

I quickly found Violet lingering on the fringes of the staggered circle, looking on with a satisfied smile. "What's going on?"

"Gerald's breaking things off with Lina." Her hushed tone didn't hide her glee. "Look at her holding her new flame's flowers while attempting to look heartbroken. Has she no shame?"

"Go ahead, Lina." Gerald's voice was chilling. "Marry him." He gestured toward the bouquet, and I scanned the hall searching for the mystery admirer. I had yet to see him up close.

"Have you met Lina's new man?" I asked quietly.

Violet jolted as if she'd forgotten I was there. "Hmm? Oh, I've seen him from a distance." She kept her gaze on the feuding couple. "Lina's protective over him. She's afraid one of us will steal him away from her."

Lina's chin quivered, and my heart ached for her. It might seem that she'd brought this pain upon herself, but I'd learned from my experience there was always more to the story.

"I'm heading home." I refused to be a spectator at Lina and Gerald's breakup. I'd had enough drama for one day, and it had nothing to do with tonight's show. This afternoon's conversation with Sterling was the final shovel of dirt on our buried relationship.

I cast my gaze forward onto a figure approaching me with determined steps. My own pace slowed, my heart taken aback in surprise. Before this moment, I would have wagered I had more of a chance being sought out by the president of Paramount rather than Sterling. But there he was.

My fingers itched to reach for him. Touch him. But my body needed to side with my head and not my heart. I squeezed my purse with a white-knuckled grasp. "I thought you were off the case?"

"I am. I came to see you."

My pulse pounded. "Really?"

He turned the brim of his hat in his hands. "I'm sorry for being angry and unkind earlier."

I bit my lip, hope rising in my chest. "Does that mean you believe me?"

He hesitated, and my spirits sank. My head was right. There was nothing between us, nor could there ever be.

"I'm done here." Lina's sharp voice broke into our conversation. She swirled in a stunning display of fury and pride and cut through the parting crowd.

I took this as my cue to leave as well. I couldn't convince Sterling to believe me any more than I could persuade my heart not to love him. Both were hopeless endeavors. "Goodbye, Sterling. I wish you well."

I retreated a step, breaking free from his solemn gaze. But in doing so, I accidentally cut into Gerald's path as he stormed after Lina. He crashed into me, and I dropped my purse, the contents spilling.

Sterling steadied me even as he glowered at Gerald's retreating form. "Are you okay?"

I closed my eyes and reoriented myself, pulling in several breaths. After the tightness left my lungs, I nodded. "I just got the wind knocked out of me."

I remembered my bag, but Sterling had already stooped. A handful of others gathered, their focus pinning to the floor as if the concrete had turned into gold.

No, not gold. But diamonds. For laying atop my silver-toned compact was a jeweled bracelet, sparkling under the hall lights.

Sterling's face hardened like granite. "Why is this in your bag?" He lifted the bracelet.

I leaned close, examining it. "I don't know. I've never seen it before." I lowered my lashes as if my rapid blinks would clear the confusion. "It's probably a stage prop."

"No, it isn't." He pocketed the piece. "This looks identical to the bracelet Mrs. Dresden reported stolen."

CHAPTER FIFTEEN

ELISE

*E*lise sat at a bistro table in the Heinz Hall courtyard garden, sipping Campbell's tomato soup from her hot-pink thermos. The temperature teetered on freezing, but she needed fresh air more than feeling in her toes. Besides, she was near the wall fountain that tapped into secret waters. It was good for her soul.

Since it was the middle of January, the fountain's pump wasn't on, but that didn't keep the view from being any less breathtaking. Icicles clung to the dark rock, catching the slanting sunshine and making the fountain shimmer as if coated with diamond dust.

Was it weird she hoped being out here would spark inspiration? She'd been stumped about her mom's love notes. After rummaging the attic the other day, Elise had brought home the box of her mother's things. She'd flipped through every yearbook, scoured each newspaper clipping, read the backs of all the photos.

Cade's identity remained a mystery.

Grancy and Pap hadn't heard of the name either.

The glass door opened, and Kinley appeared. She worked half days on Wednesdays, using her morning to volunteer at the local food bank. "There you are." She clasped a coffee cup as if it were her only heat source. Nevermind, it was.

"Kin, where's your coat?"

She took a sip of her coffee. "No time for that. How are you?" She lowered onto the bench beside Elise. "I've been texting you all morning."

"I forgot my phone at home." Her sigh was a puffy vapor.

"It's like the arctic out here." A coy smile lined Kinley's glossy lips. "I thought I'd catch you and Pierson keeping each other warm."

"Yeah, well." She finished off her soup. "I told him I was busy on my lunch break." And for dinner. She also needed an excuse for tomorrow and the next few weeks until he returned to Nashville. Her system needed a Pierson Brooks detox.

"I see." Her smile faded. "No doubt this bothers you."

"I can't spend every spare moment with a hot, rich guy."

"Yeah, you need to give those unemployed gamers a chance."

Inner cleansing mode now engaged. First step—emotional separation by examining his flaws. "Who likes an ever-present five o'clock shadow?"

"True. Friends don't let friends get pash rash."

No, no! Elise did *not* want to think about kissing Pierson. Or how her skin would react to his amazing—no, hideous—stubble. She needed to get back on course. "My eardrums can only stand so much of his deep, southern accent."

She gave a failing smile. "Sorry, no objections to that one. Ever since you two have been hanging out, I've been picturing him serenading you beneath your window with his guitar."

Elise capped her thermos and set it on the table. "I'm five floors up."

"That does complicate things." Kinley laughed and then gazed at Elise, her hazel eyes turning serious. "He's gotten to you, hasn't he?"

"My playlist went from classical to country. Namely, all his songs. On repeat." Translation: Elise had it bad.

Kinley nodded her understanding. "Which is why you told him you couldn't see him today."

"It's for the best."

"Especially with all that's happened." Kinley dug her phone from her pocket. "You knew it was going to come out sometime, right? At least it's a flattering picture."

Unease crept through her. "What are you talking about?"

"Wait." Kinley abruptly straightened, bumping the table. "Aren't we talking about the same thing?" Her eyes widened on a sharp gasp. "You don't know, do you?"

"Know what?"

Just then, Pierson strode through the same door Kinley had moments before. His brow darkened. His jaw locked. The stiff set of his shoulders revealed he was on a mission, and she felt somehow it involved her. His gaze swiveled until connecting with hers.

Down, heart. Settle. And now she was speaking to her organs like she'd command a Labrador.

He rushed toward her and then crouched, their eyes level. "Are you okay?" His voice was husky with emotion and concern.

Kinley sighed.

The soup soured in her gut. "What's going on?"

He swept up both of her hands and leaned in. "I had no idea. Believe me."

"She doesn't know," Kinley supplied.

Elise slapped her hand on the table, making her thermos wobble. "Someone please tell me."

"We got leaked." He studied her face.

"We?"

Kinley angled her phone toward Elise, and everything went numb.

"Pierson Brooks and His Girl Next Door." She read the headline. She turned her no doubt startled eyes on the man beside her. She'd warned him this would happen. But who would do this? What right did someone have to violate her privacy? She wasn't a celebrity. If Pierson was a paparazzi bull's-eye, she became a target by default? Indignation pulsed through her.

He squeezed her hand again. "She lost the bet."

"What?" Her fury extinguished. She'd only heard that phrase in connection with one person. "No. She wouldn't."

She totally would.

Elise peered at the phone as if the incriminating article would disappear. But no. With a shaky finger, she scrolled down. There was a photo. Of course there was. It wasn't a picture of them from the coffeehouse or The Outlet. "This is Grancy's attic." The image looked like something straight from the cover of a romance novel. Sunlight streaming around them, outlining their close profiles in front of the window. Pierson's hands cupping her face. His gaze. . .wait. She zoomed in. "Pierson, you're looking at my lips!"

"I'm a man, Elise."

"Way to state the obvious."

"And you have nice lips."

Kinley giggled, earning Elise's glare.

"Yes, well." Her annoying best friend jumped to her feet and snatched her phone from Elise. "I'll leave yinz to sort this out."

Elise usually smiled at the Pittsburgh-ese expression—"yinz" being the equivalent to the South's "y'all." But this was no smiling matter. Kinley gave a chipper farewell wave and all but bounced back into Heinz Hall. With a groan, Elise closed her eyes for several breaths, reopening them to find Pierson's concerned gaze. "I guess I come by my photography skills naturally. That shot looks professional." She huffed a humorless laugh. "I still can't believe Grancy would do that."

Pierson sank onto the bench beside Elise. "She didn't."

She gasped. "Dorothea?"

He gave a solemn nod. "We really need to figure a way to keep them from wagering."

"Yeah, while we're at it, we'll change the earth's rotation, perhaps stop an ocean tide or two." Elise tried to lighten the tone, but her equilibrium was off. It was unsettling to have one's picture smeared all over the internet. She glanced at Pierson. This sort of thing happened to him on the regular. How awful to never have any privacy.

He nudged her. "To Gram's credit, she didn't release your name. Just the photo and a strong allusion to my preference for the girl next door."

"I'm not even close to the girl-next-door type."

"You kinda are." He flashed his palms in defense. "That's not a bad thing."

Then why did it feel that way? She wasn't runway glam or any glam for that matter. Her sense of style came from Kinley. If it were up to Elise, she'd sport leggings, long sweaters, and topknots from here to eternity.

"Your hair's shielding most of your face." Pierson interrupted her self-deprecation session. "No one will guess it's you."

"Kinley did."

"But she's your best friend and knows we've been together." Pierson tugged her hand in his, his thumb gently stroking her knuckles. "I never meant for this to happen."

"It's not your fault. It's Dorothea's."

"Yeah, she's not even sorry."

A laugh burst from her lips. "You should write a song about two meddling grannies."

"Wouldn't they love that?"

"They'd wager how many weeks it would linger at number one."

He continued his ministrations on her knuckles. "You said you could improve my reputation. You're one efficient woman."

She put her fingers over his, making a Pierson-hand sandwich. "What do you mean?"

"My publicist called. Since the release of that photo, album downloads went up. Like crazy up. My approval rating also seemed to increase."

"Approval rating? What are you, the president?"

He wrapped an arm around her, squeezing her to his side. "I'm currently president of your heart." He ignored her pinch. "And you're obsessively in love with me. It's really sweet."

"Stop." He didn't realize how correct he was. The man hadn't yet secured presidential status, but his campaign for her heart was irresistibly strong.

"We have our own fan page."

"You're kidding. No one knows my name."

"Doesn't matter. The public loves this sort of stuff." His head tilted, his gaze layered with hotness, tenderness, and a deluge of scheming.

"No." She moved from underneath his touch. Nope, not far enough. She stood and put more cold air between them, hoping to freeze her melting nerves.

"No, what?"

"I know what you're thinking."

As if his grin wasn't wolfish enough, his eyes joined the hunt, tracking her with a flirty glint. "Couldn't possibly."

"You have that face you get when you're plotting something."

Now his legs got involved, pushing that handsome form to full height and striding toward her. "I'm definitely plotting."

"And I have a feeling it involves me."

"No question."

He caught the end of her coat's belt and gently tried to tug her to him. She stood her ground. She could always buy a new coat, but hearts were harder to come by. "We're not fake-dating to help your career."

The belt fell from his hands. "I'd never ask that of you."

Good! But then, why did *that* bother her? He'd quickly dismissed her. He should have at least given her a courtesy blink of hesitation. It was obvious she couldn't measure up to his caliber of standards. But to be so blatant about it. It only leveled her up to the next phase of detoxing—acknowledgment of insurmountable differences. "Because I'm not like the other women you've dated."

"Right."

His admission stung, but she was glad for it. Now she knew her place—far beneath him. "I have to get back to work." And hide on the balcony with a giant-sized bag of Cheez-Its. She had an emergency stash in her desk's bottom drawer and enough self-pity to do some major carb damage.

She grabbed her thermos off the table and headed for inside.

"That wasn't an insult." His voice floated over her shoulder and somehow sank into her.

Her emotions were so all over the map, she needed a GPS to track them. But the door handle was within reach, the gateway to her escape. She glanced back. "It's okay, Piers. I know all this. Which is why fake-dating a girl like me won't work."

"It would never work for me." Something in his tone stalled her retreat. "Because I want the real thing."

CHAPTER SIXTEEN

Sophie

*A*fter the bracelet spilled from my purse, Sterling suggested we take it to the police detective assigned to the robberies. An action I now regretted. Sergeant Hamilton had done nothing but toss me suspicious glares for the past five minutes. Sterling leaned against the wall behind me. The policeman had asked Sterling to remain during the interrogation.

"Now, Miss Walters." Sergeant Hamilton was handsome, seemed intelligent, and held all the power. The worst combination. But he also had something green stuck in his front teeth, which evened the field. It was hard to be intimidated when a piece of. . .spinach? Broccoli?. . .peeked at me between his snarls. "How did you come into possession of this?" His index finger grazed the bracelet, his tone baiting.

"I don't know." My honesty only made the sergeant's eyes narrow. "But I'm certain of one thing—I didn't steal it."

"Did I accuse you of stealing it?"

Oh, for Pete's sake. "No, you didn't. But that's where this chat's leading. I thought we could skip the generalities and go straight to the specifics."

Sterling coughed.

The officer's lips bent in a surprised smile. "Fair enough. Do you have any theories about how the bracelet got into your purse?"

"Anyone could've placed it there." I remembered not to fidget. Sterling had said investigators looked more at what was not verbal than what was, such as body language, expressions, and anything that could signify suspicion. I stared him in the eye, my shoulders squared, exuding confidence I didn't feel. "My bag is always left in a dressing room I share with several women. The door's also unlocked during performances and rehearsals."

He tugged a pencil from behind his ear and set it on the notepad resting on the table. "Are you accusing the other actresses?"

"Of course not." I forced a friendly tone. "I'm only stating facts."

"I see. And what about your room at the boardinghouse?"

"What about it?"

"Does anyone have access there?"

I tucked my hands beneath my thighs, keeping twitchy fingers captive. "The landlady has a key. As well as Fran Jackson. And I just recently discovered that she...uh...borrowed my room to hide Joe Neville."

Sterling shifted behind me, but I continued, "Apparently Joe was visiting another boarder and was shuffled into my room to avoid being caught by our landlady."

The sergeant scribbled something in the notepad. "So Joe Neville and Fran Jackson have recently been in your room." He glanced up, pencil poised over the paper. He was most likely jotting down the names I'd listed. "Anyone else?"

I flicked my gaze toward the ceiling, my breath slowly seeping out. She'd be furious if I revealed too much. "No one that's associated with this."

"That's for me to decide, Miss Walters."

"Greer Donnelly."

He fumbled his pencil. "*The* Greer Donnelly?"

The admiration in his tone was nauseating. "Yes. Greer and I go way back. Fellow actresses, you know."

His brows danced on his forehead as if unsure if they should rise in question or lower in confusion. Because why would a woman like Greer Donnelly mingle with the likes of me? "What did she want?"

"To visit, I guess."

"Have you seen her since?"

This was a waste of time. Greer had nothing to do with the jewel thefts. "She was at the Loew's Penn this evening, but I didn't speak with her."

The sergeant lifted my purse that was sitting on the table next to the bracelet. "Did you have this particular bag around anyone else?"

"Yes."

"Who?"

"Sterling Monroe." I twisted in my seat and innocently batted my eyes at said man. "You didn't happen to stash a stolen bracelet in my purse for safekeeping earlier, did you?"

"No."

The sergeant laughed. "Monroe wouldn't do such a thing."

"And neither would I. It's insulting to think you'd believe me brainless enough to keep a stolen piece of jewelry in my bag where anyone could find it. Trust me, if I resorted to a life of crime, I could think of a dozen better hiding places than that."

"I don't doubt it." He tapped the end of his pencil against his jaw, an amused glint in his eyes. "But maybe you were only transporting the bracelet somewhere else and didn't have enough time to hide it."

I pointed to the bracelet. "How long has that been missing?"

"At least ten days."

I huffed, stirring the lace on my collar. "If it takes me almost two weeks to find a hiding spot better than my purse, you might as well count my intelligence as another thing that's been robbed."

Sterling coughed again.

The door creaked open, and a round-faced patrolman poked his head inside the room. "Excuse me, sir, but Lina Landis is here."

Lina had come to police headquarters?

"The prima donna." The sergeant steepled his hands, pressing his fingertips together. "Well, well, what a treat. Bring her in. It's about to get cozier in here."

The officer escorted the actress into the room. With her head held high and her posture perfect, Lina equaled Greer when it came to commanding the atmosphere around her.

Once the patrolman left, Sergeant Hamilton fastened his eyes on Lina. "Miss Landis, what brings you here?"

"I heard about a stolen bracelet being found in Sophie's bag."

He adopted a bored expression. "And?"

She tilted her head as if about to perform a soliloquy and refused to be rushed. "And I came to report that I saw a suspicious man leaving the women's dressing room right before curtain call, when the entire cast was gathered on stage."

He wagged his pencil at her. "Everyone except you, that is."

She didn't appreciate the implication. "My heel broke. I had to grab another shoe. But it was a good thing I did, or I wouldn't have seen the man. I'm positive he was up to something."

I risked a glance at Sterling only to be surprised he was watching me.

"Describe this fellow, Miss Landis." Sergeant Hamilton leaned back in his chair as if preparing for a drawn-out account from the actress.

"Medium build and height. He wore a black overcoat and dark trousers. His hat was pulled low. I couldn't see his eyes. But there was a mole on the left side of his nose." She rattled off the man's details with an air of boredom like she was reciting a grocery list. "As soon as he came out of the room, he dashed away."

"Anything else?"

"Yes." She stepped beside my chair. "I vouch for Sophie's character. She wouldn't steal a button."

My jaw slacked. I expected such remarks from Fran and possibly Violet, but I didn't know Lina all that well. It was surprising and somehow more meaningful. I smiled my thanks.

After Lina left, the sergeant shifted his attention back to me. "Miss Walters, seeing as anyone had access to your bag, I can't hold you."

I straightened. "Then I may go?"

"For now. You do realize I dispatched men to search your room."

My thoughts hadn't gotten that far. My current goal was to keep from being labeled a mistress of crime. I stood and retrieved my purse. "They won't find anything." At least I hoped they wouldn't. What if something had been planted in my room just as easily as my bag?

Sterling led me out of the cramped room and through the maze of hallways. I couldn't leave this place fast enough, but the closer we came to the exit, the noisier it became.

"Wait here." Sterling strode around the corner, leaving me in the labyrinth of Policeland.

He returned within several seconds, muttering something under his breath.

"What's going on?"

"A crowd's gathered outside on the steps. Journalists, cameramen, nosy civilians." He turned to me. "They're all waiting to glimpse the Mirage."

My heart lifted. "Who's that?" Had they caught the real thief? Their capture couldn't come at a better time.

"You."

⁂

Since the crowd had gathered in the front of the police station, Sterling drove his car to the other side of the building, where I waited for him at a rear exit. I quickly rushed inside the Model-T and ducked.

My skin tingled as if Sergeant Hamilton's accusing stares left an itchy residue. My eardrums rattled by the startling shouts of the horde. And currently, my nose ached from being flattened against my knees as I hid from view. Yet it was the light pressure of Sterling's large hand on my back that finally cracked my defenses.

The courage and grit I possessed in the interrogation room faded with every pinched breath. I knew the reality of the past three hours would sink in, but I wished it wouldn't hit with Sterling right beside me.

"You can sit up now." His voice was achingly gentle. "It's all clear."

But was it? We might have escaped the pressing throng, but what happened next? I straightened, and Sterling's hand returned to the gear shift. The sergeant hadn't seemed convinced of my innocence. Would the man push for my arrest?

The Mirage hadn't left a trace for all those crimes, and the first piece of evidence to turn up turned up in my black clutch. What if I got convicted and sentenced to jail? My lungs squeezed all air from my chest, and I forced my blurry gaze out the window, tears threatening.

Sterling shifted beside me. "You were brave back there." His fingers pressed something into my palm. His handkerchief. "But you don't have to be brave with me."

I dabbed my eyes, but as one tear dried, another took its place. "I didn't steal that bracelet." I twisted on the bench, angling toward him, taking in his familiar profile. "Someone's framing me, Sterling."

"I know."

Those two words impacted me more than a thousand. "Thank you." My voice broke on a sob, and I clutched his arm, burying my face in his sleeve. "I need someone to believe me."

And not just someone. Him. I couldn't bear it if he thought me capable of those thefts.

Realizing I was still accosting his right limb, I straightened. "I'm sorry. I shouldn't—"

"It's okay." He flicked me a concerned glance. "If you need a shoulder, I hope you'll choose mine first."

My tears were on cue. This was the Sterling I'd fallen in love with. Though I was careful not to interpret too much from his kind gesture. Sterling wouldn't want to entangle himself with me again, especially now, but maybe we could be friends. I rested my cheek on his shoulder, something I'd done a hundred times.

He gently shifted gears, trying not to jostle me. "Who would want to see you pinned for these robberies?"

"I don't know." Had I made an enemy I was unaware of?

"What about the man Miss Landis saw? Know anyone of that description?"

"No." I raised my voice over the clunking floorboards as we drove along the cobblestone road. Wait. Cobblestone? This wasn't the way to the boardinghouse. "Where are we going?"

"It's dangerous to take you to your place." He glanced over his shoulder as if checking to see if we were being followed. "We're unsure where and when those jewels were put in your bag. I suspect it happened at the theater, but there's a chance they could've been planted while in your room. Which means someone has access to you there as well."

I almost reached for Sterling again. What else could go wrong?

"And if those journalists were at the station, I guarantee they'll discover where you live. Probably already there."

Was I to be hounded and pestered until they discovered the actual thief? I prayed for strength. "But I have nowhere to go."

"You'll stay at my aunt's."

Willow Courts. "Does she know I'm coming? That is, maybe I shouldn't. After all I did to you—"

"I phoned her at the station, and Aunt Helen's delighted to have you."

A sob caught in my throat. I didn't deserve this kindness. "But I can't afford her rent anymore." Which was why I stayed at Mrs. Fielding's. Her boardinghouse was nice, but Willow Courts stood in one of the best areas in Pittsburgh.

"I doubt she'll make you pay, but if so, I'm covering it."

I sat straight. "No, you can't do that." My voice pitched an octave higher. "You've already done enough."

He parked the car in the lot of the Willow Courts apartments and looked at me. "Soph, I need to know that you're safe." He spoke in a no-nonsense tone, but it might as well have been part of a sonnet the way it made my heart flip.

"There's one more thing."

"Yes?"

"Once you're settled, we need to discuss why Miss Landis lied."

Lina lied?

I didn't have time to further question Sterling, because he was already out of the car and ushering me into the Willow Courts' entrance. The inside of the apartment building looked like it had five years ago, with some fresh updates, but it felt like home and beautiful memories.

"Hello, my dear." With a dish towel draping her shoulder, Helen Parker rushed toward me. "Wonderful to have you back." Her embrace was tight and heavenly.

I almost started crying again. "Thank you, Mrs. Parker. I've missed you."

She kissed her nephew's cheek and said something to which he nodded. She faced me with a gentle smile. "Now, your old room is currently let, but I've a better option for your needs. Sterling will show you, and I'll soon be up with a tray of refreshments."

"Oh, please don't trouble yourself."

She waved me off with a motherly smile. "This is for my own peace of mind. You look too pale for my liking." She squeezed my shoulder and moved toward the back of the complex where the kitchen stood.

"Ready?" Sterling motioned with his head toward the stairs. There were twenty steps in all. I knew that because I'd jokingly made a vow to Sterling while we were together to kiss him on every one of them. And I did.

Our gazes tangled, something dark and heated in his eyes. Was he thinking of the same memories? Probably not. And neither should I. We had other issues to tackle. I followed him up the staircase and down the familiar hall lined with sconces. He led me to the last room on the right.

He withdrew a set of keys and opened the door. He'd always been the unofficial maintenance man here. It seemed that hadn't changed. He stepped inside the room, his gaze scanning the space.

I paused at the threshold. "I don't have any of my things."

He strode through the furnished room to the window and tested the lock. "Who do you trust to pack you a bag?"

I'd normally say Fran, but she was the one who let Joe into my room, risking me getting evicted. There was also Violet, but she wasn't exactly the most reliable. "I'm not sure."

"I can ask Elissa."

"Elissa Tillman?" I'd met her during my stay here. The young woman assisted Mrs. Parker with housekeeping, though her father owned the local newspaper.

"She's Elissa Parker now. The girl married my sorry cousin, Cole. Don't ask me why."

I smiled. Sterling would always tease, but he loved his younger cousin like a brother. It did my heart good to see a bit of the old Sterling surfacing. "I'm glad for them."

He sank onto the sofa and loosened his tie knot. "You'll see them soon."

I wanted to inquire what he meant but realized I had another pressing question. "You said Lina lied."

"She did."

I sat beside him. "How do you know?"

"Because she wasn't wearing her glasses."

Huh? "Lina doesn't wear glasses."

"She should," he said matter-of-factly. "She ran into me the other day and dropped her lipstick. It took her longer than it should have to find it."

I was reminded of when I delivered her bouquet in the rehearsal room. How she hadn't seen the card which was in plain sight. "Wow. I never realized." Questions piled upon questions, but one flew to the top of the stack. "Do you think she saw anyone?"

"She might have." He took off his hat and ran a hand through his hair. "But I doubt she saw the mole on the side of that man's face. Her dressing room door's at least thirty feet from the women's room. Even if she was able to see, if the man darted out of the room as she said, I doubt she'd have time to catch a detail like that."

"Why would she lie? And why go out of her way to report to the sergeant?"

Sterling capped his hat on the sofa's armrest and kicked out his legs. "It'd be easier if her ears turned red like yours. We'd know the truth in no time."

Such an annoying trait. "I should've never told you about that."

He stretched his arm along the back of the sofa behind me, his fingers feathering my shoulder. "I would have figured it out. It was my favorite place to kiss."

A shocked gasp burst through my lips. But before I could say anything, Cole Parker strolled through the door, carrying a toddler.

"Is this the recon room?" Sterling's younger cousin cast us an amused look. "Because it looks a little crowded already."

"Only because your ego sucks up all the oxygen." Sterling reached his arms out, and Cole deposited his daughter—I assumed she was Cole's child—onto Sterling's lap. "Cousin, you remember Sophie Walters."

Cole tipped his hat. "Pleasure to see you again, Sophie."

"How do you do?" I tried not to squirm. All of Sterling's relatives were present when I left him at the altar. It was more than just the elephant in the room. It was an entire herd. But my forced smile turned genuine when big blue eyes peered at me from Sterling's lap. "Hello, little one."

"This is Adaline." Sterling's massive arms cradled a sweet girl that I guessed to be around a year old. Adaline braced her chubby hands on the sides of his face, babbling and laughing.

Sterling grinned at her, and my heart swelled with warm affection.

"She's beautiful." I almost sighed at the giant man being totally smitten by such a tiny person.

"Is Ling Ling spoiling you again?" A decidedly feminine voice, one I immediately recognized, joined the conversation.

Elissa Parker had entered while I was fixated on Sterling's precious interaction with the baby. I corrected my rude manners and stood, crossing the room to greet the petite woman. "Elissa, it's good to see you."

"I couldn't believe it when Sterling told me. I'm happy you're back." She embraced me as Helen had. My heart couldn't take all this kindness. She released me and studied my face, her previous delight sobering into concern. "Cole filled me in on the way here. Are you okay?"

My heart sank. I'd been so wrapped up in the past few moments, I'd forgotten the reason I was here. "What have you heard?"

Cole ambled toward us and wrapped his arm around Elissa's waist. "Oh, nothing much. Just that we're currently in the presence of the infamous Mirage."

"Cole." Elissa gave him a warning look before turning to me. "Unfortunately, your name's been leaked in connection with the thefts. It's all over the radio. A few newspapers printed extras."

The backs of my knees quivered, and I reclaimed my seat beside Sterling. All of Pittsburgh now thought of me as the Mirage. I pressed shaky fingers to my queasy stomach. "But who. . .who told the press?" Sterling shifted Adaline to his right knee and placed a comforting hand on mine.

"Hard to say." Cole gave a sympathetic smile. "Could've been someone from the theater. Or a determined scout reporter. They've been known to weasel their way into police headquarters and badger officers for a scoop. The public eats up any headlines about the Mirage, so it's bound to get shouted everywhere."

Sterling's eyes narrowed. "But not from your newspaper, right?"

"You can relax that stern brow of yours." Cole waved him off. "The *Review* only prints the facts. Not sensation pieces." He winked at his wife as if there was a private joke between them. "But kindly advise us, Cousin, how you'd like us to proceed. Since I suspect that's why you arranged this little meeting."

At that moment, Helen Parker walked into the room, her arms loaded with a tea tray. Cole quickly relieved the burden from his mother, setting it down on the small table.

Helen tucked a grayed lock of hair behind her ear. "I'm bending the rules with allowing this to go on." She motioned among us, then dusted her hands on her apron. Under Willow Courts rules, men weren't allowed in women's rooms. "But I'll allow this exception if it means keeping our Sophie safe."

Our Sophie.

My eyes stung. I'd relayed to Sterling why I left that day, but his family was still in the dark. How could they accept me? Defend me?

After giving me another hug, Helen swept her granddaughter from Sterling's lap and left the room.

"What am I going to do?" Having my name headlined as a suspected thief? I'd always dreamed of the spotlight, but not like this.

"Tell us your side, Sophie." Elissa withdrew a notepad from her coat pocket. "Let's print the truth and see if we can hush the lies."

CHAPTER SEVENTEEN

ELISE

*T*en years ago, on this day, Elise's life changed forever.

She now stood before her mother's granite headstone, the biting wind pressing into her, her fingers clutching her violin case. With her free hand, she set the white roses on the grave and swiped the dust from the cold slab.

DEBORAH L. MALVERN
BELOVED MOTHER & DAUGHTER
Oh, Mom.

Digging into her mother's past made Elise feel more like a stranger. It gutted her. So instead of dwelling on secrets, she determined to remember the woman who'd kissed scraped elbows, overcooked mac and cheese, and sang off-key despite being the most musically impassioned person in Elise's life.

"I have an audition, Mom." She gripped her violin case. "What if I don't make it?" In many ways, her mom had been better than Elise. When her mother was her age, she was balancing raising a daughter while pursuing a career as a violinist. Meanwhile, Elise couldn't keep her aloe vera plant alive, and the thought of performing in front of a panel of judges made her reach for the antacids.

Every spare moment, Elise spent rehearsing. But it didn't seem enough. *She* didn't seem enough. *What am I doing wrong, God?*

But she didn't come to her mother's grave to focus on herself. She came to honor the life of a woman who'd loved Elise with every fiber of her beautiful soul. "Just like always, I'll play." She tugged the gloves from her hands and stuffed them in her pocket. She crouched, setting the case on the ground, and withdrew her violin.

With no one being about this early in the morning, she tucked her chin on the instrument and played. Her mother's favorite sonata poured as much from Elise's heart as from her instrument.

Her eyes slid shut, and she imagined her mom sitting perfectly poised on a stool in Elise's bedroom, listening intently as if Elise were some aficionado. If Elise squeaked out a pathetic rendition of "Mary Had a Little Lamb," Mom praised her as if she'd performed Strauss. Her mother always had a way of making Elise feel more than she really was.

The music moved at the same tempo as her thoughts, the dynamics changing with each memory flashing through her mind.

Tears streamed like drips of fire against her chilled skin. But it didn't stop her from playing. They only increased her drive to finish. She reached the sonata's end and realized she hadn't missed any fingerings. For the first time at her mother's grave, Elise performed the intricate piece flawlessly. "That was for you, Mom."

The crunch of frozen grass made her jolt. She turned, expecting to find Grancy or Pap, but instead it was Pierson.

His steps were slow and deliberate until he reached her side. He gave her a solemn nod, then lowered to place…white roses?…on her mother's grave beside the ones Elise had brought.

Each year there would already be a bouquet on Mom's grave when Elise arrived. This time, there wasn't. Elise thought the roses were from one of her relatives, but now she suspected they'd been from Pierson all along. Could tears freeze on one's eyeballs? Because the moisture wouldn't stop.

After a moment of respectful silence, Pierson spoke. "I didn't mean to intrude on your time." He cleared his throat. "I didn't think anyone would be here yet."

Four days ago, after the whole leaked photo ordeal—Malverngate—as Elise had dubbed it, she'd believed it best to stay away from Pierson. She clung to the excuse of needing to rehearse, but really he'd upended her world with that casual remark about dating. The look in his eyes had been …something. And that *something* was what she hadn't dared examine.

"Your mom bought me my first guitar." Pierson's voice was quiet. "She paid for my sessions with Meredith."

"What?" Her voice barely registered above her pounding heart. "I—I had no idea." Meredith's tutelage hadn't been cheap, yet Mom had scraped for lessons for both her *and* Pierson? Plus, she gifted him a guitar?

The imposing clouds didn't give the sun a chance this morning, but the gray surroundings only made Pierson's eyes more vivid. "I thought you knew."

She shook her head. "Mom never said a word." Elise knew her mother had met Dorothea at a supermarket and discovered Dorothea had recently lost her husband. Mom organized a meal train through the church, stocking Dorothea's freezer with plenty of food. That was also how her mom had met Pierson, who'd just arrived to stay with his grandmother. Dorothea was so moved, she started attending their church, where she and Grancy became friends.

Pierson took a step forward, shielding Elise from a gust of wind. "Your mom told me not to allow the bad songs of my past to get stuck in my head. She said I needed to trust God to give me new melodies to replace the old." He shrugged. "Looking back, I realize she wasn't talking about music. She was pointing out the only source that heals life's pain. Something I didn't figure out until lately."

Millions would trade places with Pierson in a finger's snap, but they didn't know what Elise knew. Yes, the man had all that life could give. But first he'd endured all that life could take away. While her mother had left the earth, Pierson's mom had just. . .left. No one else was there when Elise and Pierson cried together that first Mother's Day without their moms. It was one of their first deep bonding moments together. And she couldn't help but feel this was another. Her watery gaze fell to the roses. "She'd be proud of you."

He swallowed. "I hope so."

Hope. For years that word had seemed like a watered-down imitation of a wish. But what if it was more than that?

"Were you playing?" Pierson eyed her violin with a tender smile.

She nodded. "I play her favorite sonata every year. When she passed, I needed a way to feel close to her." She gave a fragile smile. "And now. . .I don't know. . .I just keep playing. Like a tribute of sorts."

"It's a beautiful way to honor her memory. With music. With what she loved."

His words curled around her heart with delicate warmth. He didn't make her feel foolish but understood. Elise returned her violin to its case and stood. "Thank you."

His head tilted. "For what?"

"For showing up. For remembering her with me."

He reached for her hand, and she placed her fingers in his. They walked in comfortable silence out the cemetery gate leading to the lot.

He shoved his hands into the pockets of his brown leather coat. "I did some digging, looking for anyone named Cade in the music world."

She stopped short. "Did you find anything?"

"Not about Cade." He exhaled a slow breath. "But one of the searches landed on a site about some random vaudeville play called the *Debutante's Cadence*."

Which would make sense considering the keywords—deb and cade. "And?" I smiled. "Did it inspire you to try your hand at Broadway?"

His lips twitched. "No." He tugged a paper from his pocket. "I found this." He unfolded what looked like a newspaper article printed off the internet. "The play starred an actress named Greer Donnelly. Take a look at her picture."

He handed her the page, and her eyes zeroed in on a beautiful woman with bobbed, sleek hair, lots of dramatic makeup, and draped in a flowing evening gown. But Elise noticed something far more significant. Her gaze snapped to Pierson, who intently watched her. "That woman's wearing the emerald necklace."

CHAPTER EIGHTEEN

SOPHIE

*I*t's sold out!" Lloyd's hair glistened with too much pomade, but it couldn't shine any brighter than his smile. The man hadn't stopped grinning since he bounded into the main-level rehearsal room for our meeting before opening curtain. "The standing areas are shoulder to shoulder."

"We all know why. Sophie became a star overnight." Joe winked at me, and several cast members nodded, voicing their agreement.

I pressed my spine against the wall beside the exit, my heart pumping so fast I feared it would burst through my chest. Today had been awful. The papers somehow got ahold of the headshot photo I'd enclosed with my information form when I auditioned for the Loew's Penn. Who would've submitted it to the press? I hated to believe Lloyd would pull such a stunt to increase ticket sales, but I couldn't shake the thought. Or maybe someone who was in my boardinghouse room took one of my extra copies. Elissa Parker brought me a bag of my things late last night. And now that I lodged in Willow Courts, I had no control over who went into my old room or through the rest of my belongings. It was troubling to ponder.

The article the Parkers published in their paper was a noble effort, but it was only a drop of truth against the flooding lies printed in other publications. All of Pittsburgh believed me a thief.

My stomach spasmed. What if the real robber framed me again? Sergeant Hamilton wouldn't be as forgiving next time around. Speaking of the odious man, Joe had said the officer was in tonight's audience.

I couldn't go on stage. Heart pounding against my ribs, I stepped forward on shaky legs. "Someone else should take my place tonight." It was such a weak protest compared to the enthusiastic mood of everyone in the room. But did they forget what part I played? I was the jewel thief!

Violet and Fran moved to flank me, offering support.

"No. Nothing changes with this performance," Lloyd continued, grinning. "This is the best publicity we've had since opening month. Stanley Theater is hosting Joan Crawford tonight. But Sophie showed them where the real entertainment is."

For years I'd craved the spotlight. Now I had it, and it was all one big mistake. "Lloyd, I really feel—"

"I'm expecting the house to be full all week." Lloyd rubbed his hands together as if he'd been informed President Calvin Coolidge was attending tonight. "Maybe next week too."

"Excuse me, please." Slapping a hand over my mouth, I dashed out the door and barely made it inside the dressing room before leaning over the waste bin. My stomach emptied its contents.

The door burst open, and Violet and Fran rushed inside.

"Oh, poor dear."

"The show starts in ten minutes."

The two women spoke simultaneously.

My hand trembled as I reached into my bag and grabbed Sterling's handkerchief from last evening. I wiped my mouth and nose, then tossed the soiled cloth into the bin, silently promising to compensate Sterling for the loss.

"It's not that bad." Violet wasn't one for reassuring sentiments. "Think of it this way. Your picture is everywhere. Your name's broadcast all over the radio. You're famous!"

"That's not the kind of fame I want." Ankles still wobbly, I gingerly stepped to the vanity to freshen up. But what was the use? How could I walk across the stage in mere minutes? I could barely move about the dressing room without stumbling.

Violet sighed. "You embody mystery and intrigue. All the men here tonight will end up fawning over you. You'll be the envy of every woman." She fluffed the ends of her bobbed hair.

Fran spritzed fragrance on me. "Soon the police will catch the real Mirage, and all this will be over."

"See?" Violet picked at her moon manicure. "Might as well live it up while all the attention is on you now. I know I would."

Violet couldn't grasp the scope of the situation. How this accusation negatively affected my life, my career, my relationships. But I couldn't focus on what tomorrow would bring. I had to get through tonight's show.

I stepped out of the shadows and into the blinding stage lights.

Over twenty-five hundred pairs of eyes locked on me. Hollers, whistles, and chants overpowered the orchestra. Some good humored. Some crude. All of it deafening. At least I wasn't booed. The orchestra played extra bars until the place quieted enough for me to walk toward Gerald and Lina.

My pulse pounded with each stride toward center stage. This was ridiculous. I'd done nothing wrong. Indignation burned until heat flushed to my pinched toes. I channeled my frustration into my lines. "You'll be sorry." I pointed an accusing finger at the couple. "I won't stand for being humiliated."

This stirred unsavory comments from some men in the crowd about the legs on which I stood. But as a true performer, I ignored the distractions and remained in character. That was, until I saw Greer in the front row.

My chest tightened. I thought she'd returned to New York. Maybe her apology hadn't been as sincere as I thought, and she stayed to gloat over my misfortune. Her fingers went ever so slightly to her decorated collarbone.

I almost gasped.

She was wearing emeralds. With all the jewelry theft happening here, why would she do such a thing? Was she hoping to be robbed for the attention? I wouldn't put it past her.

Lina repeated her line, and I realized I'd missed my cue to leave. She threw her arms around Gerald, and I stormed off the stage in a flurry of anger and jilted hurt.

The rest of the show progressed smoothly. My last scene unfolded how I expected—the crowd erupting when I was revealed as the jewel thief. The obnoxious laughter and slurs would forever pummel my brain. At curtain call, the cast stepped forward and the chanting revived.

"Encore for the Mirage!" Again and again.

Refusing to look at Greer, I swung my gaze to Sergeant Hamilton standing in the balcony, a scowl marring his face. Lloyd was right. This swell of attention wouldn't deflate any time soon. Our director had hoped for sold-out shows, but my strength could only take so much. The only way to defeat this was to find the actual thief.

And I knew where to start.

I slipped out of my temporary room and into the hall. Dressed in a black, loose-fitting frock and soft-soled shoes, I blended into the dark surroundings. I had a plan in place. One that involved an unlikely conspirator. I was to meet Greer within the hour, but first, I needed to exit Willow Courts undetected.

With quiet steps, I eased past Sterling's door. Hopefully, he was already asleep, seeing as it was half-past midnight. The staircase could prove challenging. Every other step croaked like a frog at death's door with any amount of weight upon them.

But maybe. . .

A quick wiggle made sure my bag was secure on my shoulder. I swung my right leg over the banister and centered my frame on the railing. Helen Parker was not only a gracious landlord but an efficient housekeeper, because the wood was layered with polish. I scrambled to abandon my foolish plan, but the soft fabric of my dress was no match for the slick wax.

I whooshed halfway down the banister in a teetering way that made me question all my abilities. I finally grasped control about five feet from the landing. My knuckles ached and my arms burned from clinging like a kitten to a tree limb. If I could just manage—

"What are you doing?"

Sterling! In a move to preserve modesty, I reached to clamp down my skirt only to lose balance on the railing. I grappled for the spindles in vain. My weight went sideways, and limbs went flailing.

Strong arms wrapped around me, and I found myself curled against Sterling's chest. I craned my neck, peering into his face. "Good evening."

"Evening, Sophie." His chest rumbled. Was that a laugh? "Something wrong with the stairs?"

"No, they're serviceable enough."

He gently set me on my feet. His gaze swept my frame. "Going somewhere?"

"Perhaps." I adjusted my neckline, which had shifted during my banister escapade. Thankfully, Sterling was a gentleman and flicked his attention somewhere on the sconces behind me. The man was still in his dark suit. Why hadn't he turned in yet?

He kept his tone low. "Mind telling me where you're headed?"

"Yes."

That brought his eyes back to mine. "Yes?"

I sighed and repositioned my bag to my left shoulder. "You'll disapprove. Not that I need your approval." Or his assistance. I'd already told him several of my secrets, all of which he'd sloughed off. I was glad he trusted I wasn't a thief, but he still refused to believe the truth about his partner's wrongdoings.

His brow darkened. "Ah, a rendezvous."

I stormed past him. "Why do you always suspect that?" That was the exact rubbish he'd tossed at me the night we first met again at the Loew's Penn, the evening I talked with Prudence. Sterling imagined the worst of me, just like the rest of Pittsburgh. I swirled back around, my temper rising. "It's insulting that you believe me careless with my affections. That I'd be loose with my morals, my body."

His mouth tightened.

"I thought you knew me better than that."

He took a commanding step toward me, now having to glare down since he was that much taller. "I thought so too. But I also thought you'd never leave me at the altar."

Oh, he was going to throw that back into my face? "I told you I did what I did to protect you."

He glanced at my earlobe, and that feeble restraint on my fury snapped.

"I don't have time for this." I stalked toward the front door. I'd intended to use the kitchen exit, but there was no longer a need to be discreet. I rushed down the porch steps, the cold air contrasting the kindling fire within me.

"Sophie! Wait!" Sterling called, but I only increased my pace.

I hustled down the sidewalk as footsteps sounded behind me. Sterling gained ground, but before he could reach me, I turned and stepped in front of him.

"No." My breath came out in angry vapors. "You're not coming with me. And don't even think about following me. I'm in a mood, Sterling."

"I see that."

"The past twenty-four hours have consisted of people believing terrible things about me. I've been accused of being a criminal. My name smeared. My picture plastered in papers. Tonight I was whistled and jeered at on stage as if I were a burlesque dancer."

He stiffened. "I'm—"

"Now you're acting just like them. Insinuating things I'm not. I've had enough of it."

"I'm sorry."

Some of my bluster withered. "For what? Treating me poorly, riling my temper, checking my ears for lies?"

His strong hands bracketed my shoulders, and he leaned in. "All of the above."

"And the rendezvous remark?"

He nodded. "That too." He pressed his lips together as if forcefully trapping his words, but then expelled a frustrated sigh. "It was callous of me. But I see how men look at you. This Mirage confusion only increases your appeal. You don't want to know what the officers were saying about you at the station last night. I could've throttled them all."

One breath. Two. "You speak as though you care."

The moonlight paired well with his dark eyes. "I've never stopped caring."

"You haven't?"

"It's impossible," he murmured.

I clutched his lapels and pressed my cheek against his chest. His arms came around me, and I all but melted into him. I needed to leave if my plan was to work. But I'd never been good at peeling myself from Sterling's embrace. "I've prayed for this. That we could be friends again."

He tensed. "Friends?"

I tipped my head back to look at him. "You just said you cared for me. Did I misread you?"

His hooded gaze intensified with. . .longing? "Very much."

"Sophie!"

Sterling and I jolted apart at the feminine voice. Our heads turned toward the noise of clopping heels and swishing of fabric.

"Greer." My thoughts slowly returned to the moment. I was supposed to meet her. "What are you doing here?"

Shadows twisted across her delicate features, her breath sharp gasps. "The Mirage is in my suite."

CHAPTER NINETEEN

Elise

*E*lise jumped into the passenger side of Pierson's truck and shut the door. She turned to say hey to him, but the single word died on her lips. Sunlight streamed through the windshield, cutting across the hard angles of his face, highlighting several shades of blue in his eyes, bringing out copper tones in his stubble. She'd heard a lot of songs about moonlight and starry skies, but there needed to be more about the swoony effects of daylight. "I—I don't think anyone saw me."

"Why are you whispering?"

"I don't know." She propped her violin case between her leg and the door. "Whispering feels appropriate."

With an amused smile, he shifted the truck into drive, flicked on the turn signal, and waited to enter the crazy Pittsburgh traffic. "I don't care if anyone sees us."

Thankfully, the leaked photo fiasco had quieted, but Elise wasn't eager to become a paparazzi punching bag. "You say that now, my friend."

"I'll keep on saying it. By the way, it didn't go unnoticed that you just casually friend-zoned me."

She should be annoyed with his blasé attitude about a relationship between them. Since his initial wanting-to-date-her revelation, he'd been flirty, not serious. But even if he was legit, she didn't date famous people. Famous people dated other famous people. Then they married, divorced, and restarted the process with another famous person. Keyword: famous.

Something she was not.

Sure, she and Pierson had chemistry. But that was a beast of a subject, one she'd struggled with in school. Why? Because she had no grasp of how certain properties blended with others. With her and Pierson, there was a 100 percent chance of an explosion of some kind. Most likely, it would be her heart.

Pierson pulled into the exit lane toward Legacy Towers. He'd called this morning inviting her to join him, which worked out because Elise had promised Meredith she'd swing by. Usually, she wouldn't wait this long between visits, but her life was filled with preparing for a life-changing audition, cataloging new inventory at the auction house, searching for her birth father, and digging up scandalous information about a vaudeville actress.

But instead of complaining about the lack of hours in a day or further discussing her unwillingness to date a country star, she opted for a safer topic. "I found out more about Greer Donnelly."

Pierson proved surprisingly considerate in deferring to Elise's time-frame to research the actress. Last evening, in her comfy pajamas and armed with tropical Skittles, she ran a Google search. And hit the internet jackpot. "In your world, she's the Carrie Underwood of vaudeville. Greer was the most sought-after entertainer from about nineteen fifteen to the late twenties. Then her career died down in the thirties."

He nodded. "Any connection to the necklace?"

"No." She tugged a loose thread off her sweater. "I found a lot of pictures and reviews of her roles. The woman had many affairs, but she never married. Never had children. Basically, there's nobody I can contact about the necklace."

"Bummer."

Greer Donnelly had been a stunning woman, but Elise detected something haunting in her eyes. Or maybe the secrets surrounding Elise's own life caused her to glimpse the photos through a slanted filter. "How sad to have it all and no one to share it with."

Pierson held a steady gaze on the road. "When you have fame, it's tough to find someone who gets you."

Of course he'd relate. "I see how it can be hard to trust. Like, is the person after your money? A few seconds in the spotlight? But on the flip side, coming from the typical, everyday woman, it would be tough to enter that sort of relationship. How can you even compete with an entire universe of fame?"

"You got it wrong, Malvern. You're not the definition of typical."

"Says the guy who agreed I'm the girl-next-door type." She threw back the words he'd tossed her that day in the courtyard. "Very typical. Mediocre. Average."

"Wrong again." Pierson's eyes briefly met hers before returning to the road. "Only that you have that natural look. You're pretty without the help of an airbrush or makeup artist. But you're far from mediocre." He pulled into the large lot of the senior center and faced her. "Tell me, how would *you* describe yourself?"

"How? With words." Her lips bent into a sassy smile. "I would describe myself with words. I've never been good at interpretive dance."

He chuckled. "There's that literal side I love." He tugged the keys from the ignition. "Though it's a major deflective move."

"It absolutely is." She beamed at him. "Talking about myself gives me hives. Being invisible is easier." Even if she secured a seat in a symphony, she'd be performing with a large group. Blending in was what she did best. Pierson would judge that a weakness. Another aspect in which they were incompatible.

"You want to be invisible?" He leaned, hovering over the console, his eyes piercing. "Then you're doing the world an injustice." He reached behind and grabbed his Stetson from the backseat.

She mulled over his words seconds after he exited the truck, almost missing the movement behind her. Pierson retrieved his guitar from the truck's cab, and Elise's jaw slacked. Did he plan on playing for Meredith too? She hopped out the passenger side, about to bombard him with questions, but a smartly dressed woman hustled toward them.

"Pierson Brooks? I'm Helena Kendall, head manager of Legacy Towers." Her voice held traces of awe as if she was greeting...well, a celebrity. "Thank you for stopping by. The residents are excited."

Elise's brows spiked. She and Pierson were supposed to meet with Meredith. One resident. Singular, not plural.

He nodded as he shook her hand. "I'm glad to do it. Thank you for the invitation."

Ms. Kendall was at least twenty years older than Pierson, but she was positively giddy. "I should be thanking *you*. Your generous contribution made all the updates possible. The west wing is dedicated to you, you know."

Pierson shot a glance at me before stepping closer to the woman. "I appreciate the gesture, but I asked for everything to remain anonymous." There was mild rebuke in his voice.

"Oh." Her shoulders lowered, and a faint blush spread across her cheeks. "I didn't know. There must have been a miscommunication somewhere."

Pierson sighed. "Probably on my end. I apologize. The dedication's kind. Thank you." He'd said all the right words, but his tone was suspiciously flat. His free hand settled on Elise's lower back. "This is Elise Malvern. She's a violinist."

Ms. Kendall faced her with a surprised expression as if noticing her for the first time. "Nice to meet you, Ms. Malvern." The older woman adopted a warm smile. "Are you accompanying Pierson for his concert?"

Um, what? "I don't—"

"Elise isn't my backup." Pierson's touch turned protective, sliding to her waist and slightly nudging her closer to him. "But she's welcome to take the stage and perform."

Her fingers tightened on the violin case. Why hadn't he mentioned this on the drive over?

Ms. Kendall clapped her hands in excited approval. "We have several musical enthusiasts." Her gaze bounced between Elise and Pierson, until settling on the country singer. "Like your friend, Meredith Wittenhouser. She's been a wonderful addition to the Legacy family. I'm sure she's grateful for your patronage."

Pierson's eyes darkened, and Elise suspected that was another detail that was supposed to be anonymous. Yet it all made sense now. Pierson was Meredith's benefactor. He'd supplied the cash needed to transform Legacy into the Ritz Carlton of senior centers. Without any strings attached, he cared for his aged mentor, and Elise softened a little.

They reached the entrance, and the woman smiled for the hundredth time. "I have some work to see to, but Betty at the front desk will show you where to go. I'm looking forward to the performance!"

Pierson nodded but stayed glued to his spot. "Hold on, Elise. I gotta make a call." He withdrew his cell and bounded back outside. She almost felt pity for whoever was on the line because Pierson's fierce expression looked lethal. It was also intriguing. The easygoing star was furious.

Moments later, Pierson rejoined her at the entrance. Her fingers tingled, wanting to rub away the deep lines between his lowered brows.

"Sorry." He pocketed his phone. "I had an unplanned business call."

"Everything okay?"

"Better. I fired my publicist."

She blinked. "That seems spontaneous."

"He's been going against my wishes for the past two years. I've been letting things slide. Gave a few warnings, but he continued leaking things to the press, wanting to shape my public image. Some good. But a lot bad."

"Was any of it true?"

His scowl deepened. "A little but not all." The humbleness in his eyes matched the regret in his tone. "I'm trying to be a better person. Not for publicity. But to prove to God I'm capable of being the man He created me to be."

This wasn't fair. When the right person came along, she planned on relinquishing her heart piece by piece stamped SOME ASSEMBLY REQUIRED. But the more she was around Pierson, the harder it was to hang on to all the fragments. No one warned her she'd have to superglue her heart on this trip to hold it together. "I see."

He continued as if he wasn't winning her over by the millisecond. "I told him I wanted all transactions with Legacy to be anonymous. Now I'm guessing I have a plaque somewhere in the west wing touting my good deeds."

She cocked her head to the side. "Let's go scratch out Pierson and write Garth. I'm pretty sure I have a Sharpie in my purse."

He chuckled low. "Taking on a life of vandalism?"

"Not really." She returned his smile. "I'm using your old tricks and saying outlandish things to make you feel better."

He didn't give in to lightening the moment. Instead, he stepped close. Too close. "You know what would make me feel better?"

It wasn't in her heart's best interest to ask.

"You can invite me to inspect dark closets with you."

That smolder in his eyes said he wasn't referring to cracks in the walls. And her nervous chuckle only intensified his advance. It revealed she wasn't immune to him. Or his touch. "Are you interested in structural integrity too?"

"Very interested."

"Pierson, I. . ." *Can't do this.* She couldn't get caught up in the moment. Because what would happen in a few weeks when he left? It wasn't wise to explore anything beyond friendship. "I really should thrash you for suggesting I play." It was a cop-out, and they both knew it.

Yet he took her not-so-subtle redirection with an understanding smile. "You can thrash me anytime you want. I thought this might be a convenient opportunity for you to perform in front of a less-threatening crowd. But I'd never pressure you." He released her and lifted his guitar.

"That wasn't my intention when I agreed to perform."

"Why did you?" Why offer a free concert when people would pay through the nose to attend?

"Because most here are like Meredith. They can't get out. So I'm bringing them the music." His eyes filled with purpose. "This afternoon is my gift to them."

CHAPTER TWENTY

Sophie

*G*reer's hotel was closer to Willow Courts than the boardinghouse. Which was why I hoped my plan would work.

"Come on." I motioned to Sterling. "There still might be time."

Large hands clamped my waist. "Not a chance. You're staying here."

"No."

"Yes."

I huffed and batted his fingers away. "The longer we stay here and argue, the greater the chance of him getting away."

Sterling shook his head and released me. "He's long gone by now."

"If he's gone, you shouldn't object to me coming along." I crossed my arms with a jaunty tilt of my head. "Besides, I was headed to Greer's before you were."

Greer tugged at her glove and sniffed. "Sophie was certain the robber would strike tonight." She gave me an approving nod. "She was right."

Greer was different since her apology. I hoped rather than believed this was a step in the right direction for her, but I couldn't explore that topic at present. For now, I had to convince a stubborn private detective to agree to my plan.

"Sophie." Sterling slid his eyes shut for a few heartbeats. "Don't tell me you intended to catch the Mirage."

I adjusted the bag, which had grown heavy like a sandbag. "Don't be ridiculous. I wasn't going to catch him."

"Good."

"I was going to follow him."

"Not good." His glower was impressive in the darkness.

"What? It's a sound plan." One that would be foolproof, except I hadn't counted on the thief arriving early. "I was to hide in Greer's suite. Wait for the Mirage to arrive, then discreetly trail him."

"I've seen your version of discreet," Sterling muttered, no doubt referencing the banister incident.

"Then once I knew his location," I continued as if Sterling hadn't rudely interrupted, "I was going to fetch the police so they could arrest him."

"You could've told me this." Sterling made no effort to disguise his annoyance.

Neither did I. "And you would have believed me? You haven't been putting much trust in what I say lately."

He softened at this but quickly returned to the matter at hand. "Miss Donnelly, we need to return to your apartment and see what's been stolen so we can report it to the authorities. I'll give a thorough inspection. Hopefully, he left a clue. Though I doubt it."

I looked to Greer for silent permission to confess to Sterling the entirety of our plan, but she gave a subtle shake of the head, an exchange that Sterling probably caught. He missed nothing.

"It appears you know my name, but I've yet the privilege." Greer sidled up to him, her chin lowering as she gazed up at him beneath long lashes.

"Detective Sterling Monroe, ma'am."

Greer's eyes slightly widened, and she flicked a knowing glance at me. "Glad to finally meet you. I've heard a fair deal about you." She stretched out her gloved hand as if they were greeting each other in a fancy parlor rather than on the dark streets.

"Interesting." Sterling shook her hand gently but kept his eyes on me. "Sophie hasn't mentioned you until recently."

Greer shrugged. "She can be forgetful. I've heard she forgot to attend her own wedding."

Sterling's face was void of expression. If Greer was trying to get a response from him, she was in for a challenge. But I knew what she was about. That snarky remark was cleverly intended to remove any questions about her and redirect the attention on me and my faults.

It didn't work. Sterling peppered Greer with questions as we walked toward her hotel, which was only three blocks away. "Tell me what happened and start from the beginning."

She lifted the hem of her expensive evening gown as she moved. "Sophie approached me after the show and warned me about a possible break-in."

I could feel rather than see his gaze on me. "How did you know this, Sophie?"

"It wasn't difficult. Greer was flaunting an emerald necklace. One look, and you know it's worth a lot of money." I kept up with Sterling's fast pace. "I wasn't certain the Mirage would come, but I wanted to be prepared."

He grunted. "Go on, Miss Donnelly."

"Oh, is it my turn again?" She pressed a hand to her chest with mock innocence. The prima donna was like a swan, appearing graceful and delicate but downright vicious when annoyed. "The plan was for me to leave the suite for a few hours, but before I could, I heard a sound coming from the back bedroom, like the creak of a windowsill. Then a shuffling noise." She slowed her steps. "There's a window at the end of the hall right outside my suite's door." She paused as if collecting her thoughts. "I think he climbed out that window and used the ledge to reach my back bedroom one."

Earlier when discussing our plan, Greer had detailed the layout of her suite. The door opened to a spacious parlor followed by two bedrooms—the master and a spare. Since the lone window was located in the spare, we'd guessed the Mirage would try to access her suite through there, especially considering the ledge that ran beneath it.

Sterling nodded his agreement. "Most likely. Did he see you?"

"No. I slipped out the door and rushed to get Sophie."

We reached her hotel and entered the lobby. Glittering chandeliers hung over marble flooring. The attendant had fallen asleep in a chair behind the front desk. Sterling muttered something about shabby security.

Greer swiped a complimentary matchbook from a crystal bowl on the counter. She opened her purse and retrieved a cigarette, struck a match, and lit her addiction as though she had all the time in the world. Sterling grunted his annoyance at the delay.

We climbed the stairs leading to the third floor. Sterling pressed ahead of Greer and me, his body tense, his hand on his gun holster. He'd always carried a revolver when on the police force, and I suspected the life of a private investigator proved just as dangerous. A thought that supplied little comfort.

Greer's room stood at the end of the row, and we approached with quiet steps. Electric lamps lined the papered walls, but only every other one was lit. There was an eerie hush, making me aware of my breathing, my heartbeat.

"I'll check the rooms." Sterling withdrew his pistol. "You two stay here." He inserted Greer's key and, with a soft click, unlocked the door and slipped inside.

I prayed for his safety. He was confident the Mirage had left, but what if the robber was still inside?

After several long seconds, the door swung open, and I lurched back. Greer blew out a long stream of smoke, unfazed. Sterling reappeared, and I could have launched myself into his arms with relief.

He nodded. "All clear."

"Well, that's good." Greer flicked her cigarette ashes onto the rug. "My shoes are killing me." She sashayed past Sterling, her hips swaying, but he paid her no interest.

"Find anything?" I asked.

"Not yet." His fingers wrapped mine, tugging me inside the room. "But all I did was ensure he was gone."

Sterling closed and locked the door as I took in the lush furnishings. This place was just as grand as the William Penn Hotel but a quarter its size. Richly papered walls were topped with decorative crown molding. There was a tufted settee on the far right and wingback chairs positioned in front of a cozy fireplace.

Sterling strode to the spare room where Greer had said she'd heard the noise, and Greer wasted no time stretching out on the sofa.

I joined Sterling but remained quiet, content to watch him investigate. He took his time, methodically working one side of the space to the other, pausing the longest at the window. I could see from where I sat that it was unlocked. The robber had an easy entry. During the long inspection, Greer fell asleep, her soft snores drifting from the other room.

Finally, Sterling faced me with a shake of his head.

"No trace?"

"Not that I found." The taut skin pinching the corners of his eyes matched the firm press of his mouth. Sterling wasn't a man who accepted defeat with grace. "I've a feeling Miss Donnelly's jewelry box will be empty. Did she say where she kept it?"

"Probably in the master bedroom."

Sterling palmed the back of his neck. "Let's go check, then we'll call the authorities. At least you have an alibi tonight. The police can't pin this on you. We should probably wake Miss Donnelly as well." He moved toward the door, but I caught him by the sleeve.

"There's something else I need to tell you. Something that was part of my plan too."

His forehead rippled with confusion. "What was?"

"The Mirage was on the hunt for the emerald necklace Greer was wearing." I slid my bag from my shoulder, opened it, and withdrew what would hopefully clarify everything. "But I've had it all this time." I raised it for Sterling to see.

He gave a surprised smile and then gently squeezed my fingers. "I'm sure Miss Donnelly appreciates your cleverness in keeping her necklace safe."

I darted a glance to the other room, where Greer was passed out on the sofa. Earlier, she'd shaken her head when I'd almost revealed a secret within our plan, but she couldn't stop me now. "This isn't Greer's necklace."

"Whose is it?"

"Mine."

⁓✤⁓

"What do you mean the necklace is yours?" Sterling searched my face as if the truth was written on the contours of my cheekbones, on the slope of my nose. Finally, his eyes met mine. "You didn't own it when we were together."

I lowered onto the settee by the edge of the canopy bed. "Well, no." I knew this conversation held power to destroy me. But I couldn't wear this mask any longer, even if peeling it proved painful. I set the necklace on my lap, its weight seeming to triple. "It's a long story."

The secrets had been wedged in my soul for so long. How could I pry them free? Where would I begin?

I determined to reveal the truth like I would a story. It was the only way I could detach my emotions. "Let's say there once was a struggling actress. She was young, ambitious, wanting to show the world she had what it takes. But no one gave her a chance."

He sat beside me, his gaze claiming mine, hazing my concentration.

I fixed my attention on a random spot on the rug and forced an even tone. "The actress met a gentleman. He was wealthy, powerful, and gave expensive gifts. Soon the woman discovered she was with child. His child."

A sound rattled in Sterling's throat, snapping my gaze to him. His own mask dropped, revealing anguish in his eyes.

I placed my hand on his knee. "No, Sterling." Oh dear, I was making a muck of this. "That's not what I meant."

"But you said the jewels were yours, and this. . .*gentleman* gave gifts." His voice was as hard as his steely eyes.

"No, it's Greer."

"What about her?"

"The actress I'm talking about is Greer. She's my mother."

And just like that, the silent millstone I'd been chained to my entire existence fell away.

Sterling abruptly launched to his feet, walked a few steps, then stilled. "Greer Donnelly? Your mother? We were going to be married, Soph. This is basic information a fiancé should know."

"You're right. But I couldn't tell you." I set the necklace on the cushion and stood. "Let me explain."

His frame was a stiff wall of muscle and anger. "I'm listening."

"During Greer's relationship with this man, she landed a lead role that catapulted her career. But then she discovered I was on the way. She was admitted into an asylum for unwed mothers and delivered me. Greer used a false name—Myrna Winslow. My birth certificate lists me as Sophie Winslow. Soon after, she handed me over to a children's home. And to be certain there'd be no trace back to her, she told the nuns my name was Sophie Walters."

He turned startled eyes on me. "She abandoned you?"

"Yes, but she doesn't see it that way. She manipulated my aunt Hildi into adopting me. I wasn't even supposed to know Greer was my mother. But then one day I eavesdropped on them arguing over the burden of taking care of me." I could almost hear the slap of my small feet against the hardwood as I ran to Greer and hugged her legs. But instead of welcoming me into her arms, she pushed me away, forbidding me to call her Mother. Her pretty face had twisted in scorn before she stormed out the door and left Aunt Hildi with the task of explaining my birth story. "Since then, Aunt Hildi has made it clear that I'm an intruder. You see, she's a religious woman, and to her, I'm a soiled product of sin. She allowed me into her house but never gave me a home."

A muscle leaped in his jaw. "You were an innocent child. That's not your fault."

I took pleasure in Sterling's indignation. "I know that now. But it took me a long while to find my worth." I wavered in this awkward state of freedom and hesitation. I'd never spoken those words aloud, but it seemed once the gates of my soul were unbarred, the truth pushed out in rapid currents. "Greer continued her successful career, carrying on with man after man, occasionally sending money to Aunt Hildi to appease her conscience."

"What about your father?" The tendons on his neck throbbed. "Where had he disappeared to?"

"He was a congressman. More than that, a married man. He couldn't afford a scandal."

Sterling grunted. "He should've thought about that before—"

"Yes, he should have. But he made it clear to Greer he wanted nothing to do with me. He gave the necklace as a payoff for his responsibility. He told Greer the necklace was mine, but she wore it as her own for decades. He also gave her some bonds, but I suspect she's already cashed them out."

His eyes narrowed.

"Greer's not entirely bad. She's tried to give me the necklace a few times over the years, but I've refused." I let out a humorless laugh and gestured to the jeweled troublemaker on the sofa. "I can't look at it without thinking it was a cheap payment. I would have rather had a father than cold stones set in metal."

"You could've said something." Sterling's hand framed my face. His thumb brushed a tender swipe over my cheek. "You didn't have to bear this all alone."

"Greer made me promise not to tell. There was a time I only wanted her to love me, to approve of me. I did anything she asked, thinking she'd claim me if I was good enough." I sighed. "Though if Greer acknowledged me, her career would be ruined. That was most important to her." I placed my hand over his. "There were several times I almost told you, but I was scared."

"Because of Greer?"

"Because of you."

His eyes flashed with hurt. "Why me?"

"You were the first one who ever wanted me." I gave him a ghost of a smile. "For an orphan that no one claimed, who'd been given different names to avoid scandal, it was hard for me to believe anyone would love me and willingly give me their name. I didn't want to risk your rejection with the truth."

"I'd never reject you." Now both his hands were on my face, gently inclining my jaw so I could peer into his earnest expression. "It would be like tossing away my own soul."

My heart lifted. Sterling wouldn't say such a thing unless he meant it. But he couldn't possibly understand. "It's hard to explain to someone like you who grew up in a loving, accepting home."

"Can you try?"

I couldn't look in his eyes. They were too penetrating, too tender. "You're a hero from the war. Then you became a civil servant. You're an upstanding member of the community. A devout Christian."

He lowered his hands from my face only to wrap his arms around me. "You make me sound like some kind of boy scout."

I rested my cheek on his chest. He had shed his sportscoat earlier, and I could feel the thunder of his heartbeat.

His hands flattened on my back, pressing me closer. "I'm not without fault."

Right now I thought him perfect. "But you don't have a glaring fault that shadows your entire existence."

His head dipped lower, and he nuzzled my hair. "You don't either."

"I'm..." How could I focus with him caressing me like this? Sterling was always so fiercely in control, but now it seemed his guard was down. "I'm—"

"Wonderful." He kissed my temple. "Intelligent." He pressed another to my forehead. "Beautiful in every way."

My eyes slid shut, and I savored the feel of his lips on my heated skin. His mouth trailed along the curve of my face. His arms curled firmly around me.

"I'm illegitimate."

"You're my everything."

My eyes shot wide. Sterling had never been this expressive. He'd told me he loved me only twice—the night he proposed and the day before our wedding. I wasn't prepared for this version of him. But it didn't stop me from clutching his lapels with a surprising grip. If only my heart could latch on to his words as easily.

"It's hard to explain." My lower lip trembled, but I knew I needed to voice the truth buried beneath the debris of hurt and wreckage caused by other people's actions. "From birth, I was unwanted. Nothing but a burden. People who should have loved me didn't. And growing up, I never understood what was wrong with me. Why didn't anyone want me?"

His hands bunched the fabric of my dress, and his lips covered my own. The man was fluent in the language of touch, and I quickly caught the translation. His fingers flexed, then gently pressed into my sides, anchoring me to him. His mouth was fervently insistent at just the right pressure that demanded nothing but gave most thoroughly. He was speaking to me, and his touch said—*mine.*

Finally, we broke apart, our chests heaving.

"Sophie." My name in his breathless tone was like beautiful music. "I'll do whatever it takes to convince you that you're worthy of love. And very much wanted." He gave me another lingering kiss and spoke against my lips. "I'll use words if necessary."

I smiled, knowing his actions said so much.

"If God doesn't view you as an outcast, what right does anyone else have to do so? In His eyes, you're not illegitimate. You're His beloved." His adamant tone broke through the lies. "And mine too."

Right now, I didn't care if the world saw me as a criminal, because Sterling Monroe saw the true me. Not the woman I'd constructed with careful deception and well-hidden truths. But as Sophie Winslow Walters. All my secrets were bared before him, and he hadn't turned away. Instead, he held me with a protectiveness that melted my insecurities.

His scorching gaze seared mine. I knew that look. It was one I hadn't glimpsed in over a half decade, but a girl didn't forget such an expression. The gold swirls in his eyes were like flashes of fire, igniting the memories of long-lost yesterdays and a burning hope for today. "You look like you're about to kiss me again."

An amused grunt. "Any objections?"

"No," I said, winding my arms around his neck and lifting on my tiptoes. "Just a suggestion."

"Anything."

"Do your best work. It's been a long five years."

He grinned. That rare, beautiful grin! "Don't I know it." He dipped his chin as I inclined mine. A move so familiar, like time hadn't been stretched and wasted between us. I could have sobbed at how right this felt.

When I left the day of our wedding, my soul splintered, fractured to the point of being unrecognizable. But here in Sterling's arms, I believed God could redeem anything.

CHAPTER TWENTY-ONE

ELISE

*L*egacy Towers' employees, being primarily female, clapped and danced to Pierson's songs with the enthusiasm of tweens at a boy band concert. As for the elderly residents, Elise had never seen a tougher crowd.

Pierson had said they'd be non-threatening. They were also non-participatory. Meredith was the exception, sitting at a front table in the large recreation room, smiling like a proud parent.

Pierson played the debut hit that had launched his career to stardom, and by the closing lyric, four well-meaning folks had fallen asleep. Next, he strummed his most recent single, the one that had topped the charts for three months, and by the bridge, a cluster of white-haired ladies started a game of gin rummy.

Elise's gaze zeroed on Pierson, the poor guy clearly floundering. The megastar usually required a tour bus full of guards to protect the stage, but here? Well, the man responsible for security was on his third glass of lemonade.

The staff overexaggerated their lip-syncing to get the residents involved, but the perceived consensus was the eighty-plus crowd would rather be in their rooms watching *Bonanza*. Pierson finished another song, receiving a few courtesy claps even as a loud snore echoed from the back.

Elise's marketer brain knew what needed to happen to rouse the audience, but her heart pumped the mental brakes. Her tentative gaze drifted from Pierson, who looked two seconds from waving the proverbial white flag, to her violin case. Could she?

Why was she such a wimp? No, she was worse than that—she was. . .

she was. . .looking at this all wrong. Pierson's earlier words elbowed for more mental space. Could it be that simple? There was only one way to find out. She opened the case latches with purpose. As if sensing her decision, Pierson glanced over, and relief swept his handsome features.

Who said the first step was always the hardest? Bunk! All twenty paces to the front were as if she walked against white rapids of doubt.

She nodded at Pierson and then, without introduction, jumped into a Charlie Daniels hit from the 1970s. She closed her eyes, the intense fingerings claiming all her concentration. This song was snappy and spirited. Elise played to her fullest, almost daring any senior to nod off. She braved open an eyelid, and her smile sparked.

The crowd engaged. Several men clapped along. The ladies tapped their feet. One ornery fellow stood and slapped his hand on his trousers, keeping the beat. Then there was Pierson, who strummed along as if he was her backup. Their gazes knotted, and his grin unleashed, almost knocking the air from her chest. Because only he knew the magnitude of this moment.

A rush of joy spread through her because this—*this!*—was what performing should feel like. Her pulse pounded but not in fear. No nausea. No shakiness. Just her, her violin, and a rightness only God could give. She ended the song, and the crowd applauded with whoops and hollers. She couldn't remember ever being so happy she cried.

Pierson knuckled away a tear. "How'd that feel?"

"Amazing." She leaned into his touch.

"*You* were amazing. I'm proud of you."

His words warmed her. This man played poker with grandmas, paid for wings in senior centers, supported retired music teachers, spent time with teens, and devoted hours to helping her overcome stage fright. She lifted on her toes and kissed his cheek. "Thank you."

His eyes widened in pleased surprise. "For what?"

"For being you."

"No, this is all your doing." His voice lowered as the room quieted. "I've been playing for fifteen minutes with no response. You play fifteen seconds, and people wake up. Literally."

"It's Marketing 101." She nudged him. "Appeal to your audience. For this group, you have to tap into their nostalgia. Play what they listened to when they were younger."

"You're really something." His slow wink could rival poetry as an art form. "Now. . ." He adjusted his guitar strap. "Let's have ourselves a concert." With a confident dip of his chin, he played Johnny Cash's "Ring of Fire."

As Elise predicted, he got the seniors' rapt attention. She dove in with supporting accompaniment, and by the end of the song, they were both grinning.

The hearty applause seemed to unlock Pierson's stage personality. He interacted with the audience by asking questions and taking requests. Some songs he knew, while others he pulled up chords on his phone. It was informal but personal. There was a sweet lady in a wheelchair named Lucille, and Pierson promptly sang the Kenny Rogers song of that title. The woman blushed to the tips of her silver hair.

After the performance, Elise and Pierson stayed for refreshments, joining Meredith at her table. Their music teacher pressed a hand to her heart. "You kids were wonderful. I can't tell you how much that blessed me."

Pierson responded with an affectionate smile. "Thank you, Meredith. We owe everything to you."

Elise smiled her agreement, her heart still overwhelmed. This afternoon was the first time she'd played in front of an audience in over two years. Not only had she not gotten sick, but the opposite had happened— she'd felt rejuvenated. It was a beautiful victory, giving her courage for her audition.

After spending time with Meredith, Pierson squeezed Elise's hand. "Let's work the room." He held out his arm as if they were going table-hopping at a Grammy after-party.

She loved seeing this side of him. A little too much.

Yet on their way to mingle, Pierson led her to a secluded spot to the side. "Okay. Spill it." He cupped his hand over hers. "What changed your mind about performing?"

"You did."

"Me?"

"It was our conversation in the lobby earlier. When you said this concert was a gift to the residents, it stirred something in me." She smiled up at him. "I've never viewed it that way. Using the talent God gifted me as a gift for someone else." She'd heard that in church before but never understood its depth until today. "God blesses you to bless others." That took *her* entirely out of the equation. Maybe that was her problem all along. She'd been too absorbed in herself. Her dreams. Her career. Her failures. Her stage fright. It was time to change the lens and focus on those around her. "Thank you for that."

Gone was the flirty singer. Instead, his softened expression reminded her of the Pierson of old. Her best friend. The one who'd stolen her heart. "Thank you for telling me."

Together, they greeted every resident. Pierson fielded some questions, but mostly he and Elise just listened. This seemed as much a gift as their performance—providing a willing ear and answering smile.

At the final table, Elise engaged in a conversation with a ninety-year-old woman named Claudette. Claudette wore an embroidered sweatshirt that read GRANDMA'S SWEETHEARTS, and inside each fancily stitched heart was the name of one of her grandkids. She pointed to each name and told Elise their life story. "And this here is Brenna. She lives in the Poconos. It's a charming place called Tafton."

"Tafton?" Elise perked. "My mom taught at Anders during the summer, but it was a long time ago."

Claudette smiled. "I've heard of that camp. It was quite expensive and selective."

That was something Elise knew. But she didn't have space to respond because Claudette kept talking about Tafton. The walking trails were gorgeous. There was a farm that bred miniature horses. The weather in the summer was humid but cool in the evenings. On and on. But Elise enjoyed the woman's ramblings because it gave her a glimpse of the places her mom might have seen.

"Then there was this restaurant." Claudette sipped her lemonade. "It's a little hole-in-the-wall place that serves the best fried chicken. Cade is owned by a nice woman and her son."

"Cade?" Elise tapped Pierson's elbow, gaining his attention. "You say that's a restaurant?"

She nodded. "Decent service, but the cheesecake is on the soggy side."

Her heart raced. "And how long has Cade been around?"

Claudette's silver brow dipped in thought. "I suppose since the eighties or nineties."

Elise and Pierson exchanged a look. All along they'd thought Cade was a man's name, but what if it was a place? Elise thought back to the note in her mom's music box. There were two separate measures. The first bar had her mother's name and the second one "Cade." But she'd forgotten about the six-eighths time signature beside the second bar. She looked up at the round wall clock over the doorway. What if the note's purpose had been to indicate a meeting location and time? What if the little hand was on the six and the big hand was on the eight?

Cade at six forty?

CHAPTER TWENTY-TWO

Sophie

*W*hile Greer was out cold in the parlor, I sat at the elegant desk in the corner of the spare room of her suite, pen at the ready. I'd already returned the necklace to her jewelry box in the master bedroom. No matter how much Greer would press to appease her guilt, I didn't want to take ownership of it yet. Not sure I ever would. "Okay, who do you consider suspects?"

Sterling brought his chair close to mine. "You're the best one to answer. Who would frame you?" He gave an encouraging smile, pulling my attention to his perfectly molded lips, reminding me of the heated kisses we'd just shared.

As much as I wanted to linger on that delicious topic, we needed to explore the subject of the robberies. It wouldn't do for me to be considered a criminal, though I was confident Lloyd wouldn't mind. Ah, there's one. "Our director."

His brow raised, then sank in realization. "Was the Loew's Penn sold out tonight?"

I nodded. "I asked for someone else to play my part, but he adamantly refused."

"Idiot," Sterling grumbled. "With all the theaters in town, I can see why he's desperate to remain popular."

At least a dozen playhouses flooded downtown Pittsburgh, with several more threaded throughout the city.

"Plus, Lloyd Harris is a stage name." He paused as if awaiting my shocked reaction, but I wasn't the least bit surprised. "He's really Lloyd Hendricks, a man arrested twice for rumrunning in Philadelphia."

My head whipped his direction, my jaw dropping. "What?" Lloyd had a criminal record? Moreover, he'd been threatening us if we'd dared enter a speakeasy. All the while, he had a history in bootlegging? Irony at its finest. "How do you know this?"

"I have my ways."

Right. He'd been working on the jewel theft cases before the authorities dismissed him. It was foolish of me to think he hadn't checked the backgrounds of potential suspects. "But why frame me?"

"Why not?" He shrugged. "Lina already has fame. She's not a novelty anymore, whereas you're young and beautiful and have that way about you."

"What way?" I skimmed my person as if I could discover the answer myself. My legs were long, but my torso was short. My left foot was slightly bigger than my right, though most wouldn't know. My eyes were probably my best asset, being the color of the necklace I loathed. Beyond that, I couldn't find anything remarkable about me.

He cleared his throat. "Let's just say you're desirable."

I laughed. "I don't give that impression. Nor do I encourage it."

"It's not like you can help it. You don't act suggestive or dress that way. But a man doesn't need encouragement to see what's right in front of him."

Once again, my talent got no recognition. Maybe I didn't have any in the first place. What if I'd deceived myself into thinking I had a gift and wasted my youth chasing an empty dream? "That's not the kind of attention I want."

"I know." The sharp lines of his face softened. "But I guarantee Harris sees your potential. Sold-out shows for a play he's directing is reason enough to frame you." He tapped the paper. "I've been watching him. It's safe to say he's a possible suspect."

I wrote down Lloyd's name.

"What about Joe Neville?" Sterling suggested. The former policeman's eyes conveyed just how little he thought of the on-stage one. "We know he has a drinking problem and a wandering eye." He shifted in his seat. "And he was in your room before you discovered the jewelry."

Of course Sterling would remember that detail. I scribbled Joe's name. "Fran should have never let him into my room. It makes me question our friendship. She knows I could've been evicted if Mrs. Fielding found him."

His hand covered mine. "Why did she allow Neville in there?"

"Because he was seeing—" I snapped my fingers with a new revelation. "That's it!"

"What?"

"Joe's been seeing another boarder, Hannah Price. I knew she was a maid but found out only the other day she works for the Stoneberrys. What if she talked to Joe a little too much about her employer? He's clever and would know just the right questions to ask her. Where Mrs. Stoneberry keeps her jewels, what time she falls asleep, if she keeps the windows locked. And dear Hannah's naive enough to think nothing's amiss."

Sterling listened intently.

"What if Joe wanted to hide the jewels in Hannah's room, but the landlady foiled his plan? So when Fran sneaked him into my place, he put the bracelet there, thinking he could retrieve it another time."

"That's possible. The scenarios line up." Sterling looked deep in thought. "But the bracelet is only one piece out of the dozen that have been stolen. Where are all the other jewels?"

That was true. If Joe was the Mirage, he'd have to find hiding spots for all the loot. Which meant we were back where we started—gathering suspects. Analyzing the people I spent most of my time with was uncomfortable. How could any of them resort to stealing priceless gems? A part of me couldn't believe it. But then again, someone had planted stolen jewels in my purse. Someone I possibly claimed as a friend had treated me as an enemy.

"Does Joe have a connection to Greer?" Sterling's low voice split into my troublesome ponderings.

"Joe was very pushy with his attentions toward her. She went out drinking with him last week." My gaze took in Joe's name on the paper, wondering if he'd set his predatory sights on Greer. But would Greer fall for him? Could a secret romance with Joe Neville be the reason Greer remained in Pittsburgh?

Sterling shook his head. "It's baffling to know she's your mother. The two of you are completely different. But what bothers me most is she chose her career over you, her own kid."

"It hasn't been easy." My heavy sigh fluttered the edge of the paper. "Like I said, I wanted to gain her approval. That was my initial motivation behind becoming an actress. Greer idolized the stage, and I thought she'd finally accept me if I chose the same path. But my plan backfired in New York."

"What happened?" Sterling knew I hadn't succeeded on Broadway but didn't know the main reason.

"I was up for a lead role in a Follies play. Ziegfeld himself asked Greer's opinion, and she told him I wasn't ready for the part."

Sterling's eyes narrowed. "She didn't."

"She ruined my chance." I rolled the pen between my fingers. "I was so angry, I almost ratted her out. How easy it would've been to take revenge and tell the world what she had done and who she really is."

"What stopped you?"

"My own convictions. Watching her fall wouldn't raise me any. And it certainly wouldn't bring any healing. Only God can mend the hurt."

He skimmed a knuckle along my arm. "I'm sorry."

"Don't be. We would have never met if I'd made it big on Broadway." My thoughts took a sorrowful turn. "But maybe that would've been best for you. I couldn't have hurt you by leaving."

"No." His fingers slid from my arm to my shoulder, nestling along the sensitive spot on the base of my neck. "I would go through it all again. Loving you is worth the pain."

Greer let out a loud snore from the other room, breaking the moment.

Sterling withdrew his touch with a chuckle. "Did you inherit her sleeping habits?"

I feigned offense at his teasing words and feebly pushed him. "I hope not."

That smile I adored crimped into a grimace. "This might be hard to hear, but what about Greer as a suspect?"

"She couldn't." I twisted in my seat, facing him. "I didn't see her until after the first few robberies."

"Exactly. You didn't *see* her," Sterling pointed out. "Not that she wasn't here." He hooked his foot on my chair's leg and tugged my seat closer to his. "I did some digging, and Greer arrived in Pittsburgh a week before the first theft."

"What? I didn't know." My chest squeezed. "I'd assumed her reason for visiting was to make amends with me." Maybe I'd been wrong. Greer had major faults, but I couldn't imagine her being a thief. "Why would she rob anyone? She has fame and fortune."

"She's got fame but not fortune." His hand found mine. "I know the owner of this hotel. He told me Greer's staying here on credit. I'm suspecting she doesn't have many funds."

"But she said she saw the Mirage tonight."

"Which we only have her word for."

I frowned. "She was distraught."

"She's also an actress."

True. With my mouth pinched tight, I jotted her name on the paper. "If she was low on money, she could've sold the necklace."

He shrugged. "Maybe she thought you'd call her out if she took your birthright."

"She knows I hate it." My exhaustion seeped into my thoughts, clouding everything I called truth. "It can't be her. Probably isn't Lloyd or Joe, either."

His eyes narrowed. "Why?"

"Do you still have all those dime novels?"

The dim lighting could trick my imagination, but I was fairly certain Sterling Monroe, the impenetrable detective, blushed.

A smile teased my lips. When I'd discovered several boxes of dime novels in his aunt's closet one day, it had been the first glimpse I'd gotten of Sterling as a human. I never believed this imposing, brooding man would cuddle up with a sensation serial. "Think of those mysteries. It's never the person with all the evidence pointing their way."

He pressed a kiss to my forehead. "That's why It's called fiction, sweetheart. In real life, the obvious person is most often the culprit."

I made a face. "No, it's always the *least* likely. Who do you think is the most innocent of all the suspects?"

He leaned in slow. "In that case, it's you."

I gasped. "Or you."

"So I'm a suspect now?" His lips twitched.

"It'd be a perfect plot twist if the handsome detective were the villain," I teased.

His eyes glittered with amusement, but then he shook his head. "I'm too big to fit through those dainty windows."

I gave a dramatic sigh. "Okay, then let's look at the others. Fran, Violet, Lina, and Gerald."

He stretched an arm along the back of my chair, his fingers toying with my hair. "Which of them has a motive to steal?"

"I don't know much about Gerald except he has a temper. Lina's sweet, but she isn't very loyal. Though she did come to the station and defend me." I wrote down their names anyway.

"What about Violet and Fran?"

"I've known Fran since grammar school. It's hard to imagine her doing anything like that."

"Can you imagine Violet?"

"I'm not sure. Violet is a good friend but somewhat wild. She's always looking for the next thrill. Though I can't see her stealing for the fun of it."

His hand dipped to my neck and lingered. "Plenty of sensation seekers are sleeping in jail cells as we speak."

I glanced at the suspect column on the paper. "We're only looking at the cast members I interact with. We can't forget there are understudies, extras, stage crew members, musicians, and janitorial staff. They all have access to the dressing and rehearsal rooms."

He nodded. "Which makes the hunt more challenging."

"I think. . ." I clasped my hands together under my chin, excitement building. "I think I might have a solution."

Reluctance weighted his tone. "Which is?"

"We set a trap." I launched to my feet with renewed determination. "Hold on. Let me go get the necklace and see if it still fits. It's a choker chain, but Greer's neck is slimmer than mine."

"No." Sterling bounded after me. "You're not going to be bait."

I cut to Greer's bedroom, her canopy bed vacant, considering she was still on the sofa. "It's a sound idea. I'll wear the necklace to the theater. I can say Greer let me borrow it. Surely, the robber will go after the goods. When he does, you nab him." I gave a triumphant smile. "Simple."

"I can think of a hundred ways that can go wrong."

I flipped open the jewelry box lid, my eyes blinking in rapid succession. "It's already gone wrong."

The velvet case was empty, the necklace missing.

The Mirage had stolen it from under our noses.

CHAPTER TWENTY-THREE

ELISE

If life was a highway, Elise was going in the wrong direction. And she 100 percent blamed her navigator.

"I think we were supposed to take the last exit." Pierson repeatedly tapped his phone, his confused expression distractingly adorable. "Internet's spotty here. My GPS froze on me." His crooked smile made an appearance. "That's my story, and I'm sticking to it."

"Makes for a great country song, but not so good for traveling across the state." She flicked on the turn signal and went into the exit lane. Hopefully, they could turn around and get back on track. "This is the third turn we've missed. Maybe this is a sign we should return to Pittsburgh." With her audition and Pierson's departure from Pittsburgh rapidly approaching, they'd agreed the quicker this mystery with her birth father—and hopefully the necklace—was solved, the better. So here she was, stuffed in her small car with Pierson, headed to the Cade restaurant in the Poconos.

He tried his phone again. "If I were driving, we wouldn't have missed those turns because my truck could practically drive itself there."

She rolled her eyes. He was right, of course, but she'd insisted on driving. "Next month's *People* magazine just hit the rack. Do you know who's on the cover?"

He took a casual swig of his coffee.

"It's you, and you're posing in front of your Ford. Now your beast of a truck is a tabloid target."

"Weak argument. Lots of people drive F-150s."

"It's better to take precaution." Plus, gas prices were ridiculous at present, and she didn't want to be indebted to him. Even a little.

"But your car's a roller skate." The passenger chair was back as far as it could go, and Pierson's tall frame still seemed folded in half. He probably was uncomfortable, but that would be his penalty for looking too good in the morning.

Meanwhile, she had her long hair in a braid and a ball cap to cover the frizz. No makeup, thanks to her sleeping through her alarm. Knowing she'd miss this morning's practice, she'd doubled up last night, not hitting her pillow until well after midnight. She barely had time to put on deodorant, and Pierson had the nerve to wear cologne. That woodsy scent would probably be embedded in the upholstery forever. Life was cruel. "What this car lacks in size, it makes up for in fuel efficiency and cuteness." She gave the dash an affectionate pat. "Are you regretting coming with me?"

"I'm regretting not chartering a private jet."

"This was your idea," she reminded him. "I wanted to call the restaurant."

He returned his coffee to the cup holder. "Which you did and got their voice mail. Three times."

It was four, but who was counting? "What are the odds of anyone remembering my mom? And what if this restaurant has nothing to do with my birth father? It could just be a place she went to. The note could be a private joke among her friends or something. Which means we drove five hours to *and* from for nothing." They'd been on the road since eight. They should reach the Poconos by one. Well, more likely two, considering they'd missed a few turns.

"Where's your sense of adventure?"

"I left it back at the gas station with the bag of donuts I should've bought."

"Here." Pierson reached into his bag and dug something out. The donuts! "If you looked at me the way you look at waxy processed food, I'd be driving you to the preacher."

Once again, he was being a flirt face. But today, she didn't mind. For her sanity's sake, it was best to keep things light, because she had heavy doubts about this trip. She honestly didn't think they would discover anything, but there was always that "what-if" that kept poking into her thoughts like a crazed Whac-A-Mole.

Pierson stacked his hands behind his head, but his elbow hit the window. He shifted and leaned more on the console. Her braid brushed against his forearm. "Since we're cooped up together for the next several hours. . ."

That was a suspiciously leading tone. She shoved another donut into her mouth.

His fingers idly stroked her braid. "How about we talk about us."

"There is no *us*." Another donut. If her cheeks were stuffed with chocolatey goodness, then she wouldn't be able to speak.

But Pierson was smart. He recognized her plan and snatched the bag from her lap.

"Not fair!" She spit-sprayed crumbs onto her steering wheel.

"Chew, Elise." He covered his smiling mouth with his fist. "Don't you want to address what's between us? Talk it out?"

"No." She swallowed a lump of frosting. "Because I'm better at conversational dodgeball than awkward heart-to-hearts." She upped the radio. Okay, that was rude, but it was also rude to coerce someone into talking about things they didn't want to talk about.

Unfazed, he turned down the volume. "It doesn't have to be awkward."

It was bound to get weird if Elise was part of the chat. She didn't express her feelings well. It was best to keep her emotions locked inside, with several layers of protective wrap around them. But Pierson seemed like the guy who enjoyed snapping the bubbles. She could almost hear her feelings pop beneath his heated stare.

"It's a simple yes or no."

She kept her eyes on the road.

"Are you attracted to me?"

"Millions of women already are. Why do you—"

"It's not about them. This is you and me. Yes or no?"

Fine. If he wanted the truth, she'd shovel all of it on him and bury this topic for good. "It has nothing to do with attraction. Because if so, then yes. I crushed on you when you had a mullet and sported a faded Pokemon T-shirt. The thing is, I lost my best friend for almost ten years, and it feels like I got that friendship back. I don't want to ruin it with a romance that won't work."

"The best relationships start as friends." He wasn't as deterred as she'd expected. If anything, her admission only sparked a challenge in his eyes. "We can test the waters."

"They're piranha-infested waters." She gripped the steering wheel tighter. "It will get strained between us, and. . .just no."

He scratched his stubble. "Piranhas?"

"Toss in fire jellyfish, flesh-eating bacteria, and a few ship-crunching glaciers." Her head tilted. "I could add several hurricanes, but I don't want to be melodramatic."

"Noted." He squared his shoulders, and she knew whatever he'd say next would try to penetrate her wall of resistance. "But that's not how I see our waters. It's you and me in a two-person kayak. We're—"

"Kayak?"

"If you can have flesh-eating bacteria, I can have a kayak."

"Fine. Proceed."

"It's sunrise. The water is still, but that doesn't mean boring. It's burning with color, reflecting strums of the sunrise. Mountains flank either side of the shore. Everything's breathtaking."

Oh. He meant business with such an expert delivery of his thoughts. But were those his *real* thoughts? The man wrote love songs for a living. His creative mind no doubt overflowed with pretty little lines like these, all for the sole purpose of squeezing sighs out of unsuspecting women. Well, not this woman. She sealed her lips tighter for good measure.

"On those waters, I wish I had my guitar. But then I realize I have you, and that's all the music I need."

Welp. She sighed.

"How about an experiment to see which of our versions is true." He leaned on the console, invading her space. "Let's make out."

"What?" Her shocked shriek bounced off the roof. With a jerk of the wheel, she pulled onto the shoulder.

Pierson's smile was borderline wicked. "Is that a yes?"

"No, this is for the greater good. I didn't want to have this talk sandwiched between two semis."

"Mmhmm." He made an exaggerated show of turning his ball cap around in a painfully slow rotation, giving her a clear message that he didn't want to knock brims during a smooching session.

She tugged her hat lower on her forehead.

He laughed.

This was ridiculous. "We're not kissing. We're talking."

"Not the experiment I hoped for."

Her eyes narrowed. "But what friends do."

He unbuckled his seat belt as if he planned on camping out on the berm of the highway. "Just one kiss, Elise. If it's weird between us afterward, we remain just friends." He said the last part as if the words tasted like raw eggs—slimy and full of salmonella. "No harm done. But if it's what I suspect. . ." His voice rumbled with a longing that made her blood warm. "Then we explore more in a relationship. What do you think?"

They'd already had more almost-kiss moments than the entire archive of Hallmark movies. But she was right about this. "You leave in ten days."

"Just to Nashville, not to Mars," he quipped. "Try again."

"That's the thing, I don't want to *try again*. I don't want to try to put the pieces of my heart back together because you went away and forgot about me. I don't want to try to act like life's okay when it won't be for a long time because it hurt so bad. If we go on as friends, there's no risk of that." But she feared there was a major chance it would happen no matter what. "I know we were young and immature back then, but I need more insurance than that."

All teasing left his face. "What can I do to prove I'm not that guy?"

"Do exactly that. Prove it. If we can stay in close contact after you return to your crazy world, then maybe we have a chance for more."

***

They reached the restaurant around lunchtime.

"Cade." Elise sighed. "It looks a bit run down." The sign leaned to the left, making Elise wary of parking near it. The building itself needed a fresh coat of paint or completely new siding, whichever hid the weather-beaten boards best.

But the parking lot was surprisingly full.

"Must have good food." Pierson read her thoughts.

A cold front had swept through the state, but having to drive for over ten hours today, Elise had dressed for comfort, not warmth, in her long sweater over leggings with boots. "Ready? Or would you rather stay here? So no one recognizes you."

"If I'm going down, it's not going to be inside this Barbie car."

She laughed. "Okay, Brooks. Try not to make the waitresses swoon. I'm hungry and don't want to resuscitate people to get service."

"Funny girl." He wove his fingers through hers, and she didn't object. Friends held hands, right?

A bell jingled above the door, and they were transported to the nineties. The space was cluttered with community memorabilia. A whole wall was covered in snapshots, making her photography-loving heart expel a happy sigh.

A sign by the entrance read SEAT YOURSELF. They chose the booth by the cardboard Elvis. It seemed appropriate.

An older woman with generous hips and a kind smile approached. "Hey, folks. My name's Willa, and I'm your server." She handed them menus, then pushed her teased bangs from her forehead. "Now, what can I get you to drink?"

Pierson ordered a Coke and glanced at Elise.

She bit her lip, rallying for courage. Willa seemed old enough to have worked here during the timeframe her mom would have been here. Was it too much to hope? "I'll take a sweet tea, and I'm hoping you can answer some questions I have about this restaurant during the late nineties. Can you or anyone else help me?"

Willa tapped the end of her pen against her notepad. "The only one who was around back then is our manager, Brody. I'll see if I can nab him for you."

Elise watched her round the large counter and disappear behind a swishing door.

Nerves hit.

She studied the menu as if she were getting tested on it.

"You okay?" Pierson nudged her foot beneath the table.

"My mind's going everywhere. I need a distraction." She strained for a smile. "Give me some startling gossip on Luke Bryan. Or Blake Shelton. Anything?"

He lowered his menu. "I saw my mom last month."

She jolted. That was the last thing she expected him to say. "Dorothea said no one knows where she is."

His fingers tapped a restless rhythm on the table, sending subtle tremors through the wood. Regret lined his face. Was he sorry for bringing up the subject, or was there more to it? "I hired someone to find her. I thought maybe I could convince her to come to Gram's birthday party."

Which hadn't worked, since Lorraine Brooks wasn't at the William Penn. "How is she?"

"Different," he mumbled. "I wouldn't have recognized her."

A million questions swirled her mind, but Elise had to be careful. Pierson's mom was a tender topic.

"She changed her name." He flicked the edge of the menu. Then again. "She goes by Lori Redman."

"Did she remarry?"

"No. I don't think so." He sloughed it off, but Elise knew it was a bigger deal than he portrayed. His mother left when he was a young teen and hadn't contacted him since. Elise developed stage fright from rejection, but it seemed trivial compared to the rejection Pierson had endured. "She wasn't happy to see me."

Elise set down her menu and rounded to his booth side, claiming the spot right next to him. "Listen to me, Pierson Brooks. Your dad messed up your mom's head. It was his neglect that drove her to instability. But she refused to get help." From what Elise heard, Dorothea had begged her daughter to admit herself to a mental health facility.

Elise grabbed both of his hands, holding them tight as if trying to infuse the truth through her determined touch. "None of that was your fault. You were a kid."

He nodded.

"I know you know all this. But I'm not speaking to your head." She tapped his heart. "I'm speaking to this." She peeled her fingers away from his chest, but he caught them in his.

"Thank you." He lifted her hand and kissed the inside of her wrist. "I needed that reminder. Things didn't go how I wanted, but it helped to get some closure."

She held steady eye contact with him while her mind wandered. Was this why he'd encouraged her to find her dad? To get closure? "All I can say is she missed out big time." Her lips bent in an appreciative smile. "I'm glad I know you, Brooks."

"Likewise, Malvern."

"Here we are." Willa approached their table with their drinks.

After Pierson's heartfelt confession about his mom, Elise stayed beside him. His nearness made this casual lunch seem like a date, but moving to the other side of the table felt strangely like abandoning him.

She ordered a club sandwich, and Pierson asked for a hamburger with onion rings. Before Elise worked up the nerve to ask Willa if she'd spoken to Brody, a man only a couple years older than Elise drew up, his gaze steadily on her.

"You wanted to speak with me?" His dark brows raised.

"Um, yes." She reached out to hand Willa her menu and almost dropped it in her drink. "My name's Elise Malvern." She waited for any recognition to hit regarding her last name. Nothing.

Brody's gaze strayed to Pierson. "Hey, wait." He narrowed his eyes as if trying to place him. "You look familiar. Did you play shortstop for North Bradbury?"

Pierson shook his head. "No, man. Sorry."

"Huh." He rubbed his jaw for a second, then returned his attention to Elise. "What can I do for you?"

"I'm looking for anyone who was around here in the late nineties. Willa said you'd be able to help?"

He settled his hands on his waist. "This is my mom's place. I was just a kid during that time."

"Oh." Which made sense, since he looked like he was in his early thirties. "Then there's probably no chance you might remember my mom, Deborah Malvern. I think she visited here often when she was in town."

He shook his head. "Doesn't ring a bell. A lot of people have been here throughout the years."

"I figured." She tried not to be disappointed. They'd come all this way for nothing. She grabbed her phone and held up a picture. "This is her. Anything?"

"I'm sorry, no." He gave a sympathetic smile. "Wish I could help."

"You said your mom owns this place." Pierson leaned forward. "Would she know? Is she available?"

"Her memory isn't what it used to be. But I can ask her tomorrow when she comes in. She's out all day at the hospital for my stepdad's surgery."

"I hope all goes well for him." Elise grabbed her notepad, wrote down her mom's name, and handed the slip of paper to Brody. "Can I call back and check? I know it's a long shot."

He nodded. "Sure thing. Just ask for me." He returned to the kitchen.

Elise slumped in her seat. Another failed effort. Maybe her birth father was meant to remain a mystery. She glanced at Pierson and found him watching her. "I'm sorry to bring you out here for nothing."

He gave an affectionate tug on her braid. "Time spent with you isn't wasted."

They soon received their food and ate in comfortable silence. Elise browsed the walls. They looked like they hadn't been changed in years. Was this the view her mother had seen?

Having no more appetite, she excused herself to the restroom. On the way back, she browsed the Polaroids of people wearing Cade shirts. All the varied hairstyles indicated this wall took years to complete. There were photos of pets and floats in parades. It seemed like a tribute to the residents of Tafton.

Her eyes landed on one photo, and she froze.

Mom.

Her breath caught as she took in the picture. Her mother looked to be in her early twenties. She wore jeans and a salmon-colored T-shirt, her hair long and face glowing. Elise leaned in and ran her thumb over her wide smile, her eyes burning with emotion.

Mom stood in a group of eight or so. The counselors of the music camp, maybe? But on closer inspection, the man beside her had his hand on her lower back and. . .

"Wow." Pierson drew beside her. "You found her."

She nodded.

"Look at the guy next to her, his arm wrapped around her like. . .oh." Pierson tucked her against him.

Had she just wobbled?

She wasn't sure. But she was certain she'd seen that man's eyes before. His dimpled smile. His shade of hair. All familiar because she saw them every day in the mirror.

It was undeniable.

The man in the photo had to be her father.

CHAPTER TWENTY-FOUR

SOPHIE

*A*line of electric lamps hovered over the stage door exit, providing a strong glow against the pressing evening sky. But it seemed as if a thousand spotlights glared down on me. People shouted my name. Whistles screeched. Men cupped their mouths, bellowing phrases that would make Aunt Hildi blush. Yet others disapproved of my presence. A scathing boo resounded from the back of the crowd.

Sterling stood stalwart beside me with Lina to my right.

Lloyd insisted I sign autographs after the performance, something I'd never been invited to do. Gerald usually held that honor with Lina. But now the two of them only interacted on stage. While our director saw the wisdom in keeping the feuding leads apart, he didn't have the foresight to assign me a guard for the imposing crowd.

Sterling had stepped in.

His fierce countenance wasn't for show. He'd worn a threatening scowl ever since the robbery in Greer's suite last week. He was fuming, determined to catch the thief who'd broken in, stolen the necklace, and gotten away without a trace. Greer noticed the extra pass key was gone, and Sterling deduced the Mirage had taken the key when he'd first broken in, only to use it for easier entry the second time.

But the Mirage hadn't struck since.

It had been seven days with no robberies.

Sterling believed the robber might be lying low for a stretch, but I suspected the worst. What if the Mirage had tired of Pittsburgh, stuffed a bag with his spoils, and left town? There'd be no way of recovering the necklace and, more importantly, clearing my name. Which grew more crucial by the minute. Because while the Mirage's actions had dwindled, the public eye upon me intensified.

"Hiya, baby." A gentleman pushed past a young couple, stepping before me. "I need you to sign these." He shoved a stack of posters into my hands.

I gasped. On the page was a caricature of me scantily dressed, my curves embellished, with a pile of jewels in my inky hands. THE MIRAGE OF THE STEEL CITY was printed at the top of each paper.

Sterling growled. "She won't sign those."

The man puffed up. "See here. I had these specially made. I'm going to sell them in my place." Which was probably code for speakeasy.

Great. Just what I wanted. To be gawked over in a gin joint. "I'll sign your playbill, sir. Nothing more." I stretched out my hand to return the vulgar flyers, but he grabbed my wrist. Hard.

"Sign 'em, doll. I have friends who can give you all sorts of trouble."

"So do I." Sterling got in his face. "Five very insistent ones." His thick fingers curled in a fist. "And unless you want to meet them, I suggest you release Miss Walters."

The man's eyes rounded, and Sterling's menacing smirk was something to be captured on the big screen. He was brilliantly intimidating.

The unpleasant fellow let me go and grabbed the posters with less bravado. "I'll be back."

"And I'll be here." Sterling barred his arms across his expansive chest, leveling a look of equal parts danger and promise. His eyes tracked the man's retreat through the crowd, and then he faced me. "Are you okay?" He gently caught my hand and examined my wrist.

Finding no marks or bruising on my skin, the hard lines framing his mouth softened. His thumb swept a tender stroke over the area as if erasing any trace of that awful man. The affectionate gesture was a distinct contrast to his intense mannerisms only a moment ago. But that was Sterling. Protective, loyal, and once again, mine.

"I'm better now." I gave an appreciative smile. "Thank you." Though the altercation only proved I wouldn't have any peace until all of this was behind me. Judging by Sterling's rigid posture and darting glances, neither would he.

He remained by my side while I signed several autographs. There was a slight lull in the line, and he leaned toward me. "I haven't seen Greer tonight."

"That's because she's packing," I whispered, then smiled at a young lady who waved on her way to greet Lina.

He scowled. "She's leaving Pittsburgh?" Sterling wouldn't scratch Greer off his suspect list. In fact, I believed her name topped it.

"No. I encouraged her to stay at a more modest lodging." Though I wondered if her compliance to take a room at a cheaper accommodation had less to do with my influence and more with the hotel manager demanding payment. "Greer and I reached an agreement."

Sterling raised a skeptical brow. "She's allowing you to tell others of your connection?"

"Not that." I'd accepted Greer would never acknowledge me as her child, especially now when she needed to return to work to cover her debts. "About the bonds."

"I thought you said she cashed them." Ever alert, his gaze moved about, his wide stance remaining at the ready. "That she spent them."

"That's what I thought, but she held on to the money. We decided to split the funds fifty-fifty." Though I hated to touch a cent of it, I'd agreed for Greer's sake. The only way she'd accept her portion was if I would take mine. I'd rather toss the entire five hundred dollars from the highest rooftop. But at least Greer could now pay off some of her creditors.

I needed to decide what to do with my share. My first thought was to help Prudence, but I'd received a letter from her this morning. The young lady had returned home and seemed truly happy. "What do you think about. . ." My words faded at Sterling's severe countenance. His gaze was fixed steadily on something in the distance, his chest visibly rising with each sharp breath. I followed his line of sight. "What's wrong?"

"Go inside with Lina." His head jerked toward the stage door. "I need to check something."

I glanced at the fountain pen in my hand. "But Lloyd told us to sign for at least a half hour."

Gone was the affectionate beau. The stoic detective had taken his place. "Inside, Sophie." Then, as if realizing his gruffness, he gentled his tone. "Please."

I nodded, and he slipped into the crowd, moving with purpose. What had Sterling seen? I peered out into the sea of felt derby and cloche hats. Darkness veiled those lingering at the edges of the group, but I couldn't detect anything amiss. Sighing, I moved toward Lina, who happily chatted with a young woman.

"I'd love to perform on stage one day." The adolescent peered at Lina with starstruck eyes. "But I don't think I'm talented enough. If I can even try."

"My mother had a saying that always encouraged me." Smiling kindly, Lina went on to impart generational wisdom to the aspiring actress. "In the center of life is the word *if*, but don't let that keep you from living."

Her words, while encouraging, knotted my stomach. My joints locked, keeping me from taking the final steps left to reach her.

What was wrong with me? Perhaps all the recent interactions with Greer had increased my sensitivity. Here Lina praised her doting mother, while I never had the privilege of a caring parent. But the path of self-pity always led to misery.

"Is everything okay, Sophie?" Lina watched me with concern.

I scraped for composure and forced a smile. "Sorry for interrupting. But we've been asked to return inside."

Her expression hinted at confusion, but she quickly schooled her lovely features. "Of course. Time has slipped away from us." She said goodbye to the young woman, and we walked the few yards to the door.

"Sorry, Lina." What excuse could I give? I didn't even know the reason. "Sterling felt it best for us to wrap up early."

"Fine by me. The cold air made my nose drip."

Once inside, we both retreated to our dressing areas—Lina to her private room, me to the one shared with other actresses. Violet and Fran bickered over something. A few other ladies primped in front of the vanity, getting ready for a night out after a solid performance. Me? I only wanted to go home. Though I had to wait for Sterling to fetch me.

I grabbed my bag and searched through it, ensuring I had my key, my wallet, and no incriminating stolen jewelry. But my thoughts kept straying to Sterling. Where had he gone? Had his face drained of color, or had it been my imagination?

"Aren't you listening, Sophie?"

I nearly dropped my bag. "I'm sorry, Fran. Were you saying something to me?"

Violet lowered her comb and laughed. "She's probably thinking about her new love. I told you she'd win Sterling over with those nice legs of hers."

Had Violet been spying on Sterling and me in the rehearsal room? He'd checked on me before my final stage appearance, offering support. Before he left, he kissed me soundly. But for some reason, it rankled me that Violet would eavesdrop on our private moment. Then again, what should I expect, knowing she'd done the same thing with Lina and her beau?

Fran and Violet eagerly awaited my response, wanting me to confirm or deny my relationship with Sterling. I opted for a neutral answer. "I've been distracted lately. One doesn't get used to being mistaken for a famous jewel thief." I sighed and sifted through the rolling rack of coats in search of my wrap. Where was it?

I shoved a few hangers aside, accidentally knocking a maroon cape onto the floor and causing a pair of glasses to spill out of a pocket of a wool coat. Everything I touched lately went awry. I huffed a frustrated laugh, then it hit me. "I forgot my wrap today." Here I was searching intently for something that wasn't there.

I stilled.

All along I'd been looking for what wasn't there. For what I expected to see but couldn't. Because it never existed to begin with.

And just like that, I knew the identity of the Mirage.

CHAPTER TWENTY-FIVE

ELISE

*E*lise couldn't tear her gaze from the photo of her mom and the man who most likely was her dad. She swayed, but Pierson was there, his strong body supporting her weak one. He skimmed his hands up and down her arms, rubbing away a chill, making her realize goose bumps covered her skin. Her eyes slid closed, his rhythmic touch both soothing and protective. She tipped her head back onto his shoulder, thankful for his kindness in being her pillar—figuratively and literally.

Her mom had pretty features, but in this photo, she was radiant. Her smile was wide, her brown eyes shining with happiness. The man stood close to her mom, his fingers gripping her tiny waist. "He looks older than her." Faint lines etched his forehead, and his hair, while deep auburn like Elise's, was grayed at the temples. She guessed him to be in his forties.

"There's Brody." Pierson waved him over.

The restaurant manager crossed the floor, meeting them beside the picture wall. "Find something?" His smile was friendly as his gaze followed where she pointed. "Ah, that's your mom, isn't it?"

She nodded. "Do you happen to recognize the man beside her?"

"Huh." Brody studied the photo. "Yeah, I remember him." His finger tapped the bottom of the Polaroid, fast at first, then slowing. "Wait." His gaze did a double take at Elise. "You resemble him. Is he family?"

"That's what I'm trying to figure out." There were too many similarities to call it a coincidence. They shared the same pale green eyes. Their hair color matched, as well as their broad smiles. Even their dimple was on the left side of their face. "Do you know his name?"

Brody shifted his weight from one foot to the other, as if physically balancing the question. "Not the real one. We all called him Professor. The dude taught music or something." He glanced at the picture again. "My mom *might* remember his name. But like I said, her memory's not what it used to be."

Elise's heart lurched. Professor. Could the man have been a teacher at the summer camp? Had he been an instructor at Julliard yet had a home in the Poconos? Either way, she wouldn't know his name today. And if Brody's mom didn't recall it, Elise might never find out.

⁂

During the first hour of the drive to Pittsburgh, Elise hadn't said much because her mind wouldn't shut up. She'd done the math over the years, but this time it hit hard. Her birthday was in mid-March, which meant she'd been conceived the summer of the previous year. The timing lined up with her mom's stay in the Poconos. Elise hadn't forgotten Giselle Turner's account that her mother returned to New York in the fall a changed person, making Elise assume her mom knew then about her pregnancy. Add all that to Elise's unmistakable resemblance to the man in the photo, and she was 99 percent sure the Professor was her father.

Pierson was also quiet, giving her space to process. It was as if the best friend version of Pierson had stepped up, because, just like back then, he seemed to know what she needed when she needed it. A shoulder to lean on. A steady voice in the chaos. A silent supporter giving her time to adjust to the craziness.

She opened her mouth to thank him but stopped short as snowflakes hit the windshield. One flick of the wipers cleared them away. She'd checked her weather app this morning, and the forecast predicted cloudy skies—no chance of the evil white stuff. Because if there'd been an emoji snowflake on her app, Elise would have postponed the trip.

But it was fine. She could handle a few flurries. Her heart responded with a hard thwack, calling her bull. Pushing past her choppy breaths, she tugged her hat from her head, as if that would help her see better, and reduced her speed. No problem. She could do this.

Then the heavens ripped open.

Snow. Everywhere.

Her brain spun faster than her tires. Memories crashed into her. The totaled minivan. The sterile hospital smell. The taste of stale Doritos from the vending machine. She tried to force the taunting images from her mind. Her knuckles ached from her death grip on the steering wheel. "Pierson?"

He set his phone down. "What's wrong?"

"I—I can't do this." It wasn't a whiteout, but anxiety blurred her vision, making it unsafe for her to continue. "I don't drive in the snow."

His warm hand settled on her jiggling leg. "Because of what happened to your mom?"

She nodded. "It's stupid. I know. The roads aren't even covered, but I'm struggling." She hiccupped the last word, making her sound even more pitiful.

"Pull over, sweetheart." He pointed to the gas station ahead on the left, his voice a steady calm compared to her riotous nerves.

She pulled into the gas station's lot and jumped out of the driver's seat. Pierson rounded the car and met her in front of it.

He pulled her into his arms. "It's not stupid."

She clung to him. "I usually don't freak out like this. Just with all that's happened today with my mom. It's hitting me fresh again." Her frayed emotions were already on the brink of collapse. But to navigate through a snowstorm, the cause of her mother's car accident, was all too much.

He eased back to peer into her face. "That's normal, love. It's been a rough day." He pressed a kiss to her forehead, his lips warm against her cold skin. She couldn't begin to process that Pierson had called her two endearments in a few short minutes. Or that his mouth had just been on her face. He'd only meant to comfort her, but it did crazy things to her already jumbled heart.

If anyone understood her caution with snow, it was Pierson. He'd been there during those dark days. Was beside her chair in the hospital waiting room when Grancy tearfully told her that Mom had slipped into heaven. He held her hand at the funeral. They might have changed over the years, but they shared the bond of loss and hope.

"Let's get you home." His gaze was achingly tender, his thumb brushing the snowflakes from her cheeks.

They got back into the car, and Pierson pulled to the pump. While he topped off the tank, Elise concentrated on filing down her spiked emotions. Once her heart rate chilled, she opened her weather app. The radar showed a thin band of snow heading east. Though it appeared they should drive out of it soon, she prayed for safety. God had held her steady through the years, and she relied on His faithfulness to do so again. That covered more than a fleeting snowstorm. It also covered her findings of her birth father, her growing feelings—yes, she'd finally own up to it—toward Pierson, and her upcoming audition. She needed to trust Him through all of it.

They were back on the road in minutes, Pierson driving at a slower speed.

"You were right." She kept her stare out the windshield. "It probably would've been better if we'd taken your truck."

He turned down the windshield wipers and sent her a comforting smile. "Roller Skate is holding her own on the road. I take back everything I said."

The radar proved correct. Within thirty minutes, the snow stopped and thankfully the highway stayed clear. They reached her apartment around nine. Kinley was visiting her parents, and Elise wasn't ready to be alone yet, so she invited Pierson inside to watch a movie. They settled on the sofa, and her muscles practically sighed with relief against the welcoming cushions.

She picked up the remote and flicked on the TV. "Thank you for driving."

"I'd do anything for you."

Her heart lurched at his declaration. Pierson had her changing the tune of her *maybe*. As in, *maybe* she could embrace this dizzying rhythm between them. *Maybe* she could hum along, even though she didn't know all the words or how their love song would end.

He shifted on the couch, facing her. "I think we should quit the hunt for your dad."

She blinked at his sudden switch. "But you encouraged me."

"I know." Sighing, he slipped his arm along the back of the sofa. "I just. . ." He rolled his lips as if testing the words before he released them. "I just don't want to see you hurt."

She lowered the remote onto her lap. "You think this will end badly?" Her thoughts returned to their earlier conversation about Pierson's mom. He'd said it didn't turn out like he'd hoped. Lorraine Brooks wasn't pleased to see her own son. Elise's dad might not react favorably to her either. But then, why would he send her the package?

"I care for you." He toyed with the end of her braid. "So much it's messing with my mind." His eyes deepened in intensity, zeroing in on her with an emotion she didn't quite understand.

She looked away, glancing at the television. What she saw on the screen stopped the breath in her chest. "Pierson. Look." She pushed the volume button, and Pierson muttered something under his breath.

Kinley had been the last to watch anything, and she'd left the channel on a celebrity news station. A gossip network that Elise and Pierson currently headlined. "Someone recorded us at the gas station." They'd caught her weak moment, crumbling into Pierson's chest. It was humiliating and yet. . .

"I'm sorry." He rubbed her shoulder. "I wish I could protect you from all of that."

They'd filmed him kissing her face, his arms framing her in a protective hold, his arrested gaze upon her.

"Elise?" The concern in his voice pulled her back to the sofa. Where it was just her and him in her living room. Yet right now, they were in many people's living rooms.

She jumped to her feet. "I forgot snacks. We can't watch a movie without appropriate carbohydrates." Her legs couldn't carry her fast enough to the kitchen. Sadly, it was only across the room. Pittsburgh apartments weren't known for their square footage. And soon, Pierson was at her side.

"Talk to me."

She browsed the open pantry. "I have popcorn, Cheez-Its, or my personal favorite, Cap'n Crunch."

"Please say something."

"I am saying something. Did you not hear me declare my love for Cap'n Crunch?" She reached for the box and shook it for emphasis.

The worry lining his face made her chest squeeze. "No, let's discuss what just happened on the news. Our private moment was invaded. I need to know your feelings."

"The topic of my feelings is off-limits right now." Because currently, her emotions declared war on her rational thoughts. She frowned at her shaky hands and set the cereal box on the counter. Who would think prepping snacks took that much focus? Same with breathing. *In and out, Elise. In. And. Out.*

"I know it's upsetting. I've had years to deal with it, but you haven't."

Bowls. She needed bowls! "It's not that."

His brow lowered. "What do you mean?"

"Nothing." She swirled around and grabbed bowls from the cabinet. Next, she beelined for the silverware drawer, but Pierson stepped in front of her. "You should never get between a girl and her comfort food."

He didn't seem to care about her stress-induced appetite. "If it wasn't your privacy being violated, then what's the problem?"

"You. It's you."

Her words emboldened him to step forward into her space. "What about me?"

She'd never been a fan of the game twenty questions, but it seemed she was now playing it with Pierson, and he brought a new level of smolder with each round.

His gaze intensified as if his hot stare could extract her confession.

"It was how you were looking at me." She'd had to get out of her own head to see it. Watch it from a different viewpoint to realize she'd been seeing her interactions with Pierson through a cloudy filter. It took a cheesy gossip show with Barbie-like reporters to provide a clear picture.

Pierson gently took the bowls from her and set them on the counter, his hands now free to reach for her. She didn't resist. "How was I looking at you?"

"Like you are now." Like he was in love with her. "But I'm still not sure I believe it."

"Believe what?"

No, not going there.

"Babe?"

She pushed off his chest, breaking from his touch. "Don't you 'babe' me. I don't want to share an endearment with an album title." "The Day I Called You Babe" was the name of his last release. It really was annoying that he was so famous.

He shot a disarming smile. "What can I say instead? Call you the 'wrecker of my mind,' 'captor of my senses,' 'wrangler of my heart.' Take your pick."

"Those all sound clunky." She tried to make light of it. Because keeping things surface level was easier than mining the depths of her emotions.

"Elise."

Forget every other word in the English dictionary. The way his deep voice rumbled her name was enough to detonate her heart. How much fire could be stuffed into two syllables? Hearing it defied all laws of physics, making her insides blaze with longing.

He shouldn't be able to make her feel so much. He took a step toward her in that signature swagger, a flirty smile lining his million-dollar face. Pierson Brooks, casual and unflustered. At this moment, all she desired most was to knock him off balance. To rock his core, like he'd shaken hers.

Her fingers bunched the front of his hoodie in determined fists.

She yanked him to her and kissed him hard.

Pierson's lips stiffened with shock as she employed her best moves on the contours of his perfect mouth. Her plan had succeeded. She'd stolen his composure. The Nashville king stumbled off his high throne. Slipped into the bog of discomfort. Nosedived into—

His arms crashed around her, and he pulled her flush against him. His mouth, so unpliable a second ago, molded to hers with powerful finesse. He'd recovered quickly. Too quickly.

Her retaliation mission failed.

Because now he tilted his head, taking over with a fervency she wasn't prepared for. She was at odds with herself, her feet backpedaling while her lips pressed against his, demanding more.

Her shoulder blades hit the refrigerator, blocking any retreat. Not that she wanted an escape. No wait, yes, she did. Because she was melting. Her defenses. Her iron resistance to never fall for Pierson Brooks.

Oh, she didn't just fall. Her heart did an all-out faceplant into his waiting palms. And it was. . .wonderful.

His fingers hooked her waist, but his knuckle must've smacked the ice dispenser because several cubes rattled against her, onto the floor. She chuckled against his lips.

He took her teasing as a challenge, upping the smoothness of his delivery, sliding his hands to frame her face, angling her just so, devastating her with his touch. His mouth skimmed her cheek, traveling a delicious route to her ear. "Is this your way of saying you're into me?"

She tilted her head, giving him better access to the curve of her neck. "This was supposed to be a revenge kiss."

His chest shook with laughter. "I approve of your method of vengeance."

"You make me feel things I don't want to."

He groaned. "Now we're even." He tugged her to the left and lifted her onto the counter, bringing her even with his gorgeous eyes. "Because I've felt for you since you threw yourself into my arms at the hotel."

She wound her arms around his neck. "That's not an accurate account. I tripped."

"Tripped. Flung. Launched." He pecked her lips. "Doesn't matter. The end result made me a happy man."

She smiled. "You're ridiculous."

"I'm crazy about you."

Those words jump started her dream-fogged heart, revving it straight back onto the road to reality. "You're leaving soon."

He seemed more interested in nuzzling her hair than confronting the fact that in less than ten days they'd be in two separate states. "We'll figure it out."

Doubt crept in. Elise worked business days at Heinz Hall and helped Pap at the auction house every other weekend. There was a possibility of seeing Pierson only four days out of the month, minus travel time. And that estimate was if he was available. Undoubtedly, his life would be more chaotic than hers. "You know my take on risks." Careful not to smack her skull on the upper cabinet, she eased back, disentangling from his arms. "And this one's huge. It involves my heart."

"I'll tuck yours safely next to mine."

Her heart pounded its approval. "For this to work between us, we need to be completely open with each other." She ran her fingertips along his jaw, his stubble against the pad of her thumb feeling as good as she'd imagined. "Communication is key."

"I think we've been communicating very well." He winked. "But seriously. I'm all in with this relationship. All I ask is you give us a chance."

CHAPTER TWENTY-SIX

SOPHIE

*S*terling needed to know what I'd discovered. I dashed outside the theater side door. The alley had emptied of its previous occupants, a few crumpled playbills the only residue of the previous commotion. My gaze swiveled in all directions.

No six-foot-something detective.

I cut a hustled path, rounding onto Penn Avenue. Several gas lamps cut into the darkness, though not enough light to ward off the chilling shadows. My gaze snagged on Sterling's car, sitting empty on the corner. I frowned. Where had he gone?

Since I had no inkling when he'd return, it would be best if I went back to the theater and phoned a taxicab to drive me across town to Willow Courts. Hopefully, Lloyd would allow me to make the call. I wrote Sterling a note, informing him of my plans, slipped it through the narrow gap in the window, then turned toward the Loew's Penn.

I entered the backstage area swarming with activity and weaved my way through the hall. Some stagehands were roughhousing, playfully shoving each other. Not wanting to get pummeled, I paused near the prop room door, allowing them to pass even as a thought struck.

There *was* a way to uncover the truth.

Trying not to draw attention, I moved toward the large folding screen beside the stage entrance. The portable partition was intended for actors with quick changes yet not enough time to run to the dressing room. Though now it would serve as my hiding spot. I slowed my pace and casually skimmed my fingers along the rolling rack of costumes next to the screen. I feigned interest in a beaded frock, examining it from all angles. My gaze cut to the left, then right.

No one was looking.

I ducked behind the dressing screen. Lina had complained about a small crack in the third panel. Within seconds, I found it. The gap was no larger than the size of a raisin. It was risky because if I could see out, others could see in. But since the stage performance was over, no one would expect me behind here.

Now all I had to do was watch and wait.

I jerked awake with a start.

Disoriented, I grasped for my sheet, only to clutch my frock. My gaze bounced around. I wasn't in my bed but on the hard concrete behind the dressing screen. I blinked away the fog in my mind, wondering how much time had passed.

A sigh escaped my lips. My plan had failed again. I was a lousy detective.

Confident the Mirage would sneak into the theater, I'd waited several hours crouched behind the boxy partition. By the time I'd resigned hope, the overnight cleaning crew arrived with their buckets and brushes, ready for several hours of scrubbing the theater.

I'd been trapped. Because what excuse could I give if I was caught hiding behind a changing screen well after midnight? With no other options, I'd curled against the wall, waiting for housekeeping to enter the auditorium and leave the hall clear for escape.

But I'd dozed off.

Inclining my ear, I now listened for noise from the auditorium. Nothing. The cleaning crew must have come and gone. Eyes still bleary, I peeked through the crack in the panel. Certain the space was vacant, I grabbed my heels I'd shed earlier and padded down the hall, cold from the stone floor seeping through my stockings.

I glanced at the prop room. More specifically, at the door that had inspired my impromptu hiding caper. Hours ago, when I stopped to avoid the rowdy stagehands, I'd noticed a piece of cloth was shoved in the lock, which would keep the bolt from fully clicking shut.

Someone wanted access to the props.

My mind traveled to the instance a few weeks back, when I found the room unlocked the afternoon my paste necklace was missing. No longer did I believe that a coincidence. The cluttered prop room would be an ideal place to stash stolen jewels. Seeing the cloth in the lock made me suspect someone would try to break inside it this evening. Had they come while I napped behind the screen? If so, why hadn't they removed the stuffing from the bolt?

With a stabling breath, I eased inside the room and closed the door behind me. My fingers scrambled in the darkness until I found the light. A soft glow filled the space.

Now to hunt for. . .anything.

I rushed over to the tower of metal drawers and yanked open the one marked COSTUME JEWELRY. How easy it would be to disguise the genuine among the fake. No one would think twice about a gaudy ring or pearl necklace lying about. But how would I know the difference? Of course I'd recognize the emeralds, but as I sifted through, nothing struck me as suspicious.

On to the next drawer.

It was crammed with prop weapons. Knives with dulled edges. Revolvers with soldered cylinders. I glanced at a fake pistol, and my heart jumped.

This one hadn't been welded shut. Was it real?

I stepped more fully into the light and opened the steel cylinder. No bullets. The chambers were empty. I breathed deep with relief. Though it would be wise to hang on to the piece, considering it wasn't supposed to—

Door hinges groaned.

Someone was coming!

My gaze darted. There was nothing close to duck behind. I raced toward the filing cabinets on the other side of the room and stumbled over a fake sword. I quickly righted myself, but it was too late for any chance to hide.

A cart rattled through the entryway, pushed by a janitor. I recognized the gray hair and trembling frame. It was the same cleaning person I'd encountered the afternoon I'd discovered the prop room unlocked. It all clicked into place.

Startled eyes met mine. "Y–you shouldn't be in here, miss." The weak voice dissolved into an abrupt cough.

My shoulders squared. "Neither should you, Violet."

CHAPTER TWENTY-SEVEN

ELISE

*E*lise's destiny would be decided tomorrow. At half past noon, she'd play before a panel of judges for her audition, then three hours later, Pierson would board a chartered plane taking him to Nashville for a meeting with his record label. She'd be tested in two forms tomorrow— her worth as a violin player and her ability to adjust with Pierson being 562 miles away.

These past ten days had consisted of rehearsing, her day job at Heinz Hall, and more rehearsing. In between, she'd squeezed in dinners with Pierson. But even with all her increased practice time, she didn't feel prepared.

"Elise?" Grancy's voice drew her back to the kitchen table in her grandparents' home. Grancy and Dorothea had called an emergency poker match in a futile attempt to distract Elise from all the emotions concerning tomorrow.

"Oh, sorry." She grimaced at her cards and laid them face down in front of her. "I fold."

Grancy sighed. "This is the third hand in a row you've folded, sweetling. And you're not eating your dessert." She shoved the ceramic plate with an insanely huge slice of cherry pie closer. "You look too thin. Have you eaten at all this week?"

"Here and there." Food had lost all appeal. Even her beloved cereal. If it wasn't for Pierson's prodding while they were together, she probably would have eaten even less.

Everyone at this table knew the magnitude of tomorrow and had been supportive in their own way. Grancy helped Pap at the auction house so Elise could use those extra hours practicing. Dorothea messaged her scriptures each morning. And Pierson? He brought her food every night after work, encouraged her with swoony pep talks in his southern drawl, and overwhelmed her with kissing she could spin poems about.

Even now, he reached for her hand beneath the table. She glanced over, and his gaze was steady on her. Yeah, his mind wasn't on the poker game either.

They finished the round with Dorothea as the winner, her smug smile an exact replica of Pierson's. Her grandson might be the reigning champ in the ring of flirting, but when it came to the gambling arena, Dorothea held the title. With the haughtiness of a card shark in Vegas, she hauled in her winnings—ten packets of peanut butter M&Ms.

Grancy collected the cards and started shuffling the deck. "Have you heard back from Cade's yet?"

Elise poked her pie with her fork. "Nope. Not a word." She'd phoned the day after their trip to the Poconos, and the line was busy. When she tried again, it went straight to a generic voice mail. The computerized voice followed by a beep had been the response every attempt since.

"Maybe they haven't called because they can't help." Pierson twisted a lock of her hair on his finger. "It might be for the best."

She set her fork down, earning Grancy's scowl. "I just want to finally have closure." Before Elise had left Cade's restaurant, she'd snapped a picture of the Polaroid on her phone to show Grancy and Pap. Neither of them recognized the man beside her mom. Elise revisited her mother's Julliard yearbooks, poring over the faculty sections. Nothing.

Pierson's hand slid to her neck, his thumb grazing her collarbone. "It'll all work out." He leaned over and kissed her temple.

"There's no PDA in poker, young man," Grancy scolded as she dealt the cards. "But at least this time it's not on television."

Grancy might disapprove of the celebrity gossip channel, but Elise couldn't be upset that their gas station scene was featured. It had opened her eyes and brought her and Pierson together. Hopefully, they had what it took to survive a long-distance relationship. Her head had doubts, but she was learning to rely more on her heart.

Her grandmother sniffed. "But I'll overlook it since the two of you getting together won me a month of free car washes."

Dorothea picked up her cards with a grunt. "Only because I bet they would be a couple *sooner*." She shot Pierson a reproving look. "You should've upped your game for my sake."

His grin was stuffed with mischief. "Not my fault Elise took her sweet time realizing she couldn't live another waking moment without me."

Dorothea clucked her tongue. "Took your grandad and me only a week to reach that point. Young people nowadays move too slow." She turned to Elise. "Are you certain you got the right number, honey?"

"Huh? Oh, the number to Cade's." Dorothea had an interesting habit of resurrecting past conversations when others had moved on. "The Google number matches their website and their social media pages. It's all the same." She should have verified the phone number with Brody while she was there, but ever since seeing her mom and probable dad on the restaurant's wall, her brain was on parental shock overload.

Cade's number might have changed without being updated on the internet. If that was the case, how would she get in touch with them? She didn't have time to jump in her car and drive across the state. Wait. In her car!

That was it!

"Excuse me a sec." Elise shot from the table, ignoring the displeased grunts of the grandmas having to delay their game. She rushed into the garage, threw open her car door, and sat in the driver's seat.

She had tossed the receipt from Cade in one of the cup holders.

Got it! She unfolded the paper and sure enough, the number—a different number!—was on the bottom. Heart pounding, she dug her phone from her pocket and dialed.

"Cade Family Dining." A female voice greeted her.

"Hi, this is Elise Malvern. I'm calling to speak with Brody if he's available."

"Please hold," the woman said before a loud click.

Elise impatiently tapped the steering wheel. Whatever she found out over the next few minutes could possibly change her life. But then again, Brody's mom might not know the man's name, leaving Elise in the wilderness of the unknown. She hated that place, even though she'd been a lifelong resident.

"Thank you for waiting." The woman's bored tone wasn't encouraging. "Brody's on grill duty. He can't field any calls."

"Oh." She hid her disappointment and left a detailed message for Brody or his mom, then provided her cell number. After thanking the woman, Elise hung up.

It took several minutes for her choppy breathing to even. All this spiked emotion over a phone call. Perhaps Pierson was right. Maybe this wasn't a good idea. But one question bothered her more than she liked to admit. If her father sent her the ornament, why hadn't he tried to contact her since?

This was it.

Elise arrived early before her audition to compose herself and warm up. She worked in this building. Had walked this very hall countless times, yet today the space felt different.

Pierson kissed her temple. He'd insisted on accompanying her, and she was touched by his support. A few people glanced their way. More like glanced Pierson's way, but his focus was on her. "I'm proud of you."

"I haven't even auditioned yet." Her gaze bounced to the rehearsal room. She should probably go inspect her violin and keep her fingers warm.

"You're here, facing your fears, going after what you want." His voice held traces of pride. "You overcame your stage fright."

That was yet to be determined. Dread poked its tormenting reminder of previous auditions. Where she'd failed because of fear. But she couldn't dwell on the past. She needed to trust in God's faithfulness to bring her through.

She glanced at the violin case in her hand. Her mother's instrument. The day after Mom passed, Elise vowed to secure a seat in the Pittsburgh Symphony, to carry out her mother's dreams. She wanted to make her mother proud. But if Mom were still alive, would Elise have chosen this same path?

And why was she questioning her life choices now? Thirty-eight minutes before her audition?

A slight shake of her head didn't dislodge the mental block, but it did cause Pierson to give her a look of concern. "It's fine," she told herself more than him.

He swept up her free hand and kissed her fingers. "I'll be here when you're finished, and we'll celebrate before my flight."

She really loved his confidence in her but really hated he was leaving for Nashville. This would be their first test as a couple. Pierson seemed as invested in the relationship as she was. What worried her was how he would navigate the crazy vortex of the stardom universe all while trying to keep her a part of his world.

Her cell buzzed in her pocket. Ugh, she should've left her phone in the car. But one quick glance told her it was Cade's Restaurant.

Her heart jumped.

She shouldn't answer. This was focus time! But would she be able to focus if she bypassed this call? Probably not. With a sigh, she answered.

"Hi, is this Elise Malvern?" It was definitely not Brody. The feminine voice had the gruffness of a five-pack-a-day smoker. "I'm Pamela. Brody's mom. He tells me you want information about one of our customers from years back?"

"Yes, Brody said you called him Professor." She took Pierson's hand, needing his touch. "I was wondering if there was any chance you remembered his real name?"

The woman laughed. "I could never forget a man like Professor. He was that kind of guy you should never fall for but do anyway."

Elise knew the feeling even as *that kind of guy* gently squeezed her fingers. "So you remember his name?"

"Of course. It's peculiar, but one that never leaves a lady."

Elise held her breath.

"Dax Wittenhouser."

No.

It couldn't be.

Elise barely managed ending the call with Pamela and lowered onto a seat against the hallway wall. She'd only heard his name in connection to one other person. If what Brody's mom said was true, no wonder the man in the Polaroid had never married Elise's mom. He was already married ...to Meredith.

This could all be a misunderstanding. A mistake. But deep within, she knew. *She* was the mistake. Among the wreckage of her mind, two thoughts emerged from the debris of emotion and shock:

She was the result of an affair.

And her father couldn't have sent the ornament because Dax Wittenhouser was dead.

CHAPTER TWENTY-EIGHT

SOPHIE

$\mathcal{J}$he was dressed in a workman's uniform, her black hair concealed beneath a scraggly wig. Her creamy complexion was burdened with cosmetics. I guessed she'd used a specific brand of greasepaint, which, after applied heavily, would harden and form wrinkles, giving an aged appearance.

But under all the layers of disguise and deception stood Violet Salter. The Mirage.

We'd shared a stage, a dressing room, and a boardinghouse. More than that, we'd shared moments of laughter and friendship. She was integrated into almost every facet of my life, making this side of her difficult to believe.

But very much true.

Violet's rounded gaze dropped to my hand. "I'm not armed. No need to aim a gun at me."

Oh, the prop. I still clutched it. Though maybe it was wise to allow her to think this was a real firearm. "How can I believe you? You've been lying about everything." Her skin was currently masked, but she'd been wearing a false face for a long time. "You've mentioned how you'd do things for the thrill of it, but stealing? How could you?"

Eyes turning sad, she yanked off the threadbare cap, followed by the scraggly wig and glasses. She tossed them onto the cart. "It's not for the thrill of it."

"Then why?"

Her deep scowl made the hardened lumps on her forehead crack. "It's none of your business."

"It became my business when all of Pittsburgh blamed me for *your* crimes. Only hours ago, I stood outside for autographs only to be accosted, and poor Lina. . ." That earlier nudge in my brain twinged, realization finally dawning. My mouth popped open in surprise. "There's more to this, isn't there? Lina's in on this too."

She scoffed. "That's absurd. You know I can't stand the woman. She's—"

"Your sister."

Her hand flew to her chest. "I've never. . .when. . ." She heaved a sigh. "How did you know?"

"Lina was talking with a young lady tonight."

"So?"

"I overheard her passing on wisdom from her mother. She said, 'In the center of *life* is always the word *if*, but don't let that keep you from living.'"

Violet took a sudden interest in peeling the crud off her chin.

"I've heard that before. Because you told me on the walk back from the speakeasy. Only it was *your* mother who'd come up with that advice."

"We're sisters." Violet puffed her cheeks, then released the air slowly. "We thought if we pretended to hate each other, no one would make the connection." She moved closer but kept a wary distance. "How did you piece it together with the thefts?"

"For starters, the glasses." I gestured to the spectacles lying on the cart. "They fell out of your coat pocket earlier when I was searching for my wrap. I remember seeing those same thick frames not on your face but on an old man's. A janitor." Dressing up as the part of the cleaning crew gave her the ability to come and go without drawing attention.

"Stupid mistake," she scolded herself.

"But it was more than that." Speaking it aloud helped me see clearer. "Tonight you flippantly remarked about my 'new love.' But I never told anyone of my relationship with Sterling. I thought you snooped on our secret meeting in the rehearsal room. But you couldn't have. During Sterling's visit, you were on stage." I watched her expression crumple. "You didn't spy on us in the theater but in Greer's suite."

She nodded.

"You took the emerald necklace." I couldn't keep the aggravation from my voice. "You took it while we were all in the suite."

"I'm not proud of it." Her bottom lip quivered.

That was the evening I told Sterling about Greer being my mother.

Had Violet overheard? I was about to question her, but the stark anguish on her face stopped me.

"Don't tell anyone. Please, Sophie." She made a frantic gesture toward the cart, where I suspected this evening's haul was stashed. "You can't say anything about the stealing or Lina being my sister. It'll ruin everything."

"You're breaking the law." I couldn't hide my disbelief. How could she demand that of me? "This isn't some parlor game. You've been stealing."

"I had to!" Her anguished eyes welled with tears. "I had to do it."

Her muffled sob tore at my heart, but then. . .she was a performer. I refused to be manipulated by her antics. "You need to turn in the jewels. All of them." I started toward the cart, but Violet grabbed my arm with a desperate grip. I shook her off. "If you return them anonymously, I suppose I won't—"

She jumped in front of me, blocking the cart. "I can't give them back. He'll hurt her. I swear he'll even kill her." She hiccupped on a sob. "You don't understand."

Her entire frame shook. Gone was the confident young girl with the world at her fingertips. In front of me stood a broken spirit bound with fear.

I tossed the gun prop aside, wrapped an arm around Violet, and led her to a bench piled with ribbons and lace. I shoved them aside so we both could sit. "Tell me everything."

She gave a fierce shake of her head. "Nothing good will come of it. He won't stop."

"I might be able to help." Though I probably wouldn't be able to keep her from facing jail time. "Who's upset you?"

She shuddered. "My brother-in-law."

Whoa. "Lina's married?"

"Ten years ago, they eloped." Her tears carved tracks in her makeup. "I was really young at the time. I never met the man. My parents were so angry with Lina, they wouldn't let her come home."

I remained quiet, straining to connect everything, but it was like trying to put together a puzzle without all the pieces.

"I missed Lina. I ran away from home to go see her. I arrived at her house only a day after her husband left for the war. But when I saw her, she was covered with bruises." Her eyes closed as if trying to block out the painful memories. "The man was violent."

My heart broke even as my anger soared. Then I remembered the incident in the rehearsal room when Lina flinched at Gerald's raised hand. It all made sense now.

"I hated seeing her like that. The man not only beat her body, but he crushed her spirit. She wasn't the same Rose anymore." She gave a sad smile. "Rose is her real name."

I dipped my chin in a compassionate nod.

"I needed to get her far away from him. I made her run away. Since he was off at war, it was the best time. She changed her appearance. I helped her cut and dye her hair. She got rid of her glasses and put on makeup. Then she reentered the world with a different name."

"Lina Landis."

"Yes." She sniffled. "We worked a lot of jobs. A producer saw her waiting tables at a restaurant and offered her a small part in a show. It didn't take long for her to get larger roles."

"And you got into acting too?" I wanted Violet to get to the part where she'd assumed the life of a robber, but clearly she had more secrets to spill.

Her body had been tense and rigid, but the more she spoke, the more her posture loosened. "Lina was a natural, and she worked with me, teaching me what she learned along the way." Violet wiped the heel of her hand across her nose. "When she got the role here in Pittsburgh, I auditioned too. Lina insisted we pretend to hate each other. She was always scared her husband would find her, and she didn't want him to know I was her sister."

"But he did find her?"

"In Pittsburgh of all places!" She started crying again. "Why is he even here? They lived in Georgia. That was why I pushed Lina to move up north."

"But how does this tie in to the jewels?"

"He's blackmailing her." Her fingers bunched the loose creases of her trousers, her voice brimming with disgust. "He's threatening to expose her and cause a scandal. He'll paint her in the worst light because she left her soldier husband and carried on with other men." She released the worn fabric and took in a rugged breath. "My sister will be ruined."

I was reminded of Greer. How she'd lived the past two and a half decades in fear of being disgraced and losing her career. Yet Lina's situation was different. If her husband had mistreated her, she was a victim. But who would believe her? Society wouldn't. She'd be shunned without mercy. "What can be done?"

"I don't know." Her youthful eyes turned weary. "He taunts her with roses. That's how he sends his blackmail messages. Each bouquet says how much money he demands. He told her if she gets him all the cash, he'd leave her alone for good. But we really—"

"Wait." I flashed my palm, needing a second for my mind to adjust. "The man we all thought her admirer is her husband. He's the one who gives her the flowers?"

"The flowers are from him, but he mostly sends his 'errand boy' to deliver them." She scoffed. "Her husband has only visited her twice, to make sure she complies." She peered at me beneath glistening lashes. "Remember when she was upset about her costume? She'd refused to give him any more money, and he started pushing her around and tore her dress. She had to invent an excuse why it was ripped."

Understanding dawned. "That was why she accused you." Lina had stormed into the dressing room blaming Violet for her damaged costume, but it was her husband's fault. Lina also claimed the bruises on her arm occurred when she bumped into a door. Another lie to cover up her husband's attack. Such a man couldn't get away with this.

But then, Violet had robbed several families. Justice would demand that she pay for her crimes. This was all a mess. But first things first. "We can stop him." We had to go to Willow Courts and retrieve Sterling. No doubt he'd be there by now after the note I'd left. He'd know what to do.

"No, you can't stop him." Her voice was adamant. "A man like Percival Simmons cannot be stopped."

I pressed my fingers against my temples, my vision graying at the edges. Everything was blurry, especially my mind.

What was going on? Had Violet truly claimed Percival Simmons was her brother-in-law? Percival's wife had left him while he was at war, and that was why Sterling brought him to Pittsburgh. That wife had been Lina?

"But Percival Simmons is dead," I blurted out.

Was someone acting as his imposter? I needed to know more, and only one person could give me this information. His wife. "Let's go see Lina." I stood on shaky legs. "It's important I talk with her."

Red-rimmed eyes blinked back at me. "What do you mean, he's

dead?" Unfortunately, Violet didn't possess the same sense of urgency.

"Percival Simmons was killed two years ago. His body was found in the Ohio River."

"Huh?"

"Come on." I gently tugged her hand until she stood. "Where's Lina?"

"I'm supposed to meet her in the stage door alley." Her gaze lowered. "She's meeting Percival in a few hours to pay him off."

My pulse pounded. That didn't give us much time to plan. We needed Sterling. How would he react to this news? What if he wouldn't believe me again? "We have to go. Bring the jewels with you."

"I planned on it." Violet bustled about the room collecting the valuables from different hiding spots. A ring tucked inside a hat band. A necklace behind a mantel clock. She tipped over a vase, and several glittering trinkets fell into her hand. I must have had a shocked expression, for Violet shrugged and said, "We chose to store them in here because if anyone found them, they wouldn't be linked directly to us."

"I'm guessing it was you who took my prop necklace."

"Yes." She unscrewed a candlestick and pulled a brooch from its brass base. "Mrs. Stoneberry's necklace has unique settings. I thought it would be easier to sell if I removed the real stones and put them in your necklace. It didn't work."

"I see." That was why my necklace was returned the same night it had gone missing. "What about the bracelet in my purse? Were you purposely trying to frame me?"

Violet had the grace to redden. "No. I'm really sorry." She paused her treasure hunt. "Lina can't see well without her glasses. She tried to pawn the bracelet earlier that day to a dealer, but he wouldn't give her much. She thought she returned it to my bag but accidentally placed it in yours. She felt awful about what happened."

Which was probably why Lina went to the police station with the bogus story about a man with a mole.

Violet finished gathering her stolen items.

"Please hand over Greer's emeralds." I pointed to the large bag of spoils. "I need to return them."

"Lina wanted to give them back to you. She didn't tell me where she put them." Violet tucked the bag under her arm. "She feels bad that I took it. Especially knowing Greer is your mother." Violet waited for my reaction to her knowledge of my secret, but I had no response.

This evening had my brain scrambled to where I couldn't untangle truth from fiction. Was Percival alive? Was Violet being honest? How easy would it be for her to fabricate a story? I couldn't remember if Sterling and I talked of Percival in Greer's suite. If so, maybe Violet overheard and concocted this most ludicrous tale.

But why would she do that?

Hopefully, Lina would clear things up.

Being careful not to run into any cleaning staff, Violet and I moved through the hall and outside to the dim alley. The lights above the door were off, leaving the gas lamp on the corner our sole source of illumination.

Lina stepped out of the shadows. She saw me and bristled.

Violet rushed toward her sister and embraced her. "Sophie knows everything."

It was odd seeing them this way. For months, they'd been nothing but hostile with each other. But it had all been a show.

Violet briefly explained my presence to Lina.

Only half of Lina's face was visible, but I caught her sad smile. "We never meant for you to get caught up in this."

"Violet told me the bracelet was placed in my bag by mistake." I pressed a comforting hand to her arm. "I need to ask you a few questions. Are you certain that the man who's been blackmailing you is Percival Simmons?"

Her brows lowered. "It's him. I'd know him anywhere."

I nodded. A wife would know her husband, but for clarity's sake, I had to know one more thing. "Percival Simmons had a tattoo on his shoulder. Do you know what it was?"

"A rose. He got it because that's my real name." Her mouth pinched. "Before I knew he was a monster."

Lina was telling the truth. But many questions remained. The tattoo was used to identify Percival's dead body. If Percival was still alive, who was the man found in the river? "Was your husband here tonight?"

Her soft sigh was barely audible. "Yes. He leaned against that wall right there." She pointed to her left. "He gets cruel pleasure from taunting me. He sneered at me while I signed autographs, but then he left suddenly."

I gripped my stomach. The spot Lina indicated was the exact place Sterling's gaze had been.

He'd seen Percival too.

That was why he'd acted strangely. Why he'd dashed off. Had Sterling caught up with him? Where was Sterling now? At Willow Courts? Had he taken Percival to the authorities? I hoped it was the latter. Then all Lina and Violet would have to do was return the stolen jewels. There was only one way to find out. "Come on. We can talk as we walk."

Lina and Violet exchanged looks but said nothing.

I increased my pace. "When are you supposed to meet Percival?"

"At four thirty."

"In the morning?"

"I don't know why he picked that time."

Violet scoffed. "Probably because it would be most inconvenient for you."

"Probably." Lina shook her head. "He hates me for what I did to him."

My anger spiked as my steps clipped against the sidewalk. "What about what he did to you? You're the victim." But she was not the victim when it came to the robberies. "Though I disagree with what you've been doing lately. Stealing is always wrong in my book."

"It was once wrong in mine too." The voice that had entertained thousands grew feeble. "I gave Percy all I have. He took my savings, my earnings, everything. We've been living on Violet's wages, but that doesn't go far. Gerald was helping until. . .well, recently."

"Does Gerald know?"

"No one knows but you." She dashed a tear away. "Gerald thought I made a bad financial move, which in a way I did. I married Percy." Her laugh held no humor.

"What are we going to do about these?" Violet held up the bag of stolen loot.

"Give them to him." Resignation tinged Lina's tone.

Her words shocked me. "What? You can't give him those jewels." That would give the man even *more* incentive to blackmail her. He could turn her in for stealing, and I believed he would, especially if it meant ruining Lina. "Does Percival already know you're paying him with stolen goods?"

"Not yet. He doesn't know anything about the thefts." Violet wound a supportive arm around her sister as they walked. "But we don't have a choice. There's no one we trust to sell the jewelry to. It's getting too risky to take them to pawn shops. We can't come up with any more money. We have to give him the jewels."

Money. Wait. "How much are you supposed to give him?"

"Three thousand."

That was more than I had. "I can give you five hundred. Do you think it would stall him?" We turned the corner and Sterling's car came into view, still parked on the avenue. Dread curled in my stomach. There was no chance he would have left it here.

Both women gaped at me, but I didn't have time to explain my remark about my money. Because the problem had grown more complicated. "Sterling's disappeared. And I fear Percival had a hand in it."

Lina gasped.

I quickly explained how Sterling knew Percival and my dealings with the dice joint owner. How Percival had threatened me, using Sterling's life as a bargaining chip. "If he wasn't afraid to kill Sterling then, he wouldn't have any qualms now." Even more because Sterling could call the law on him.

Please don't let it be too late.

My fingers flattened over my heart as if I could physically keep it from pumping so hard. "Percival's been bribing you this entire time, holding things over your head, when he has just as much to lose by being exposed."

"That rat," Violet fumed. "What are we going to do?"

There was only one option left. "We need to go to Sergeant Hamilton."

"No!" Lina gripped my arm, her tone desperate. "Percy warned me not to go to the authorities."

Of course he had. "But he's the only one who can help right now." But could we trust the sergeant? It was hard to determine which officers were honest. Percival was once a cop. Were there policemen who knew he was alive? Were they on his payroll? I quickly changed my mind. I couldn't take that risk.

Lina shivered, shadows twisting across her face. "We have to come up with something ourselves."

"Then we need to figure out where he's taken Sterling." I shoved all the hope I could muster into those words. I had to find him. He had to be okay.

"No doubt Bert's watching him, since Lina has an 'appointment' with Percival." Violet glanced at Lina, then me.

"Who's Bert?"

"He's a large ruffian who works for Percival," Lina answered. "He usually delivers the bouquets."

He must be the "errand boy" Violet referenced earlier. My pulse, so jumpy a second ago, slowed to a dull thud. As if one sinister man wasn't tricky enough, now we had Bert the Brute to contend with.

Violet lifted her head in determination. "Let's go."

"Not you." Lina adopted a motherly tone. "I don't want you near that man."

"But—"

"Percy doesn't know who you are." She framed Violet's lean cheeks and kissed her forehead. "You are the most important thing to me, and I won't risk your life."

Yet Lina allowed her little sister to go about Pittsburgh in the dead of night thieving? Wasn't that equally dangerous? Violet could have been hurt or even shot by a homeowner or the police. But I wasn't about to mention that contradiction. It was obvious neither of them had been thinking clearly for quite some time. Which left it to me to devise a plan to save Sterling, outmaneuver a blackmailing husband, and subdue his brutish righthand man.

The odds couldn't be more stacked against me. Those men were strong, cruel, and most likely armed.

And what was I? An actress.

God help me.

CHAPTER TWENTY-NINE

ELISE

*E*lise's mind replayed a hundred different scenarios. It all made sense. Now she understood why her mom hadn't told a soul the identity of Elise's dad. Why Pap said Mom's eyes had always been a mixture of regret and pain whenever her father was mentioned. Why her mother poured all her extra money into Elise's trust fund since the day she was born, overcompensating for an absent father and to provide for Elise if the worst should happen.

The worst had happened.

And kept happening. It was like she'd lost her mother all over again. And now her father. She'd never met Dax Wittenhouser but had heard Meredith's ex-husband died three years ago of a heart issue. Her mother was a homewrecker. Dax Wittenhouser had been a man in his fifties when he seduced a woman in her twenties.

Had her father even known of her existence? Did Meredith know? Her music teacher had gotten divorced long before she taught Elise. Was Elise the cause of their split? If Meredith was aware all this time, why hadn't she mentioned it to Elise? No, it was more likely Meredith didn't know. Especially if Elise's mom hadn't told anyone. And she doubted Dax Wittenhouser fessed up to the affair. He obviously hadn't been a man to own his mistakes, since he'd ignored Elise from birth.

She was going to be sick.

What about her audition? How would she be able to play her mother's violin, using the techniques Meredith taught her, and not crumple into a heap of sadness? This wasn't supposed to be this way.

She turned to Pierson for support, but her throat squeezed tight as realization hit. He hadn't heard the phone conversation with Brody's mom, so she understood why no shock registered on his face. But there was something else noticeably missing—curiosity. He hadn't asked what Pamela said, but his features were somber. As if. . . "You knew, didn't you?"

He stuffed his hands into his pockets and dipped his chin. "I wasn't for sure certain, but yeah."

Her heart sank. "How?"

He stepped toward her, but she moved back. "I made a quick trip here in early January to instruct the movers taking Meredith's stuff to Legacy. I came across a black-and-white wedding photo. I didn't think anything of it until I saw the picture at Cade's, and it was the same guy." He sighed. "I didn't draw the connection to you until I saw the Polaroid."

"You promised." Her chin quivered. "You promised we'd be open with each other, and you kept something huge from me. Huger than huge." Her voice crept to an uncomfortably loud decibel, but she couldn't help it. "You knew who my father was." She felt stupid. These past two weeks, she'd been agonizing over the phone call from Cade's, nervous about what it would reveal, and her own boyfriend had the answer the entire time.

"I wanted to protect you."

"Oh, that worked well," she scoffed with an exaggerated sweep of her free hand. "Because instead of giving me a couple weeks to process and cope, I discover my dad's identity only minutes before the most important audition of my career."

He looked pained, but it didn't justify what he'd done. Or rather hadn't done, and that would be telling Elise the truth. He'd purposely withheld the thing he'd first encouraged her to find. She wouldn't have searched for her dad if it hadn't been for Pierson's urging. To help her get over her stage fright. Ha! She'd be lucky if she could walk into the audition room, let alone play.

"I'm sorry, Elise."

"Me too." Her temples pounding, her lungs burning from staccato breaths, it seemed every part of her ached. But nothing more than her heart. "I knew better." She draped a wobbly hand over her forehead. "I totally knew better than to believe this could work between us."

He flinched. "You're breaking up with me?"

"You should've told me." She hardened herself to the anguish lining his face. "I'd rather hear the news from someone I care about than a twenty-second phone call from a stranger." He'd no doubt banked on Brody's mom's ill recollection. How could he have done this to her?

He held out both hands in a plea. "I didn't say anything because I knew it would hurt you."

"Yes, it does hurt. Big time." She turned and brushed a tear from her cheek. "But what you did hurts just as much."

"Elise, I—"

"There's nothing you can say that'll make this okay."

A shaft of air cut through his firm lips. "There's the out you were searching for."

She popped a balled fist on her waist. "What's that supposed to mean?"

"I mean, you were never really sold on the idea of us." He matched her scowl. "You were hesitant from the beginning. Now you see a way out, and you grab it."

"Don't turn this on me."

"Instead of hearing me out—"

"I would've totally heard you out *two weeks ago* when you first knew about all this. But what did you do? Instead of telling me answers to a lifelong question, you tried to talk me out of my search." She pointed a sharp finger at him. "You broke your word."

"I planned on telling you after your audition. You've been stressing about it, and I thought the news could wait until you got through today."

Easy for him to say now. She doubted the sincerity of that excuse. But more than that, she hated that from here on out, she'd have niggles of doubt with everything he'd tell her. "And you get to be the judge of what I can handle or not?"

"Because I didn't want you hurt." He slashed a hand through his hair. "Because I love you."

She got in his face and shout whispered, "You don't tell a girl you love her in angry tones!"

"You're right." Still angry. He took a deep breath, and the storm settled in his eyes. "You're right. I said that out of frustration. Because I *know* you love me too."

She did. Which was why his decisions broke her. "How can I trust you again?"

He advanced slowly. "You're scared, and I get it. Everyone but your grandparents have left you one way or another."

Another tear fell, but she didn't bother sweeping it away. "You're leaving too."

"But you're keeping my heart." His eyes begged her to reconsider. "Don't give up on us. Not yet. Letting someone in is hard when you're used to no one showing up. I know that better than anyone."

Pierson had a long backstory of rejection and pain. But didn't this only confirm her theory that they were incompatible? Two broken people with acceptance issues. How could that work in the long run?

He exhaled. "It's hard to trust."

"Especially when you literally just broke it." She hated to replay that particular song, but the lyrics were fresh in her mind. He'd cut her to the core with his silence about her father. "I need time." Those were always her go-to words, and she hated that she went there. "I can't right now."

He nodded, a defeated smile lining his solemn face.

Her phone alarm went off. Twenty minutes until her audition. She silenced her cell. "I gotta go."

She walked away from him.

CHAPTER THIRTY

SOPHIE

*T*he entire city believed I was the Mirage, and tonight, I'd play the part.

My plan seemed flimsy, far-fetched, and something Hollywood producers would toss in the rejection bin for its ridiculousness.

And yet. . .the absurdity was the exact reason I believed the scheme could work.

I retrieved the cash from my room in Willow Courts and changed into a loose-fitting frock, wishing I owned a pair of trousers. I proceeded to Rumrunners Row, where Percival lived, which was also the meeting place for the impending payoff. Lina would keep her appointment with her husband, and Violet would remain as far from the scene as possible, per Lina's insistence.

Sterling wasn't at Willow Courts. I'd hoped I was mistaken about his disappearance and would find him waiting in the parlor, ready to scold me for being so late. But the sitting area was vacant as well as his room. I was fully convinced Percival had taken Sterling. But whether he'd taken Sterling to his shoddy lodgings in this crime-ridden district, I was less certain.

My nose wrinkled at the stench of mildew and garbage clogging the dank alley. Inclining my chin, I studied the layout of the rundown apartment building. According to Lina, her husband lived in the corner apartment on the fifth floor, and a fire escape was conveniently located near his back bedroom window.

My gaze followed the chain of vertical ladders attached to horizontal platforms leading to Percival Simmons's domain. But the question was, how would I access the fire escape? The lowest landing was at least twelve feet up. There were several discarded wooden boxes I could stack and climb on top of, but it wouldn't be high enough.

Keeping alert of my surroundings, I searched the dim alley for something I could use. A dumpster stood against the building, about twenty feet away. But it wasn't as if I could push the large metal contraption beneath the fire escape. I scanned the area just above the dumpster lid.

A ledge!

I squinted at the narrow strip of stone that ran alongside the length of the building. If I managed to climb onto the dumpster, I could pull myself onto the ledge, then walk the stony beam to the other side of the building where it met the fire escape. I'd need the agility of a panther, but feared my dexterity was that of Mrs. Fielding's three-legged housecat.

My shoulders drew back with a steadying breath. *I can do this*. For Sterling. For those women. And even for myself. Percival had ruined enough lives.

I dusted my hands on my dark dress and scaled the side of the dumpster. Simple. Hoisting myself onto the ledge would take more skill. The stone edge met my chest. I flattened my palms on the coarse surface and pushed my weight up.

I clung to the brick building, refusing to glance down. The ledge spanned only a foot wide, leaving no room for error. Several deep breaths cleared any dizziness. With a prayer on my lips, I forced my legs to move.

Left foot. Right foot. Hug the wall.

I repeated this process until I finally reached the fire escape.

After facing the hazards of the ledge, climbing the five stories to Percival's level was a cinch. The window was covered except for a sliver of space along each side of the curtain. I hunched low, keeping my silhouette from darkening the window and giving me away. Cautiously, I lifted my head and peeked through a narrow slit between the curtain and sill.

I bit my lip, stifling a gasp. Sterling was bound to a chair. His left eye was almost swollen shut, his mouth busted and bleeding. I looked away, grappling for composure.

Sterling was breathing. He was alive.

With quiet movements, I tried to lift the sill. Locked. Of course. A craggy voice drifted from inside, causing me to duck. Someone was in the room with Sterling. I braved another look and caught sight of the bodyguard Violet had mentioned.

Bert the Brute. His broad build wasn't as large as Sterling's, but the hard glint in his eyes made me reconsider my ludicrous scheme. Too late to back out now. Not that I would. Sterling needed me. I only hoped Bert's boxy head framed a dull brain.

This wasn't a fair fight. I only had one weapon in my meager arsenal—my acting ability.

One deep breath. Then another. I prepared for the most important performance of my life. Stepping into character, I straightened to full height and tapped on the window.

It took three loud raps to get Bert's attention. He drew back the curtains and cursed.

I rolled my eyes and huffed. "C'mon. Open up." I held his gaze and tapped again. "I won't stand out here all night."

The man jolted open the window, and I was greeted with sinister eyes and a revolver's barrel. I fought against a tremble. For this to work, I had to appear obstinate and confident. Two things I didn't feel.

Bert's lips peeled back from his teeth in an impressive snarl. "Who are you?"

I was thankful I'd grown accustomed to Sterling's scowls and glowers, because I was oddly unaffected. Though the gun aimed at my heart proved unnerving. I gave a snarky smile. "Don't recognize me? How refreshing."

He sucked air through his teeth, clearly unamused. "Who are you?"

"Didn't the boss tell you about me?" I rolled my gaze heavenward with a light shake of my head. "I was invited. Why else would I be here? Do you think I randomly assault windows at four in the morning?"

He pulled back the hammer, the cylinder rotating, positioning a bullet with my name on it.

I couldn't look at Sterling. The emotion on his face could make me falter. "Looks like you don't read the local news." I bent in an embellished bow. "I'm the Mirage."

A spark of respect lit his eyes. People were so strange.

"But you can call me Sophie. Since I started introductions, it's your turn, big fellow. Though I'm fairly certain you must be Bert. Percy told me about you."

His gaze raked me over, down then up.

I popped a hand on my hip. "We both work for Percival Simmons Enterprises. But. . ." I peeked over his shoulder at Sterling. "It looks like I get to handle the prettier goods." I lifted my other hand to show him the gaudy string of diamonds on my wrist. "I don't suppose I can leave this with you and skedaddle?"

His wide eyes locked on my wrist.

I gave a dramatic sigh. "I suppose not."

The more I spoke, the more Bert's fiery guard cooled degree by degree.

I gave the windowsill a friendly pat. "Percy ordered me to come through this back window since he's expecting another guest." I hoped my casual tone was convincing. I double-hoped that Percival couldn't hear me talking from the other room. Since Lina had visited Percival's apartment before, she'd explained to me the layout. He'd demanded Lina come to his place at four thirty, which was only minutes from now. I prayed Percival wouldn't check in with his underling before the meeting.

Traces of reluctance lingered in Bert's eyes.

"Look, if you don't believe me, take me to Percy." *Don't take me to Percy.* "Though he won't like the interruption. His 'guest' is some dame he's trying to weasel money out of." I nodded toward Sterling. "I'm guessing you've been banished to the back bedroom too, huh?"

He gave a tight nod. "Yeah."

"It's all such a bother. But hey, as long as I get my Benjamin Franklins at the end of the day, it's worth the extra hassle."

He lowered his gun and held out a hand to assist me inside.

My preposterous plan worked!

I slid my fingers into his strong grip, ducked low enough not to scrape my back on the window frame, and entered the room.

He angled to close the window, and I glanced at my bewildered beau. I mouthed "Trust me" and swiveled forward before Bert turned around. Hopefully, he wouldn't drag me by the elbow to verify my story with Percival.

I relaxed a little when he seemed content stalking about the room like a caged tiger.

I flicked a glance at the door. Lina should be arriving soon. "Did Percy mention how long this shindig would take?"

Bert shook his head.

"Too much to hope." I glided toward a table in the corner as if I owned the place. "Might as well get comfortable." I could feel both men's gazes on me, almost hear the questions in Sterling's mind. "Care if I have a drink? Scaling walls at night is enough to parch a lady."

I hiked the hem of my skirt and removed the flask from the bulky garter. *Do not blush, Soph.* The thick band, borrowed from Violet along with the flask, was positioned just above my knee, but the gesture felt scandalous.

"Simmons lets you drink on the job?" Bert's thick lips pressed into an indignant slash.

"No, I'm done working." I shrugged. "But to show my gratitude for you not poking bullets in me, I'll share." I extended the flask to him, then reconsidered, pulling it to my chest. "Don't drink it all. This stuff costs a fortune."

His eyes brightened as he accepted the steel bottle. He raised it to his mouth and chugged.

Sterling shifted in his chair, but I didn't glance over. It was paining me not to communicate with him, but one shared look, and we'd be sunk.

Bert lowered the drink and wiped his mouth with the back of his hand. "Lady, whoever you bought this from cheated you." His face pinched with a coarse cough. "It's diluted. Not the strong stuff."

It wasn't alcohol at all. But a near beer with a pinch of cayenne pepper to give it a kick. "Let me see." I snatched the flask from his meaty fingers and sniffed it. "You're right. That's what I get for switching suppliers. Might as well dump out the rest." Feigning disgust, I moved toward the window, but Bert blocked me.

"It's not that bad." He gave me a coaxing smile. "I'll take it off your hands."

"Fine by me." I surrendered the flask. "But you might want to turn your back in case Percy comes in."

"He won't for a while."

Good to know.

Bert downed the rest of the contents. *Atta boy. Drink up.* I moseyed to the extra chair by the table and sat down. The faint sound of voices drifted through the door.

Lina was here. Hopefully, the cash I gave her would be enough to stall Percival, and Violet wouldn't forget her part of the plan. I sent up a prayer and glanced at Bert. His hooded gaze was on Sterling, then drifted to me.

The flask fell from his hand onto the floor. He bent over to pick it up and nearly lost his balance. With an effort, he straightened and took a step toward the table.

"You look done in, Bert." I stood and made a show of dusting off the seat. "Take a load off. I'll watch your prisoner." I sent a look to Sterling.

"I might do that." His words slurred. He lumbered toward me, almost stumbling in the process. Then his heavy body collapsed onto the wooden chair.

I reached out and caught his head before it smacked on the table. "Sleep tight," I whispered, then pinched his shoulder, hard, testing his exhausted state. He didn't even flutter an eyelash. Good.

With that, I relieved Bert of his gun and rushed toward Sterling. His wounds looked worse than I'd first thought. "I don't know how much time we have." I stooped, set the gun on the planked floor, then focused on untying the bindings around his feet.

He peered at me through his right eye. "There's a lot I want to say to you."

The thin rope sliced my skin as I worked the knot free. "I know it was foolish of me. But I couldn't think of any other—"

"No, you were brilliant." He kept his voice low. "I mean about Percival. I'm sorry. I should have believed what you told me."

My chest squeezed at his apology. "All that matters is getting you out of here."

He gingerly tilted his head toward Bert. "Do I want to know what was in that flask?"

I tilted my face at him with a small smile. "A giant dose of Lina's sleeping powder. He'll be okay after a long nap." I loosened the rope at his ankles. "There. Now to get the rest." I stood and rounded to the back of the chair. His arms were stretched behind him, the ropes digging into his wrists, but it was his knuckles that caught my attention. They were puffy and discolored. Sterling had put up a fight. "There are some things you should know."

"Maybe start with those rocks on your wrist. Where'd you get them?"

"Violet's the Mirage. But she stole because Percival's blackmailing Lina. Lina is Violet's sister."

"What? I thought they hated each other."

"It was all a ruse." I tugged at the stubborn knot. "And Lina is Percival's wife."

A noise rattled his throat. "The one that left him?"

"He beat her."

Sterling mumbled something.

"Lina should be in the other room with Percival now." A soft grunt broke through my lips as I used all my strength to pull at the bindings.

"She's supposed to give him some cash." I tugged harder. "Got it." My voice warbled on a relieved exhale as I worked to give his hands some much-needed slack.

"What's next in your plan?"

I stood and wiped my sweaty palms on the fabric of my skirt. "Well, I hadn't—"

The door flew open, and Percival Simmons stood in the entryway.

CHAPTER THIRTY-ONE

ELISE

$\mathcal{M}$eredith had asked Elise to visit Legacy Towers after her audition, and Elise vowed she would. But first she had to get out of her car.

She checked the time on her dash. Four forty-five. Pierson was on a plane, returning to his glittering world, while Elise's lay in shambles. She'd powered down her phone at her audition and had kept it off since. If Pierson called or texted, it would be difficult not to answer. If he decided she wasn't worth the effort and didn't contact her, it would be. . .more difficult.

The sun glinted off the steel high-rise where Meredith resided. How could Elise face her? After performing, Elise had taken a long drive, needing to process. Because in the span of thirty minutes, she'd experienced the shocking news of her father, the shame of realizing she'd been a result of an affair, the devastation of her breakup with Pierson, and the emotions involved with the results of her audition. She'd postponed several sobbing sessions because she didn't want to arrive at Meredith's door with a soggy face. But there was an epic ugly cry in her near future.

She tugged her keys from the ignition and exited her car, the blustery wind curling around her. The walk inside reminded her of Pierson, of their moments in the lobby, the halls, the elevator. This place was stamped with Pierson prints, but then again so was her heart.

Elise forced her legs to keep going, though every part of her screamed retreat. She was about to chat with the woman her mother had wronged. How did one even approach that subject?

Her fist raised, poised to knock, but Meredith's door swung open.

A nurse, arms loaded with bedsheets, stood in the entryway. "I'm sorry, but Mrs. Wittenhouser isn't here."

"Oh." Elise nodded. The complex had several dining areas, recreation rooms, a movie theater, and spa. Meredith could be anywhere. "I'm sure I can find her if you steer me in the right direction."

"No, honey, Meredith's in the hospital."

There were two constants in Pittsburgh—the word *yinz* and construction on Highway 376. Elise currently battled the latter on her way to see Meredith, each minute in traffic spiking her blood pressure.

The Legacy Towers nurse said she'd had difficulty waking Meredith this morning, and when Meredith finally roused, she'd been alarmingly disoriented. An ambulance took her to the nearest hospital. While Elise was at Heinz Hall testing her musical merit, Meredith was at the University of Pittsburgh Medical Center undergoing her own tests.

Elise burst through the hospital doors and charged toward the front desk. The kind receptionist took pity on her, quickly relaying Meredith's room number. With rushed steps, Elise located the elevators and stabbed the UP arrow.

Come on. Come on. She tapped a staccato rhythm on her thigh. Finally, the doors dinged open.

Pierson stood inside.

He was typing on his phone, his eyes squinting, but those blues raised to her. His head tipped back in surprise. "Hey."

Shouldn't her lungs be expanding and contracting with oxygen? Breathing was a basic life function. Like blinking. But her eyelids joined the revolt, refusing to lower with Pierson Brooks in view. His presence had a direct hit on her vitals. He was the last person she'd expected to see.

He stepped out of the elevator, his gaze training on her. As if a reflex, his arms reached for her, but then the light dimmed in his eyes, and his hands fell to his sides. "I've been trying to call you."

Yeah, her phone was still off. But she couldn't think on that when all her focus was on getting her lips to form words. "Why aren't you in Nashville?"

He gently cupped her elbow, alerting her to the handful of medical professionals waiting to get onto the elevator. He led her to the side, then dropped his touch. "I swung by Legacy to say goodbye to Meredith and found out they brought her here. I postponed my flight."

But what about his meeting with his record label? Elise had no idea how that side of the industry worked, but she suspected missing an appointment with top-level music execs wasn't a career-advancing move. Though maybe he still had time to catch another flight. Not that it was any of her business. Not anymore. "How's Meredith? Is she okay?"

"She seems all right." He nodded, but there was a tightness around his eyes. Elise wasn't certain if his strained features stemmed from their earlier friction or the scare Meredith had given them. "All her tests came out fine. The doctors can't find anything."

"Oh good." Her relieved exhale could probably be heard four states over. "I've been stressing since I heard." Hopefully, Meredith would be able to return to Legacy soon.

"She'll be happy to see you." His mannerisms were off, just as hers were. She hated the weirdness between them, but there was no way to repair the damage done. "You're all she's been talking of."

Why did that suddenly make her feel guilty? Elise knew she wasn't at fault for her parents' sins, but shame snaked around her with a suffocating force. "I'm glad you were here for her." Her voice was thready.

"How did your audition go?"

She shook her head. "I can't right now." Because talking about the audition brought back the events surrounding it. A strange sense of grieving had taken hold of her. She mourned the death of her naive thinking regarding her mom, any hope for a reunion with her father, and the loss of her relationship with the man before her.

He dragged a hand over his crumpled face. "I'm sorry." His choked tone crushed her. "I never meant to ruin your audition."

His distress seemed to cast an invisible hook into her heart, making her sway toward him. But she caught herself and braced a hand on the wall.

"I planned on telling you afterward, but I also wanted the right way to break the news. I messed up on both accounts." He tugged something from the front pocket of his hoodie. A folded note. "It doesn't make up for my jerk decision, but this might explain more." He handed it to her.

She glanced at her name written in his handwriting. Her curiosity rose, but she couldn't read anything from Pierson minutes before seeing Meredith. Her composure was already thin, and his words and downcast expression were like a sledgehammer to tissue paper.

The mouth she'd kissed so often over the past two weeks barely lifted into a sad smile. "The only thing I can add to that. . ." He motioned at the note she held. "Is that mine is yours to keep, not to borrow."

Her brow lifted in question, but he gave her a parting nod and walked away.

Elise entered the hospital room and succeeded in not bursting into tears. "Hey, Meredith." Her voice was somewhat robotic, but she hoped her mentor wouldn't catch it. "I came to check on you."

Meredith sat in her bed, her back propped with pillows, a peaceful smile gracing her face. "Hello, my dear. I'm well." While her voice carried wisps of strength, the rest of her appeared weak. "I don't need all this fuss." She cut a judging glance at the beeping monitors.

"Your nurse at Legacy seemed concerned." Elise's gaze dropped to Meredith's age-spotted hand, specifically her bare ring finger. Her teacher never wore jewelry, and now Elise wondered if that preference had started with the removal of her wedding band. Elise bit the inside of her cheek, a feeble attempt to regain composure, and claimed the chair closest to Meredith's bed.

"You must've spoken to Nora." Meredith shook her head with a soft laugh. "She worries about everything."

Elise leaned forward, resting her elbows on her knees. "Not waking up is kinda a big deal."

"No, dear." Elise had heard that gentle rebuke for three-quarters of her life. *No, dear, don't play with a limp wrist. No, dear, adjust your posture. No, dear, that note's flat.* But this one was different because her gaze turned wistful. "If I don't wake here, I get to wake in a far better place."

Elise swallowed. "You have some time yet."

Meredith responded with a gentle smile, then studied Elise's face. "Do you have some news for me?"

Warmth drained from Elise's cheeks. Meredith meant the audition, but the word *news* sank into her like talons. She couldn't tell her teacher what she'd discovered. Not while she was this frail. "I advanced." But as a person, Elise had regressed in many ways. She was one giant lie. How did one cope with something like this? She'd only known this life-shattering factoid for four hours. How was she to bear the weight of this secret the rest of her days?

Meredith's head tilted. "To the next round?"

"Yes." Telling Meredith would be a betrayal to Mom. Which provided yet another reason why Elise couldn't speak of it. Though Mom had betrayed Meredith first. And then her mother had the nerve to place Elise under Meredith's tutelage. What was the reasoning behind that? "The callback is set for tomorrow morning."

Her eyes brightened, her thin arms spreading for a hug. "Oh, that's wonderful!"

Elise stood and carefully embraced Meredith, disliking how fragile the older woman felt. It would be unfair to burden her with the heavy truth. Meredith was too weak. By keeping quiet, Elise could protect her from heartache. She blinked. Then again. That was precisely what Pierson had done. Hadn't those been his exact words? That he'd wanted to protect her from getting hurt?

Suddenly, his reasoning didn't seem that far off.

Meredith patted Elise's back. "You took several minutes to mention your audition. I assumed you got cut. I'm glad I was wrong."

Elise was the one who was wrong. Everything about her, straight from conception, was the result of wrong choices.

Meredith still clung to her. "Deb would've been so proud."

A sob erupted in Elise's throat. Meredith's remark lit the fuse to her powder keg of emotions. Hot tears exploded on her face, her shoulders shaking.

"That's not a happy cry." Meredith's tone was quiet, but worse, it was knowing. She eased back, her eyes taking a long inspection of Elise. "You finally found out."

What? Meredith couldn't mean. . .could she? Elise could play dumb, but that wasn't fair to either of them. "About my mom?"

Meredith nodded. "And my husband."

Elise mopped her cheeks with her sleeve. "You knew?"

Meredith brushed the hair from Elise's face, such a motherly gesture that it almost broke her. "I've known since before you were born."

Huh? She lowered onto the edge of Meredith's bed. Elise could hardly be shocked, given how much she resembled Dax. But she was surprised that Meredith had never mentioned anything, especially since her mother died. "Why didn't you tell me?"

"Because Deb asked me not to."

"Wait. Mom talked to you about. . .this?" Then had the nerve to ask for Meredith's silence? Elise's stomach twisted. How could Mom request anything from Meredith after treating her so cruelly?

A wrinkly hand slid over Elise's fist. "I'm not sure of all you know, but let me tell you my side. It might bring more clarity."

Elise nodded, her mind like a ball of knotted barbed wire. Would untangling it all prove painful?

"My husband, Dax, was prominent in the music field. He was highly educated and highly sought after for his talent. He was also very handsome. And he knew it." Her face crimped with sadness. "He had the kind of charm that made you feel special." She squeezed Elise's hand. "Your mother wasn't the first woman he took advantage of nor the last. He was only faithful to his music."

"I'm sorry, Meredith. But that doesn't make what my mom did any less wrong. She was raised with morals." Something Elise knew because Grancy and Pap had parented her when Mom died.

Meredith nodded. "When she met Dax, she didn't know he was married. She was devastated."

"I'm somewhat surprised by the age gap. He was more than twice her age."

"He looked and acted younger than he was. I don't think your mother intended to get swept away, but Dax sweet-talked her. Told her things every starry-eyed girl loves to hear. He made promises of pulling strings and getting her an important seat in the symphony where he lived so they could be together. All lies." Sadness entered her eyes, making the lines of her face appear deeper. "It was the same stunt he pulled with all his flings."

Elise put her hand to her chest. "And you knew about his affairs? How could you bear it?"

Meredith shrugged. "I didn't suspect at first. But as the years wore on, I noticed things and confronted him. He was always repentant but never changed. He had a knack for saying what a girl wanted to hear."

Pierson had that talent. Even now, his letter seemed to burn inside her pocket. She guessed it was filled with a flowery apology. Perhaps he'd written her a song. But how could pretty lyrics mend broken trust?

"We went on to live entirely separate lives. I followed my career, and he followed his. It wasn't until your mother came to me that I realized enough was enough." Her gaze softened on me. "I wasn't able to have children. It hurt when your mother told me she was pregnant, because then I knew the barrenness was on my end."

The tears started again. "I'm so sorry."

Her dull eyes sharpened. "No, child. Don't apologize for your existence. God formed you in your mother's womb and called you His." Her tone was comfortingly adamant. "For years, I got my worth from my musical ability. And then from my marriage to Dax. It took my failings to find Jesus, but when I did, I realized my value came from Him. So does yours." She reached for her water on the side tray and took a dainty sip. "I regret to say, Dax never assumed responsibility."

"So he did know about me?"

Meredith nodded. "Your mom was a counselor at the summer music camp where he was on faculty. Apparently, she told him that final week of summer camp, and he ended their relationship."

Elise's chest tightened. How heartbroken and scared her mother must have been.

"Then Deb returned to Pittsburgh, where I'd recently accepted a position at the symphony. There was an article about my hiring in the *Gazette*, listing my marriage to Dax. That was how she discovered he was married." She shook her head. "I will never forget your mother's broken sobs. She begged me to forgive her."

In those fifteen years Elise was with her, she'd never seen her mother cry. It was hard to imagine. "But if Mom was so upset, why did she have you teach me?" Talk about rubbing salt in the wound.

"I asked to tutor you."

She blinked. "Really? I'd think you'd never want to see me. Especially since I look so much—"

"Like Dax. You certainly do." There were traces of relief in her tone, her worn features. One would think this would be difficult for her, but it was almost as if this conversation brought her healing as much as it did Elise. "But you have your mother's sweet spirit. Her goodness. She knew she'd made a mistake. I've never seen someone struggle with forgiving herself and accepting forgiveness more than her."

That made sense. Mom had never seemed interested in dating or relationships. It was almost as if she'd remained alone as penance.

"I told her if you were interested in music, I'd like to teach you. And that was how the whole mentoring program started." Her tone was nostalgic, and Elise was thankful Meredith could reflect on good memories. "You see, God gave me many kids I was able to pour my heart into. You and Pierson and others over the years."

Pierson. Her chest squeezed. This conversation helped sand the sharp edges of her heart. Yeah, he'd messed up. But if anyone had a right to hold a grudge, it was Meredith with her mom. Yet she hadn't. She'd revealed the heart of God, extending grace when it wasn't deserved. As a result, Meredith had become one of the dearest people in Elise's life. "I still can't wrap my mind around my mom confessing everything to you, a complete stranger. That had to be hard for you both."

"It was." She scratched her arm. "And it only got tougher for a while. After her first visit, I spoke with Dax. I told him he needed to step up and be a father to you."

"He refused."

A soft sigh escaped her lips. "He wouldn't assume responsibility for anything. I'd never been so angry. And oh, how I would pray for you. My father was everything to me, and I hated that you grew up without one. When Deb passed, I was already divorced but wrote Dax and pleaded with him to step forward."

Elise knew where this was going.

"He never responded. He died three years later." She slumped against the tower of pillows. "He lived only for himself. That in itself is a tragedy."

Elise noticed her weary posture and leaned to kiss Meredith on the cheek. It was time to let her rest. "Thank you for sharing the truth."

She smiled. "The *real* truth is that you have a heavenly Father who loves you. That's why I sent you that ornament. I wanted you to know your worth comes from God."

"That package was from you?" The violin ornament. What had started this search to begin with. It had nothing to do with her birth father. "There wasn't an address on the box."

"I thought I included a note." Meredith's head tilted. "Perhaps it fell out. It was a hectic time. I arranged it to be sent when I was moving to Legacy. I included my mother's coat, since you mentioned gathering items from the Loew's Penn." She gave a fond smile. "My mother was an actress, you know."

"Wait. Your mother is Sophie Walters?" Elise's head spun. "That means the necklace belongs to you."

Meredith's eyes widened. "What necklace?"

CHAPTER THIRTY-TWO

*P*ercival Simmons, with his handsome looks and regal bearing, fit the mold of a fairy-tale prince, but he had the soul of a villain. He stopped in the doorway, eyes widening at the sight of me.

The last time I saw this man, he threatened all I held dear, and now with his right hand clutching a pistol, it was the second act of the same play. His other hand clamped Lina's wrist, pinning her to his side as if she were a disobedient puppy. Dread pooled in her eyes.

Percival took in Bert, still passed out in a chair, the flask lying in front of him. "Drunk," he muttered, and before he could assess the thug any further, I threw my right hand over my chest and gasped, commanding his attention.

"Y–You're supposed to be. . ." I threw a tremor in my voice.

"Dead?" His brows lifted as if amused, but currents of darkness ran in his deep brown eyes. "Things are easier to get away with when the world thinks you're gone." He trained his gun on me as if to emphasize his point. By faking his own death, he could get away with murder, run illegal operations, basically anything. "Nice to see you again, Miss Walters."

"Leave her alone." Sterling's low warning set Percival to laughing.

A quick scan of the floor had me wishing I'd planned better. *Think, Sophie.* One trick of my profession was manipulating the audience— guiding their focus toward something unimportant to camouflage what was right before their eyes.

Keeping my eyes forward, I gradually tucked my left hand behind my back.

Percival caught the movement, and his mocking grin tightened to a scowl. He leveled me with a severe look. "Hands up where I can see them."

I gave a tight shake of my head.

"No?" A muscle jumped in his stony jaw, his gaze fusing to my arm. "What are you hiding? Come here."

"I still can't believe it." I shuffled a step forward. Perfect. Exactly where I wanted to be. "You're alive." Keeping him engaged with my theatrical remarks and mysterious hand-behind-the-back scheme, I hoped to keep his attention from lowering to the floor.

"Are you disappointed?" Percival taunted. "It was simple to hand over my identity to a chiseling bootlegger. Rid the world of a crooked rumrunner and become invisible."

The hair rose on my neck. He'd used a substitute. The newspaper said the body was ravaged in the river, the only identifiable marking the inked rose on his shoulder. "But the tattoo."

His eyes darkened with annoyance. "Not hard with the right tools." There was a faint wildness in his tone. "Now quit stalling. What's behind your back? Show me, or I'll put a bullet in his head."

Sterling's hands flexed behind the chair. He hadn't had time to wriggle out of the bindings before Percival barged in. From Percival's viewpoint, it appeared as if Sterling was still tied up, though his hands were nearly free. Not that it helped anything at the moment.

"No! Don't shoot!" I lifted my hand, revealing the sparkling bracelet, and could practically see greed sharpening his glare.

Lina shifted behind Percival, keeping her wary gaze on her husband.

Percival clucked his tongue. "Not nice to keep things from me." He cut a glance to Sterling. "One thing about women, old friend, is they can't be trusted." He jerked his arm, forcing Lina forward. "Right, wife?"

"Let the women go, Simmons," Sterling commanded.

"You're not in a position to give orders." Percival kept his gun on Sterling and spoke to Lina. "When I say three thousand, that's what I expect to get." He yanked her closer and ran his nose along her cheek. "Not five hundred."

Lina squeezed her eyes shut. "I couldn't get the money. I need more time."

Percival pulled away, his face twisting in disgust. "Know what I think? I think you're trying to pull one over on me, just like Sterling here. I had to sic Bert on him to show he can't sneak up on me. Now, you, Sophie, hiding your hand as if I wouldn't notice what's on your wrist." His voice grew devilishly quiet. "People should know better than to try to outsmart me."

The tendons on Sterling's neck tightened.

"Sophie." Percival's dark smile put me on my guard. "You have two seconds to hand me your bracelet before I shoot Sterling."

"Please don't." My hands fumbled the gold hook in frantic motions as I tried to rush forward. My shoe caught the leg of Sterling's chair. I stretched out my hands, breaking the fall, even as my kneecap smacked the hard floor.

All pairs of eyes were on me, one brimming concern, one in silent approval, and the last filling with cruel laughter. Pulling air through my teeth, I shifted and writhed.

"Behold your hero, Monroe. A genuine klutz." His coarse laughter erupted, and I took the opportunity.

The gun fired.

Lina screamed.

The revolver fell from Percival's grip and onto the floor. Sterling kicked it across the room, out of Percival's reach.

"You said it, Percy." I pulled back the hammer on Bert's gun, turning the cylinder. "Women can't be trusted." Earlier, I'd set down the revolver to untie Sterling. When Percival entered the room, the gun was in plain sight. I'd distracted him with my bracelet, successfully blocking the weapon from his view before pretending to fall so I could retrieve it. "Hands high, Percival, or this next bullet won't just graze your hand." Years ago, Sterling made certain I learned how to operate and shoot a gun.

Percival cussed but did as I ordered.

Sterling shimmied out of his ropes and gave me that smoky look. "Well done." Nothing flowery about those two words, but still, his husky approval infused warmth. "Keep your aim trained on Simmons while I tie him up."

I nodded.

Percival didn't put up a fight. Not that he could. Sterling outmatched him in size and strength. Lina's husband now sat in the chair Sterling had occupied. Within minutes, the captor became the captee.

I handed the gun to Sterling. "Sergeant Hamilton should be here any minute." Despite Lina's objections, I'd asked Violet to alert the officer.

Sterling's gaze dropped to my wrist. "Get far away from here."

Oh. Right. The stolen bracelet. We still needed to discuss what to do with the jewels, but now wasn't the time.

"I'll handle the rest," Sterling vowed.

I kissed the cheek that wasn't swollen, gathered Lina, and fled.

Back in my room at Willow Courts, I stood guard near my window, watching the fringes of dawn push through the cracks of night.

"Sophie really shot the gun out of his hand?" Violet's tone held the kind of admiration reserved for Hollywood starlets. She perched on the edge of the sofa, enraptured with Lina's account of the past two hours.

"She did." Lina's subdued smile split her exhausted features as she lowered beside her sister. "I just want to be free from him."

I released the curtain, allowing the soft fabric to fall back into place, and turned toward the women. "There's a train leaving Union Station for New York soon. You two are going to be on it."

Violet draped her arm around Lina. "New York's not far enough. We need somewhere quiet and away from everything."

My every muscle and joint protested, reminding me I'd been awake for twenty-four hours. I claimed the seat adjacent to the sofa. "If you and Lina leave the jewels—"

"We can't." Violet launched to her feet. "We don't have any other money. That rat took it all."

"Listen." My voice was equal measures compassion and firmness. "If the jewels are returned anonymously, then perhaps this Mirage situation will naturally quiet down." I presented it as if they had a choice. They didn't. There was no chance Sterling would allow them to traipse away with the stolen goods.

Forty minutes ago, he'd phoned from the police station, ensuring we'd arrived at Willow Courts safely and informing me he intended to contact all the stolen jewelry owners. He'd negotiate a safe return of their heirlooms in exchange for them not issuing any legal charges.

I faced Lina, appealing to her. "You don't want your sister always watching her back, wondering if the law will catch up to her. Return it all. Keep my five hundred dollars and leave the country. The SS *Belgenland* sails from New York to Belgium at the end of the week."

Lina pressed her handkerchief to her heart, her eyes widening. "You've done so much already. We can't take your money."

"But you're willing to take other people's priceless heirlooms?" I sure hoped Sterling was having more success getting others to see reason than I was. "Please take the money. I never considered it my own anyway."

"But to leave the country?" Violet pouted.

I eyed the bag of jewels in her lap. "It's the best solution. Percival Simmons will face judgment, but we all know the system is corrupt, especially here in Pittsburgh." Cops and city officials were given graft money to turn a blind eye to illegal activities, while judges were bribed to dismiss cases. "Sterling said Sergeant Hamilton is on the level, but we can't guarantee the honesty of everyone else."

Lina wrung her handkerchief in her lap, and Violet's lower lip remained protruded.

"I'm not trying to frighten you, but you need to hear the truth. Percival could be sentenced, or he could walk. If he goes free, he'll hunt for you again." It was possible he held friends in prominent places, yet I hoped he'd created enemies even higher up.

A knock sounded.

I rushed to open the door and found Sterling there. The left side of his face was swollen, and the bruising had purpled, but the corner of his busted lip lifted into a smile. I had almost lost him again to Percival's evil plans. But God had other ones.

I launched into his arms, and he grunted with the impact. I drew back. "I'm sorry! I didn't consider you having injuries elsewhere." Bert could have broken his ribs, and here I was, throwing myself at him!

He chuckled. It was such a beautiful sound. "I appreciate your thoughtfulness, but I'm fine. Sore, yes, but not too broken up that I can't hold my girl."

I beamed at him. His girl. That was a role I'd cherish all my days. "Is everything set?"

He nodded. "Simmons is in custody, as is Bert. Unfortunately for Simmons, his henchman is singing like a canary to Hamilton about his boss's underground dice joints. With all the crimes stacked against Simmons, it'll be hard for a judge not to convict." He looked over my shoulder at Lina and Violet. "But you can't be certain nowadays."

I agreed. "What about the others you spoke to?" I didn't need to expound further, because Sterling's gaze drifted to the bag of jewelry cradled in Violet's hands.

He gave a brief nod. "Everyone cooperated."

Relief washed through me. The owners of the jewels wouldn't press charges upon the safe return of their belongings. The plan was coming together nicely on Sterling's side. I wish I could say the same for mine. Because as of yet, the two sisters hadn't fully committed. "Is anything going to happen to me? I told Bert I was the Mirage." I'd used the facade to gain entry into the apartment, but had that been the wisest?

Sterling gave a reassuring smile. "We kept Percy and Bert separated, so Percival doesn't know you claimed to be the Mirage. And if Bert spills it, all you have to say is you pretended it all to save me."

A throat cleared behind me. Cole Parker lingered in the doorway. "Tell me, Sterling, how does it feel to have a woman save your sorry hide?"

Something sparkled in Sterling's eyes, and I felt like I was witnessing an inside joke. He bumped Cole's shoulder as his cousin brushed past, stepping inside the room.

"Ladies." Cole tipped his hat, and I made quick introductions.

"You work for a newspaper?" Violet's petite frame froze in suspicion. "Why are you here?"

Cole withdrew a notepad from his pocket and a gold-nibbed fountain pen. "I've come here to verify a scoop that the stolen jewelry has been anonymously turned in. Thus putting an end to this Mirage charade, so my straitlaced cousin won't have to marry an alleged criminal." He cast a look at Sterling. "Though I suggest waiting until your face heals. You'll scare small children."

Sterling grunted, but I detected his amusement.

The men's scheme was subtle, but I could see right through it. To guarantee Lina and Violet forfeited the jewelry, Sterling had summoned Cole to represent the press, basically forcing the women's hands. If they refused to surrender the jewelry, I assumed Cole would write an entirely different article. One that would incriminate them—and Sterling would be bound to take them to Sergeant Hamilton.

Lina stepped forward. "Yes, Mr. Parker. I request that our names not be published, but here are the stolen pieces." She retrieved the bag from her hesitant sister and handed it to Sterling.

The tight band between my shoulders relaxed.

Sterling glimpsed inside. "My clients will be grateful to have their heirlooms recovered." He shot me a look, and I knew he'd be certain to account for all the jewels before he allowed them to skip town.

Cole scribbled something on his notepad, then with a clap to Sterling's shoulder and a gentlemanly goodbye to us ladies, he left.

Sterling closed the door behind him and addressed Lina and Violet. "I'll see you two home so you can pack your bags, then I'll escort you to the station." That was Sterling's polite way of informing them he'd make sure they were on that train and out of Pittsburgh.

They both nodded.

I retrieved the envelope filled with my inheritance and pressed it into Lina's hands.

She looked as if she'd refuse but then, with a soft sigh, placed the money into her bag. "Thank you, Sophie."

"I'm just glad this all worked out." Everything. Percival locked away so he couldn't hurt them. The jewels returned to their proper owners. The two women getting a second chance at life.

She leaned forward and whispered, "Your necklace is in your coat." Then with a squeeze of my fingers, she turned toward the door.

What? I glanced at my burgundy overcoat, hanging on the wooden rack. Had she placed the necklace in one of the pockets this morning? Or maybe when I'd worn it to the theater?

Violet pulled me into a hug, her thin arms squeezing tight. "Goodbye, friend. I'm sorry about the world blaming you for the things I did."

"All is forgiven."

Violet blinked, incredulously. "How can you say that so easily?"

I smiled at her. "I know what it's like to do anything to protect someone you love." My eyes locked with Sterling, and I knew he grasped my meaning.

"Time to go, ladies." He adjusted his hat and hooked an arm around my waist. "I'll be back after I take care of the jewels. Don't run off on me." He winked the eye that wasn't bruised.

"You can't get rid of me now, Detective," I teased even as he dropped a light kiss on my lips.

The door closed, and I grabbed my coat from the hook, searching the pockets. Nothing. Had Lina meant the hideous duster I'd worn for a costume? I'd check when I returned to the theater. Though I couldn't care less if I found the emeralds, because I'd discovered something more valuable.

For years, I'd chased the spotlight, believing my talent was what gave me worth. I was wrong. I didn't need the world's applause because someone was cheering me on all along. God's love taught me I was never alone, and Sterling's love revealed the joy in second chances.

And that knowledge was more beautiful than a thousand jewels.

CHAPTER THIRTY-THREE

ELISE

A necklace." Meredith's rheumy eyes fastened on Elise. "Was it an emerald choker? On a platinum chain?"

Elise dumbly nodded.

The older woman's hand, though connected to an IV, pressed to her wrinkly cheek, her stupor lasting only a second before her mouth spread in a beautiful smile. "You found my mother's necklace. It's been hidden for decades."

Awe spread through Elise. "The emeralds belonged to your mother?" Pap had estimated the antique to have been made around the 1900s. The dates certainly matched. "Sophie Walters, right? You said she was an actress at the Loew's Penn."

Her narrow chin dipped. "Yes, Walters was her stage name."

The mystery of the hidden emeralds was solved. At least one thing had gone right today. "I'm relieved it belongs to you. I was nervous I'd found something stolen."

"It was stolen." Meredith paused. "By the Mirage."

Elise blinked. "I remember that nickname from an article I found. But I thought it was a rumor."

Meredith shook her head. "I'll tell you what my mother told me." She went on to relay a detailed account of how Sophie had been framed for the thefts and how the real jewel thief, another young actress, robbed to help free her sister from the clutches of an evil man. Sophie had a hand in returning the valuables and aiding the two women's escape. But jewelry wasn't the only thing taken. A romance sprouted between Sophie and the private detective who had stolen her heart years before.

Elise listened, captivated, her mind going to a certain man who'd stolen her own heart several years earlier.

"Where did you find it?" Meredith's question brought Elise back to the moment.

"In the overcoat you sent. Someone sewed the necklace inside the liner."

Her surprised laughter made Elise smile. This conversation seemed to energize her dear friend. "Lina must have hidden the jewels in the duster and left it there for my mother to find." Meredith's heart monitor increased in activity as she continued. "Lina is the actress I was talking about. She and her sister, Violet, were behind all the thefts. She told my mother to check her coat. Though to be honest, I doubt Mother searched very hard. She wasn't fond of the necklace."

"Why not?"

Meredith turned hesitant. "My mom was the result of an affair."

Oh.

"Her father didn't want anything to do with her and gave Greer Donnelly the necklace as a payoff of sorts."

"Greer Donnelly? The vaudeville actress?"

"She's my grandmother." Meredith softly laughed at Elise's shock. "Though she never acknowledged she had a daughter."

Elise shifted in her seat, bewildered. She felt a strange sort of connection to Sophie Walters. They both had fathers who'd abandoned them. And while she and Elise were not related by blood, they were linked by Meredith. "It's all surreal."

"It's how God works." A wave of wonder swept over Meredith's delicate features, making her appear more youthful. "This is an answer to prayer."

Elise's day had been filled with heartbreak on many levels, but this moment infused peace in her soul. "I'll bring it as soon as I can."

"No, honey." She patted Elise's hand. "I wasn't praying about the necklace for me. But for you. I want you to have it."

"No way." She lifted her hand. "That thing's worth a lot of money." Pap hadn't given Elise a specific amount, but she was confident it involved several zeros.

"Even better."

Elise opened her mouth to protest, but Meredith silenced her with that familiar teacher look. "Through Dax's selfishness, you were robbed of a father. I've been asking God for a way to make up for all that Dax should've done. I want you to have it."

"But that's not your responsibility. It was Dax's."

Thin fingers wrapped Elise's. "I don't have biological kids to pass it on to, but I've always thought of you as my adopted girl. You and Pierson will always be my kids."

Meredith had taught them more than just music. "Pierson should be here for this conversation," she said. "He encouraged me to find the person who sent the package."

"Oh." The wrinkles on her forehead deepened. "Well, we'll have to wait for the rest of our talk. I believe he left for the airport."

Her gut clenched. He'd postponed his chartered jet, not canceled it. Which meant he was gone by now. His note was still in her pocket. Unread. It could easily be a goodbye letter.

"Though I'm sure you need to go practice."

"Huh?" Elise's head tilted. Oh, the callback for her audition. "Yeah. I probably should rehearse."

"Not much enthusiasm, dear." Meredith gave a knowing smile. "You know, your mother never expected you to make a career of it. She only wanted you to find something you love."

"I love the violin." But Elise loved a lot of things. Her camera. Digital storytelling. Pierson's voice. The look in his eyes when he said her name. His—

There was a trend here.

And it all involved a man who'd dropped back into her world four weeks ago and changed the rotation of her heart.

"You need to follow what's inside." Meredith pressed a hand to her chest. "Don't settle for anything less. Because you'll never be happy chasing someone else's dream."

Was that what Elise was doing? Following her mother's dream? Or had it been her own? She had a spark of doubt before her audition today, and Meredith's words had just doused it with kerosene. "Thank you, Meredith." She carefully hugged her. "For everything. Though we need to talk about this necklace more. I really don't think I should accept."

"It's yours. You'll find I'm a stubborn woman when it comes to getting my prayers answered." She settled back against her pillows. "Now I can finally rest."

Sensing Meredith's exhaustion, Elise said goodbye, exiting into the hall. She tugged Pierson's note from her pocket and unfolded it. She didn't know what to expect. It could be anything from a song of apology to a farewell note. What she hadn't counted on was seeing her own handwriting. Pierson had given Elise a letter she'd penned ten years ago. She gaped at the bubbly letters, complete with her short-lived phase of dotting the i's with little hearts.

I'm sorry about your dad. I know it hurts. I wish I could let you borrow my heart until yours feels better. Don't forget God's the best Father, and He won't leave you.

Elise remembered writing this. It was summer, and Pierson's dad was supposed to pick him up for a fishing trip, but he never showed. Pierson was devastated. Elise recalled feeling stupid when she handed him the note.

Yet he'd kept it all this time?

In the letter, Elise said she'd loan Pierson her heart until his felt better, but this afternoon by the elevators, Pierson amended that part.

"Mine is yours to keep, not to borrow."

Tears stung. How could she respond to that?

Only one way came to mind.

This was reckless. A total un-Elise move.

But it was also right.

She felt it all the way to her marrow. She also felt annoyed that her phone had died. No cell meant she couldn't call or text him.

Her plan was formed before she exited the hospital lot. It was sketchy at best. She'd drive to the terminal for charter aircrafts and check if Pierson had left. Well, that part of her scheme was already busted. She hadn't reached the first gate alongside a stretch of fenced-off tarmac before someone flagged her down, making her turn her car around. The only information she'd received from Chandler, the guard, was that a private jet left twenty minutes ago.

Phase two? Book a flight to Nashville. It was extreme. Crazy. She hadn't packed a thing. Didn't know if there was even a departing plane. Didn't know where Pierson lived. The what-ifs piled her mind like clutter on the luggage carousel, reminding her of the heavy baggage between them.

Frustration gathered in her chest, making her breaths heavy. She should just go home and call him later.

But that didn't seem. . .enough.

She could at least see if there was a flight to Nashville and go from there. With her phone still dead and unable to check departures, she eyed the commercial airport in the distance and then shifted her car into drive. The main lobby was packed, but she snaked her way to the giant screen of arrivals and departures.

She hastily scanned the list.

A plane was scheduled for the country music capital at seven thirty with the longest layover in commercial flight history. Better than nothing. Six weeks ago, her cowardly soul couldn't force her finger to click submit for an audition application. Could she force herself to board a plane, forfeiting her chance tomorrow morning with the symphony, with no guarantee of a future with Pierson? He'd told her she had his heart. Was there fine print on that? The possibility of takebacks?

She straightened her spine, determination shoving aside doubt. Today, she wouldn't let another opportunity slip without a fight.

It was the Hail Mary with two seconds left on the clock. The nineties rom-com with an absurd grand gesture. The poker game where she shoved all her chips to the center of the table.

It was the risk that would now define Elise Malvern.

Where she'd chased what *she* wanted. Pursued the one who—

"Elise?"

See? Even his voice was embedded in her brain. Another confirmation she was doing the right thing.

A large hand cradled her shoulder, and she jolted.

Pierson stood there in his signature ball cap. The brim was pulled low, but it didn't hide the surprise in his eyes. "You're browsing departing flights."

She bit her lip with a nod.

"Planning to take a trip?"

"I was going after you." In romance novels, those words sounded epic, but from her mouth, they came out on the lame side of awkward.

But it drew Pierson close. "After me? You were planning on going to Nashville?"

Another nod. When devising her plan, she probably should've rehearsed what she would say. "How did you know I was here?"

"Funny thing." He shoved his hands into his pockets, his gaze set on her. "I was finishing up business with my pilot when I spotted this young woman jumping out of a red Barbie car at the gate and pleading with the attendant." He stepped toward her. "A few well-placed questions with the guard, and he told me a lovesick fan was begging to speak with me."

"I deny begging." She picked at her thumbnail. "It was more of a passionate appeal to Chandler's sensitivities. He's a calloused man."

His knuckle stroked her cheek. A cheek that may or may not have had a few tears on it. "But you don't deny being lovesick?"

Her lips went comatose. Though her silence seemed all the encouragement he needed.

He moved in, hands at her waist, eyes hot on hers. "I followed you here. On the way, I called to check on Meredith. She told me about your audition tomorrow."

Elise nodded.

"Yet you're taking a trip to Nashville?" His hands slipped up her arms, cupping her shoulders. "You can't give up that audition. The symphony is what you've been working toward. I won't let you waste your chance on me."

"It hurt more to lose you than an audition." And there it was. The biggest gamble she'd ever wagered because she stood the very possible chance of going broke. "There's no music without you."

His gaze darkened with intensity, then his lips were on hers. In the middle of the noisy airport, they created a song between them, sharing that beautiful rhythm of give and take. He pulled back only to kiss her again with so much fervency she hoped it wouldn't be broadcast on the nightly news.

Then again, she didn't care. Let the world know how much she loved this man.

When they finally broke apart, he took her hand and pressed his lips to the inside of her wrist. "Just so you know, I'm not headed to Nashville tonight. I canceled."

"But what about your meeting?"

"I asked to reschedule." He shrugged as if it was no big deal. "I hated leaving things between us as they were." He pulled her to him. "I've filled my life with many things, and I can walk away from all of it. But I won't walk away from you."

CHAPTER THIRTY-FOUR

Sophie

This second chance was a beautiful gift.

Elissa Parker, resplendent in a blush pink matron-of-honor gown, delicately lowered the sheer veil over my face. "Cole bet me two dollars that Sterling cries when he sees you."

It was I who held back tears. Here I stood, in a lace-layered gown, in the same church from before, about to pledge my life to the man who'd held my heart for so long it beat only for him.

Sterling's aunt made a disapproving noise behind me. "You two and your wagers." She rounded to the front of me, stepping past a child's wooden rocking horse. We'd employed the church's nursery as the bridal changing room. "You look stunning, Sophie."

"I told you that cut of dress is perfect." Greer handed me the bridal bouquet with a knowing smile. Our relationship had improved over the past few months. She still forbade me to call her Mother, but she insisted on accompanying me for all the motherly duties involved in wedding preparation, including shopping for a gown. I didn't tell her about the emeralds because. . .well, I didn't know what had happened to them. I'd searched every coat I owned and found nothing.

I hadn't heard from Lina and Violet, except for a postcard informing me they'd arrived in Belgium. Because I was Lina's understudy, I stepped in for the leading role for the show's final two weeks and subsequently resigned. Lloyd allowed me to keep that bulky duster jacket as a parting gift. The hideous costume wasn't worth the hanger it hung on, but to me, it held sentimental value. It was what I'd worn the night Sterling walked back into my life. As expected, the returned jewels quelled rumors of the Mirage, but accusations against Percival Simmons surged.

It was revealed that Percival continued his underground dice joint these past years, and men he'd swindled were stepping forward by the droves. Lina wasn't the only person he'd blackmailed. The man had so much evidence against him that Sterling believed he'd be locked away for a long while.

I took a final glimpse in the mirror. I would no longer be Sophie Winslow, the orphan, or Sophie Walters, the actress, but soon a Monroe. Sterling would give me his name as wonderfully as he'd given me his affection.

The intro to "The Bridal Chorus" floated through the doors, and I took a deep breath. "I'm ready, God." I may not have had an earthly father to give me away, but I had a heavenly one whose presence was as tangible as the fragrance of gardenias filling the foyer.

The doors opened, and with my head held high and my heart soaring even higher, I finally—finally!—walked down that aisle toward the man I loved.

The pews brimmed with family and friends on their feet. Well, mostly Sterling's family, but today I would gain a family I'd been robbed of for so long. My gaze connected with Sterling's and held. His hands folded in front of him, his shoulders squared, and his stance wide as if ready to chase after me if I bolted.

The song's tempo decreased, making me slow my steps to match the sluggish pace. Then to my dismay, the march reduced to a crawl. The sweet organist was in her mid-eighties, with significant hearing loss, but I'd waited long enough to reach this moment and wasn't about to let anything hold me back. I pressed my bouquet into an unsuspecting guest's hands and took off toward Sterling. If he had any doubts about my hesitancy, my mad dash down the aisle removed it all.

His smile broke free, and he opened his arms as I reached the front. I fell into him and found myself lifted off the ground.

His lips brushed my ear. "I thought you'd never make it to the altar." There was a dual meaning I felt to my soul.

"Nothing's going to stop me from becoming your wife." I curled one arm around his neck and flattened my other hand against his vest. The buttons that had belonged to his father pressed into my palm. Everything felt right.

His kiss feathered my temple as he set me down. "I love you, Sophie."

Fusing my gaze to his, I realized Cole had won two dollars.

CHAPTER THIRTY-FIVE

*M*eredith had gone home.

Not to Legacy Towers but to her heavenly residence.

Two days after Elise's audition, she'd received the call relaying her mentor's passing.

Now I can finally rest, Meredith had said after their conversation about the necklace.

Elise had taken it in the physical sense, but considering how peaceful her friend had been, she should have recognized the tug of the eternal on Meredith's aged soul.

An entire month had passed. Elise woke this morning a year older, a tad wealthier due to her trust fund, and a degree on the somber side. This was not only her first birthday without Meredith but also her first with a full awareness of her parents' history. She'd been studying scriptures on identity, which helped ground her. God didn't see her as a mistake but as the apple of His eye.

Of course, Pierson overcompensated, arriving in Pittsburgh at the beginning of the week and packing each day with delightful distractions. Like during her lunch break today, he'd surprised her with street tacos arranged in the number twenty-five, earning him boyfriend bonus points. Though he'd been curiously cryptic about their plans for this evening.

Pierson had informed others of the top-secret date. Elise arrived home from work, and Kinley immediately activated primp mode. By the fourth hair product and facial treatment, Elise was officially suspicious. But Kinley's Best Friend Loyalty card must have expired because the woman wouldn't divulge a thing, fussing over Elise until she was "runway chic." Kinley's words.

With her sleek hair and pristine makeup, Elise looked more suitable for the red carpet than for going out to dinner. Though she did feel attractive in her classy black dress hugging all the right spots.

At seven that night, her doorbell rang.

Pierson stood in a gray suit, tailored to perfection. His gaze swung over her in masculine appreciation, sending a bolt of warmth through her.

He swallowed. "You look. . ." Another sweep of her form. "Amazing. I may have to cancel our plans," he teased. "I don't want to share you tonight." He wrapped his hand around her waist and pulled her to him. "So are you going to tell me about your decision?"

Her Heinz Hall internship ended next week, forcing her to think about her future. "Only if you tell me what you're hiding behind your back." As if she wouldn't notice his left hand tucked away.

"Deal. But you go first."

She agreed. "I'm done pursuing a career in music."

His smile dropped. "You sure?"

She pressed her cheek against his shoulder. "It's the right thing." She tipped her chin to look into his face. "I'm glad I followed through with the callback audition because if I hadn't, there would always be a "what-if" hanging over my head. But when I didn't advance the second round, I wasn't heartbroken like I thought I'd be." Her performance wasn't flawless, but it was her best effort. "I've learned a lot these past two months."

She toyed with the edges of his lapel. "I realized I've been trying to keep my mom alive through this dream. I played her violin. Wanted to perform on the same stage she did. The same section." Saying this aloud brought healing.

His free hand slid over her back. "And now?"

"She'll always be a part of me, but I'm going to pursue what I want."

His gaze zeroed in on her. "And what do you want?"

"Not a music career. When I was coping with Meredith's passing, I didn't reach for my violin."

"You grabbed your camera."

"How'd you know?" She'd spent the nights Pierson was away snapping photos reminding her of Meredith. The old church where they'd held their recitals. Meredith's favorite restaurant. And her last house, where Elise came to know her as a friend rather than a teacher. It had helped her through the grieving period.

Pierson pressed a kiss to her forehead. "I told you in your grandmother's attic, remember? You're a storyteller. And your camera is your medium."

She smiled. "I always thought photography was my hobby and the violin was my career, but I'm seeing I had it reversed." Elise had ideas for her own marketing business, and without the overhead of a building, she could start up anywhere, like in Nashville.

"Speaking of reversed, I'm taking us back several years." He finally brought his arm forward, revealing what he'd been hiding.

"Is that. . .a corsage?" She gaped at the beautiful white and pink flowers.

He cracked open the box. "I know I'm nine years too late, but will you go to prom with me?"

This was what he'd been planning? "Hmm. The last guy who asked me to prom ended up giving me the silent treatment for almost a decade. I don't want history to repeat itself."

"We're rewriting history, darlin'." He slid the corsage onto her wrist and grinned. "Come to prom with me." His voice dropped to a low, sizzling whisper. "There's a whole snack table dedicated to every flavor of Skittles."

She laughed. "With temptations like that, how can I refuse?" But first she had to retrieve something.

She glided to her bedroom and returned with the emerald necklace. "In honor of Meredith." And Sophie. The women, Elise included, had been forgotten and abandoned by the men who were supposed to love them. For Meredith and Elise, it had been Dax, and for Sophie, her father. An emerald symbolized rebirth. Like the newness of spring after a long winter. So on her birthday, Elise would wear the necklace as an outward show of her rediscovered joy.

Pierson led her to his truck and opened the door. She didn't have time to question where they were headed because, within seconds, they were there.

Heinz Hall.

Her mouth dropped open. "You rented the lobby?" The beautiful space was often booked for weddings and engagement shoots.

He nodded with a downplayed smile.

They parked, and he escorted her inside. She paused in wonder at the atmospheric grandeur. The glittering chandeliers were bright, casting crystal flecks onto the glossy marble floor. Gold sconces were lit along the base of Corinthian pillars stretching into the arched ceiling.

But as beautiful as this venue was, the people who filled it were more so. Elise hugged Grancy and Pap. Then Dorothea. Kinley waved from beside the dessert table. A live band was set up on the other side. Her gaze lifted to the balcony where a sign hung reading ELISE MALVERN'S PROM. She laughed even as her heart swelled with affection. "Thank you." She pressed a soft kiss to his lips. "I love you, Brooks."

"Likewise, Malvern." His arms wrapped around her like a promise.

Then they danced while Pierson crooned love songs in her ear.

God's plan hadn't seemed to make sense, but then again, neither did sheet music at first glance. To most, it only looked like varying dots smattered across lines. But those notes were deliberate, placed for a specific purpose. And when all strung together, a song was created. He was the masterful composer of Elise's life, a beautiful melody to her days. By His grace, she was more than willing to sing along.

AUTHOR'S NOTES

*W*hile a lot of old-time theaters have legends and folklores tied to their names, the Mirage at Loew's Penn is entirely from my imagination. But there are some fun truths that I was able to insert into the story.

The Loew's Penn opened its doors on Tuesday, September 7, 1927, to a waiting line of guests stretching down the street and around the corner. Many referred to it as the "Temple of Cinema" because it was the grandest theater between New York and Chicago. Loew's Penn ran nightly live stage performances followed by the latest silent movie. The theater hosted many popular traveling acts. Bing Crosby did indeed perform at the Loew's Penn when he toured the country with the Rhythm Boys.

The Loew's Penn Theatre boasted a large pipe organ designed by Robert Morton. At the time, it was the largest organ in Pittsburgh, earning the billing as "the greatest musical instrument the world has ever known." The organ could produce the sound of every orchestra instrument with the volume of a fifty-man orchestra played by Dick Leibert in the 1920s. Sadly, there was a historic flood on St. Patrick's Day in 1936, which wrecked most of downtown Pittsburgh. Many theaters had shut down due to the devastation, and while the Loew's Penn building survived the flood, the organ was destroyed.

The Loew's Penn continued falling into disrepair until the mid-sixties, when it was purchased and restored by John Heinz. On September 10, 1971, the theater reopened as Heinz Hall for the Performing Arts. Heinz Hall is now owned by the Pittsburgh Symphony Orchestra.

Pittsburgh's fourth river is also a little-known fact. There really is an ancient aquifer that runs beneath the city. The wall fountain in the Heinz Hall courtyard taps into the secret waters, and I thought it'd be so much fun to incorporate that into the story.

The William Penn Hotel is an elegant, historic hotel in downtown

Pittsburgh. It's true that during Prohibition, there was a speakeasy beneath the lobby, which had a secret tunnel leading to the street in case of a raid. The speakeasy has been restored and is open to the public inside the hotel.

On a personal note, I really enjoyed setting both timelines in Pittsburgh. I grew up only a few minutes north of the Steel City. My middle school field trip was to Heinz Hall, where we attended a symphony performance. Little did I know that twenty-five years later, I'd be setting a mystery in that beautiful theater.

ACKNOWLEDGMENTS

This is the part where I get to brag on all the awesome people who helped make this book happen. Let it be known to everyone that this story is a product of the grace of God. No question. One thing after another came against my deadline to the point that if I listed it all, it'd take up most of this section. Just know that God helped me BIG time.

A huge thanks to my agent, Julie, who always champions my stories and is always there when I need help. You're the best, Julie! Also, a huge shout-out to the Barbour team. Thank you for embracing my story, designing an amazing cover, and just being so wonderful to work with. And to Ellen, my editor, who is ever so patient with me and probably strained a finger muscle highlighting all the lines containing independently moving body parts. Thank you!

Elise Winterseller, thank you for the inspiration for my heroine's name. Ashley Johnson and Abbi Hart, I always appreciate your feedback. And Abbi, thanks for letting me use your grandma's name, Dorothea, and her story of working at the William Penn! Amy, Joy, and Crissy, your constant encouragement means more than I can say.

I wouldn't be here in writing or in life without my support system. Rebekah Millet, my critique partner and sister of the heart, "thank you" never seems adequate, but I'm still trying to figure out how to send you a tractor trailer's worth of Pop-Tarts. One day! To my husband and best friend for life, Scott, there's a part of you in every one of my heroes. Thank you for loving me on my best and worst days. To my kiddos, Drew and Meg, I'm pretty sure it always seems I'm behind my laptop. Thank you for allowing me to follow my dreams as I encourage you to chase yours.

Rachel Scott McDaniel is an award-winning Christian romance writer. Her stories inspire with faith and heart yet intrigue with mystery and suspense. Her first novel was nominated for the ACFW Carol Award for best debut. She's also the winner of the ACFW Genesis Award and the RWA Touched By Love Award. Rachel can be found online at www. RachelScottMcDaniel.com and on all social media platforms. Her work is represented by Julie Gwinn of the Seymour Agency. She enjoys life in Ohio with her husband and two kids.